THE CADE CLAN

LAWRENCE CADE

Copyright © 2024 by Lawrence Cade.

ISBN: 979-8-89465-086-9 (sc)
ISBN: 979-8-89465-087-6 (e)

All rights reserved. No part of this publication may be reproduced, distributed, or transmitted in any form or by any means, including photocopying, recording, or other electronic or mechanical methods, without the prior written permission of the author, except in the case of brief quotations embodied in critical reviews and certain other noncommercial uses permitted by copyright law.

This is a work of fiction. Characters, names, places, businesses, incidents, and events are either the products of the author's imagination or used in a fictitious manner. Any resemblance to actual persons, living or dead, or actual events is purely coincidental.

Printed in the United States of America.

Integrity Publishing
39343 Harbor Hills Blvd Lady Lake,
FL 32159

www.integrity-publishing.com

INTRODUCTION

"There is in this world no such force as the force of a person determined to rise." W.E.B. DuBois

America is so incredibly young. Some of us can remember great-grandparents who lived during the Civil War. We had grandparents who survived the carpetbaggers and the reconstruction of the South. Our parents lived through violent racism, and we struggled under Jim Crow laws that seemed impossible to change.

Somehow, we survived—we are still here.

This is my story. It is written to honor all who have gone before me… and all who will follow.

CHAPTER ONE

Rob Callaway woke to the sound of his wife screaming. Little Shirley was crying in the hallway, her terrified face illuminated by the dim early light.

"Daddy! Daddy! You must do something! Mama is going to have a baby!"

"Honey, are you going to be all right?" He sat up in bed and stroked his wife's forehead. Rachel just rolled her eyes back in her head and nodded. She was used to birthing by now. After all, this was their tenth child.

"I am going straight over and pick up old lady MacKay," he soothed. "I'll be back as fast as I can."

Rob threw on his pants, his arms through his shirt and flung open the front door. He pulled the crank handle from the car's trunk, and with a half turn, the engine came alive. Gravel flew as he jammed out onto the main road.

By the time the midwife arrived, Rachel had all but pushed the child from her body. The baby popped out in the blistering heat, its cry of jubilation. It was a boy; Rob and Rachel now had eight boys and two girls.

CHAPTER TWO

Two of Rob's youngins were born on the same day, two years apart. Rob had some explaining to do. He knew his family disapproved of his ability to create life at such a rate. For several weeks, everyone had been quizzing him whether his wife Rachel was pregnant or only regular North Carolina fat. Still, his family predictably increased.

Every October, he spent day after day at the animal auction in South Carolina. It made him randy as hell. He could not help himself. When he came home, he only wanted to screw his wife several times a day, damn the consequences. He was a man after all and Rachel, bless her heart, almost always conceived. The way Rob saw it, he could take care of a wife and kids, so why should anyone judge him? People, he thought, even family, should mind their own damned business.

His children were always beautiful, and this baby was no exception. Rob took a look and announced, "I am going to name this one Jacob."

Jacob Foster was an old white man who had taken a liking to Rob since he was a young boy. He had told Rob early on that he was the type that could stand firm against any discrimination, prejudice, or the like. He was the man who encouraged Rob to start his blacksmith shop.

"Boy, you have what it takes to make it," said old man Jacob with his usual authority. "I ain't seen any nigger that's got what you have." He shook his head and pronounced, "You can go a long way in Callawaytown."

He looked over at Rob, his blue eyes intense against his sunburned skin. "Just start a blacksmith shop, and you'll get the horse and mule-shoeing and wagon repair work from around here." Jacob was certain of his thoughts, and his voice got louder. "Yep, once the respectable whites start taking their work to you, it won't be long before the crackers, Indians and niggers will give you all their business." Crackers are what everybody called poor white folks who were considered trash. Their skin looked spotty, like a soda cracker. Some called 'em rednecks.

But Rob had a problem to deal with before starting that blacksmithing shop. His daddy had married a woman seven years younger than him. With no warning either. Rob was sure his stepmother would stand in his way over pretty much anything he wanted to do. They never got along. He just could not bring himself to accept the fact that his father, whom he worshipped, could have married such a young woman so soon after the death of his mother. The old man's marriage to the young woman shocked everyone in Callaway town and the surrounding communities.

Bent had been running down to Dillon, South Carolina, to see her. One Friday night, he got married without even mentioning it to anyone except Edmund Foster, the old white man who lived a few miles up the road. Bent knew that he could trust Edmund to keep a secret; they had been exceptionally good friends since they were boys, playing together in Edmund's mother's yard and fishing in the Lumbee River.

When Bent approached Edmund, he was more than willing to help. What Bent wanted to do didn't make sense to Edmund, but if his nigger friend wanted help, he would certainly give it to him. Anyhow, he looked forward to seeing how Rob would react to the news! In the end, Edmund would have the biggest laugh.

Sure enough, when they returned to North Carolina, everything went as Edmund thought it would go. Rob went crazy! He was certain that the gal had married his dad for his money. Rob could not believe someone that much younger would marry him for love. It had to be for money. He stood out in the yard, yelling his head off. "If I only knew who talked Daddy into going down to Dillon and marrying that gal, they'll have hell to pay!" Rob knew full well his father could not have driven himself. Someone had taken him. Still screaming, he vowed to personally break the son-of-a-bitch's neck.

Edmund had indeed laughed, but he was also concerned. He owned a little shop at the point where Callaway town Road and Highway 72 crossed. If Rob ever found out that he had helped Bent, he'd stop coming to the shop. That would only be the beginning. Rob was considered the leader in Callawaytown. If he told folks not to shop at Edmund's, they wouldn't, and Edmund would go flat out of business.

For now, Edmund's business was going quite well. He had most of the niggers' business except those who went to Bent's sister-in-law's shop. Linda had a shop in Callawaytown, and she captured a lot of customers. In Edmund's opinion, that was because she was always willing to give credit to poor crackers and niggers. Edmund shook his head ruefully. Linda was not someone he got along with.

Privately, he thought it was shameful when Bent's youngest brother Richard married Linda. He had always believed a Callaway could get any nigger gal in the county. And he knew for a fact that more than one white gal around these parts wanted to be screwed by a Callaway. The Callaway's were exceptionally light and red-skinned niggers with curly hair. They were a mixture of Lumbee Indians, and niggers. Even white foster blood flowed through their veins. They were quite different from all the other niggers in the county and maybe the state.

The word was out all over the county, that a white gal did not have anything to brag about if a Callaway hadn't piped her. Why, he was downright shocked when Richard married Linda. She was blacker than a moonless night. Why did such a good-looking nigger marry someone so black?

Now, he knew she had been stealing his business by talking bad about him to the poor crackers and niggers. Only Richard and their youngins was closer to Linda than Rob was. Now that Edmund had helped Bent, he prayed to God that he and his new wife would keep their mouths shut.

CHAPTER THREE

Bent was proud of his oldest son Rob, and they had always been close. Rob had purchased a piece of land near the swamp, repaired the old house, and started a family. Bent felt sure his son would be around to help him with the farm for the rest of his days. Today, they were working side-by-side in the heat. He knew that something was on Rob's mind. He was fairly itching to ask him something.

Finally, Rob spoke. Trying to sound casual, he said, "Daddy, you know I've been doing horseshoeing work for some time when I am not here helping you on the farm. I have been doing it for free- even fixed some wagons for people around here." He paused and glanced over at his father. "I've been doin' it all for free."

Bent answered patiently, "What's wrong with doing things free for people when you have the time? It's good to be able to do good deeds every once and a while."

"Well, Daddy," replied Rob. "I agree with all that. But I have been thinking about starting my blacksmith shop." He kept working, sparing a look over at his father. Then he stood straight and pointed, "If you would let me put up a shed over there, I could get a business off the ground in no time. I know plenty of people who would pay me good money to shoe their mules and horses, repair their wagons and buggies."

Bent slowly wiped the sweat off his face with an old red handkerchief, then, grinned. "Guess you could do that and still be around when we need you for the farm."

Shocked by his father's positive response, Rob stood silent. Bent continued, "Over where you pointed would be fine. But if I were you, I would have put it further toward the swamp. That way, you will have plenty of room for folks to turn around when they come in to get work done."

Rob never dreamed his daddy would approve of the idea. At the very least, he thought his father would consult with his stepmother. But no! The decision was made, and he could move forward with his plan. Sure, enough, one fine day, Rob, his father, cousins, and older sons went to work. They got the shed up and all the equipment installed.

The business quickly became a great success. As Rob had predicted, folks came from as far north as Virginia and south as Georgia. Even though he could only work during his spare time, Rob could construct a buggy in about three months. Soon, his waiting list was exceedingly long. When the shop was five years old, folks had to wait two years for a buggy.

Rob was a careful businessman. In October 1989, the stock market crashed. The effects had rippled all the way to North Carolina. Rob had lost the few dollars he had put in a bank. That day, promised to himself that he would never totally trust a bank again. Even though folks said the federal government now guaranteed the banks, it did not matter to him. He had decided the most he would put in any bank would be $3,000.00. He purchased a safe where he kept the deed to his property and the bulk of his money.

As the years went by, Rob grew closer to his father. He never did get over his resentfulness towards his stepmother.

CHAPTER FOUR

Rob's wife Rachel was from Carriton, around fifteen miles east of Lakeville in Bull County. Her father was black as tar. However, it was no secret that Rachel's mother was almost white. Her grandfather held a lot of land in Bull County. Everyone within a hundred miles in any direction was or wanted to be old man McBride's friend. He was, without a doubt, the most powerful man in the area.

McBride kept a mistress- an Indian girl who worked in his mansion. At first, having sex with her was only plain fun. But after their second child came along, McBride took responsibility for his actions.

He said that the Indian girl and her two children belonged to him. His slave foreman built her a shack just out of sight of McBride's mansion. Once that word spread throughout the area, no troubled them. Because of McBride, Rachel's mother Sarah was spared most of the horrors of the Civil War.

Everyone knew Sarah was old man McBride's daughter and that no nigger should dare come near her. Jason Pope came along and married her, and she had just about been lynched. He was out of his mind in love, and that put his entire family and all of his friends in jeopardy. McBride was furious. Truth be told, some of Jason's family had had their shacks burned to the ground and their crops and livestock destroyed. The KKK had gotten all riled up, and there was no one in the county with the will to stand up to them. The poor white trash hopped on board, and they were responsible for the destruction. But the colored folks and Indians protected Jason. He went from shack to shack, hiding until things cooled down.

As time passed, old man McBride accepted that Jason had indeed married Sarah. People watched them when they were out together, but no one dared say a thing.

Eventually, things got back to normal in Bull County. In due time, Sarah gave birth to a baby girl, Rachel. Jason and Sarah went on to have nine more children.

Rob followed in Jason's footsteps. He took Rachel away from her home and straight to Dillon, South Carolina, to marry her.

On a Sunday afternoon in late August 1924, Rob repaired his car, washed up a bit, and put on his only suit. He drove to Jason and Sarah Pope's home with the excuse that he wanted to sample some of Jason's newly made home-brew. The fact was Rob was head over heels in love with Rachel.

The two men sat out on the porch, happily drinking together. Jason's home-brew was good that day. Home-brew was somewhat unpredictable and made by fermenting grain, fruits, yeast, and anything else that carried the hope that it would taste good. It sat in a wooden barrel for several days or weeks depending on the weather, until the aroma was extraordinarily strong. Then it was screened through cheesecloth. Sugar was added and it was left to ferment for several more days until it was ready for consumption.

After Rob had several drinks with Jason, Rachel offered them some limeade. She was exactly what Rob had been waiting for. Rachel looked good that day. Just eighteen years old, she was 5 feet two inches tall and 110 pounds. To him, she was perfect. That long black hair hanging down her back convinced him she was the girl he would spend the rest of his life with. There was not another girl around that came close to her beauty.

Rob sat there talking with Jason while his mind worked overtime trying to conjure up a way to get Rachel alone. He was certain she had feelings for him, but she was very much her father's little girl.

Propelled by love, Rob's mind was devious. He had to have Rachel as his wife. He was more determined about that than he had ever been about anything in his life. His mind worked at full speed, trying to formulate his thoughts into words, words into sentences. Rob struggled to keep up with Jason's small talk- he asked appropriate questions ranging from how Rob's father was doing to how the weather was in Mills County. The fact was, he only cared about Rachel.

To separate Rachel from her father, Rob knew that his timing had to be perfect. One bad move, and Jason would know what he was up to. He would make sure that Rob never got close to her again.

Finally, Rachel came outside. She held out a plate of pound cake and said, "Papa, do you and Rob want some?" Rob thought she was the most beautiful creature on the face of the earth.

"No, I don't want no cake," answered Jason crankily. "How about you, Rob? Do you have a taste for it?"

Rob was having trouble finding his tongue. "Nope, don't believe I do," he managed to say. Before he could unscramble his thoughts, Rachel went back into the house. But, a few moments later, he overheard her quietly arguing with her mother.

"But mama, I am sure Rob will take me to get some ice cream if I ask him," Rachel murmured.

Sarah's response was sharp and swift. "You shouldn't bother Rob. He came to visit your father. He's not interested in you."

Rob could not stand it any longer. What if Rachel believed her mother? "Sarah," he called out. "I'd be glad to take Rachel to get ice cream. Just let me finish this little bit of home-brew I have here." He hoped he sounded casual.

Jason did not feel the need to protest. He liked Rob well enough. But he looked over with his dark and piercing eyes and said, "You take care of my little girl and drive safely, you hear?"

"We'll be back," Rob said as he emptied his glass. He complimented Jason on his home-brew. He hoped the good Lord would not judge him too harshly. After all, he would bring Rachel back to see her parent's again- just not for a while. Rachel came out of the house with her small hand-made purse in one hand and her knitted sweater over her arm. Rob opened the passenger door, and Rachel got in the car.

He took the crank and gave the engine a half turn to get it started, and walked back around the car. Once again, he reassured Sarah and Jason that their daughter was in good hands. He got in the car, put his foot on the clutch, placed the car in gear, and away they drove.

Jason pulled his watch from his vest pocket and noted that the time was five minutes past three o'clock. He watched the old car disappear into the dust. Taking his seat again, he called to Sarah for another quart of home-brew. He finished his third quart and then had a few winks of sleep. Finally, he roused himself and looked down the dirt road. The sun had gone down, and it was getting dark. Feeling the far edge of alarm, he wondered what time it was. He drew his watch from his pocket. It was ten minutes before nine.

"Rachel! Come and bring me a glass of water!" he called. When he did not get a response, he raised his voice to a shout. "Rachel! I said bring me some water!"

Sarah had already figured out that Rob and Rachel were not coming back. Taking a cool glass of water from the just-drawn well bucket, she walked out on the porch and gave it to Jason.

Without thanking her for bringing him the water, Jason asked, "Didn't Rachel come back yet?"

"No, they're not back," Sarah quietly replied.

"Well, it couldn't take this long to get ice cream," grumbled Jason. "Where in the hell are, they?" Then realization dawned, and Jason shot up in rage. "That son-of-a-bitch stole my little girl! I'll kill that son of a bitch when I see him again!" Jason was fit to be tied, but he could do nothing. Instead, he rumbled and cussed for several hours, then finally went to bed.

Meanwhile, Rob and Rachel were having the time of their lives. They *had* stopped by to purchase the ice cream, but that was only the beginning. They had gone on to drive the dirt roads all over southern Bull County and ended up in Mills County.

Rob had already asked Rachel if she would marry him. Caught up in the moment, she grinned over at him and said, "Yes!" They had been hugging and kissing from when they'd disappeared down the dirt road.

Although he wanted to find a secluded place and find out exactly what was below Rachel's waistline, Rob was an honorable man, even if he had been somewhat devious. As they approached the state line, he made his final decision. He would continue to Dillon, South Carolina, and marry Rachel before a Justice of the Peace. He briefly considered returning to Rachel's home and asking her father for her hand. But he knew he would be lucky to escape from Jason with his life. Instead, he murmured sweet things to Rachel as he held her hand.

In less than three hours, they were married.

Once Rachel was his, Rob was thrilled. There was nothing her father or anyone else could do about it. He knew he was about to have the best night of his life. He had been with other girls before- he was, after all, a grown man. But Rachel was going to be special. He knew Jason had guarded her since she was old enough to be noticed. Rob was sure that he had married a virgin.

At about nine in the evening, Rob and Rachel arrived in a little town called South of the Border. Almost all the lodging was for whites only. In fact, only the rich whites traveling from Florida to New York and back again could afford the one dollar per night cost of a room. But Rob had found a place to stay there before. He had been there with a gal from a nearby town.

Rob parked his car behind a motel. Rachel waited in the car as he got out and walked around to the front of the building. The person at the front desk was someone he knew from Callawaytown. His father was the man's landlord. Although the man was white, Rob thought he had a good chance of securing a room for the night.

The man looked up lazily and asked, "What can I do for ya boy?" Then he looked closer. "Ain't you old man Bent's son"?

"Yessir," Rob replied. "I am his oldest son. I am the one that worked with my daddy on the farm and with Mr. Jacob shoeing mules and horses and repairing wagons and buggies." At that moment, Rob leaned closer to the man's ear so he would not have to speak so loudly. "I was thinking that maybe I could, you know, get one of their rooms at the back." Before the man could respond, Rob added, "I'll pay you the dollar and give you a quarter for your help."

The man looked at Rob, shook his head, and said, "You know I could lose my job if anyone found out that I let a nigger stay here." Then he sighed, "But do not get me wrong. I don't mean that you're like all them blackass niggers. We all have respect for you, Callaway's. But if I let one nigger in, it will just be a matter of time before every blackass nigger in Mills County will want to get a room here".

Rob looked over without blinking. "I'll pay for the room and give you four bits."

The man saw that Rob had already drawn a dollar and fifty cents from his pocket. It was too much for him to resist. The four bits were more than he made in a day. He ignored his resistance and took the money. He held out a key with 101 on one side and "South of The Border Motel" on the other side.

"This is the last room on the corner of the ground floor," he whispered, although no one else was around to hear. "Go straight to your room, stay there all night, and be sure you're gone before daybreak." He wrinkled his face. "I'll tell you now, if I get caught letting niggers stay here, you ain't going never to hear the last of this. And if I lose my job, I ain't going to have no way to pay Uncle Bent his rent."

"Uncle" was the term whites used to refer to certain black folks. If white folks were nice and kind, they referred to black folks as boys or girls until they were forty. After forty, they referred to them as uncle and aunt. But poor white trash, or mean people, referred to all black folks as niggers.

Rob took the key, looked the man in the eye, and thanked him. Then he added quickly, "If you ever need me to do anything for you, anything at all, just let me know."

He walked around the back where Rachel was waiting. When he was sure she could see him, he held his arm parallel to the ground and shook the key. "I told you I'd get a room here," he said proudly.

Rachel was extremely nervous. She twisted her hands and said, "I don't know if we should go inside a room here." Her voice wavered, and she looked like she was going to cry. "You know colored folks can't stay in a place like this. What if we get caught? Just tell me what are you going to do if we get caught?"

Rob's mind was racing ahead to other things. "Well, we ain't going to get caught. When we get in the room, we aren't leaving until just before daybreak. We ain't got nothin' to worry about."

The room was only a few steps away from the car. He helped Rachel out, and they flew toward room 101.

By now, Rob was fully aroused. He reached out and eagerly fondled Rachel's breasts. When she shivered and leaned toward him, he knew she wanted him as much as he wanted her. Urgently, they held each other and kissed before landing on the bed. Rob could not wait any longer. He didn't take the time to remove his trousers. Instead, he spread Rachel's legs and within moments slipped her on like a tight glove. He thrust inside her a few times, drawing moans from Rachel. But it was only a minute before he burst inside her.

As brief as it had been, making love with Rachel brought up feelings that Rob had never felt before. Still inside her, he told her how much he loved and was proud to have her. Looking down at his beautiful wife, her breasts caught up against his chest, her long black hair around his neck, Rob wasn't surprised to find he was ready again. This time he decided he would really give her the experience of her life. But he could not hold on. Before he knew it, he let go a second time. He felt the blood beneath them. He had just taken a virgin. They lay together until dawn broke; giggling and whispering, they drove away.

In the light of day, Rachel considered what they had done and became indeed and well upset. "What will I tell Mama and Papa?" she wailed. "They'll kill me when they find out I ran away and got married!"

Rob held her hand and said calmly, "We'll tell them the truth. We will say that we talked after getting the ice cream and decided to get married. We thought the best way to do it was to go straight down to Dillon and tell everybody about it when we returned." Rob reached over and held her hand tightly.

"I don't know what Papa will do to you," said Rachel, hiccupping with tears. "What if he shoots you?"

Rob managed to look confident. "I'll take care of Jason," he said quietly. "Don't you worry. I'll talk to him when we get there." Inside, Rob was scared. Rachel's parents were going to be furious. And they should be angry, he admitted to himself. They must have been going through hell. They probably thought there had been an accident.

On the other hand, Rob convinced himself that Sarah probably knew why they had not returned. And Rob bet that Jason also knew that he had taken Rachel to Dillon, South Carolina, to get married. Maybe it would not be so bad after all. The bottom line was that he had accomplished his mission. There would be some hard feelings and maybe a few harsh words, but now the chips would just have to fall where they may.

Hearts pounding, Rachel and Rob headed down the road toward Jason and Sarah's house. Rob came to a full stop in the yard. Before he could utter a sound, Rachel flew out of the car and ran into the house. He knew she wanted to make it possible for him to get away quickly if he needed to do so. Rob put the gearshift into reverse and positioned the car to head out the driveway. Suddenly, Jason was right in his face. Rob pushed the car door and nudged it into Jason's chest. Putting his left foot out the door, he pressed it further, and Jason moved back a half step. As he did, he raised a shotgun.

"Where in the hell have you been with my daughter?" yelled Jason, pointing the weapon at Rob's head. Without thinking, Rob grabbed the barrel of the shotgun and tried to wrestle it away from Jason. There was not a sound as Rachel's sisters and brothers watched from the porch in horror. A shot exploded in the silence. Sarah and Rachel ran out of the house.

"What's going on out here?" Sarah shouted across the yard. "Stop it now. Y'all are acting like boys!" Surprisingly, both men stopped and looked over at her. "Put that shotgun down and come to your senses," Sarah commanded. "Rachel is over eighteen years old. I know how much you love and care about her, but she is a grown woman now. She's gone and married Rob."

Jason shook his head in disgust. "Who in the hell said she is married?"

Sarah's hands were on her hips now–a familiar sight to Jason. "Well, while you and Rob were out here making fools of yourselves, Rachel told me that she and Rob went down to Dillon and got married last night." Jason stared at Rob, who now had the very beginnings of a grin on his face.

Sarah continued, "So, just back off and let Rachel live her own life." Sarah was a practical kind of person. As she saw things, the marriage was a fact, pure and simple. It was Monday morning, and they were already three hours late getting down to work. Everything was already said and done, as far as she was concerned. Now it was time to get everyone out of the house and on to their normal chores.

But Jason didn't see it at all. He had just lost a daughter. Truth be told, he worshipped the ground she walked on. Although he had other daughters, Rachel was so special to him. So, Jason angrily rambled on, not making a whole lot of sense. Everyone else ignored him. Finally, when he noticed that he was the only person speaking, he stopped. "Well, Rob," he said belligerently. "What do you have planned for my daughter's future? How do you plan to support her and a family?"

In an instant, Rob flew from a dangerous present into a non-existent future. He had not expected Jason to hit him with such a question. He could not believe that they had leapfrogged from Jason trying to murder him to plans. He gulped and said cautiously, "Well, you know I am not one to do much work for anybody else. Jason frowned, and Rob hastily continued. "But I have been working in Mr. Jacob's blacksmith shop, and I do some blacksmith work at my papa's place." Jason just stared at him. Rob went on, "I don't know if you know about that piece of land down by my papa's place." Jason nodded, his lips still tight with anger. "Well, Kenny Hooker owned that land and the house. I heard that he's not been paying old man C.G. Baily for the last few months. And you know he ain't even been doing any work for them. So, what I was thinking was that I'd go down to Lakeville and talk to old man Baily and see if he would let me have that land. That way I will have a house for me and Rachel, and we could add-on to it later."

Rob stopped to take in some air. When Jason still did not say a word, he added, "I also have a few dollars in the bank. I just want you to know that I really love Rachel. I have loved her since the first time I met her. We are going to be okay. Just you wait and see."

Jason was both irritated and impressed at the same time. Rob had stolen his oldest daughter. How could he accept such a thing? If he let this jackass get away with this, where would it all lead? Then he thought about how Rob had everything all worked out. Shockingly, Jason smiled! He was still angry, but Rob had impressed him. He could hardly be mad at Rob when he had just about done the same thing with Sarah. But Rob had planned things far better than Jason had.

Things could have been quite different for them and their families if he had thought things through the way Rob had. So, Jason gave in. Rob and Rachel were truly in love. Why should he be an obstacle to a God-given natural event? He decided to smooth the way. "Well, will y'all be staying here until you have a chance to meet with old man Baily? Or will you be going back to Mills County and living with Bent and Louise?" Jason expected they would be going back. Louise was not in good health, and having Rachel there would help.

Sure enough, Rob replied, "We'll be going to Mills County. I do not think it will take long to get things worked out with old man Baily. One of his sons told me if I came up with one hundred dollars, it would be a deal. And you know what? I already have the hundred dollars." He chanced a smile over at Jason. "I'll go down today and see if I can get something going. If I cannot get it settled today, I am sure mama would love to have Rachel live with us until we can get everything straightened out."

Jason suddenly grabbed Rob's arm and hissed, "You son-of-a-bitch, if I ever hear of you mistreating her, your ass is mine! I will hunt you down like a goddamn mad dog and blow your damn fool brains out." He let go of Rob's arm and stepped back. Then he commanded, "Do you understand me?"

"Yessir! I understand," Rob answered loudly. Then he added quietly, "But I do not know why you have to talk about that, Jason, because just as I said, if I did not love Rachel, I wouldn't have married her. So, you aren't got anything to worry about sir."

Jason cooled a bit after he was sure that Rob respected him. From then on, he accepted that he had lost the battle. He would have to save face and cooperate the best he could. "Sarah," he called. "Get Rachel's things together. They've got to get to Mills County in time to go and see old man Baily about that land."

Rob let out a full breath. He was still alive, and Jason seemed to accept the marriage. If everything worked out as planned, he could honestly say that this had been a perfect weekend. Rob could hear Rachel and Sarah through the front door. They were talking about things that were of little interest to him. He wanted to get in the car and get the hell out of that yard.

Now that the crisis was over, he leaned against his car and waited for Rachel and Sarah to come outside. Rob thought about his own father. Even though he was 31 years old, he had never left home without telling his father. As a matter of fact, he always waited for his father's nod of approval before he went anywhere. Now he was bringing home a wife!

Finally, the screen door squeaked as Sarah pushed it open. Rachel appeared and handed Rob a simple brown paper bag. It contained all her earthly belongings. He placed it in the rear seat of the car and opened the door to the front, and Rachel stepped on the running board and sat down on the seat. Rob closed the door and walked around the front of the car, grabbed the crank, and made a half turn with his right hand. The old car shook as the engine fired up with a roar and a couple of backfires. Rob replaced the crank, waved a "see you later" to Sarah and Jason, got into the old car, and they drove down the dusty road.

Taking Rachel's hand and holding it to his lips, Rob said, "Well, we made it. It's our life now. We'll make what we want out of it."

Rachel sighed and thought of her future. "We are going to have a lot of children," she smiled shyly. "Many boys and some girls. Just you wait and see." She looked over at her new husband with pride. Nobody had ever taken Jason on. She was impressed with her new husband.

Rob looked over at Rachel, but his mind was on what lay ahead. He would drive directly to his father's house and explain things. He was not too worried about that. His father would love Rachel. What was there about her that anyone could not love? After he calmed the storm at home, he would go straight to Lakeville and talk to old man Baily about the house and piece of land. He would ask his father if he would go with him. That would give Rachel and his mother time to get to know each other.

The old car rumbled on down the road, and dust floated in all directions. Soon they would be in Callawaytown, and a new life would begin.

CHAPTER FIVE

After what seemed like an eternity, Rob made the turn into the driveway where Bent and Louise lived. Now, there would be four people living in the house. Rachel was used to her father and mother and several brothers and sisters. Rob, Bent, and Louise were a small group. His brothers and sisters were all away from home, married, and had their own families. Rob's father and mother had always given him a free reign. He had always respected them by always letting them know where he would be. Now he would have Rachel to think about.

Bent really was a wonderful father. He had his quirks. Bent had the habit of going behind the barn to where the Rabbit tobacco grew wild. There, he would strip off the leaves of several branches, and stuff the leaves into his corncob pipe. With the strike of a match, he would be puffing what smelled like burning, dried, half-rotten cedar wood. At that moment, everything else would take second place to the enjoyment he received from the Rabbit tobacco smoke. Bent loved to smoke Rabbit tobacco. He had been doing it since he was a small boy, just after the great civil war. As a matter of fact, it was a Yankee who first gave him a puff from a pipe.

In fact, Bent had made several trips behind the barn last evening. He had been worried about Rob. Louise had given him her standard speech about the tobacco. She hated it and badgered him to stop. She had made him promise that he would not smoke Rabbit tobacco in the house or when they had visitors. Sure enough, he had limited his enjoyment to behind the barn. Louise was pleased. In her heart, she knew he'd never stop altogether. But she'd had enough power to slow down his use of the tobacco.

Now Bent and Louise stood in front of Rob's car like centennials. Bent's eyes were red. They were so red that they looked like two cherries in a glass of milk. He had just finished off his third pipe of the day, and it was still not quite mid-morning. Before Rob could get the door open, Bent spoke firmly. "Boy where you been? Louise and I have been worried stiff about what had happened to you! You never stayed out like this before. What happened?"

But Bent could see for himself exactly what had held Rob up overnight. Jason and Sarah's oldest girl was sitting right there in the car. Bent started to smile. Finally, he thought! He and Louise thought Rob should have had a wife a long time ago. Now, here she was. A good choice, too.

Rob could see his marriage was not going to be an issue. He wanted to get on with securing the land and house. "Papa!" he said smiling broadly. "Would you go with me to Lakeville?"

Bent knew well enough that Rob had something important he had to get done. "What are you going to do in Lakeville on a Monday morning?"

"I am going to go down and talk to old man Baily about that piece of land down there," responded Rob as he pointed towards the swamp. "I heard that Kenny Hooker didn't pay for it like he was supposed to. He is not even there anymore. He moved in with his aunt." Rob waited for his father's response. When nothing happened, he continued, "If I could just pick up where Kenny left off, that would be good. It would not take much to get the house in livable condition. That way Rachel and I would have a place to live."

Now Bent looked at his son with approval. "Boy, it looks like you have everything under control. I might as well go with you today. There is always a few things I can get down there in Lakeville." He grinned over his shoulder at his wife.

Louise was also happy that Rob had finally taken a wife. Not one to make a fuss, she called out, "I need some little things that I can't get down at Annie and Richard's place or at the crossroads."

"Boy, you really have done it," said Bent happily as they drove off. "I didn't even think you were interested in that Pope girl. You know you really kept that a secret from your mama and me. How come? You know that you can always tell us what's on your mind. There's no reason to keep us in the dark."

Rob shrugged, feeling a little ashamed that he had worried his mama and daddy. Bent added, "We both think that it's good that you got married. And you know what? If old man Baily needs me to stand for you to buy that place down there on the swamp, all you have got to do is ask…just you come on out and let me know. Cause all I want is what is good for you."

He listened to his father ramble on for several minutes as they drove the dirt road toward Lakeville. He did not comment on anything. His mind was fixed on the situation at hand. Bent continued to offer his support. "You have been living with your mama and me for all your life, and there ain't nothing we won't help you with. Just let me know if you need anything."

Rob had grown up overnight, and this was one of the most important days of his life. He was married now, and he had to have a place of his own to live in. Getting down to Lakeville and meeting with old man Baily was the most important task of his life.

CHAPTER SIX

They approached the bridge that crossed the Lumber River. Both men were flooded with memories. Bent thought about the terrible things that had happened to that bride while he was growing up. Just in his teens, he had heard the screams of a colored man as he came near the bridge. Those screams were forever engraved in his memory. The poor man had been hung from the bridge and skinned alive. The sight was unbearable. Bent remembered that he had held his head down and almost passed out.

Terrified, he told his father what he had seen. He had been told to never talk about it again. That was how it had to be. It was a reality that colored folks had to deal with. Several days later, he heard that the body hanging from the bridge was that of a colored man who was in the town of Lakeville and had just happened to look at a white woman. For that reason alone, he had been hung by his big toes and skinned alive.

The Klux Klan had done it. The organization was extremely strong in North Carolina. As a matter of fact, there was a sign on Highway 301 right on the border from Virginia, which stated in bold letters: "NORTH CAROLINA, HOME OF THE KKK GRAND DRAGON." This was not an informal sign–it had been placed there by the state government.

The Civil War had not been that long ago. Bent had been just two years old when the Union troops came to the old plantation homestead where his mother and father worked as domestic slaves. What happened that day would remain forever in the souls of black folk.

Around ten thirty in the morning, he was holding the apron his mother was wearing as tight as his little hands could hold.

A tall man in a dark blue uniform approached them. "Good morning, ma'am," he said respectfully. Right there, they knew something was radically different about this particular man. "Is the miss of the house home?" he continued.

"Good morning, sir," his mother had replied with her head down. "Yes some, she is just upstairs. Can I go get her for ya?"

He nodded. "Please go and get her for me."

For the first time in his short life, Bent was very, very frightened. His mother pushed his hands away from her apron, led him to a chair, and told him to sit there until she returned. Bent wailed as the Union soldier moved toward him. "Don't be afraid," the man told him. "I'll not harm you or allow anyone else to harm you. Your mother will be right back."

Bent calmed down right away. Something about the man told him he could trust him. It was the first time that someone with a white face had spoken to him with kindness. The soldier paced the floor and looked carefully around the room.

The miss arrived. "Good morning! What can I do to help you?" she said sarcastically. "You Yankees have destroyed everything we have. What more do you want from us?" Her head was held up high.

"We're consolidating this area," the man had replied patiently. "I want to know if the slaves are being freed as they should be."

The miss just stood up taller. "We don't have any free niggers in this county," she said defiantly. "And you know what? There will never be any free niggers in this county."

The Union soldier moved to what looked like a coat hanger. A huge leather strap, which had two rows of parallel holes, hung on it. "Miss, what is this?" He took the strap from its place.

"That's what we use to keep the niggers in line," said the miss matter-of-factly.

"Have you ever thought of how this feels when it hits a bare back?" asked the soldier. His face twisted with disgust.

Exasperated, the miss said, "Now tell me, how do you think a white woman who owns slaves would know how that feels?"

Immediately, the soldier grabbed the woman by the arm and pushed her to the floor. "Well, I think it's about time that you know what it feels like," he said coldly. As she attempted to free herself, the soldier lashed her several times with the strap. The woman screamed louder than anyone Bent had ever heard before. It was the first time that he or any other slave had ever seen a white person bleed. When the soldier finished his business, he said to the miss. "I hope that you can now understand what you put these people through."

The big house was never the same again. The master of the house had gone to help in the war, and so had all the other able-bodied white men. All the white males from the plantation who were of fighting age had gone off to fight in one of the many North Carolina militia units. Many would never return home. They had gone to fight for their way of life. They knew if they lost, the South would never be the same again.

As time went by, the ex-slaves were given a mule and forty acres of land. Bent's father was put in charge of the distribution of the land that had been a part of the plantation. Starting with the land just around the big house, Bent's father gave forty acres to all his family. Next, he gave land to the domestic helpers. Desperate, the miss had asked Bent's father if he would stay on at the big house. He had agreed, but the stay was short-lived. When Sherman's troops came up from South Carolina, the big house was right in the center of their forty-mile-wide search and destroy mission. The troops seemed to really enjoy burning or destroying everything that could be used by the rebels to prolong the war. And that they did!

When they arrived at the big house, they gave the ex-slaves just moments to gather their belongings and clear out. Afterwards, the house was razed.

With the assistance of other ex-slaves, Bent's father built a house for himself. Even though it was much larger than the usual houses in the area, it was nothing compared to the plantation house.

Bent's brothers and sisters were born and raised there. Once the Civil War ended, they carefully contended with Jim-crow, white crackers, and racism.

CHAPTER SEVEN

Rob and Bent arrived at the shop of old man C.G. Baily. Bent went in first. "Good morning, Mr. Baily."

"Good morning, Uncle Bent. Is that your oldest boy behind you there?" responded Mr. Baily. Not waiting for an answer, Baily decided to make a speech. "I can't get over how you niggers can make things work for you when most of those blackass niggers don't seem to be able to make it on their own. Most of them niggers out there will never amount to nothin.' They really need a white man to keep kicking them in the ass. Most of them are just lazy and do not do no work. I cannot believe that some of them even want to go to some sort of college. You would think it would be enough to help them learn to read. But no, that is not enough. You give them an inch, and they're going to take a yard. Now do not get me wrong, Uncle Bent, you Callaway niggers ain't no way like that. It would be really good if we had more niggers in this county like you Callaway's."

Bent knew by now that he had no choice but to let Baily ramble on until he was good and through. "Who in the world do they think is going to crop the tobacco, pick the cotton, pull the corn, and all the other things that have to be done if their black asses are in school?" rumbled Mr. Baily.

Today was worse because Baily was in a complaining mood. "Every time I look at how you Callaway's have made it. I just can't keep from wondering what's wrong with those blackass niggers. I have tried to help many niggers in Callawaytown, but it never works out. Just take that house and piece of land down by the swamp, aside from your farm. You know I sold that land and house to Uncle Kenny. That nigger gave me something down, and I made five payments, and that was it. I finally had to tell him to move out of the house and off the land. How can you help when niggers will not pay?" said Mr. Baily, as he puffed on his old corncob pipe.

The old man was smoking golden leaf tobacco. Just about every farmer in Mills County grew it. By rambling, Baily had given him all the information he needed to go forward with Rob's plans. "Yessir! That is my oldest son, Rob. He just got married yesterday, and we were thinking that maybe he could buy that land and house that you sold Kenny Hooker and had to take back. He added carefully, "That would be mighty nice if Rob could buy that land and house."

Baily leaned over his desk and looked over at Rob. "You mean you want that land and house that I sold Kenny?"

"Yessir! That would be good of you if you would let me have it at a good price," said Rob. He knew he had to look casual about the whole thing. A white man could do whatever he wanted to do.

Mr. Baily was feeling generous today. "Well, boy, if you can pay me what Kenny Hooker owes me on it, it's yours."

"How much does he owe you on the place, Mr. Baily?" asked Rob.

"Well, let me see here." He turned around in his chair and started fumbling through papers on a side table. "He bought it for five hundred dollars, and he paid me one hundred dollars down. That leaves four hundred, and he made five payments of twenty-five dollars each. So, he still owes two hundred and seventy-five dollars. But I will tell you what I'll do. If you can come up with two hundred dollars this week, you can have it."

"Yessir! I know I can come up with that much by Friday," said Rob, as he looked over toward Bent.

"Okay", said Mr. Baily. "Let's say I see you Friday around the same time."

Knowing well how things worked, Bent felt compelled to say something. He looked over the desk to Mr. Baily. "Thank you for letting Rob have that land and house. We really appreciate what you're doing."

Mr. Baily looked up. "Well, Bent, you Callaway niggers have always been straight with me and my family. We have never had any trouble with you niggers. And when that's the case, I don't have any problem helping when and where I can. Who'd Rob marry?"

"He married Jason and Sarah Pope's oldest girl… from Carriton, you know, in Bull County," remarked Bent.

Baily looked a little shocked and turned as red as a beet. "Ain't that the granddaughter of old man McBride?"

Bent was surprised that he knew the story about what had happened in Carriton so long ago. He hurried on, "Yessir, that's her, and Louise and I are happy to have her as a family member."

"I guess it's all right that she married your boy. She would have to marry someone, and I'd rather see her marry your boy than marry a blackass nigger."

Accepting that statement, Bent said goodbye and left the office to enter the shop where Rob had already started to gather some goods. They needed a few things now that Rachel would be living with them. Bent paid, and within minutes, he and Rob were on their way back to Callawaytown.

"We got it. We got it!" Rob cried as he raced into the house and pulled Rachel up off her feet.

"You did it?" She laughed in wonder at her new husband. "I am so proud of you!"

Rob and Rachel worked hard and made a home down on the land. As the years went by, they had many children.

CHAPTER EIGHT

After having a baby every other year for eighteen years, the birth of one more was not overly exciting for Rachel. At least this birth had been the easiest she had endured. With a full head of curly black hair, the boy had almond-colored skin. His eyes were wide open and looked black as tar. This baby did not arrive screaming as all the others had. That made him immediately special in Rachel's mind.

Mrs. MacKay cleaned him up and wrapped him in the diaper which had been hand sewn by his grandmother. Then she handed him to his father, "Here he is!" she exclaimed. "Now you've got eight boys and two girls. How many more times will you bring me over here?" she teased. "One more boy, and you will have your baseball team!" Because Mrs. MacKay was practically a member of the family by now, she felt free to admonish Rob. "Rachel is a strong woman and, she is very healthy, but she needs a rest, so just take it easy, okay?"

Rob held the boy in his arms and paid little attention to what Mrs. MacKay said. She had said the exact same thing at each of the last four births. Rob looked down at his son and put his right forefinger out so the baby could grab it. He played with the cheeks of the small baby. He did this for several moments before he got a response. The baby finally opened its little left hand and grabbed Rob's finger. Rob looked up at Mrs. MacKay and said, "Look, Miss MacKay. He just grabbed my finger."

Mrs. MacKay had helped at so many births that she gave little thought to what Rob had said. Instead, she looked over at Rachel and, in her no-nonsense way, said, "I will have to register him with the county the next time I go to Lakeville. So, you need to decide on a name before then."

Rob stated firmly, "We already decided on a name. I promised the old man, Jacob Foster, that if the next one was a boy, I would name him after him. You register him as Jacob Callaway."

"That was fast!" Mrs. MacKay said it in astonishment. "It usually takes you and Rachel weeks before you make up your mind." With that, Mrs. MacKay took the baby and handed him to Rachel. "This baby's going to be starving. You get on and feed him."

Rachel thought silently that she did not need to be told what to do. After all, this was her tenth child. But that was just Mrs. MacKay's way. Hungry he was the baby locked onto her breast and did not let go.

Jacob's birth was the only thing to celebrate that year. It was a bad time in Callawaytown… and the United States. Europe had been at war with Hitler and Germany for more than two years. After Japan bombed Pearl Harbor, the United States entered the war. The President placed the nation under a state of emergency. That meant most foods and clothing were rationed. All produce and livestock had to be registered with the federal government. Anyone who didn't report everything they had would be charged and punished.

Rob had his two oldest sons, Ernie and Lonnie, count all the animals on the farm, and he reported the number to the federal government in Lakeville. As always, Rob made sure that he looked out for the wellbeing of his family. He hid two of his finest fattening hogs in a special pen under the barn. No one outside of the family knew about it. He did not know how bad the war would be or how long it would last. He wanted to be able to feed his family if things really got bad. He was willing to take a huge risk–if the federal government found out, he'd do jail time.

At school, Ernie and Lonnie listened to the other boys talk about how their families were coping with the war crisis. One boy mentioned that his uncle was going into the Army. It was very possible that they would have to move back to his grandfather's home because they were running out of meat. The word "meat" lit a spark in Ernie and Lonnie. They couldn't help themselves and blurted, "We ain't got to worry about no meat. Daddy put two of our fattening hogs in a pen under the barn." An immensely proud Lonnie added, "He sure did." He crossed his arms and added, "He put them there so nobody will ever find them. We're going to have meat when nobody else is got it."

By that time, several boys had gathered around Ernie and Lonnie. Louise and Shirley walked by with their friends. They were dismayed to hear their brothers, and they carefully steered everyone away.

When school was out, the boys returned home and did not tell anyone what they had talked about at school.

The evening and night went by, and the next morning was quite normal. Rachel got up as usual, prepared breakfast, and worked with Shirley to get the small kids ready for school. At around seven forty-five, all the schoolchildren were out of the house. Rob had his last cup of coffee before going over to the blacksmith shop. Rachel changed the baby and started doing the things she did every day.

But when Rob got to the blacksmith shop, he looked up and saw what looked to be two official vehicles. The vehicles had "U.S. Government" stamped on the sides. Rob's heart began to pound. White men in an official vehicle could not mean anything good. Before he could gather his thoughts, eight white men, four from each side of the vehicle, got out and came straight into the shop. "Good morning. Are you Rob Callaway?" asked one of the men pleasantly enough.

"Yessir, that's me. I am Rob Callaway."

Another man then barked, "We have a federal warrant to search your place." He glared at Rob. "We'll do it by force, if necessary."

Rob tried to evade the inevitable. "This is not my place. This is my father's place. I live down the road on that little island near the swamp."

"Yes, we know, but we figured that you would be here at the blacksmith shop."

"Well, here I am," Rob said with a demeaning smile. "But there's no need for the search warrant. I have nothing to hide."

One of the men pulled a folded sheet of paper from his inside coat pocket. "Read and sign this," he demanded.

Rob read the sheet of paper. Sure enough, the problem was those hogs. How in the hell did the Feds find out about the hidden hogs? Rob thought frantically. Who had told them? Having no other choice, he signed the document and handed it back to the man.

"Okay, boys, you know what we have to do. Let us get it done," said the man who had the document. The men walked straight over to where the hogs were hidden and pulled back the cover.

"Well, Mr. Callaway, by the powers vested in me by the United States Government, I am placing you under arrest for holding back farm animals from the federal government," said the man rather triumphantly. Rob did not say a word. One of the other men took a pair of handcuffs from his back pocket and placed his hands behind his back.

Rachel looked up from her work inside the house and saw the white men. Scared to death, she went outside and saw that Rob was handcuffed with his hands behind his back. Trying to contain her panic, Rachel asked softly, "What's going on, officer?"

"We're going to have to take him in for violating a federal statute," replied the man in charge.

"What has he done, officer?" asked Rachel. When white men came and took away a black man, they never even had to have a reason. She feared the worst.

"He's got two hogs that he didn't report to the federal government. We found them just where our informant told us we would. We're going to take the hogs for evidence."

Her heart pounding, Rachel was so terrified that she could hardly get the words out. "Will he be able to get out on bond, sir?

The white man seemed almost kind. "Yes, we just must take him down to the federal building in Lakeville, book him, and then he can post bond. After that it's all up to the judge." The men left with Rob and the hogs that had been put into his trailer.

Just before lunch, Bobby Baily pulled up with Rob in the car. Bobby had gone over to the federal building that morning for some routine business and noticed that Rob was there. Bobby paid the two-hundred-and-fifty-dollar bond to get him out. Rob immediately went over to the bank and withdrew the money to pay Bobby back. "Rob, how in the hell did the Feds find out about those hogs?

Rob shook his head in disgust. "I don't really know Mr. Bobby. Only three people knew about it. That is me and my sons, Ernie and Lonnie."

"Well, somebody had to tell them, or they would not have come out there this morning," said Bobby, his face wrinkled up in the sun. "If you want me to, I'll represent you before the federal judge. It'll cost you one hundred dollars."

"Yessir. Thank you." Whew, thought Rob. Bobby was good at what he did. "Right now, I need to get out to Callawaytown. I got to lotta work to do."

"I can drive you out there if you can wait until I go to the office and tell them where I am," said Bobby.

As they drove towards Callawaytown, Rob wondered who had told. Or maybe someone saw him, and the boys put the hogs in the pen. Well, now he was out of two of his finest hogs, two hundred and fifty dollars, ands maybe much more once he appeared before the federal judge. He would have to find out who told the story and deal with it.

When he arrived home, Rachel was standing on the front porch, feeding the baby. She was amazed she had any milk after pacing up and down, worried out of her mind. "What happened? Rob, are you okay?" she cried as she flew toward him.

Bobby responded, "He's okay." He watched Rob and Rachel for a moment. "You must have been worried sick."

"Yessir!" she said, looking to Rob for an explanation. "I just didn't know what the Feds would do to him," replied Rachel.

"Well, they took him down to the federal building and booked him. We posted bail. We'll have to meet with the judge when the case comes up," said Bobby. "I'll be representing him."

Since Rob still wasn't talking, Rachel asked Bobby, "What about the two hogs?"

"Well, no telling what they will do with them, but for sure you won't get them back. I hope the rest of the day goes better for you," Bobby called as he got back into his car.

Rachel was getting mad by now. "Rob, why didn't you report them two hogs? You know how it is," she sighed. "I know. I know, during the First World War you could put things aside for a rainy day, but now the Feds are everywhere!"

"I guess so," said Rob. "But what I don't understand is how they knew where to look and what to look for. Somebody had to tell them. Cause, when I signed that sheet of paper letting them search this place, it said that they were looking for two fattening hogs. So, somebody had to tell them. That's the only way they could have found out."

Rob continued to talk with Rachel as he walked back behind the house to the water pump to wash his hands. They sat down at the table and silently ate their dinner. When Rob finished eating, he got up and walked out of the house and up the dirt road to the blacksmith shop. Several men were waiting to get one thing, or another done that day. No one knew what had taken place that morning.

He worked until late in the afternoon. Although folks attempted to make small talk with him, his mind was on what had happened with the Feds. It just did not make sense to him; how could the Feds know so much about where to find the two fattening hogs?

When he was finished for the day, he closed the shop and walked back to the house. He had not spoken very much with the older boys Ernie and Lonnie. They worked in the fields after school. The two younger boys Rob Junior and George, were always around him. Rob Junior and George like to turn the blower, which provided air to fuel the fire in the iron furnace.

When they were all sitting around the dining room table waiting for supper, Rob said the grace, and everyone began to load up their plates. Rob always went first, and then Rachel would serve the younger kids before passing the dishes to the older children. Rob Junior said to Ernie, "Don't take so much meat because you know Bubble said that they didn't have any fattening hogs saved like we have. So, we might have to give them some meat."

Instantly, Rob was furious! His eyes brightened up and got really narrow. "What do you mean Bubble said they didn't have any fattening hogs like we have? Who was talking about fattening hogs?"

Rob Junior looked up at his father and back over at Ernie and Lonnie. The boy was very frightened. He did not know what to say next. He looked back at his father and just stared at him with his mouth wide open.

"I said," Rob paused and looked menacingly at his sons, "who was talking about fattening hogs, and how did Bubble get into that conversation?" At that point, Ernie and Lonnie knew that they were in deep trouble. Suddenly, they remembered that Daddy had told them no one should know about those hogs.

"We were just standing there, and Ernie and Lonnie were talking about the two fattening hogs we have," said Rob Junior, trying to deflect some of his father's anger.

Rob looked over at Ernie and Lonnie with blood in his eyes. He could not believe his ears. He had hammered the point about not talking about the hogs to anyone. Not only did they disobey him, but they did it outside of the family. "You mean to tell me that Ernie and Lonnie were talking about fattening hogs at school with Bubble and other boys?"

"Yessir, there must have been five or ten boys standing around when they were talking," Rob Junior squeaked.

Rob looked over at Ernie and Lonnie and said, "I told you boys not to mention anything about those fattening hogs to anyone, and you disobeyed my orders. You just finished your supper, and I am going to teach y'all a lesson that you will never forget!"

Ernie and Lonnie were clearly frightened. For that matter, everyone at the table was scared. No one knew what "a lesson you'll never forget" really meant. But one thing was for certain: everyone knew that Ernie and Lonnie were in for something bad.

Rob took a couple more bites of food and got up from the table. Rachel stood and pursued her husband. "Rob! Rob! What are you going to do?" she pleaded. No matter what they had done, Ernie and Lonnie were still her babies.

"This is a matter that I am going to deal with by myself. I don't need any help from you!" said Rob angrily. He went outside and slammed the door behind him.

He went down to where he always slaughtered, cleaned, and dressed the hogs during slaughter season, between Thanksgiving and Christmas. He had already completed the hog killing for that year. The hogs were always shot, butchered, and hung up by their hind legs on a log that was held up by two fork trees about six feet from the ground. He had a plan about how he was going to punish those boys. He went to the barn and got two ropes and his bullwhip.

When he came back towards the house, Rachel and all the kids were crying; then they started screaming. "Rob, please don't do it," Rachel begged. "They're just boys. They made a mistake." She was frantic now, "Just talk to them some more. They made a mistake."

Rob did not say a word. He continued to work with the ropes, removing any knots that the kids had put in them. When he had finished, he took his bullwhip and went back over to the area by the barn and gave it a few test cracks. The cracks were so loud that it sounded like someone had fired a pistol. He rang the whip and laid it down near the log where the hogs were always hung. He walked back over to the house.

Rachel was hysterical. She started pulling on Rob to try to get him to come back to reason. But Rob would hear none of it. He was going to teach those boys a lesson, and no one was going to stop him. "Ernie, you and Lonnie come on out here!" he commanded.

A terrified Lonnie ran toward his grandfather's house, but Rob caught him and threw him to the ground. "Boy, don't you ever run from me! I am your daddy!" Rob growled. He tied Lonnie's hands in front of him with one of the ropes, and then he put him up over the log where the hogs were hung. The boy was shivering and whimpering with fear.

"Daddy, we didn't mean any harm by talking about the hogs at school," begged Ernie. But Rob tied him up as well. Both boys were now hanging by their arms with their toes barely touching the ground. The boys were still fully clothed and were screaming at the top of their lungs.

Rob grabbed his bullwhip, took several steps back from the boys, and gave the whip a couple of loud cracks. Then he gave the boys several cracks with the whip. He was good with the bullwhip and knew exactly where he wanted to strike. He hit them between the buttocks and the knees. Every time he cracked the whip, the boys screamed. Their clothes were ripped away, and bits of flesh flew from their bodies.

Rob gave each boy ten cracks with the whip. When he finished, he untied them, and their limp bodies fell to the ground. Horrified, Rachel and Shirley ran over to them. They removed their bloody clothes and cleaned their wounds. Rachel was appalled at Rob's behavior. The boys should not have talked, but the punishment didn't fit the crime. There was nothing Rob could do to bring back the hogs. And he'd have to pay the fine. After all, it was Rob who had broken the law! He had punished the boys for something he'd done.

Rachel didn't talk to him for days. For a long time, it was very tense in the house. Eventually, she softened up and talked to him. Before long, they were the best of friends again. Bobby Baily got Rob out of the mess with the Feds without a fine. The federal judge heard all the good things about Rob and the Callaway family and decided not to put a black mark on Rob's record. It also helped that the federal judge was C.G. Baily's brother-in-law. So, he let Rob off with a warning, but they kept the hogs. Ernie and Lonnie never again mentioned anything that was said to them at home.

The war went on, and so did life in the Callaway family. Rob's nephew was drafted into the Army and sent to France. His brother, Richard, became an officer in the Navy. Another nephew volunteered for the Army and was given a commission.

Thomas was the youngest son of Bent's baby brother Richard and his wife, Linda. Linda had always stressed education at any cost. She had worked hard to ensure that her children got through high school and went on to college. Even though Rockville Elementary School only went through the eighth grade, Linda found ways to get her children through high school and on to college. Thomas was a fine example. He had gone through the eighth grade at Rockville Elementary School and had lived with one of Linda's brothers in Fairbluff to complete high school. Afterward, he was accepted into Morehouse All Negro College in northern North Carolina. And now it was paying off, for he would probably be the first Army officer from the Callaway family.

Thomas came back from the war without a scratch. However, Richard was not so lucky. Somewhere off the coast of Africa, the Germans blew his U-boat out of the water. He survived but had a gaping hole in his head. He was never the same again.

CHAPTER NINE

As Jacob grew, it became apparent that he was quite different from the rest of Rob and Rachel's children. Everybody could see it. Jacob was exceptionally bright. Rob had made the statement at least once that Jacob always had a lot of questions. Rob was correct. The boy would never take a one-word answer for anything. He always wanted to know more.

Two years older than Jacob, his brother George was chubby, slow, and laid back. Both boys were born on July 16. George was Rob's favorite son. He took special care to work out problems with George, but he would explain things once to Jacob and the other boys and move on to the next issue. No one ever really knew the reason. Rob never discussed it. And no one would dare to question him on the subject. George simply accepted the answers he got to his questions. It was good enough for him. He never was interested in getting to the depth of anything. Before he had even started school, Jacob was far ahead of George.

When George did start school, he had learning difficulties that were not addressed as they should have been. During his first year in school, George's greatest accomplishment was his 100% attendance. He had achieved this even though he had come down with the flu in February. The teacher allowed Rachel to take him to school each day for a week so that he would be counted present when the morning roll was called. His grades were poor, but the last thing that the teacher wanted to do was keep Rachel and Rob's favorite son from going on to the next grade the following year.

Bent Callaway had given the community a school, but it only went through the eighth grade. Having only one room and one teacher, it managed to provide education to any child who wanted it. If the teacher did not promote George, she'd most likely have to look for a job in another state. The Callaway family was a force to be reckoned with.

George did even worse his second year in school. His mother and father, not to mention his older siblings, had spoiled him rotten. George took full advantage of the situation. He could see no need to study or do any homework. Rob justified his behavior by saying that this boy would be just like him. He would stay on the farm and take up the blacksmith trade.

Both George and Jacob worked in the shop with their father. They were responsible for turning the bellows used to keep the fire going in the iron pit. After a few minutes, George would get bored and give the job to Jacob. That would be the last anyone would see of him until Jacob tracked him down. While Jacob worked, George played. Rob would call for help when the fire went down. The first name out of his mouth would be Jacob, not George. The last person who kept the fire going was always responsible for it. So, of course, Jacob was the one who was called. He put in two or three times the work that George did.

Rob would take the boys fishing whenever he wasn't working in his blacksmith shop. Both enjoyed going with their father. There was a fork where the Ralf Swamp River met the Lumber River. Rob and Rachel's house sat right between the two rivers. There was never a shortage of good fishing spots. However, one spot was for Rob alone.

Once a poor white cracker tried to challenge local tradition about who fished where. Bent simply passed the word in Lakeville that the poor white cracker's daughter was screwing around with one of the blackass niggers from out of town. She was married to a poor white cracker from another county. The gal had a baby boy that had curly hair and brown skin. The whites tried to pass it off by saying that she had been scared by a mule when she was carrying the kid.

All the black folks knew why she had the colored child. That is why they just laughed when the tale went out. All the blacks in and around Callawaytown knew she would be "been scared" by that black mule a whole lot of times.

The preacher in the white church in Back Swamp had told the gal not to bring the baby to church because the congregation would be upset and there would be problems. The word had gotten to the Ku Klux Klan about the man's daughter. It had been just a matter of time before he was completely isolated from everyone in Callawaytown.

Bent did not like the KKK or anything they stood for. But he was smart enough to know that they were a reality, so he used them to his advantage. They were the only group with the will and resources to get that bastard off his property. He knew that no one would ever dare to question him. If he were the source of the information, everyone would take it as gospel. The best thing to do was to get the child out of Mills County right away. If he stayed, a disaster would befall all the good niggers and white folks in the County.

Bent waited and let time take its course. Soon, the white cracker said that he would be returning to Mississippi. "It's not a place for me and my family. I can't live in this state; niggers ain't in their place up here," he had ranted. "I can't see how any good white person can live with niggers like this. Hell, look at you! Here you are a goddamn nigger, and I gotta pay you rent. Now you know that ain't right. If anything, you should be paying me rent. I just do not understand how white people can let niggers have land and houses like this. There must be a law against this type of thing. In Mississippi, you never see a thing like this."

Bent did not care about what the poor white cracker said about black folks or anyone else just as long as he got out of his house, and, for that part, out of Callawaytown. It was not exceptionally long before Bent rented the house to someone who paid on time and was a Callaway or related to the Callaway's in one way or another. Rob knew his daddy had greased the skids so that there would not be a confrontation between Rob and the poor white man. The Callaway's had their own set of rules. They never started any trouble and never "rocked the boat."

CHAPTER TEN

Just before Jacob turned six, the teacher at Callawaytown Elementary School noticed that he always followed George to school. Although Jacob was not old enough to attend, clearly he wanted to go. His brother George used to tease him about what went on in school. This made it just that much more interesting for Jacob. He wanted to see for himself what was happening.

Miss Lee noticed the youngster came to the school with the other kids in the morning and would always be there when the final bell sounded. "Little boy, what's your name?" she asked.

Before Jacob could utter a sound, George responded, "His name is Jacob. He is my little brother, but he will not be six until July 16. On July 16th, he will be six, but I will be eight."

"So, he won't be old enough to start school until next year," the teacher replied kindly. She thought for a moment and looked down at Jacob. "Do you think your mother would let you come to school for the rest of this school year? Just to try things out," she added. "It's already May, and school will be out soon."

"Yessome, I sho will ask her and see what she says," answered Jacob. He was afraid to get too excited. He wanted to go to school more than anything in the world.

"Okay, if she says yes, you are welcome to come to school starting tomorrow," replied Miss Lee.

Jacob was so excited that he could hardly contain himself. He ran for home. George was startled. He liked having the status of being able to go to school while Jacob had to stay home. "But, Miss Lee, he can't come to school yet. He ain't six years old yet, and mama said that he might not be able to start next year, even though he'll be six, because she said he won't listen to what anybody says." Wanting to make his case, he added in a rush, "You know, everybody says he's just like Billy Raymond."

Billy Raymond was the son of a poor white cracker who lived further up the road. His father and mother were half sister and brother. He had two sisters named Kitty and Molly. All three of the Raymond children were only plain dumb. There was nothing inside their heads. People in the neighborhood considered them the biggest idiots in the entire county. Jacob's family had teased him about "acting like Billy Raymond." Jacob was different, and his family could not understand it.

Miss Lee looked solemnly at George and said. "I don't think he's like Billy Raymond at all. He is different, but that is what makes this world such a good place to live in. We have so many different types of people, which makes everything remarkably interesting." When George continued to look dismayed, Miss Lee added kindly, "When you get home, tell your mother that Jacob should come and attend class for the rest of this year."

George looked at Miss Lee like she had just stolen something very precious from him. As he turned to start his journey home, which was only about one hundred yards from the school, he thought, that I will never do! I will do whatever I can to keep that little stupid brother of mine from coming to school.

George knew he was his parents' favorite, even though he never mentioned it straight out to Jacob or anyone else. Rachel and Rob would never tolerate that. But if Jacob could start school now, he would certainly have one up on George. And even though Miss Lee had let him slide last year to the second grade and he had made a perfect attendance record for the previous year, Miss Lee had already met with Rachel and Rob. They had all agreed that George should spend an additional year in the second grade.

When Jacob arrived home, he ran straight to his mother. Pulling her apron, he shouted, "Mama, mama, I was at the school this afternoon, and you know what?"

"What?" Rachel asked patiently.

"Miss Lee said I could come to school for the rest of this year if it's okay with you and daddy," he cried.

"Well, I am pretty sure she was just teasing you," said Rachel. "You won't even be six until July 16. Next year you can go to school," she said dismissively.

Jacob was heartbroken and walked away crying. At just that time, George came into the house. "Mama, you know what?" said George.

"What?" Rachel asked.

"Miss Lee is doing something wrong. She said that Jacob could come to school, but he ain't six yet," he complained.

Rachel looked up, now interested. But she did not say anything. By then, Jacob's older sister, Louise Ruth, came into the kitchen. She had heard what Miss Lee had said and had heard the conversation between Jacob, her mother, and George. "Mama, you know Miss Lee did say that Jacob could come to school for the rest of this year if it was all right with you and daddy." Right then, Louise Ruth decided to take up Jacob's cause. "He wants to go so bad. You always say he is always into something. So, this would be a good way to get him away from the house for some time every day. You will not have to worry about whether he's into something. I'll help you get him dressed, and I will make sure that he behaves like all the other kids when he gets to school."

Rachel looked down at Louise Ruth. "Do you really think he would be okay in school?"

"Yessome, I really do think it will be good for you and for him. At least we can try," replied Louise Ruth. "If he starts acting crazy, I will just ask Miss Lee if I can take him home."

Rachel thought for a moment that she could use some freedom from that boy! She had never been so busy as she had been since she gave birth to Jacob. All the other kids were easy to handle, but Jacob was truly a different child. And since his birth, she had given birth to Mandy and was due to give birth again sometime in the summer. At this point, anything to get that boy out of her hair would be good for her. "Okay, we will try it tomorrow and see what happens."

Jacob heard what his mother said and ran out to tell the news to George. "George, you know what?" shouted Jacob.

"What?" said George sullenly.

"Mama said I could go to school tomorrow!" replied Jacob with a wide grin. George just frowned. He did not think it was right that Jacob should be allowed to start school. In fact, he was downright hurt about it. He would lose every bit of control he had over his younger brother.

Jacob went to bed early that night. He could not fall asleep for at least an hour, thinking about what the next day would bring.

He was the first person out of bed in the morning. Shortly thereafter, Rachel, Louise, and the whole family were out of bed getting dressed, preparing lunches, and getting ready to sit down for their usual big country breakfast of stewed ham, sausage, bacon, biscuits, grits, and eggs.

Jacob's first day in school was remarkably interesting. He was terribly busy all day, just trying to understand what was going on and how he would fit in. He received his first coloring book and a box with eight different colors of crayons. The coloring book had all types of animals in all shapes and sizes, as well as landscapes, houses, trucks, and cars. It was the most exciting day of his life. He did everything that Miss Lee showed him to do and even more. He was terribly busy from the time he arrived at school until the bell sounded for the close of the day.

George resented Jacob and the attention he got. For the remainder of the spring and summer, Jacob was the topic of conversation on Sunday afternoon when all his aunts, uncles, and cousins came to visit. Everyone would ask about Jacob and how he was doing. The word was out that he had started school even before he was six and was doing well. That did not go over well with George, and it went to Jacob's head.

One afternoon, when the kids had returned from school, their uncle came by the house. Sonny Winsey lived on the other side of the road and was married to one of Rachel's younger sisters. He was the kind of man who always wanted to start something. He looked at Rachel, who was standing on the bank of the Lumber River washing some clothes. Jacob was standing behind her as she bent over to scrub the clothes against the washboard.

Sonny walked over and started some small talk with Rachel, but she was busy. So he walked over to where Jacob was standing. "Howdy Jacob. How today you are doing boy?"

"I am doing okay, uncle Sonny," responded Jacob.

Sonny reached into his pocket, pulled out a nickel, showed it to Jacob, and said, "You can have it if you push Rachel off the rock." Jacob was too little to understand that pushing his mother into the river was wrong. He looked at his mother and then back at the nickel. If Uncle Sonny said he should do it, it must be okay. He took the nickel out of his uncle's hand and wedged it between his right forefinger and thumb. He thought about the candy he could get down at his Aunt Linda's shop and placed the nickel in his pocket. Without a sound, he walked over behind his mother and gave her a big push.

Rachel fell headfirst into the river. She could not swim, and the water was about two inches over her head. Sonny let out his biggest laugh ever. Rachel was about to go under for the second time when Sonny reached out, grabbed her arm, and pulled her from the river.

Jacob now knew he had done something bad. He knew that his mama would beat him with a branch from the old willow tree nearby. Rachel would make him go and get the branch and bring it to her. She was upset with Sonny for what he had done. But that did not excuse Jacob's behavior. He would have to be taught that you must make your own decisions…and live with the consequences. She would have to teach that boy a lesson.

Rachel dried herself and changed clothes, and then she came out of the house. Before she could utter a word, Jacob started talking. "Mama, Uncle Sonny gave me a nickel to push you. I didn't want to do it, but a nickel is a lot of money."

She just glared at him. "Boy, you go down to that old willow tree and get me a branch. And you go and get it now." Jacob went down to the willow tree, picked out a branch that he thought would satisfy his mother, but it was a ridiculously small and short one. He brought it back.

Rachel looked at the branch and then back at Jacob. He could see by the look in his mother's eyes that the branch was not to her satisfaction. "Boy, you go back to that old willow tree and get me a branch that I can use."

Jacob went back to the old willow tree, and this time he picked a branch that was more to his mother's liking. Within a noticeably short period, his backside hurt. He told himself that he should have never done what he did, even for a nickel. And for sure, he would never do anything like that again.

Meanwhile, Sonny was having the time of his life. Some of the Foster boys who lived near the crossroads came down to the fork to do some fishing. The incident had taken place just a few minutes before they arrived. When they approached the house, Sonny met them and said, "You know that crazy Jacob pushed his mother in the swamp for a nickel. Can you believe he would do a thing like that? The more I think about it, the more I know that that boy is just like Billy Raymond. How could he do a thing like that just for a nickel?" continued Sonny. At the same time, he gave out a big laugh, which could be heard all the way down to where Rob's Uncle Winson and Aunt Linda lived.

One of the Foster boys looked at Rachel and joked, "Well, Rachel, you finally had a bath," and busted into big laughter.

Rachel was not amused. She thought it was a shame that her sister's husband could pull such a trick on an innocent five-year-old. But she was extremely concerned about why Jacob let someone talk him into doing something that was so wrong. She simply disregarded what the Foster boys had said. She had known the Foster family ever since she and Rob were married. They were considered by blacks and whites alike to be poor white trash, which was no better than being a redneck or cracker. Whatever they said always went in one ear and out the other.

Soon, Rob came in from his shop. When he was told about what had happened, he got really upset with Sonny. If he had not been married to Rachel's sister, Rob would have thrown him out of his house and told him not to come back. But he just gave Sonny "the Callaway look." Once you got that look from a Callaway, everyone knew things would never be the same again. There was nothing you could do to resume your former place in the world. Rob didn't have to say a word. His look spoke for him.

Still, Sonny tried to justify his actions. "You know that crazy Jacob pushed Rachel in the swamp just for a nickel. How stupid can a boy be?"

Rob gave Sonny a very cold stare and responded, "What do you think he was going to do? He's only five years old. At least he earned the nickel. If it had been you and you were only five years old, you would have probably taken the nickel and run away. You know, when a grown man doesn't have anything better to do than stand around and pull a trick on a five-year-old, it would sound more to me that the man was the fool," continued Rob.

Sonny was stunned. He never imagined he would get that kind of talk from Rob. Hell, he was only trying to have some fun. There was nothing to get upset about. No one got hurt. Rachel only got wet. As far as he was concerned, it was no big deal.

But from that point on, Sonny knew where he stood with Rob and behaved accordingly.

CHAPTER ELEVEN

School was over, and everyone was planning for the start of a hot and humid summer. Jacob had performed very well during those few weeks he could attend school. He could hardly wait until September. This would probably be the longest summer he had ever lived through. But there were a lot of things to look forward to. Rob's sister and brother would come down from Baltimore, MD. Every summer, they spent two weeks in North Carolina and brought all their children to visit.

They would live between Rob's and Bent's houses. Most of the time, they would stay with Rachel and Rob because they really didn't like Maddie. Everyone thought it was sad that Bent had married that young girl.

There would be a steady flow of visitors from mid-June to Labor Day. It was the best time of the year for Jacob. He would be able to play with all his cousins and just be a part of the big group. Now he had school to look forward to in the fall. This really made this summer special. He looked at the calendar every day and asked his mother how many weeks it would be before school started. When he got that answer, he would ask how many days that was.

Late that summer, Bent became extremely ill. Rob took him to the doctor several times, but there was nothing he could do. In his mid-nineties, Bent had finally become an old man. He had had an incredibly good and simple life. He had fathered ten children by his first wife, Louise, and two by his second wife, Maddie. He had the largest tract of land in the area. All his children are married and doing well, except for the ones that are already dead. He was ready to go.

Bent lay on a cart in the hallway, smoked Rabbit tobacco and talked to himself. Jacob took him some water and tried to understand what he said. It had something to do with riding a witch and floating through the air.

On a Friday afternoon, Jacob took the old man some water and noticed that he did not move. Jacob placed the water on a small table near the old man's head and looked at him for a few moments before touching his forehead. Bent's head was cold as ice. Jacob almost panicked when that cold feeling went through his fingers, up his hand, arm and through his body. He ran into the kitchen. "Grandma! Grandma! Something is wrong with grandpapa. I gave him some water, and he is lying still. I touched his head, and it's awfully cold," shouted Jacob.

Maddie looked at the boy and knew that Bent was probably dead. She walked into the hallway and knew, even without touching him, that he was gone. She immediately turned to Jacob and asked him to go over to the blacksmith shop and tell his father to come over to the house.

"Papa! Papa!" Jacob shouted. "Grandma said you've got to come over to their house. There's something wrong with grandpapa."

Rob immediately put down what he was doing and walked over to the house. When he arrived, Maddie was kneeling over Bent and crying. Rob pulled her up and consoled her. He could see that the old man was dead. They walked into the kitchen and, after a while, talked about the practical things that would have to be immediately addressed.

Jacob was told to go down to Aunt Linda's and tell her that Bent was dead. Then Rob told his cousin to go down to Barry Evans' Funeral Home and tell Barry to come out and pick up his father. Rob walked back into the hallway and closed Bent's eyes. He placed a penny on each eye to make sure they stayed closed. Maddie got Rob a white bed sheet, which he placed over the body. He left, went home, and gave the news to Rachel.

Rachel wept as she remembered how the old man had helped them so many years ago. He was a truly kind and caring person. Everyone who knew him loved him.

Rob comforted Rachel for a few minutes, then got into his car and drove to the Western Union in Lakeville. He sent all his brothers and sisters a telegram informing them that Bent had died.

In Mills County, having a funeral on any day other than Sunday was unheard of. The old man's body would have to be preserved for a minimum of seven days. Rob could not make any decisions about the funeral until all his sisters and brothers were notified and given time to put in their two cents worth. It would be next week before a decision could be made about what kind of casket they wanted. The only decision that Rob could make at this point was that the funeral would be on Sunday of the following week.

Rob's four sisters, who lived in the nearby towns, were the first to arrive. They were very upset that they had not been told that their father was so ill. Rob would not listen. He raised his voice. "You all knew that Daddy was sick. He's been sick for some time now. You all come here every weekend, but the only thing you are interested in is what you can take back with you. You were never interested in how Daddy was doing."

His sisters were visibly angry, but they were not about to make a scene. They got down to the business of figuring what to do about the funeral. The family decided that it should be at Big Swamp Baptist Church and that the body should lie out at the house starting on Thursday. The wake would be on Friday and Saturday, just before the funeral.

Jacob hovered in the background and listened to the grownups. Tears rolled down his face as he thought about the fact that his grandpa was dead. Now his body was all laid out in the living room–that was so strange. The grownups were talking about a wake and then the funeral. There were so many people around all the time. He just could not put it all together. Everybody was talking about Grandpa going to heaven, and it was so great to go to heaven and be with God.

But if that was true, he wondered why they were all crying. Some of them were even screaming and kind of falling. It just did not make any sense to him. He did understand that the old man was cold when he touched him that Friday. After the funeral, everyone left. It would never be the same without Bent.

Jacob's grandmother, Maddie, was still living in the old house, but she wanted to leave and go back to her family, who lived in another town. By law, she had a lifetime right to live in the house and be the administrator of the estate. However, she was not interested in anything in Callawaytown. She had born Bent two children, a son, and a daughter. The son was killed in a car accident, and the daughter died of pneumonia. The town held nothing for her. She just wanted to get away from the place.

A few months after Bent's death, Maddie went out to the blacksmith shop where Rob was and said she wanted to talk to him when he had the time. Shortly thereafter, he closed the shop and went over to the house, where Maddie was sitting on the porch. "What's on your mind?"

"Well Rob, I was thinking…" Maddie paused and took a deep breath. "I really don't like living here since your father died. I would like to go back to where my family lives. I know that you were Bent's favorite. He would really be pleased if you got this place, you know, if you were living here with Rachel and your children."

Rob just looked at her. He knew that she had little time for him and was not about to put herself out for him, so he was waiting for the punch line.

Maddie walked to the door, looked out over the garden and fields, turned back to Rob, and said, "If you would give me five hundred dollars, I will sell you my lifetime rights here. That way, you can move into this house with Rachel and the children and rent your house out. All you have to do is give me a little something out of the rental property every month."

Rob looked at her in amazement. He could not believe that he could have the house that he had always wanted. He would have to be incredibly careful. He did not want to be saddled with paying an income every month. However, he knew he'd agree to give her something.

He walked out of the house and into the backyard without uttering a word. Maddie followed. "I don't think it's wrong for me to want to have something out of all this," she said. "You got to give me something."

Rob could be a hard man. "Yes, I know you need something. But what we must do is decide what that something should be. I'll tell you what I can do, and you can agree or disagree." Maddie just looked over at him.

"I can give you three hundred dollars right now for your right to live here, and I will give you ten dollars a month from the rental property. But I do not want you to take any of Papa's things from this place. And that means that you can't give or sell anything to anyone."

Maddie could not do anything except agree with him. "I ain't going to take nothing from this place that don't belong to me. I know that all Callaway's going to want all Bent's things, and that's okay with me." She shrugged her shoulders. "When can I have the three hundred dollars?"

"I'll go down to Baily this afternoon and get the papers drawn up," Rob answered. "You can have the money as soon as you get out of the house."

"Okay," Maddie said as she slumped a little. "I'll start packing now. I'll send word to my brother to come and pick me up."

Rob left the house and went straight to his old car. Within half an hour, he was in C.G. Baily's office. "Hi, Mr. Baily," he said with a smile. "Is your son here today?"

"Yes he's in. What can we do for you, Rob?"

"Well, I wanted to talk to him about some property."

"What property is that, Rob?" asked Mr. Baily.

"Well, it's my daddy's estate. Maddie does not want to stay there any longer. She wants to move away since my daddy is dead."

"Yes, I heard about Bent," replied Mr. Baily. "That was really bad. Bent was one good nigger. He never gave anybody any trouble. If all the niggers were as good as the Callaway niggers, we wouldn't have any problems in this county."

Rob listened to the old man as he continued to ramble on about Bent and what he thought of the Callaway's, other niggers, good niggers, bad niggers, and so forth. Rob could care less about what he said if he got what he came for. Even though Rob was truly not interested in hearing all that nonsense, he knew he would have to go through the process if he was going to get what he had come to Lakeville for. His only objective was to see Bobby Baily.

Both of Mr. Bailey's boys were lawyers. They had gone to an all-white Christian College just north of Lakeville. Now they were working at the family law firm. Bobby was Rob's favorite. He was always the one that Rob would ask for. After listening to C.G.'s rattling, Rob was told that Bobby would be with him in just a moment. Before Rob could get settled into his chair, Bobby came out of his office.

"Hi Rob," said Bobby. "Come on in. What can I do for you today?"

"I want you to draw up some papers for my stepmother," responded Rob. "She wants to leave the old place, so I am going to buy her lifetime rights to the place. I have already discussed the deal with her. I wrote it all down here." He handed Bobby a sheet of paper. "I am going to give her so much in cash, and she will get so much a month from the rental properties. What do you think about the deal?" Rob asked.

Bobby read for a moment. "Well, it looks good to me. It looks like you made a real good deal with her. She must have really wanted to get away from that place pretty badly."

"Well, you know how it is," said Rob.

Bobby nodded his head. "She ain't got no family in Callawaytown, so she's going to move back down to where her brother lives."

"Yes, she has already written a letter to her brother telling him that he can come pick her up. I told her that I would have the money for her today," Rob said.

"You really move fast. You want these papers today?"

"It doesn't have to be right now," Rob assured him. "I got to go to the shop and buy some things for the house, and I can come back by when I finish if it's okay with you."

"Yes, that's okay. I see you have all the information I need. It should be finished when you return. It will cost you ten dollars, and of course you will have to have the money you are going to give Maddie when you return," said Bobby. "And oh, Maddie will have to sign the papers before we can record them over at the courthouse."

Rob was dismayed. He had not thought it would be necessary to have her sign anything. Maddie could not read or write. All she could do was draw an X, and at least two people would have to see it He was annoyed that his plans would have to change. He would have to think of how to do all the things he planned to do and still have time to make the trip out to Callawaytown, pick up Maddie, return to Lakeville, get the papers signed and recorded, and do his chores.

After Rob had gone to the bank and completed his shopping, he drove to Callawaytown. Maddie was waiting on the front porch. "Do you have the money and the papers?"

"Yes, I got everything taken care of. You'll have to go to Lakeville to Bobby Baily's office with me to sign some papers before we can have them recorded at the courthouse."

"Oh no!" Maddie exclaimed. "You know I can't do that! I can't read or write. How am I going to sign any papers?"

"Well, you don't have to worry about that. Bobby will take care of everything. All you got to do is go down to Lakeville with me and go to Bobby's office. But we got to do it now. I want to get this all taken care of today."

Maddie returned to the house, went inside, removed her apron, made a few adjustments to her dress, and returned to the car. Within a short period, she and Rob were in Lakeville. They went straight to Bobby Baily's office. Bobby had the papers prepared. Bobby had a good idea that Maddie was unable to read and write. He read through the papers and asked if she had any questions or if there was any part of the agreement that she did not understand or disagree with.

When Maddie nodded, Bobby said, "Just put your X here and everything will be finished." At that point, Rob reached into his pocket and pulled out the amount that they had agreed upon. Rob had already counted it out and had it separated from the rest of his cash. He handed it to Bobby, who counted it on his desk as Maddie and Rob watched. When Bobby was finished, Maddie picked up the cash and placed it in her bosom. Bobby looked up at Rob and said, "You two have a deal. I will go over to the courthouse and record these papers, and you can pick up your copy the next time you are in town, Rob."

They left the office and went to the car. Rob droves back to Callawaytown and parked near the blacksmith shop, where a lot of people were waiting to have work done. Maddie got out and walked over to the house. Right away, Rob started with the first person in line and worked until everyone had been taken care of. Finally, he closed the shop and walked the few yards home.

He said casually, "Rachel, we'll be moving up to papa's house soon."

Startled, Rachel asked, "What do you mean we will be moving up to papa's house? I will not move into that house with your stepmother. I just as soon stay here where we are. We have enough room here, and we live alone. It's better this way, so you can forget about moving."

Rob laughed. "Rachel, if you will just listen for a minute, I'll tell you what's going on." When he had her attention, he said, "The other day, Maddie asked me if I wanted to buy her lifetime rights to the house, and I told her I would. So today I went down to Lakeville and talked to C.G. Baily's son, Bobby. He was able to take care of everything. We have the house now for as long as Maddie is alive. I have already paid Maddie what she wanted. She wrote to her brother and told him to come and pick her up as soon as he could. So, I'd say she should be out of the house before the end of next week."

Rachel was overjoyed. "Oh Rob! Really? You're sure?" Rob just grinned over at his wife, enjoying her enthusiasm. She threw her arms around him. "Now we'll have room enough for the girls to have their own rooms. And we will have our room and two bedrooms for the boys!"

"You should have seen her face when I gave her that money," Rob said into Rachel's shoulder. "She could not wait to get home and start packing. I know she will be on her way down to where her family lives as soon as that brother of hers can get a truck to pick her things up. I'd say by the middle of next week she will be out of Callawaytown."

Rachel jumped up and down. "I'll start packing!"

"That's good," Rob said ruefully. "Because I think she will probably take everything that's in that house with her. She didn't bring anything with her when she came after Mama died, but you can be sure that she will take everything with her when she leaves."

Rachel was so happy about the house. She didn't care about anything else. "We have everything we need, and there will be just enough room once we spread everything out." For the first time since they were married, they would have room for all of their twelve children. Once Maddie moved out, Rachel would take their oldest daughter, Shirley, and the middle daughter, Louise, up to the house and give it a good cleaning. Depending on the condition of the house, she might even ask Rob's cousin Maddie-Jean to help her.

Maddie-Jean lived across the swamp and had twelve children. She was several years younger than Rachel. Her mother had died when she was born, and her aunt Linda, who was Bent's youngest sister, had raised her. When she was only twelve, Linda forced her to marry an older man named Kenny Hooker. Kenny had been renting a room from Linda, and she thought that would be the best thing for Maddie-Jean.

Now, they lived just over the bridge in an old farmhouse, which was owned by someone in the Baily family. The house sat on a large farm. They were sharecroppers. A sharecropper worked the land and received one-half of the net profit. Depending on the situation, people could wind up owing the landowner at the end of the year. However, Kenny and his family were able to tend the farm and still have time to spare.

When Rachel approached Maddie-Jean, she immediately agreed to lend a hand. So, it was set. The following Saturday, Maddie-Jean would walk over the bridge to where Rachel and Rob lived. They would probably chat for a while, have some mint tea, and then walk up the few yards to Bent's house.

On Tuesday of the following week, Maddie's brother came with a truck he had borrowed from the farm where he and his family worked as sharecroppers. They loaded up Maddie's belongings and were on their way by mid-afternoon. Rob stopped what he was doing in the blacksmith shop and went over to the house just as they were preparing to leave.

"Well, y'all have a good trip home and drive carefully," were the last words Rob said to his stepmother. When the truck was around the bend and out of sight, Rob walked inside the house. Despite their agreement, Maddie had done exactly what he had expected. The house was empty. Rob shook his head and accepted reality. He went through every room in the house and noted what he would need to repair or replace before he and Rachel moved in with their family. But in the end, there was little that had to be done. He walked back out the door and thought what a great deal he had made with Maddie. Now she was out of his father's house and out of his life as well. He closed the door and walked back to the blacksmith shop. It was all over. He and Rachel would be moving in over the weekend.

He hoped they could do it on time. He had promised old man Jacob that he would go with him to the auction in Bennettsville, South Carolina. This was the single largest auction in the Carolinas.

Rob had a special talent when it came to purchasing livestock at an auction. He could tell the age of just about any large animal by taking a good look at its teeth. Although old man Jacob had taught him the trade, Rob had long since surpassed his abilities. Now, he was not only getting older, but he was also losing his sight, memory, and hearing. He depended on Rob to do his bidding for him.

He decided he would just have to tell Rachel that the house would have to be cleaned by Saturday. That way, they would have Saturday and Sunday to move in. That would free him up for next week and not interfere with his obligations. He shook his head. Sometimes, Rachel was a hard woman to convince.

"Is that you, Rob?" shouted Rachel when he entered the house. "You're home early today. Were things slow at the shop?"

"Nope, just decided I would close early today. Wanted to come home and be with you and the kids some before we eat," Rob said casually. He knew how to work his wife. "You know Maddie moved out today. I went through the house to see what needed to be repaired or replaced. It did not look too bad. As a matter of fact, I am going to take Ernie and Lonnie over there with me tomorrow when they get out of school. We will get everything done. I was thinking that maybe you and Shirley can go down on Thursday and see what you have to do to get the place cleaned."

Rachel looked up at Rob in amazement. "You know I have already talked to Maddie-Jean, and she is coming to help me clean that house on Saturday."

"Yes, I know," answered Rob. "But if you and Shirley just go down and see what you have to do to get the place cleaned, you could have that out of the way." Noticing that Rachel was less than pleased with the point he was attempting to make, Rob walked over to her, put his arms around her, and sweet-talked her.

After a while, she sighed and said, "Okay, I'll go up there Thursday and see what's got to be done as far as cleaning is concerned." In a short while, they sat down with the twelve kids and had an exceptionally good North Carolina country dinner.

The next few days were remarkably busy for everyone. Rob, Ernie, and Lonnie made the repairs that were needed. Rob instructed the boys to put a bag of lime in the outside toilet after they had completed the repairs. The next day, true to plan, Rachel and Shirley went up to the house to see what had to be cleaned. When they arrived, they could see that Rob and the boys had already done much of the cleaning as they completed the repairs.

Rachel walked through the house and did a little dusting here and there as she moved from room to room. Before long, the place was almost entirely cleaned. At that point, she thought, why not go ahead and just get the job done? Then the only thing left would be moving in.

Rob did not know how he did it, but he got the job done, and he and Rachel were still on good terms. Now his plan for next week would not be interrupted. Everything would go as he wished. Just one more day, and they would be making that move.

The following morning, the family was up bright and early. The move went well. By the late afternoon, everything was just about in place. Everyone knew where they would be spending the night. Shirley and Louise were putting things away in their bedroom.

The boys were all outside playing horseshoes.

At around six-thirty that evening, Rachel and the girls had prepared a very nice meal for the family. Rice, potatoes, pork, chicken, fish, cornbread, biscuits, brown gravy, and oceans of cool-aid and limeade were set on the table. It was the first meal that they had in that house without Bent and Maddie. It seemed a little strange.

The family was happy, but Bent was sorely missed.

CHAPTER TWELVE

The summer of 1947 was one of the hottest in many years. None of the family members from outside of North Carolina came to visit that year. Everyone had come during the late spring to attend Bent's funeral. Most of the family were wage earners or had their own businesses. No one could afford to take more time off. It was a good thing for Rachel. She was happy that she would have the summer to herself, Rob, and the children.

The weekend before school started, Rachel and Rob took George and Jacob to Lakeville. They needed clothes for school. Each year, they got two pairs of blue jean overalls, two blue jean shirts, two pairs of socks, a pair of brogan high top shoes, and a blue jean jacket.

They left Callawaytown for Lakeville around noon that day. It was not very long before they were parked in Rob's regular parking space on Fourth Street, near the area where folks took their mules and wagons to town.

It was the first time Jacob had ever gone to Lakeville. When Rob opened the door for Jacob and George to get out of the car, little Jacob's eyes brightened up. He had spent his short life on his grandfather's farm and had not been exposed to the outside world. Jacob looked around; to him, this was the biggest place in the world.

Of course, it was practically the only place he had ever been. He had been to Carriton in Bull County, where Rachel came from. But they had never stopped in Lakeville or any other town along the way. Everything looked so big. Over by the market on Fourth Street was a water fountain made of white marble. Over the fountain was a sign that read, "WHITES ONLY." Just to the left of the fountain was a gourd cup with a sign over it that said, "COLOREDS ONLY." On the other side of the fountain was the same set-up with a sign that read, "INDIANS ONLY."

But little Jacob could not read.

He freed himself from his mother's hands as she talked to someone she knew. The boy ran over to the fountain and began to drink. He had barely started when a big redneck came over to the fountain, grabbed him by the neck, and threw him up against the wall. "Nigger! What are you doing? This fountain's only for white folks!" he shouted. "If you want water, you drink from the gourd for niggers."

Jacob was shocked out of his mind. His parents had sheltered him from the harsh reality of racism in North Carolina. The white cracker did not stop there. Turning his head and looking around, he shouted; "Who is this goddamn nigger with?"

Rob heard what was going on and walked over to where the cracker was standing. He did not recognize him.

"Is this your nigger boy, nigger?" said the redneck belligerently.

"Yessir, that's my boy," said Rob carefully.

"Well, you better teach that nigger son of yours some manners," snarled the redneck.

"You know no nigger is supposed to drink out of that fountain."

"Yessir, I know. This is the first time my son has been to town," Rob said, hoping to defuse the situation. "He's never been off the farm before. He just doesn't know any better." Rob was standing face-to-face with the redneck. "I'll teach him all about what he can and can't do. Just let me have him." The white cracker still held the boy by the throat, pressing him against the wall.

Rob could see that Jacob was terrified, so he began to plead with the cracker to let his son go. By that time, a crowd had gathered between Rachel and the fountain. Someone wiggled through to Rachel and told her that something was going on over at the fountain between Rob and a cracker. Rachel quickly wormed her way through the crowd. When she saw that Jacob was very frightened and completely helpless, she began to plead with the cracker as well. But as the crowd continued to swell, the cracker held his ground and continued to talk about a nigger drinking from the fountain. Rachel started to scream in terror as Rob tried to keep his cool.

He glanced quickly over at Rachel and said, "Run inside and ask Mr. Baily to come out here." Tears streaming down her face, Rachel ran through the crowd and into his office. As he looked up, he could see that Rachel was frightened out of her wits.

"Rachel! What's wrong?"

"Mr. Baily!" Rachel cried. "You got to come out to the fountain now! A white man has our son and won't let him go. Please, please help us."

Without making a sound, Mr. Baily came from behind his desk and swiftly went out the door toward the fountain. Rachel was right behind him. A lot of people had gathered around. Mr. Baily cut through the crowd and made his way to where the cracker still held the boy by the throat. "Let the boy go," he said with authority.

"That nigger was drinking out of the fountain. We can't have this in Lakeville," the cracker snapped back. "That nigger needs to be taught a lesson."

"I said let the boy go," Mr. Baily said firmly.

Mr. Baily stood more than six feet tall and weighed more than two hundred and fifty pounds. When the cracker still refused to let the boy go, he hit him on the side of his head with one hard blow. The cracker released his grip on the boy and hit Mr. Baily in the chest. Mr. Baily shook off the blow and gave the cracker a hard right hand, which landed him on the ground.

The whites in the crowd were offended. They shouted that the cracker was just doing what any other full-blooded American should do. The nigger was wrong for drinking from the water fountain. They thought that, as a white man, Mr. Baily should have supported the cracker instead of the nigger. In any case, Mr. Baily should not have hit the man.

Mr. Baily looked quickly around to see if he could identify anyone. He knew that nobody wanted to be on the wrong side of the Baily family. They owned just about everything in Mills County.

Once Jacob was released, he wasted no time in getting to his mother. Rachel immediately grabbed the boy in her arms and held him close to her breast. The crowd was beginning to break up when a Negro ran over and started drinking from the fountain. A long gazing line of Negroes and Indians followed him.

A white man named Tom yelled from the crowd. "I guess you see what you have done. Now we will have trouble with all the niggers and Indians in the county!"

Mr. Baily just stared at the man. "Tom, what are you doing down here? Do you have your tobacco in for this week? What about the tobacco that you were supposed to have ready for the market this week? If you have time to be down here with all these stupid people, I know you have time to come into my office so we can discuss what we should do about the following year and how you plan to pay the Baily Company what you owe."

Tom looked down at his feet and shuffled, "Well, Mr. Baily, you know I am behind you in whatever you do in this county. I just thought that the nigger should be taught a lesson."

"I know how you feel, Tom," said Mr. Baily. "But do you know who this is? This is a respected member of the Callaway family out there in Callawaytown. The Callaway's are the most respected niggers in the County. I know there is an explanation for what took place here today."

At that moment, everyone thought about what Mr. Baily had said. There wasn't a single person who wasn't in debt to the Baily's in some way or another. The family provided the only way to get through the winter. Just the threat that their grain, feed, and food would be taken away was enough to make them shudder. Right away, everyone shifted their attention to whether or not they would be on Mr. Baily's shitlist.

As the crowd dwindled, Mr. Baily looked up and saw that niggers, Indians, and whites were using the fountain. He looked back at Rob, Rachel, and their two sons and started walking toward the shop. "Come on, Rob. Rachel, would you stay out here with the boys while I talk to Rob?"

Rachel had just stopped shaking. "Yessir, I got to buy the boys some school clothes."

Now in the office, Mr. Baily said, "Sit down, Rob. You know that was a crazy thing to do out there."

"Yes, I know Mr. Baily. But I can explain everything," answered Rob. "My son Jacob just came to town today for the first time. God knows he did not know that he was not supposed to drink from that fountain. If he had known, I can tell you he wouldn't have done it."

Surprised, Mr. Baily asked, "Rob, you mean that you have not explained how it is in the South?"

"Yessir, Mr. Baily, we talk about it all the time when we're home. But you know how it is with youngins. In Callawaytown, they never see anything that's going to get them in trouble. So, the youngins never run into anything like that. We have our own school and church, so we don't ever have a chance to get into trouble."

"Well, I am glad that I was here. I don't know if my sons could have handled that or not. Now that that's over, did you want to talk to me about anything else?"

Shaking off the remains of his anger and fear, Rob answered, "Yessir, I was thinking about that tract of land that you have on the other side of Flat River. The Jones' are tending that land now, but I think there can be more pounds of tobacco out of that land if it was tended better."

Mr. Baily was interested. "How much do you think you can get out of that tract?"

"Well, I don't know how much land there is, but I'd say you could probably get ten thousand pounds from each acre," responded Rob.

"How much will you make from that land of Bent's?"

"Well, we still have one, maybe two croppings left, and we've already sold more than ten thousand pounds for every acre," replied Rob.

"That's good. I think we can do some business next year. I'll tell you what. If you think that you can bring that land up to around ten thousand pounds an acre, that would be good." Then he thought a little more. "What about your father's farm? Won't that be too much work for you and your family with you working full time in your blacksmith shop?"

"Nope, it won't be too much work," Rob said confidently. "You know I have Ernie, Lonnie, and Rob Junior."

"You had an older son, didn't you?" asked Mr. Baily.

"Yes, his name was Richard," replied Rob. "However, he became ill and died a few years ago. But we have Shirley and Louise who can help out if we need them in the fields."

"I am going to be out there early next week to talk to old man Jones. We'RE going to have a man-to-man talk," said Mr. Baily. "I am going to tell him that he can live in the house, because you don't need it."

Rob spoke up. "If I am going to tend that land, I don't want them living there if they won't be doing anything. That means they will be stealing from the land and selling it to Indians in the area. That I can tell you now, Mr. Baily, I don't want that to happen."

Mr. Baily thought for a moment. "I understand what you're saying. I'll tell them that they can live there if they agree to look out for the crops and help you when you need them. We can just split the profit from the sale of the tobacco and corn. Everything else that you grow is yours. When you order the seeds, fertilizers, and other things that you will need to get going, just order for my land as well. The only thing that we will charge you for is what you buy for your farm."

"That sounds good to me Mr. Baily," replied Rob. He looked over at Mr. Baily as a pleased son would look over at his father. "I just want to say that Rachel and I really appreciate what you did for us today. I really don't know how to say thank you in any other way."

"Don't worry about it, Rob," replied Mr. Baily. "You know how it is with them poor crackers. They just must show off from time to time. Good niggers and we decent white folks have got to work together, or else we will be swallowed up by poor white trash and blackass niggers. Don't get me wrong. I wouldn't have done what I did for any other niggers I know. Cause we got to make sure that them blackass niggers know their place and don't cross over the line."

"Okay Mr. Baily," replied Rob. "But I sho hope that we won't have any trouble later on with any of those white folks that was out at the fountain."

"You don't want to have any trouble, because anybody that was out there today is thinking what I am going to do about whatever debt they owe," stated Mr. Baily.

Rob put out his hand as he left the office. Mr. Baily took it and placed his left arm around Rob's shoulders as they walked from the office to the shop.

By that time, Rachel had finished her shopping and was ready to leave. Rob paid, and they walked from the C.G. Baily shop over to the fish market. Rob bought four pounds of Spots, his favorite saltwater fish.

They got into the car and headed back to Callawaytown. Jacob asked, "Mama, why was the man so mad at me just for drinking some water?"

"That's something you will understand as you get older," Rachel said grimly. "For now, just remember that we have three types of folks in Mills County. We have whites, we have Negroes and we have Indians. All of these folks are separate. They have their own schools, churches, and everything else that they need, separate from each other."

She looked down into Jacob's innocent black eyes. "What you did was against the law. The law says that Negroes, whites, and Indians have separate places to go, to eat, and to drink. The law is wrong. There is nothing we can do about it. We just have to live with it."

Jacob looked up at his mother in stark amazement. "If it's wrong, why's it the law, mama?"

"Well, it's a long story," Rachel sighed. "One day you'll know all about it. Right now, you just do what I say."

George did not understand either, but he knew an opportunity when he saw one. "Mama, Jacob got into trouble because he is always getting into trouble, isn't that, right? Isn't that right, Papa? He is just like Billy Raymond. He is just crazy like Billy Raymond. Isn't that right, Mama?"

"No, that's not true," replied an exasperated Rachel. "Jacob just didn't understand that he was not supposed to drink from the fountain."

"But mama, I don't ever get into anything," protested George. "Why is it always Jacob who gets into trouble?"

"Well George, Jacob is different," explained Rachel. "Everybody is different. You will never find two people who are the same. I don't want to hear you calling your little brother Billy Raymond again." She could see that Jacob was sad and hurt. George was making it worse. If everyone living in the county was treated equally, as they should be, there would not be any problems. But reality was reality. She would have to make certain that young Jacob understood the situation. "His name is Jacob, and that's what your daddy and I named him, and that's what we want you to call him," Rachel said firmly.

George looked like someone had poured a bucket of cold water over his head. His mother had never taken such a strong stance against him. It was a shock. George sat back in the car and was silent the rest of the way home.

Jacob was still thinking about what had happened and why. He did not understand any of the things his mother had said. All he wanted to do was get back to Callawaytown, where he could live as he chose: play, help his dad, fish, and have the run of the land. The day had turned from one of joy to tragedy and back to joy again. It was far too much excitement for a six-year-old.

The news about what had happened was all over Callawaytown and the county, for that matter. Everybody knew what had taken place that day in Lakeville. From that day forward, anyone, regardless of the color of his or her skin, could go up and drink water from that fountain. No white cracker ever challenged the authority of Mr. C.G. Baily again.

There were members of the Baily family who thought old man C.G. Baily had gone too far, but no one said anything. As time went by, the signs came down, and no one asked why they were not replaced. It was a landmark in race relations for Lakeville and Mills County.

When folks visited Rob to get repairs done or get their horses and mules shoed, they would try to engage Rob in a conversation about the subject. But Rob would not respond. As far as he was concerned, the matter was over. He did not want to get caught up in the middle of some sort of racial problem–that would be far too dangerous.

CHAPTER THIRTEEN

Life went on in Callawaytown. On weekends, folks came from all over the county to Rob's place to pitch horseshoes. Between three in the afternoon and dark, their yard was full. That was a time when most Negroes, Indians, and poor whites who lived in and around Callawaytown forgot all the problems they had had over the previous week and had a few hours of enjoyment.

There were two large grapevines in Bent's front yard. They grew in an L shape. One produced red grapes, and the other produced white grapes. After Rachel and the girls had gathered what they needed for preserves, Rob would make wine from the rest. The two vines yielded a sixty-gallon oak barrel of wine each. There was always enough to last throughout the fall, winter, and into the next season. During the horseshoe games, Rob would sell the wine by the glass. His brother, Jim, would bring homebrew with him. Most times, he brought six to twelve quarts, depending on how much he had consumed himself during the week. No one ever talked about what percentage of alcohol the homebrew contained. One thing was certain: no two batches of homebrew contained the same alcohol percentage.

Mills County was a dry county. It was against the law to buy, sell, make, or have alcoholic beverages. But that did not deter Rob or most folks from making a little something for themselves. Rob would even supply most of the big shots in Lakeville with wine. The police would always look the other way.

By six o'clock in the afternoon, the men in the yard felt rather good. Sometimes they would get a little noisy, but for the most part, they did not disturb the peace of the women who sat in the house or on the porch.

Rachel would not have invited that many people to come every Sunday. That was one of the disadvantages of living in Bent's old house. It was not that bad. Rachel had company as well, and the men did not cause any trouble. After they had been drinking white lightning, homebrew, and wine for several hours in the hot sun, they would get pretty rowdy, but it was something Rachel could live with. At least her man was home, and she could always look over the grapevines and see what was going on.

Rob's brother Jim always thought he should have been the son who lived in Bent's house. He had the same size family as Rob, and furthermore, Rob had his own place on that little island. He and his family were living as sharecroppers. Bent had offered to give Jim a tract of land and help him build a house, but it was something that Jim never got around to deciding about. Now that Bent was dead, everything was in Rob's hands.

Rob thought that everything was rightfully his. He always said that all his brothers and sisters left home, and he was the only one around to watch out for his father. So, everyone usually stayed quiet, just like the eye of a storm. After many hours of hard drinking, Jim would sometimes challenge Rob. The result would always be the same. Rob would give Jim a black eye, or Jim would give Rob a black eye. They would be separated. Jim's sons and wife would take him home, and Rachel, Ernie, and Lonnie would take Rob inside. The next time Rob and Jim met, it would be like nothing had happened. They would be the best of friends.

At the end of summer, Rob was doing well with his blacksmith shop and the farm was going well, but for some reason he was not satisfied. He gave a lot of thought to the discussions he had had with Jim about his father's property. If there was some way to help Jim, he would do it. Rob was the leader of the family. He would do what he could to ensure that the family stayed close, just like it always had been. Still, he had made it crystal clear that he would never break up his father's property. Rob declared that anyone was welcome to come and build a house on Bent's land, but it would always be under the name of Bent Callaway.

School always opened at Rockville Elementary School the day after Labor Day. It was an incredibly special day for little Jacob. It would be his first official day in school, and he was really looking forward to it. The little boy hardly got any sleep the night before. He was the first one in the house that Tuesday morning. As his siblings got themselves dressed for school, Jacob pestered his sister Louise, "What's it going to be like? What do I do when I get there? What if I don't do something right?"

Before she could respond, George interrupted, "It's going to be like any other day. All you got to do is do what you see me doing, and you won't have any problems."

Jacob loved school, and he was better at reading and math than George. By the end of the first three months, Jacob had completed all the work required of a first-grade student. Miss Lee sent a note home to Rachel and Rob, in which she said that she would like to discuss a few things concerning Jacob when they had time. Rachel read the note first and gave it to Rob.

"What has that boy done now?" asked Rob. "He just can't seem to stay out of trouble." He called for Jacob. "Boy, why does Miss Lee want to talk with your mama and me?"

Jacob couldn't stand still. He had no idea what his father was talking about, but it didn't seem good. "Well Papa! I- I- I really do not know. I try to do everything Miss Lee says to do, and I even do more, so I don't know what I've done wrong."

George hurried into the conversation. "I know what he's been doing. He is always doing other things than what Miss Lee says we should. He's already finished all of his books, and Miss Lee hasn't even told us how to do all of the things he's doing. He's just like he is at home. He just can't wait and will just do what she says."

After supper, Rob laid on the bed and played with his two youngest children, Mandy and Pope. Mandy was two years old, and Pope had just arrived on July 16. When they had fallen asleep, Rachel moved them to one side of the bed and got in between Rob and the two kids. She said wearily, "Rob, what are we going to do with that Jacob?" She sighed. "He must have done something very bad for Miss Lee to want to talk to both of us."

"I want to go up and talk to her the first thing tomorrow morning," Rob answered firmly. If there was a problem to deal with, he wanted to get on with it.

"I think that's a good idea," said Rachel. "It shouldn't take long. She'll just say what he did wrong, and we'll tell her that we'll take care of it. I'll deal with him when he gets home from school. "

The next morning, Rachel and Rob went to school with the kids. When they arrived, the schoolhouse was still closed. They were there for about ten or fifteen minutes before Miss Lee arrived. "Good morning, Mr. and Mrs. Callaway!" she smiled. "I won't take much of your time. I just wanted to talk to you about Jacob."

"Yes, I know," replied Rob, bracing himself for bad news. "We got the news yesterday and wanted to come right away to see what trouble he was in."

"Oh! No! Mr. Callaway! Jacob is not in any trouble," Miss Lee said quickly. She leaned over and retrieved some tablets and books from her bag. "Just look at this! Jacob has done all this work just since school started. He's already finished all the work that the county allocated for the first grade, and we still have over half of the year left. This boy is doing so well that I wanted to talk to you about getting him moved up to the second grade."

When Rachel and Rob just gaped at her, she added, "If we do that and he continues as he is going, I am sure he won't have any problem completing the second grade by the end of the year."

Rachel wanted to make sure she had understood Miss Lee correctly. "Does that mean that he'll be in the same grade as George?"

"Yes, that's what it means," Miss Lee replied. "It would put some pressure on George to do better. That boy could do much better than he is doing now. To have them in the same grade would at least make him want to stay up with his little brother."

Rachel was clearly worried about putting the boys in the same grade. Maybe the teacher was giving Jacob more attention than she was giving George. Still, the facts were clear. Jacob was smarter than George. Adjustments would have to be made. But she did not want to make a decision on the spot. This was something that she and Rob would have to discuss alone.

Rob looked down at Miss Lee and said, "Miss Lee, what do you really think?"

The teacher's eyes were bright when she responded. "George could certainly do better than he is doing now. But I do not think he will ever be as good at reading, writing, and numbers as Jacob. Having them in the same grade will surely give George the encouragement he needs to do all his work. He won't want to be left behind a grade when he is two years older than his little brother."

Rob looked at Miss Lee with amazement. He had once read something about a child who was so smart that she plumb went crazy. Could that be what was wrong with Jacob? Maybe it would be better to keep him out of school for a year or two until he cooled down a little. If Jacob was so smart that he was going crazy, that could be the reason for the water fountain problem. Maybe moving him up a grade would make the problem with the boy even worse.

In the end, he decided that Miss Lee was the expert on school, and she knew what was good or bad for kids. So, he would support her and work the details out with Rachel. Forthright as ever, he told the teacher, "Well, you know more about what's good for youngins than me and Rachel, so I guess it will be okay to move him up to the second grade if you think it's the best thing to do and you think it will be good for George as well."

Rachel was shocked. How could Rob make such an important decision without first checking with her? Rob had never done a thing like that before. She would certainly have a word with him when they got home. But Rachel just looked over at Miss Lee and said, "We can try him in the second grade and see how it works out, but I don't want him under a lot of pressure. If you find that it's too much for him, can we place him back in the first grade?"

"Yes, Mrs. Callaway, that's just what I am suggesting," answered Miss Lee. "If we feel later that it's not good for him, we can just put him back. I will get that cleared with the county. In any case, the only thing that will really change is that he will be using the second-grade books, and the county will be notified. You know they always want to know when one of our students is doing really well, or really bad for that matter."

Rob and Rachel left the school with a done deal. Their son, Jacob, would be moved up to the second grade. They were immensely proud. For the first time that either one could remember, they had received a report on Jacob that was not bad. Maybe the boy was not as bad as everyone in Callawaytown thought. Maybe this would be something that would keep him busy and out of trouble.

However, Rachel was visibly angry with Rob, and she let him know it as they walked down the road. "Why did you agree with Miss Lee without even talking with me first?" she sputtered.

"Well, I didn't think it was anything that we would not agree on, so I thought it would be good to just get it over with," Rob said, calm as ever.

As time went by, things turned out just as Miss Lee had predicted. Jacob did very well in the second grade, and George worked harder to ensure that his little brother didn't get a grade above him.

Each day, the boys came home from school, changed their clothes and went out to the blacksmith shop to do whatever their daddy told them to. They were great at keeping the blower so that the furnace would continue going to keep the iron hot. When the boys were around, Rob was free to work twice as hard at getting his work done. From time to time, their cousin Arthur, who was one of Maddie-Jean and Kenny Hooker's sons, would join them.

Linda and Richard's grandson, J.D., would also come around. J.D. was George's age. Sometimes George and Jacob would let the other boys take turns turning the blower. But, for the most part, George and Jacob had a monopoly on it.

As fall came and went, George and Jacob received the same gifts for Christmas that year. Santa Claus came down the chimney and gave them a stocking full of fruit, candy, and a bag of mixed marbles. Rachel had even started to dress them identically. When people met them for the first time, they thought they were twins, even though they were two years apart. Rachel never corrected anybody. Folks were free to think as they liked. She never volunteered any information on the subject. The boys had fun during their Christmas holidays. They played out in the yard with their friends, and many marbles changed hands. Jacob always lost when it came to shooting marbles, which was just fine with George.

One day Jacob and the boys were playing out between the house and the blacksmith shop. It was approaching noon, and Rob was getting ready to close the blacksmith shop for dinner. He wanted to have one of the boys come over and turn the blower so that the furnace would continue to stay hot while he took a break. "Jacob, come over here for a minute," said Rob. "I need you to turn the blower a few minutes for me."

"I'll do it, Mr. Rob! I'll do it!" cried J.D. Before Rob could respond, Jacob was there standing on the block of wood and turning the blower.

"Don't touch anything else," Rob ordered. "I am going over to the house for dinner. I'll be back in about an hour. Just turn the blower for a few turns until you see the coals turning red. When you see that, you can stop." The instructions were mostly for the other boys. Jacob had performed that task many times. Rob left the blacksmith shop and proceeded to the house.

J.D. came over to the entrance of the blacksmith shop. "Jacob, look!" Jacob turned his head to look and got the surprise of his young life. J.D. had taken out his penis, held the skintight end, and forced it full of urine. When Jacob turned around, J.D. let go and spread urine into Jacob's face. Jacob stopped turning the blower and wiped his face with the sleeve of his shirt. George and Arthur were laughing. J.D. ran up the road to his grandparents' house. Jacob cried as he walked over to the pump, where he washed his face and hands. Unfortunately, what had landed on his clothing would carry a stench until he changed clothes, which would not be until Thursday!

After the clothes were washed, the boys would take baths in the used wash water and be dressed in clean clothes. Jacob did not think about what would happen if George and Arthur said anything about what J.D. had done. If Rachel or Rob found out, they would be upset. Rob already had little use for J.D.'s mother and father. Both had gone through college and had good teaching jobs in Charlotte, North Carolina. They thought that they were better than other Negroes in Callawaytown. That rubbed Rob the wrong way. He was always short with them and never spent more time with them than was necessary. To hear that their little bastard had pulled such a stunt on one of his children would be just what he needed to go up to Linda's shop and tell them what he thought of them. So, Jacob kept the secret to himself and hoped that Arthur and George would do the same.

CHAPTER FOURTEEN

Winter was over, and the fields were prepared for the next growing season. Groundbreaking took place all over Callawaytown and the other villages throughout the county. Rob cut back on his activities in the blacksmith shop and spent more and more time fishing with George and Jacob. He was teaching Ernie the blacksmith's trade. He had just turned fifty on Christmas Day. For all practical purposes, life was full. He had settled into his father's house and rented it out, so there was not much to worry about. His three oldest sons were old enough to tend the fields under his supervision, so all was going quite well.

School was out, and Jacob had proven himself to be a great student. He had a perfect attendance record for the year and excellent grades. Next school year, he and his brother George will be going to the third grade. As always, the relatives from Baltimore came down to Callawaytown for two weeks. The house was full of aunts, uncles, and cousins. That was the best time of the year for the boys. When they finished their chores, they could go down to the river fork, where there was a sand bar that was used by Rockville Baptist Church for baptizing the saved. Revival meetings took place there every August.

Jacob could not wait to go down and try to swim. He always pretended to be swimming, but he would be kicking from the bottom with one foot. Rob would go down with the group of boys and men from time to time. He would always make it a point to find out which of his sons could swim and which could not. The great test would come when Rob took a youngster under his arms and threw him off the sand bar.

The water would be over the youngster's head. Then the child would swim, or he would go down two times. In the end, Rob would always come to the rescue. This tradition greatly motivated the children to learn to swim and most of them could.

On this day, Rob decided to accompany the gang to the sand bar. He jumped into the deep end, stayed under water for a few seconds, came up for air, and swam over to the low end of the sand bar. George, Jacob, and the other boys were playing in the shallow end when Rob grabbed George by one hand and Jacob by the other. They began to scream as Rob continued to drag them along the bank towards the deep end. Disregarding their screams, he pitched both boys into the deep end of the sandbar. As they came up for air, Rob yelled, "Kick! Paddle!"

The boys were doing their best. They went under twice. On the try, Jacob started to stay afloat. He was kicking and dog paddling, as he continued to get his breath and make his way to the shallow end of the sand bar. "Come on, boys, I know you can do it!" Rob shouted.

It wasn't easy. Both boys looked exhausted, but no one made a move to rescue them. That was Rob's department. Nobody would come and help until Rob made a move.

Jacob was the first one to make it to the shallow water. Everyone thought that it was a cruel way to teach a youngster to swim, but it worked. No one could convince Rob to do otherwise.

Meanwhile, just away from the sand bar, the teenage boys and girls were having the time of their lives. Ernie, Lonnie, and Rob Junior were always pleased when summer came, and their cousins came down. Rob's brother Lee had an older son and daughter and two beautiful granddaughters named Carol and Lesley. The granddaughters were the same age as Ernie and Lonnie. They were considered tomboys because they always played with the boys instead of the girls. And play they did. Noise came from behind the bushes, but Rob was busy talking with the other men. Jacob looked over behind one large bush and could not understand what he saw. Ernie was lying on top of Carol, and her legs were in the air! She was making terrible noises, like she was in pain. Just around the corner from that bush were Lonnie and Lesley, almost in the same identical position.

Jacob tried to decide whether to pull Ernie off Carol or maybe Lonnie off Lesley. George shouted, "Jacob! Jacob! Come on over here to the deep end of the sand bar and let's take a big jump from the tall tree." Now that they could swim, it was fun. It seemed much more fun than watching two people do weird things and make strange noises. Jacob forgot about what he had seen and ran back to the deep end of the sand bar.

When dusk came, Rob yelled out, "I am going to go back to the house. George, yosu, and Jacob can stay here and come home with Ernie, Lonnie and them." In Rob's language that meant that they could stay if Ernie, Lonnie, and Lee's two granddaughters stayed. It also meant that Ernie would be responsible for the wellbeing of the young boys until they arrived home again.

Ernie staggered out of the bushes, followed by Carol, Lonnie, and Lesley. All four swam for a few minutes before Ernie told everyone that it was time to go home. They walked towards the house, which was across three bridges. The bridge closest to the house was small and just a few steps from the old house where Rob and Rachel's children were born. The kids used that area to get into all types of trouble.

Jacob approached the bridge and ran down the bank to see if he could find any pike fish relaxing in the shade. No one seemed to care about what he was doing. They continued to walk toward the house. Jacob heard a noise. It was like what he had heard earlier in the afternoon in the bushes near the sand bar. He tiptoed toward the noise. Rob Junior and Candie Lee Winsey were doing the same thing he had seen earlier that day. Her legs were in the air. Rob Junior had his arms under her knees as they pushed at each other. Candie Lee went up as Rob Junior went down. To Jacob's disgust, they were kissing each other. He watched for a few seconds before he went up the bank to the main road.

This was an incredibly special day for Jacob. He had learned to swim. Now he had seen two things that just did not make sense to him. He totally forgot why he went down the bank in the first place. After what he saw down there, nothing else mattered.

As he continued his walk home, he noticed that his Uncle Sonny's car was parked by his house. Everyone was either on the back porch or in the backyard. Rob and Sonny were discussing what the results of the upcoming election might be. Dewey had won the nomination for the Republican Party, and it was almost a certainty that Truman would be running against Dewey for the Democrats. There were still several months before the election.

When Jacob approached the yard, Connie came out. "Jacob, did you see Rob Junior and Candie down at the sand bar?"

Ernie immediately broke in on the conversation. "No! We did not run into them. We must have missed them. They probably took the short cut through the woods."

Jacob was amazed that Ernie could talk that fast. He knew that what Ernie said wasn't true. He had seen the whole thing. Rob Junior and Candie Lee never made it to the sandbar. They had stopped at the first bridge, gone under it, and were lying on the bank underneath the bridge. Jacob didn't want to get in the middle of anything. He was not about to volunteer any information.

A short while later, Rob Junior and Candie Lee came up the road toward the house. Rob Junior said casually, "We must have missed y'all. We went through the woods. We thought that would get us down to the sand bar before y'all left. But I guess we were too late, as y'all were gone when we got there. We didn't go into the water. We just decided to walk back. There were a lot of Indians down there from across the swamp."

Candie did not say anything, but she held her breath. The story Rob Junior gave seemed to satisfy everyone. Jacob looked at Rob Junior and Candie Lee. He didn't know what to do. Rob Junior was lying.

Jacob wondered how he could just stand there and tell such a big lie like that. Why didn't he just tell the truth? Maybe they had done something wrong. Maybe they were all doing something wrong. There had to be something special about what was going on. What was it all about? Well, he decided he would best stay quiet. One day, he was sure he would find out all about it. He would just have to wait.

Throughout the summer, Jacob saw the cousins having sex, and he saw other people too. Once, he saw Rob's nephew with Shirley and Louise with Thomas Junior.

In 1947, everyone had come home to attend Bent's funeral. Some thought that the occasion had split the family. In some ways, it had. Rob worked to keep the family together. He had made it clear to everyone that he would not tolerate any discussion about the farm or rental properties before the funeral. Once that point was made, Rob's brothers and sisters adhered to Rob's wishes and did not bring up the subject during that sad time. Now, a year later, things were different. Rob's brother Jim had died, and the only brother left was Sandy. Sandy and his wife were divorced but were still good friends. They both lived in Baltimore, and at times, shared a bed. Some wondered why they ever got a divorce.

Except for Rob's sister May, all the family lived around Mills County. They would visit the old home place at least once a month. In some cases, they would all converge at the same time. When that happened, it was on Sunday afternoon, after church was finished. Rachel, Shirley, and Louise would prepare a feast. Biscuits, cornbread, three different meats, potatoes, rice, gravy, and oceans of lemonade, cool-aid, and iced tea would all come out onto the table. The men would pitch horseshoes, drink home-brew and white lighting. Around four o'clock, the food would be ready, and then the men would be almost drunk. After dinner and a nap, everyone would return to their homes for another week of work in the fields.

CHAPTER FIFTEEN

On an early Saturday morning, Jacob and George were on their way down to the bridge that crossed Flat River. They had a favorite spot near the bridge where they fished for perch, catfish, and redbreast. Today, they noticed that there was a fifty-pound burlap bag lying in the ditch on the left side of the road. Jacob pointed to it. "Look over there. What do you think that is?"

Never curious, George shrugged and said, "I don't know."

But Jacob insisted they investigate. "Let's go over and see what's in that bag."

George looked up and saw Mr. Buddy Brown standing on the Flat River Bridge. No one liked Mr. Brown. He was always drunk. In a dry county, there was a special stigma attached to being a drunk. No one knew where he got his whiskey from, but some folks thought he helped Benny Blackfoot make white lighting some place in the swamps near Callawaytown. When he visited families in the area, he was always drunk and had a pint in his pocket. That Saturday morning was no exception. When Buddy saw the boys retrieve the bag from the ditch, he walked down to where the boys stood.

"What's you got there, boys?" Mr. Brown, slurred.

"We just picked up this bag from the ditch, Mr. Brown," George answered. Both boys could smell the whiskey on Buddy's breath. They pulled the bag from the ditch.

"Let me see what you got there," said Buddy. He took the bag out of their hands and immediately opened the bag. Quickly concealing his surprise, he was amazed at what he saw. There were stacks of hundred-dollar bills, fifty-dollar bills, and twenty-dollar bills. "I see someone dropped this bag from a truck or car," Buddy said casually. "I'll just take it and make sure that it gets back to the people who lost it."

He pulled the string on the bag and made it as tight as he could. Then he swung it over his right shoulder. He turned around and started to walk away. No one really knew where Buddy Brown lived, but he did have a hut up the river somewhere. The fact was that he lived anywhere he could spend a night.

George and Jacob continued their walk down to their favorite fishing spot as the older man disappeared around the bend in the road. The boys placed their lines in the river. It was not long before both boys had caught several fish. After about two hours, they were ready to return home. They gathered their fish and started to walk. It was just before noon when the boys arrived. Rob had just finished up his work at the blacksmith shop and was preparing to close for the weekend.

Their sister, Louise, walked outside and yelled, "Daddy! Daddy! Dinner is ready."

"Okay," he shouted back. "Tell your mother I'll be there in a few minutes."

About fifteen minutes later, Rob arrived at the house. After washing his hands at the back porch pump, he dried them with a towel that always hung on a nail on the porch's inside wall. Afterwards, he walked into the kitchen and sat down at the head of the table. He turned the old vacuum-tube console radio on. The tuning dial already pointed to 6:40 AM. That was Lakeville's only AM station. As Rob turned the volume up, he could hear the announcer's excited voice. "This is a special bulletin! The Flathead National Bank was robbed this morning! It was carried out by a lone gunman–probably a professional bank robber by the name of Lenny Blackfoot! You might remember that Lenny Blackfoot, an Indian, was just released from the state prison last Friday after spending five years for attempting to rob the Southern Bank of Red Spirit."

The announcer continued with his commentary. "I don't know when these Indians are going to learn that they must work for their living just like the niggers and white people in this county. Oh yes, it was also reported that the robber got away with close to one million dollars! He got away with five US Treasury bags containing twenty, fifty, and hundred-dollar bills. The truck was seen heading east on Highway 72. Someone reported seeing the truck make a left turn at the Back-Swamp intersection, heading towards Callawaytown.

At that point, Rob turned the volume knob down a little and said to Rachel, "That Lenny Blackfoot will never learn. You'd think that after spending so many years in prison he would try to get a job and straighten out his life."

Rachel looked up at Rob but didn't say anything. Rob continued, "You know, Lenny's father has that farm up the swamp from that road which leads from the middle bridge. I bet Lenny was going up that road to his father's farm. There would be several places that he could hide that money in those swamps."

Rachel finished the food preparation and set the table. All of the kids were seated, and Rachel took her place at the far end of the table. Rob said grace, "Good Lord, make us humble and thankful for all that we are about to receive into our bodies, Amen." The rest of the family murmured their Amens. The food was passed from person to person until everyone had a bit of everything. As everyone was eating and enjoying themselves, Rob looked up at George and Jacob. "Did you boys have any luck at the sand bar today?"

"Yessir," George blurted before Jacob could get a word out. "We caught a few perch, some redbreast, and a few catfish."

Jacob looked up at his father. "Daddy, we found a bag that had something in it. Mr. Buddy Brown came along and said we should give the bag to him. He said the bag belonged to the U.S. Government and that he would see that it was returned."

Rob stopped eating and looked seriously over at the boys. "Did you open that bag?"

"No, we didn't look in the bag, but Mr. Buddy Brown did. He pulled the strings tight again, threw the bag over his shoulder, and walked back across the long bridge."

Thoughts ricocheted through Rob's head. That bag probably contained $200,000.00! Humm, Mr. Buddy Brown was now likely a rich man. The family ate their dinner without further comment. Afterwards, Rob went out to his spot on the front porch. With a pillow under his head, he laid down for a nap.

A few hours later, Rob awakened to see that two policemen from Lakeville were standing near the porch. He sat up abruptly. "Hi Rob. We don't want to bother you, but we'd like to ask you some questions, if you don't mind."

"Yessir, just go right ahead and ask me anything you want," Rob said carefully.

"Well, we don't know if you heard the news on the radio today, but Lenny Blackfoot robbed a bank this morning in Flathead. He got away with about a million dollars. He was seen driving east toward Lakeville on Highway 72. We know that he made a left turn at the intersection of Back Swamp Road and Highway 72. We caught him at his mother and father's house up the swamp from that middle bridge. We found four bags of money. One bag is still missing. We just want to know if you or any of your youngins saw anything this morning?"

"No, we didn't see nothin'," Rob answered. "I just turned on the radio, and there it was. The announcer said that a bank was robbed. He did not say too much about what was happening, so I did not pay any attention to it. But we did not see a thing. I've been around here all morning and I didn't see a thing."

"You mind if we look around to see if we can find anything?" the policeman asked. "He had to hide that bag somewhere between the turn at Back Swamp and Highway 72 and the turn at the middle bridge. It's got to be someplace along the way."

"Yessir, help yourself. My three older boys will give you a hand."

The policemen started their search for the missing bag of money. They covered every inch of ground between Highway 72 and the third bridge. Looking on both sides of the road, they turned every can, barrel or bush along the way. They found nothing. Afterwards, the policemen came back by the house and thanked Rob for his cooperation.

When the policemen had gone, Rob called George and Jacob over. "You know that the bag you found this morning was probably what the police were looking for? You should have brought that bag home and given it to me or your mother."

Rob shook his head. "I bet the police will never find that bag of money. I know for sure that that drunken Buddy Brown will not turn himself in to the policepolice. He's probably on his way back up north. But I think I will drive over to that shack where Buddy lays his head and see if there's any action over there."

"Rob I wouldn't get involved with that if I were you," Rachel cautioned. "Just let it go. The police do not think our family knows anything about the robbery or what happened with the money. It's not your business."

Rob answered stubbornly. "No, I am going to drive by just to see if he's still around. That's a lot of money, and my boys found it. Just think of what the reward might be. I am not going to let that drunken bastard get away with all that money."

He got in his car, backed out of the driveway, and headed down the road toward the three bridges. When Rob arrived at Buddy Brown's shack, he saw that it was empty and the door was wide open. There was nothing valuable there–only a chair in one corner, a mat on the floor, and a dirty army dish and cup in a bucket on a small table. There was no sign of him or any of his belongings.

At that point, Rob knew that he would never see Buddy Brown or the bag of money. If he had told the policemen the story, they would never have believed that the boys had given the bag of money to a total stranger. They would have certainly thought that he was holding something back. It could have been a disaster. They would not have been able to find the bag of money or the drunken Buddy Brown. This would leave them with the only logical conclusion: The Buddy Brown story was a fabrication and that the bag of money was still hidden someplace in Callawaytown. They would tear the place apart. Just the thought of what would happen in that quiet community was enough to make Rob's skin crawl. He turned into the driveway and parked his car in the usual place.

"Well, what did you find?" said Rachel.

"Not much, but the place was clean," answered Rob. "That old drunken bastard is out of here. No one will ever find him again."

"I told you so," said Rachel. "You can't say I didn't tell you. You just would not listen. I told you that it would not do any good to go over there. You could just as well have gone back to the blacksmith shop and worked for a few more hours. At least you would probably have made some money. He is gone for good. What would you have done if you were in Buddy's place? Would stay around if you had a bag full of that much money? Would you?"

"I don't want to hear any of your shit now," said Rob wearily. "That son-of-a-bitch took money from my sons. It really should have gone to us, if not back to the bank. I would just like to get my hands on that son-of-a-bitch. I would teach him a thing or two. The asshole never did a day's work in his life, and now he took the money that my sons found." He shrugged his shoulders to get rid of his disgust.

Rachel knew she had pushed too far. She tried to smooth things over. "No need to think about it now. It is over and done with. There ain't nothing you can do. So, you might as well forget about Buddy Brown and the bag of money, and just thank God that you didn't mention anything to the policemen." She stepped off the porch and went out into the yard.

"Well, it's always better if you make your money yourself. Then you don't have to worry about somebody coming along to take it from you," said Rob. "That's how I got the money that I have, so I ain't going to worry about what I could've had or anything like that."

George and Jacob came over to their father as he sat in his favorite rocking chair. They jumped on his lap and said, "Papa, we're sorry. We did not know there was money in the bag. Mr. Buddy said he would turn it into the police."

"It's okay, boys. I just want you to know that the next time you find anything, the first thing you do is take it to me or your mama. Do not give it to anybody. Just remember what I say."

"Yessir, we understand," they replied.

The radio confirmed that Lenny Blackfoot was indeed the robber. Some folks said the police were torturing him to find out where he had hidden the missing bag. But Rob knew that that missing bag of money would never be recovered. Sure enough, the police never found the missing bag of money or the drunken Buddy Brown. It seemed he had disappeared from the face of the earth. Rob remained irritated that Buddy would never have to work again. He would have one comfortable life with two hundred thousand dollars in cash.

CHAPTER SIXTEEN

It was late August 1948. The weather was hotter than normal. The crops were withering, and most farmers were scrambling to harvest their last crop of tobacco for the year. Rob's family had already made their yearly summer visit and returned home. He was getting ready to take a load of tobacco to the warehouse in Lakeville, where it would be auctioned off to the highest bidders.

The large cigarette manufacturers would pay the least amount of money they could get away with for the farmers' tobacco. The politicians in North Carolina were in the pockets of the tobacco companies. The tobacco growers had virtually no say about what their tobacco was worth. The cigarette companies stole tobacco from everyone, regardless of their color. The average price for unblemished golden leaf tobacco was 3 to 15 cents a pound; the cigarette companies sold cigarettes for between 25 and 55 cents a pack. They were making a killing off the backs of the tobacco farmers.

Rob always managed to land on the high end of the price scale for his tobacco. He graded his crop. At the top was an unblemished golden leaf, which would bring between 10 and 15 cents a pound. Next came the blemished golden leaf, which would bring between 6 and 10 cents a pound. The third grade was considered trash. It would bring between 3 and 6 cents a pound. Most of Rob's tobacco fell in the first grade.

Rob cured his tobacco with care. It was kept at a constant temperature of 75 to 85 degrees for two to three days until the leaf was golden. Afterwards, the heat was turned up to 200 to 250 degrees for a day or two, until the leaf was dry. When the stems were dry, the heat was removed from the tobacco barn, and the tobacco was allowed to air out for a couple of days. Then it was taken to a barn to be graded. Rob had years of experience growing and processing tobacco, as did his three oldest sons. His tobacco would nearly always be perfect.

This had been a good year for Rob. He had done very well with his blacksmith shop, and most of his tobacco had sold as first grade stuff. There hadn't been any major windstorms or hail. He was pleased with his work. He had only one more cropping left, and the tobacco season would be over. The tobacco buyers would move on up to Virginia. Rob would make the deadline. He could then concentrate on getting the hay and corn in before the fall and winter set in.

He had money in a trunk under his bed, and he had money in the bank in Lakeville. There was not much for him to worry about. His sisters and brother had not given him any trouble about his father's property. The youngins would soon be going to school. His oldest daughter, Shirley, had finished the eighth grade and moved to be with his sister so that she could attend the high school for Negroes in Fairbluff, North Carolina.

The high school in Lakeville was for whites only. The nearest school for Negroes was about ten miles from Callawaytown in Big Branch. The school bus for Negroes did not go out to Callawaytown. The official word was that there were not enough children to justify sending a bus. But the real reason was that the County Board of Education didn't feel they should pay to send niggers to school. The eighth grade was enough schooling for niggers. It was agreed that they should be trained to read and write so that they could easily understand what the white folks ordered them to do. But no one wanted them to get the idea that their place was anywhere except the fields.

However, Mr. C.G. Baily let Rob know that once his son was old enough to drive, they would consider letting him drive a bus out to Callawaytown. Ernie was almost old enough, but since his birthday fell in November, it would be too late for him to get his driver's license, get all the paperwork completed, and get permission from the State Board of Education to drive a school bus. Shirley would have to go and stay one more year with her aunt and uncle so that she could attend high school.

Ernie would be finishing the eighth grade this year and would miss school until he was old enough to drive the bus. With ten children of her own, Mary couldn't take in one more person.

Just before it was time for school to start again, Rachel and Rob took the children to Lakeville to buy them their school supplies. Rob did not believe in spending his money on nonsense. In his opinion, buying school supplies or new clothes was nonsense.

The day before school, little Jacob could not go to sleep. He was overly excited about the next day. He would be in third grade!

Rob Junior was the first one up. It was his job to make a fire in the kitchen stove. When it was cold enough, the three older boys, Ernie, Lonnie, and Rob Junior, took turns getting up and making a fire in the living room where Rob, Rachel, and the two smallest children slept. Everyone knew what was expected of him or her and acted accordingly.

When the heater was hot enough, Rachel got up, dressed, and prepared their usual breakfast: eggs, grits, bacon, ham, sausage, and biscuits. When the food was almost ready, she would wake up the children. On the first day of school, getting them out of bed was not a problem. Everyone was ready to go. Rachel only had to make sure that everyone had breakfast. Jacob was always the first to go and the last to get home. He loved school and could not get enough of the three Rs.

The days, weeks, and months went by. Before long, it was Thanksgiving, and then Christmas was on the way. Rob's behavior changed. He spent less time in the blacksmith shop and more in and around the house. He looked as though he was searching for something that was beyond his reach. Rachel got worried and tried to get him to go and see Dr. Bitman, but he would not do it.

One day, Rachel was standing in the kitchen and could see that Rob was standing outside in the yard, looking into space. "Rob! Rob!" she shouted.

He simply turned around and looked at Rachel as if in a trance "What do you want, Rachel?" he said absently.

Rachel ran out of the kitchen and into Rob's arms. "Honey, I love you, and I only want what's good for you," she said softly. "I can see that you don't feel well. Why don't you go and see Dr. Bitman?"

Stubborn as always, Rob answered irritably, "There ain't nothin' wrong with me. I just need some rest."

But Rachel was not about to give up. "Please, Rob, go talk to Dr. Bitman. Tell him how long you have been feeling like you do. Just see what he says. He'll probably give you some medicine, and in no time, you will be your old self again."

To her surprise, Rob gave in. "I can tell you it will just be a waste of money, but if it will make you feel any better, I will go by and see him the next time I have to go to Lakeville."

Rachel gave him a big hug. "That's good. I already feel better now that I know that you will go. Several days went by before Rob had any business in Lakeville. Then he was true to his word and went to the doctor's office.

"Good morning, Rob," said Dr. Bitman. "How are Rachel and the children doing?"

"Well, Dr. Bitman, they're doing just fine. All of them are in school now except the two little ones. You know Mandy and the baby, Pope Junior. They're just two and four years old."

"That's good. And Rachel is doing okay?" asked Dr. Bitman.

"Yes, she's doing good. As a matter of fact, that is why I came by today. Rachel has been saying that I should come by and let you look at me."

Surprised, Dr. Bitman gestured for Rob to follow him to a room. "Come on in, and I will get to you in a few minutes."

Rob sat down and started to look through a newspaper that was on a small coffee table. Dr. Bitman came in and checked Rob's temperature and vital signs. "Do you ever have headaches?" he asked.

"Yessir, that's one of the things I wanted to talk to you about. Sometimes my head hurts so badly that I cannot hardly stand it. Sometimes I just have to stand still."

Dr. Bitman looked concerned. "When was the last time you had such a bad headache?"

Rob thought for a second, then answered, "Well, it was just a few days ago. I was standing outside the house in the yard. I was just going to feed the horses and mules when it hit me all at once. The next thing I knew, Rachel was yelling at me. She came out of the house and told me I should come down and see you. And the funny thing is, it went away just as fast as it came on."

The doctor did not respond for a moment. "I don't think it's anything serious. You Callaway's are a strong bunch. How old are you now?"

"I'll be fifty on Christmas Day."

"I'd say that you should take it easy and get plenty of rest," advised Dr. Bitman. "Stay away from that hot furnace in that blacksmith shop for a few days. I want to get you an appointment to see a specialist at Duke University in Durham. It's only about a two-hour drive from here."

When Rob looked over at him, the doctor quickly added, "I don't want you going home and worrying Rachel. This is between you and me. I do not think there's anything to worry about, but I do want to get you checked out as soon as possible. As a matter of fact, I have a meeting at Duke University tomorrow. I will talk to the specialist about setting up an appointment. If he is not too busy, I will try to have him see you next week. I do not know what day it will be, but I will promise you that it will be in the mid-morning. That way you will have time to leave home in the morning, drive up there, see the specialist, and drive back the same day."

Dr. Bitman took some pills out of a drawer, gave them to Rob, and told him to take them for the pain. "Come by here in a couple of days. I will give you information on the specialist you will be seeing and the directions on how to get there. For the meantime, you take care of yourself and stay away from that furnace for a few days."

Rob shrugged into his shirt. "Okay, I will."

When he got home, Rachel was full of questions. "How did it go with Dr. Bitman?" she asked. "Were you able to see him? What did he say?"

He wasn't about to tell her anything. "Yes, I was able to see him. And like I said, it was nothing. Everything is okay with me. He said that I would be okay. It's just that he thinks that I should not spend so much time so close to that furnace in that blacksmith shop."

Not able to help herself, Rachel gave a big sigh and said, "I have been telling you that for, I don't know, how long, and you never listen. You spend way too much time in that shop, and I do not know why. We have enough money to live off. We do not need nothing. So why don't you just take it easy for a while?"

Softening now, she added, "You can spend more time fishing with the boys. You know George and Jacob just love to go fishing with you, and we ain't had no fresh-caught fish in some time now. So, why don't you say that from today on you will tell folks that you just can't work as hard in that blacksmith shop."

"I know what you mean, baby," Rob protested. "But there's a lot of work that I have got to get finished before I can take any real time off. I have had wheels that have been here for some time now, and they keep coming in from as far north as Virginia. You know, I get folks who come from as far south as Columbia, South Carolina. I just can't stop like that without letting folks know what's going on."

He stroked her arm. "Ernie and Lonnie are helping me a lot now. That Ernie can shoe a horse and mule as good as I can, and Lonnie ain't bad. He's been shoeing them too. I work on the hard stuff and let Ernie and Lonnie do all the easy stuff. Okay, honey?" he pleaded.

Knowing just how far she could push her husband, Rachel gave in. "I want you to take care of yourself."

They left the subject as quickly as they had started it. Rob went directly to his blacksmith shop. Rachel saw him do it and shook her head. She wondered if he even remembered the conversation, they had just had. She thought to herself, "there is nothing I can do with that man of mine." He is going to do just as he wants to do, and if he wants to do it, so I might as well let it go. She walked back into the house and started to prepare supper.

The week went by, and Rob went to Lakeville to get supplies for the blacksmith shop. He went to Dr. Bitman's office. When he arrived, it was still early in the morning. He and Dr. Bitman got out of their cars at the same time. "Hi Rob! How are you feeling today? Have you had any of those bad headaches that you were telling me about since last week?"

"No, I ain't had any headaches at all since I was in your office. And I've been feeling really good."

"Well, that's good," said Dr. Bitman. "I had a chance to talk to the specialist at Duke University the day after we met, and he said he'd make time for you. He is a good friend of mine. I told him that you were a special nigger–one of the most respected niggers in the county. So, he is going to put you right at the top of his appointment list.

The two men walked toward the medical office. "It's good you came by today, because he's got time to see you on Wednesday of this week. I told him that it was something that we wanted to keep between you, him, and me. So, you don't have to worry about anybody finding out that you went to see a specialist. If you leave home around 6:30, you should be at his office around 9:30 or before. He can see you between 10 and noon. That way, you will be back home by midafternoon. You can just tell Rachel that you have to go to Durham to pick up some supplies for your blacksmith shop. You know, something that you can't get here in Mills County."

"Yessir, I will go there tomorrow," Rob said with a smile. "I really do appreciate what you are doing for me."

"Don't worry about it, Rob. I am a doctor. I'd even do that for a blackass nigger, and you ain't that by a long shot," replied Dr. Bitman. "I've been thinking about buying a horse and buggy for my daughter. When I make up my mind, I will be coming over to you to get some advice. I know that you are the best blacksmith in Mills County. He paused, "Come to think about it, is there even another blacksmith in this area?"

"No sir, I am the only one with an account in any of the three joining states," said Rob proudly. "I've got folks who give me orders as far north as Richmond and as far south as the Georgia state line. Maybe there's a blacksmith out there somewhere that I don't know about, but I can tell you they ain't nothin' compared to me. You know, Mr. Jacob Townsend taught me the trade, and he was the absolute best. There ain't nobody as good as he was."

"Is he still in the business?" asked Dr. Bitman.

"No sir. He even sends his folks over to me now. He's so old that he doesn't do much of anything anymore."

"Well, I have heard a lot of good things about him," said Dr. Bitman. "My father and uncles used to take their horses and buggies to him years ago. They always said he was the best."

"Yessir, I can say to you that he was the best, and I worked for him for a lotta years. He is the one who helped me get into business. And you know what? For that, I named a son after him. Yes, that is right. I named one of my sons Jacob after him. Cause if it weren't for him, I'd have never learned about being a blacksmith and would never be where I am today."

Rob walked out of Dr. Bitman's office and got back in his car. Shortly, he was well on his way out to Callawaytown. As he drove, he thought. What would happen when he went to Durham the following day? How would he explain to Rachel that he had to go to Durham on such short notice?

Rachel was a smart woman, and there was no way that he could tell her the whole story. He wished he could just drive home and lay it on the line for Rachel, but that was not possible. If he told her the whole story, she would just get all upset. Dr. Bitman had said that there was nothing to worry about. He just wanted to make sure that everything was okay. Sure, he had felt bad sometimes, but it had been weeks since he'd had a headache. Chances were that there was absolutely nothing wrong with him at all. He decided that he would not tell Rachel or anyone else, for that matter. He would do just as Dr. Bitman had advised. He would just say that some of the materials he went to Lakeville to get today were not in. If he went to Durham, he could get what he needed the same day. She knew that he was working on some special jobs and she would believe the story. That is what he would do.

Rob really wanted her with him. She could go into the doctor's office with him and listen to what he had to say. But that was not possible. It would be too much for her to bear. This was something that he had to do alone.

When Rob arrived home, he parked the car and went straight into the house. "Honey, I got some fresh fish from the market," he called. "I'll dress them, and you can fix them for supper."

Rachel came into the room. "Rob, that was really nice of you. Now I don't have to worry about what to fix for supper. I will have the boys go out and get a mess of taters, some onions, and pick some green beans. We can have some collards with the fish too." The boys understood what to do when their mother instructed them to make a mess of something. It meant that they should get a peck bucket full of whatever she had asked for. They brought everything back to the house, and Shirley and Louise washed and prepared the food for cooking. A few hours later, the food was ready.

Rob closed the blacksmith shop and came over to the house. He washed his hands, took his place at the head of the table, and said grace. Rachel prepared plates for the small children, and the food was passed around the table. About halfway through the meal, Rob spoke. "You know, I am going to have to go to Durham tomorrow. They did not have some of the materials I needed to complete that one job. They told me that I could get it if I went to Durham."

Surprised, Rachel asked, "Is it far away from here?"

Rob answered quickly. "No, not really. I'll leave early in the morning and be back before dark." It was clear to everyone that he had already made up his mind about driving to Durham.

Rob got up and went outside, as he always did, to check on the horses, mules, and other animals after they had finished eating. He did not give any indication that he was preparing to visit a specialist at Duke University in Durham the following day. Rob was not the type of person to complain about his ailments. Visiting the specialist was a decision that he had made with Dr. Bitman. The men had promised each other that they would keep the visit a secret. Furthermore, Rob decided, there was no reason to get anyone all worked up when it was nothing serious anyway. He was only going to see the specialist as a precaution. Dr. Bitman had already told him that it was probably nothing. Although the thought of telling Rachel went through his head, he would not. When he had finished, he came back to the house and sat down in his favorite rocking chair. There, he twiddled his thumbs until late in the evening. No one knew what was going through his mind, and he wanted to keep it that way.

The next morning, Rob was the first person in the family out of bed. That was quite unusual. He usually only gets up after the fire in the heater starts. That morning, he made the fire and went out and took care of all the chores that were usually done by his older sons. He came back to the house and had breakfast while the kids were getting ready for school. Then Rob said good-bye to Rachel, got in his car, and was on his way to Durham.

As he drove the twisting roads, he wondered what the specialist would do for him. How would it go? What questions would he be asked?

CHAPTER SEVENTEEN

It took Rob the better part of four hours to drive to the clinic. He had no difficulty finding the specialist's office. He had traveled to Durham several times, but this was his first trip to Duke University.

The campus looked quite different from what he was used to seeing. Even the folks were nicer than any white folks he had ever met before. Hell, these white folks were even calling him "Mr." Any white person had never addressed him as "Mr." before.

He walked into the clinic and went up to the window, where a blond woman sat in what looked like a glass cage. "Can I help you, sir?" she asked.

"Yessome, my name is Robert Callaway. I was sent here today to see a specialist for my head."

"Yes sir. Oh! Yes, I see," the woman exclaimed. "We had you down as Rob Callaway."

"Yessome, everybody calls me Rob."

She bobbed her head in understanding. "Well, we have you here, and the specialist will see you in a noticeably short while. I know you need to get back to Lakeville. Just take a seat, and the doctor will see you in a few minutes."

Rob sat down beside a white man. There was a woman sitting on the other side of him. She leaned her head over and whispered something into his ear. He looked over at Rob and got up. He and the woman moved one chair over, leaving an empty seat between them and Rob.

That did not bother Rob. He'd grown up with racial prejudice. The only place he felt safe was in Callawaytown. A Callaway, or someone related to a Callaway, owned everything in Callawaytown. There, everyone felt safe.

The specialist came out of a side office and called, "Mr. Rob Callaway!"

"Yessir," answered Rob.

The specialist offered his right hand to Rob, and Rob put his right hand forward. "My name is Dr. Knox. Dr. Bitman talked to me about you. I will be doing some tests and asking some questions. Afterwards, I would like to discuss your case with other specialists in the hospital."

Rob was totally confused. Dr. Bitman had told him he was going to the university, but it was really a hospital. Dr. Bitman had told him that he would be seeing a specialist and now this fellow Knox had told him that he was a doctor. What was going on? Had Dr. Bitman tricked him into coming to a hospital? He had thought he could trust Dr. Bitman. But it was just like his father and grandfather had told him many years before–you could never trust a white man.

Now, he was stuck. Dr. Knox started examining him and asking questions. Rob wondered what was going to happen next. He decided to speak up. "Sir, Dr. Bitman said that I was going to see a specialist, and now you say you're a doctor. He also said that I was going to Duke University, and now you tell me this is a hospital. What is going on here? Is this a hospital or a university? Are you a doctor or are you a specialist?"

The doctor looked at Rob with a smile on his face. "Mr. Callaway, this is a university. One of the things we do best here is teach men and women how to be good doctors. I am a doctor, but I am a special doctor. That is why some people call me a specialist. I specialize in the study of the brain and the nervous system. Dr. Bitman is a general doctor. If he feels something might be going on with a person, he sends them to another doctor that specializes in whatever that ailment is. That is why he sent you to me. After we finish with the examination and all the tests,

I will review the information with other specialists. I will be able to tell Dr. Bitman why you have these headaches. Once we find out what causes them, we can treat them. Do you understand now?"

Rob released his breath. "Yes, sir, I understand. I am glad that you explained everything to me. I really thank you a lot for that."

All the tests and questioning were finished within two hours. Dr. Knox told Rob that he would get in touch with Dr. Bitman in a short while. Rob left the building and proceeded to his car. He was glad it was all over. As he drove out of the parking lot, he wondered what the tests would show. What was Dr. Knox looking for?

Many thoughts went through his mind as he followed the winding road leading back to Mills County, Lakeville, and eventually Callawaytown. Should he tell Rachel? How could he tell her? How would she take the news that there was a possibility that he could be sick? If Dr. Knox thought he was sick, Rob rationalized, he would probably have told him right away.

He tried to shake off a growing concern. Dr. Bitman had said all these tests were just to make sure everything was okay. Furthermore, he had gone several weeks without having headaches. He decided not to worry. He would not tell anyone anything. He had gone to Durham to get those blacksmith supplies that were not available in Lakeville or Mills County. His attention shifted to the fact that he was getting hungry.

A few hours later, Rob arrived home. He drove straight to the blacksmith shop parking lot. He got out of the car, opened the trunk, and took out the items, which he had purchased several days earlier in Lakeville, and put them in the blacksmith shop.

Afterwards, he went to the house, where Rachel fell into his arms. "I missed you today. Did you have a good trip to Durham?"

"Yes, it was good," Rob answered quietly. Before she could ask him any more questions, he said, "You know that's a long way up there. I almost forgot how long a drive it was from here to Durham. You can spend the bigger part of a day just driving up and back. I was able to get all the supplies I needed. Tomorrow I can get some work done." He walked over to the stove and took a drumstick that Rachel had just taken out of the hot grease. "God! This is hot!" he shouted.

"Good enough for you," laughed Rachel. "You know I don't like when you pick at the food before I put it on the table. If you do that, the kids will grow up wanting to do the same thing."

"You know, I ain't had nothing to eat since I left home this morning," Rob complained. "I wanted to get back before dark, so I didn't take any time to eat." He pulled the drumstick through his mouth from one side to the other. When the bone came out on the opposite side, all the meat was left inside his mouth.

Rachel slapped at his hand playfully. "Supper will be ready in a few minutes, so don't take anything else from the stove. Okay?"

Not long afterwards, Rachel called out that supper was ready, and kids came from every direction to share in the last meal of the day. When everyone was finished, one by one, the kids excused themselves and left the table. Rob and Rachel were left alone. Rob could sense that Rachel wanted to say something to him. He shifted uncomfortably in his seat. If she didn't have the courage to speak out, it would be all the better for him. As long as there were no questions, he would not have to provide any answers. They sat at the table for a few more minutes, chatting about trivial matters. She never asked any substantive questions.

CHAPTER EIGHTEEN

"Papa! Papa! Mr. Kenny Hooker is coming down the driveway," shouted Jacob.

Rob looked over at Rachel and said, "I wonder what he wants this time in the evening."

"I don't know," shrugged Rachel. "Maybe he just wants to visit."

Kenny was sure to be in some sort of hurry. He looked very worried and depressed. Rob and Kenny's eyes locked on each other as Kenny raced up the steps of the porch and through the kitchen door. "Lee Kenny just shot Charles in the back," he said frantically.

Completely shocked, Rob asked, "Where is Charles now?"

"He's lying on the bank of the Flat River. It doesn't look like he can make it. But Maddie-Jean and I would be glad if you would drive him to the hospital."

Rob was already on his feet. "I'll drive him home. Let us go."

Rachel was stunned. Why would a brother shoot his brother? Kenny and Maddie-Jean had always given their kids a free reign. There were never any limits on what they could or could not do, she thought. Somehow, the Lord would work everything out.

When Rob and Kenny arrived, they saw that Ernie and Lonnie had taken Charles to the bank nearest the road. There was blood everywhere. Rob looked down at Charles and tried to assure him that everything would be all right.

"He shot me! He shot me in the back," cried Charles.

Rob replied firmly. "Don't talk. We will get you to the hospital in just a few minutes." They got to the emergency entrance of the hospital within a short period of time. Rob parked and walked into the hospital. The person at the entrance had to first check and see if there was a room for colored folks available before they could admit Charles into the hospital. Heaven forbid that a black person should go on an operating table that was reserved for whites only. They had to wait for almost an hour before arrangements could be made to take Charles into the hospital, get a surgeon, and set up a table for treatment.

After they admitted Charles to the hospital, Kenny stayed there, and Rob returned to Callawaytown to pick up Maddie-Jean. As Rob drove from Lakeville to Callawaytown, he thought of how long they had to wait in the waiting room before the folks there would even see Charles. If Charles were white, they would have had him in that hospital and on the operating table right away.

When Rob arrived at Maddie-Jean and Kenny's house, he got out of the car and walked over to the porch, where she was standing on the steps. "How is he doing?" she sobbed. "Will he be okay?"

Rob answered carefully. "He lost a lot of blood, but he seemed to be in good spirits. He is in the hospital now, and they said they'd operate on him right away. Kenny is still there. I told him that I would come out and drive you back to the hospital."

As Maddie-Jean got into the car, Rob cranked the car vehicle, turned it around, and headed toward the main road, which led back to the hospital. As they drove towards the bridges, they could see a commotion at the middle bridge. The sheriff's car was there, and several other police cars were parked near the site where the shooting took place.

"Oh! God! They have Lee Kenny!" Maddie-Jean shrieked. Rob did not say anything. The police had handcuffed Lee Kenny and were leading him toward one of the police cars. Maddie-Jean wanted Rob to stop the car. Thinking it best, he refused and continued toward the hospital.

When they arrived, Rob took Maddie-Jean to the waiting room. Nearly hysterical, she ran over to the front desk. "My son was shot. They brought him here, and I want to know how he's doing."

"Is he the nigger that they brought in here about a hour ago?" asked an overweight white woman behind the counter.

"Yessom," Maddie-Jean said, trying to calm down. "They brought my son in here about an hour ago. His father was with him."

The woman behind the counter looked over her shoulder at another woman that was sitting at the back of the office and asked, "Was the tall nigger that Uncle Kenny?"

"Yes, I think that was Uncle Kenny," replied the woman in the back. Clearly, she did not care.

The woman behind the counter looked back at Maddie-Jean and said, "Yes, there is a nigger in the operating room now. I will go and see if I can find out what time he will be out."

She came back shortly and said, "They have a nigger on the operating table named Charles Hooker. Uncle Kenny is waiting outside the operating room. If you want to, you can go in and wait with him. I don't know how long it will be before they're finished."

Once Maddie-Jean was in the waiting area near the operating room, Rob left the hospital and returned to Callawaytown. Rachel and the older kids met him. Ernie was the first to speak. "Papa, you know the sheriff came out and picked Lee Kenny up at the middle bridge. They were asking him what happened, and he was saying that he shot Charles because he stole his boat. The sheriff just looked at him and shook his head."

Rob called all the boys over to the porch to talk to them. "You see, boys, that's why your mama and I don't want you being with them Hooker youngins. You see what that Lee Kenny did to his own brother? He shot him just because he took his boat. That's plain and simple crazy."

"Nobody in their right mind would shoot their brother over anything, much less a boat. Kenny and Maddie-Jean just let them youngins run wild. Half the time they do not even know where those youngins are. I will tell you boys one thing: You always must listen to your mama and me. We always know what's best for you. We will always be around to help you, but you must listen and learn from other people's mistakes. That is the only way you can make it in this world. You can see what happened to those Hooker boys. It's a shame before God and man that Lee Kenny shot anyone over a boat. It's even worse that he shot his own brother."

"All those white folks think colored people are lazy and crazy. When something like this happens, that just makes them more convinced about it. I want you boys to learn from this experience. Remember, you should never do anything foolish like what Lee Kenny did. Now he is in jail, and his brother is lying in a hospital bed. That looks bad for Callawaytown and colored folks. I cannot understand why he would do a thing like that. That's something I will never understand if I live to be a hundred years old."

The boys looked at their father in amazement. Finally, Lonnie asked, "Why didn't Lee Kenny just come home and tell Mr. Kenny and Miss Maddie-Jean that Charles had taken his boat?"

"That's just what I am saying," Rob emphasized. "They never listen to anything Kenny and Maddie-Jean say. Their boys always want to take the law into their own hands. It is bad, but that's the way they were brought up. And I'll tell you right now, I don't want you boys growing up like that. I want you boys to have respect for your mama, me, and each other. That's the only way you can make it through this world and stay out of trouble."

The next morning, Rob was up bright and early. He did most of the chores that were usually reserved for the older boys. He felt good, and he had had a well-deserved good night's sleep. After breakfast, he would go to the blacksmith shop and get caught up with his work. Around noon, the mailman came and brought the county newspaper. Huge headlines read, "Nigger teenager shoots brother for taking boat."

Rob could not believe what he was reading. The newspaper stated that Lee Kenny was not remorseful for what he had done. He told the newspaper that if he had it to do over again, he would do the same thing. He was not sorry. The only thing he regretted was that his brother was still alive. Rob had to put the newspaper down and think about what he had read. He threw the paper on the table and looked over at Rachel. "I can't believe what I just read. You know that Lee Kenny said he wasn't sorry for what he did to his brother, and the only thing that he was sorry about was that his brother was still alive? And if he had the same thing to do over again, he would make sure that he killed him. That boy should go to the electric chair for shooting his brother!"

Rachel looked up at Rob. "Ain't you glad that we don't have boys like that?"

"Yes," he sighed. "It's good that we have such good and kind boys. They have done things that I did not like, but overall, they are good boys. You know, Rachel, I never thought it was a good idea for Maddie-Jean to marry that Kenny Hooker. Nobody knows what type of family he came from. I think that has a lot to do with how boys come out. If they come from a really good family, most of the time they turn out okay. If they come from a bad family, there is no telling how they will come out. But I will tell you, Rachel, if that were my son who shot his brother, I would personally shoot him myself. That's just the way I feel about the whole situation."

Rachel could see that Rob was terribly upset. Maddie-Jean was his first cousin, and the whole situation reflected badly on the Callaway family. Although the core of the Callaway family did not treat Maddie-Jean as family, after her marriage to Kenny Hooker, the fact was that she remained a Callaway by birth.

Rob and Rachel had drawn a line in the sand by instructing their children to speak to Maddie-Jean and Kenny as Mr. Kenny and Miss Maddie-Jean. Those terms were totally unheard of when referring to members of the family, no matter how distant the relationship.

Maddie-Jean and Kenny did not seem to feel badly about the way they were treated by the Callaway's. They accepted everything in good spirit. They always knew that no matter how the Callaway's treated them in public, they could always rely on their assistance in times of need and trouble. And that was a true statement.

In the late afternoon, when the children were back from school, Rob and Rachel drove Kenny down to the hospital to visit Charles. Maddie-Jean had been there since the previous day. When they arrived at the hospital, they found that Charles was doing quite well, considering all the blood he had lost and the operation he had endured. He had been shot with a twelve-gauge shotgun containing buckshot, which was the size of ball bearings. Not many men survived that type of wound. Charles was awake and in good spirits. He was weak, but he looked as if he was on his way to recovery.

Rachel suggested to Maddie-Jean that she go home and get some sleep. Rachel would spend the night at the hospital with Charles. Maddie-Jean would have none of that. He was her son, and she would be the one who stayed with him during his recovery. Rob gave Rachel a look that suggested she not press the issue. They stayed at the hospital for about an hour before they said good night to Charles and Maddie-Jean and returned to Callawaytown.

The next morning, Kenny came over to visit Rob and get some new shoes for one of his mules. While he replaced the shoes, Rob looked up at Kenny and asked, "Did Lee Kenny really say what the newspaper said?"

"I don't know what the newspaper said."

Rob remembered that Kenny could not read. Now he was stuck and had to report the news himself. "It said that Lee said he meant to kill Charles, and if he had it to do over, he would make sure that he killed him."

Kenny looked down at Rob and said sadly, "Yes, that's what he told me when I went to the jail to visit him."

Rob could not believe what he had just heard. "When are you going down to the jail to visit him again?"

"Well, I planned to go today, but I have so much work to do that I don't have time to go way down there with this mule and wagon," replied Kenny. "It will take the bigger part of the day to go down there and return. I just, you know, don't have the time. As much as I'd like to go down and see him, I've got too much to do out here."

It was still very early, and Rob really wanted to see Lee Kenny himself. He wanted to hear him say the words he had read in the newspaper. Looking up at Kenny, Rob said, "You know, Kenny, I'd be glad to take you down to the jail in Lakeville. I want to see him."

"Okay, that's a deal as far as I am concerned, but you know I ain't got nothing to do with who sees Lee Kenny or not. It's going to be up to whoever is the jailer," answered Kenny.

"Well, we can try." Rob shrugged. "Just as soon as I am finished with this last shoe, you can just leave your mule here, and we will drive down to the jail." Within five minutes, they were on their way over to the house. "Rachel, I am going to drive Kenny downtown. I will be back in an hour. If anybody comes while I am gone, just tell them I'll be right back."

Kenny was incredibly surprised that Rob would take the time to drive him to Lakeville, but Rob had his own agenda. He wanted to know for himself if Lee Kenny had said all those terrible things that the newspaper said he had said. They got into Rob's car, and within a few minutes they were parked in the jailhouse parking lot. They made their way up the steps and into the jail. Kenny talked to the jailer. "I am here to visit my son."

The jailer was a real redneck, cracker, and white trash. "Are you the father of that nigger that shot his brother over some goddamn boat?" he asked. "I don't know about you niggers. It looks like all you want to do is shoot and cut each other up. If you would spend that time working, you wouldn't have time to get into trouble."

Kenny dropped his head and did not respond to the jailer. However, Rob looked at him and said, "We would like to talk to Lee Kenny Hooker. He was arrested a couple of days ago. He's in this jail."

"Okay, come on back here with me," the jailor sneered. He searched them for weapons and then let them into the cell area. He pointed down the hall. "He's all the way down to the end. I'll be back to pick you up in about fifteen minutes." Rob and Kenny walked down the long cellblock until they saw Lee Kenny.

"How are you doing, son?"

"I am okay."

"You know Charles is doing very well after the operation," said Kenny.

"I don't care about how that son-of-a-bitch is doing," Lee Kenny snarled. "I tried to kill the bastard, and if I had it to do over again, I would make sure I killed him. He stole my boat."

Rob wanted to reach through the bars and do Lee Kenny bodily harm. But he held his temper and just listened to what that asshole was saying. Before long, the jailer was back, and they were on their way out of the jail.

As they drove home, Rob looked over at Kenny and said, "Kenny, I don't know what you have done to your boys, but whatever it was, it wasn't the right thing to do. That Lee Kenny is crazy. They need to put him in prison and throw away the key. If he were my son, I would personally take matters into my own hands. Just think of how he talked to you even while he was in jail. If he keeps speaking like that, the judge will put him away for a long time, and that will be a good thing."

Kenny did not respond. All he wanted to do was get out of that car, take his mule, and go home. That is exactly what he did when they arrived back at Rob's blacksmith shop.

Rob went to Rachel's home and inquired whether anyone had visited while he and Kenny were in Lakeville. She told him that it had been quiet and no one had come.

"You know what that Lee Kenny said to his father when we were at the jail?" asked Rob. Rachel shook her head. "He said that he wanted to kill Charles, and if he had it to do over again, he would make sure that he did kill him. I tell you, if that were my son, the judge would not have the opportunity to send him to prison. I would take care of him myself."

Rachel wanted to calm him down a bit. "Well, Rob, you don't have to worry about our boys. They never give us any trouble, and I thank God for that. But you know it's got to have something to do with the way we treat them. We do a lot of things as a family, and you're a very good father to them."

But Rob just could not accept the fact that someone could shoot his brother, or anyone else for that matter, just because a boat was taken. Throughout his fifty years on this earth, he had never seen anything like it. He was even more distressed that it had happened in Callawaytown.

After supper, Rob drove Rachel, Kenny, and a couple of their youngins to the hospital. They found Maddie-Jean sleeping on the side of Charles's bed. Charles was wide-awake and in a great mood. He looked so good that it was hard to believe that he had almost died just a few days before. In fact, the surgeons had almost given him up for dead before they took him into the operating room. The blast had just missed his spine.

When they arrived home, Rob turned on the radio to listen to the 9 o'clock news. The announcer said that the sheriff had charged Lee Kenny with attempted murder. He would be tried immediately. Rachel heard him say, "By the time he gets out of prison, he won't want to shoot his brother or anyone else. It serves him right to be charged with attempted murder."

This had not been a good week for Rob.

The next morning, Rob got up and performed his chores. Afterwards, he got in his car and drove to Lakeville to get some supplies. On his way through town, he decided to stop by Dr. Bitman's office.

The doctor was standing at the counter talking to one of his nurses. "Hi Rob," he smiled. "I've not heard anything from Dr. Knox. It will probably be a few more days. How do you feel? Have you had any of those headaches lately?"

"I've only had one, maybe two, since I saw you the last time. And you know, Dr. Bitman, I do not want to be a bother to you. I know you are a busy man, so I don't want to hold you up when I know so many folks are here to see you."

"Don't you worry about that." Dr. Bitman said firmly, "I can always take time out to see you. I have been the doctor for the Callaway's since I can remember, and I do not plan to stop now. So, you just stop by any time. How are Rachel and the kids doing?"

Rob laughed. "They're doing simply fine. If they were doing any better, I wouldn't be able to live in that house."

"Well, you give them my regards, and I'll probably see you sometime next week." With that remark, Dr. Bitman turned and walked back into his office.

When he arrived home, he took all the materials he had purchased to the blacksmith shop and walked over to the house. It was almost time for dinner. For once, he'd be there before Rachel had to yell for him out the window. Today, he would be standing on the porch when she raised the window to call for him.

When Rachel came out of the kitchen, Rob met her, and they sat down to a very hardy dinner. She had made some of his favorite foods and didn't chastise him about eating so much meat.

He picked up the day's newspaper to see if there was any additional information on the shooting. There was an editorial that blasted his community. It did not mention the Hooker boys by name, but it did have lots to say about how niggers shot and cut each other up. Rob did not raise the subject with Rachel.

After Rob had finished reading the newspaper, he lay on the bed and got a few minutes of well-deserved rest. Rachel shook and let him know that somebody was over at the blacksmith shop. Rob got up, went to the porch, primed the pump, and pumped out a few strokes of ice-cold water. He took the gourd dipper that was hanging on a nail near the pump and took a few good swallows of water. He put his head under the pump and pushed the handle up and down a couple of times. He shook his head and took a towel and dried his head, face, and hands.

Now he was wide awake and ready for the rest of the day. When he got over to the blacksmith shop, he could see Edmund Foster waiting to get something done on his wagon. The wheel was worn, and the rim needed to be replaced. It was not a difficult job; Rob did it regularly. He barely got started when Edmund brought up the Hooker boys.

"You know I can't understand what's wrong with them Hooker niggers," said Edmund. "Callawaytown is not the same since Maddie-Jean married that Kenny Hooker nigger. It looks like those youngins are always into something. They just can't keep their blackasses out of trouble."

Rob did not respond, so Edmund continued to rant without any interruption. Rob thought that it would be best not to comment on the subject. He could not care less about what Edmund thought. To Rob, he was just poor white trash with a red neck. They were all basically the same. They were at the bottom of the white economic ladder and needed someone that they could look down on.

The Hooker boys were far from ideal, but that had nothing to do with their race. There were plenty of whites in the county with problems. But he could not speak his mind if he wanted to keep the business that the poor white trash brought him. He finished the wheel, and Edmund paid him and left.

Shortly afterwards, Kenny came over and asked Rob if he could drive him to jail. He had heard some talk that Lee Kenny was being mistreated. A distraught Kenny told Rob that he needed to see his son with his own eyes so he could sleep at night.

Rob agreed, and they were in his pickup truck and on their way to Lakeville. They didn't have any problems with the jailor this time. They went in and talked to Lee Kenny right away. He had looked like he'd been beaten, but he didn't admit it. He continued to trash talk to his brother.

Under normal circumstances, Rob would've been outraged at the thought of a Negro being beaten in the county jail. But this was different. Lee Kenny deserved it.

There was silence in the car as they followed the dusty dirt road from the jail in Lakeville to Callawaytown. Finally, Rob could not take it any longer. "Kenny, what do you think was going through Lee Kenny's head that caused him to shoot Charles? That was a really crazy thing that he did. Why on this man's earth would a boy shoot his own brother just because he took his old boat?"

Kenny sighed heavily. "I don't really know. But you know that Lee Kenny just bought that boat a few weeks ago. It was new when he bought it. I know that does not make any difference, but Charles should not have taken the boat in the first place. If Charles had not taken the boat, I can say that this would not have happened. I tried to tell Charles long ago that you do not mess with something that does not belong to you. But that boy does not ever listen to anything that I say to him. He just goes on doing just what he wants to do and never thinks about what's going to happen when he does it."

Kenny rambled on about the boat being new, and Charles was not listening. Rob looked over in disbelief. Even Kenny was more interested in the boat being new and Charles not listening than he was in what Lee Kenny had done. Hell, Lee Kenny had always done what he wanted to do. He had no direction at all from home. Kenny was always away, working either on the farm or doing small chores for well to do whites in Lakeville. Maddie-Jean was always taking care of the little ones. She had a baby every eleven to twelve months. She had two sets of twins in the same year. She certainly did not have the energy or time to give her youngins the guidance they so desperately needed.

Rob finally broke in. "Well, it looks like he's going to have a hard time when he gets in front of the judge. I happen to know Judge Maddox. I know he does not like Negroes. He's hard on every Negro that comes before him. I remember when that boy, Johnnie Williams, caught his wife with another man. He didn't do anything when he caught them. He didn't even let on that he knew about it. When they were supposed to meet the next time, he was ready for them."

Kenny just looked at him, so Rob continued, "Remember? He just got that forty-five-caliber pistol, came home, got under the bed, and waited for them. They were in bed talking about what Johnnie would do if he found out about what was going on. His own wife said, 'He's a fool. He'll never find out.' You remember the story?"

"Yeah," said Kenny quietly. "That was really bad what happened."

Rob went on. "Johnnie got out from under that bed after what his wife said and started screaming, 'So you think I am a fool?'"

"I think he started shooting at that time. He killed the man on the spot. His wife made it out of the house and down to the cornfield before he shot her. Remember, the judge said that he could understand how he could shoot them both on the spot. He thought he should have had time to change his mind while he was running her down in the cornfield. Judge Maddox gave him forty years for that. I think he's still in prison somewhere."

Kenny looked over at Rob as if someone had just poured a bucket of cold water over his head. Rob knew at that point that he had gone too far with the discussion. He dropped the subject and started talking about other things.

It was not awfully long before they were back in Callawaytown. Rob wanted to go inside the house and discuss everything with Rachel, but there was already a line of customers waiting for one thing or another. So, he parked the truck, said good-bye to Kenny, and walked straight over to the blacksmith shop.

After putting shoes on a few mules, Rob pulled on the chain that connected to his pocket watch, which was deep in the bottom of his side pocket. As he checked the time, Rachel called to say that dinner was on the table.

"Yeah! I hear you, baby. I'll be right over. I just have to finish this one mule's back hoof. I'll only be a minute."

Just as she usually did, Rachel said, "You better get over here now, else everything is going to be getting cold."

He finished shoeing the mule, and the last customer thanked and paid him. Rob walked over to the house, stopped at the pump, walked into the kitchen, and sat down at the table.

Rachel brought food to the table. She knew not to bring food to the table until after Rob sat down. He never left the blacksmith shop in the middle of a job. She passed the dishes of food around, and he helped himself from every dish.

He looked over at Rachel to see if she was prepared for him to say his usual grace. She had her hands together over her face with her head bowed. He folded his hands over his face and said, "Good Lord, make us thankful for what we're about to receive into our bodies, Amen."

Rachel repeated, "Amen."

Rob took one bite of the food and looked up at Rachel. "I drove Kenny down to the jail today. I couldn't believe what he had to say. That boy is a damn fool. If he tells the judge what he's told Kenny and me, he's going to get some real time. I'll bet you he'll get at least one, maybe two years of hard labor in the state prison."

"Why do you say that?" asked Rachel.

Rob shrugged. "He still says that he meant to kill Charles. He said that the only thing for which he was sorry was that the son-of-a-bitch was still alive. I could not understand how he could say such a thing about his own brother. Kenny just stood there looking like a damn fool. If it had been my son who said such a thing, I would've kicked the hell out of him. I really don't know about that Hooker family."

Rachel couldn't believe what she was hearing. How could Lee Kenny say such a thing about his own brother again and again? Why wasn't he sorry for what he had done? But there was nothing they could do about it. They might as well enjoy the food she made.

When Rob and Rachel had finished eating, he got up from the table and went out on the porch, read the headlines of the Millsian newspaper, and took a short nap.

CHAPTER NINETEEN

That evening, when Rob had finished work at the blacksmith shop, he came over to the house and got ready for supper. Just as he finished saying grace, the screen door opened, and Kenny stood there. Before anyone could make a sound, Kenny said flatly, "Charles just died." Rob collected himself in the cold silence.

Finally, he sputtered, "What do you mean, Charles just died? He was doing fine when we were down there at the hospital yesterday."

Kenny was in shock. "That is right. He was doing well this morning too. I do not know what happened. Mr. Baily just came by the house, and he told me that Charles just died." He shook his head sadly. "Lord, I don't know what they're going to do to Lee Kenny now."

The whole Rob Callaway family was sitting at the table and heard the sad news. Rachel got up and went to Kenny. Putting her arm around his waist, she said, "Kenny I am sorry for what has happened. But do not you and Maddie-Jean worry. The Lord is going to take care of everything. It's now in God's hands, and let me tell you, God knows what he's doing. Everything he's doing is for the best, and there is always a reason for it."

Kenny started to shake as tears rolled down his face. Rob got up from the table and embraced him. He whispered into his ear, trying to comfort him. The children continued to eat, their eyes big and round. Finally, Rob took a breath and said, "He's at Barry Evans' funeral home, isn't he?"

"Yes, that's who we always use, so I am sure that's who Maddie-Jean had the hospital call," Kenny answered brokenly.

Looking over at Rachel, Rob asked. "Do you want to go with us?"

Rachel answered quickly. "Yes. I should be with Maddie-Jean now. I can just imagine what she is going through now. Just let me clean up a little, and I'll be ready." Rachel looked over at Shirley and said, "You take care of putting everything away. Make sure you put the food that your children do not eat in the icebox, wash the dishes, and make sure all the children get to bed early. Louise, you give Shirley a hand, and all you kids be good and do what Ernie and Shirley say."

Rob added, "You boys make sure you feed the hogs, chickens, mules, horses, and cows. And don't forget to give them plenty of water. I don't want to see one empty trough when I get back."

They approached the counter with Rob leading the way. There was a big, fat, redneck cracker woman behind the counter. "What can I help you folks with?" she asked.

"I am Rob Callaway, and this is my wife, Rachel, and Kenny Hooker."

The woman scoffed, "I know who y'all are. I've seen y'all around Lakeville all my life."

Kenny stepped over to the counter. "My son Charles was in the hospital here. He- he- they said he died this afternoon." Kenny's voice cracked. "So, we just came down to pick up my wife, Maddie-Jean, and see who y'all called to take the body."

The woman looked up at Kenny and said dispassionately, "There was a young nigger boy that died this afternoon. Was that nigger your boy?"

"Yes, he was my son," said Kenny.

The woman peered over the counter. "Well, we called Barry Evans to come pick up the body. I think Maddie-Jean went with them. They just left here. They can't be gone more than ten or fifteen minutes." For some reason, she felt compelled to add, "You know I can't understand some niggers. Now take you Callaway's," she looked up at Rob and Rachel, "now y'all never have any trouble with anybody. I can't imagine a

Callaway nigger shooting his own brother, but look at what just happened with those Hooker niggers. How can you have that kind of niggers living in the same neighborhood with you?"

Rob and Rachel's mouths were about to drop open. How could this woman possibly be so unkind at a moment like this? But they had learned long ago to try to ignore what was said by poor white trash. After an awkward silence, Rob said, "Well, I guess we might as well get going over to the funeral home and see if there is anything we can do."

By now, Kenny was struggling to stay upright. "Yes, it'd be good if you would drive me over there. I know for sure that Maddie-Jean is at the funeral home because we always use Barry Evans. He's the only one who will take care of everything for us. Cause I ain't got no money to pay no undertaker now." They left the hospital and headed toward Rob's car.

Rob shook his head, still in disbelief. "I didn't think Charles was bad off enough to die from those buck shots. After seeing him the other day, I thought he was going to pull through."

Rachel tried to help. "But you don't know how bad he was when they took him to the hospital, and you never know what they had to do when they got him in that operating room."

Kenny was completely speechless when they got in the car. Rob drove toward the funeral home. Kenny said brokenly, "I don't know where I am going to get the money for no funeral. Maddie-Jean and I don't have a nickel at home."

"Don't you worry about a thing," said Rob. "We're going to make sure that everything works out okay. I will go in and talk to Barry Evans myself. If he doesn't want to do the funeral for you on credit, I will stand for you. We have always used Barry Evans. There won't be any trouble."

Rachel knew that Rob had stored their money somewhere. He never seemed to worry about money, and the family always had enough for its needs. She never asked about their money situation, and Rob never volunteered for any information. Everyone knew he wasn't a man to waste money. He had heard Bent say that if you had the almighty dollar, you would not run into any problems that could not be resolved in one way or another.

Still, Rachel could not believe what Rob had just said. How would he be able to stand for Kenny to get Barry Evans to take care of the funeral? The money would have to come from somewhere.

After making their way through the winding roads across town, they arrived at Evans Funeral Home on Fair Bluff Highway. They all got out and walked into the front entrance. Rachel went straight over to the waiting room, where Maddie-Jean sat in a chair weeping. Putting her right arm around Maddie-Jean's shoulders, she looked at her and said, "Do not worry, everything is now in God's hands. Jesus is going to make everything all right. Just wait and see. Charles is now in heaven with Jesus. He is all right. I know how you feel, but you've got to leave everything in God's hands now."

Maddie-Jean laid her head on Rachel's shoulder and continued to cry. "I know what you're saying is right, but, Lord, I don't know why my burden is so heavy to bear. Now I have lost two sons. I know that the judge is going to put Lee Kenny in prison for sure now that Charles died. And he was doing so well just last night. It's hard to think about him being dead the way he was laughing and carrying on in that bed last night."

"Just don't you worry," Rachel said soothingly. "The Lord knows what he's doing, and everything he does is for the best. We can't see it now, but I know there will be some good that comes out of all this bad. You just leave everything up to God and Jesus, and they will surely take care of everything."

Rob and Kenny talked to Barry Evans, and he agreed to take care of the funeral. Rob had given his word that he would pay if Kenny and Maddie-Jean could not. Barry Evans said that the body would be prepared for viewing by the end of the week. They could have the funeral on Sunday. The kinfolk up north in Baltimore and Washington, D.C., would need time to come down.

Looking over at Rachel and Maddie-Jean, Rob said, "Well, I guess it's about time we get back to Callawaytown. There ain't nothin' else we can do here."

Kenny's face looked relieved as he said, "Rob, me and Maddie-Jean really thank you and Rachel for all y'all are doing to help us. I don't know what we would do if we didn't have y'all next door."

"That's okay," said Rob quietly. "We know how hard it is for you now. So, don't y'all worry about a thing. I know y'all is thinking about what's going to happen to Lee Kenny now that Charles has died. There's no telling what Maddox is going to give him in the way of time. But you and Maddie-Jean do not think about Lee Kenny now. They aren't going to do nothing until after the funeral. Take one thing at a time."

As they drove up to the house, Ernie was standing there with Lonnie behind him, followed by Rob Junior and the rest of the children in descending order. Rob could see that Ernie and Lonnie had done all the chores he had told them to do.

"Papa," Ernie babbled anxiously, "is everything going to be all right? Where did they take Charles? When are they going to have the funeral?"

"They took the body to Evans Funeral Home," Rob answered, "where your grandpa was."

Rachel added, "Barry said that the body would be ready for viewing by the end of the week. And I think Kenny and Maddie-Jean want to have the funeral on Sunday. Isn't that what you want to do Kenny?"

"Yes," he answered soberly. "I think everybody who wants to come down for the funeral will have enough time to get here. We'll have to let 'em know right away. I got to go by the Western Union so Maddie-Jean and me could send them folks a telegram."

"That's okay, Kenny," answered Rob. "You and Maddie-Jean go home and get some sleep. I will drive you down to the Western Union in the morning."

"There's no need to think about the Western Union. Kenny," Maddie-Jean said. "Because I don't have any addresses with me. I got to go back home first so I can get the addresses. I don't have their addresses in my head."

Kenny and Maddie-Jean turned and walked silently into the night.

"I don't know what's happening with them," Rachel said as she looked over at Rob.

Rob answered, "Well, there could be many reasons why folks have such bad luck." He shrugged his shoulders. "You never know why things happen, but you just have to roll with the punches and don't let nothing get you down."

He walked over toward the barn to make sure that the boys had done all the work he'd asked them to do. He walked over to the stables and saw that the horses and mules were well fed. He walked down the path to where the goats, cows, hogs, and pigs were located. He checked to see that they too were well fed. When he had concluded that his instructions had all been obeyed, he returned to the house and entered from the back porch.

"Do you want something to eat or drink before you go to bed?" Rachel asked as she got ready for bed.

"No, I am okay until tomorrow. It's late now, and all I want to do is get some sleep." He sat on the bed and removed his shoes and woolly socks, turning them inside out before tossing them under the bed. Within seconds, he was fast asleep.

CHAPTER TWENTY

The next morning, Rob was out of bed before dawn. He got dressed and did his usual morning chores. He returned to the house, where Rachel had already prepared the breakfast meal and dressed the smaller kids for school. Everyone sat down for the morning meal of grits, eggs, ham, bacon, sausage, brown gravy, and molasses. Rob said the blessing, "Good Lord, make us humble and thankful for the food we're about to receive into our bodies. This we pray in Jesus' name, Amen." Everyone at the table repeated the "Amen."

Breakfast was the one meal where everyone was at liberty to eat as much as they could hold. It was considered the foundation for the rest of the day. If someone got a full stomach in the morning, they'd be able to put in a full day's work.

When Rob finished eating, he got up from the table and made his way out of the kitchen, through the porch, and over to the blacksmith shop. About the time he had arranged things as they should be for the day's work, he looked up and over to the road. He could see Kenny walking toward the blacksmith shop.

"Good morning, Rob."

"Hi Kenny, did you sleep well last night?"

"Yes, I slept well, but the youngins kept Maddie-Jean up most of the night. I don't think she got much sleep at all."

"Well, you and Maddie-Jean got to lot on your minds these days," Rob answered as he put his tools down. "I guess you want to go down to the Western Union and send that telegram."

Kenny nodded his head. "Yeah, that would be nice of you if you could drive me down there. With that old mule I've got, it would probably take me the bigger part of the day."

"Okay, just give me a few minutes to finish up on what I am doing now, and then I'll drive you down there." He had not expected Kenny to arrive before eight. Rob wanted to catch up with his work.

He did not open a conversation about Charles and Lee Kenny. The situation was painful. They did not know what would happen next, so he thought the best thing to do was not bring it up.

Rob walked over to the house and called out to Rachel. "I am going to drive Kenny down to the Western Union to send a telegram to them kinfolks. I will not be gone for more than an hour. If anybody comes by for work, just tell them that I'll be right back. Okay?"

"Okay," said Rachel as she stepped out onto the porch.

Rob and Kenny drove to the Western Union office. Kenny did not even have the funds to pay for the wire. "Do I have to pay to send this telegram?" Kenny asked in disbelief. "It's not my fault that my son is dead. Why should I have to pay?"

The man behind the counter was poor white trash. He was in his late fifties or early sixties. He really took advantage of the situation. Looking up at Kenny with an expression of disgust, he answered, "I don't know where you come from, nigger, but if you want to send a telegram from this Western Union, you've got to pay like everybody else." He added, "I can't understand why you niggers always think everything is free. Don't you niggers ever learn anything?"

At that point, Rob had heard enough. He looked over at the man and abruptly asked, "What's the cost to send the telegram?"

"Well, it's going to be one dollar and fifty cents. You niggers are bound to have that much between the two of you."

Rob just reached into his pocket, took out a roll of bills, took one dollar, and handed it to the man. He added two quarters from his right pocket. Clearly, the white man was shocked to see that Rob had such a large roll of bills. He had never seen a black man with so much cash before. After putting the money in a drawer, he wrote out a receipt and handed it to Kenny. Since Kenny could not read, he handed it over to Rob. Within a few minutes, the men were on their way back to Callawaytown.

It was an incredibly sad time. The funeral was set for that following Sunday at the Middleview Baptist Church. All the kinfolk from up north were notified. Charles had not been baptized, so no one knew what the preacher would speak about. Somehow, he would have to find something good to say about Charles.

Barry Evans came to visit Kenny and Maddie-Jean and finalized the details for the funeral. They chose the spot where Charles would be laid to rest. Barry told Kenny, "I don't have anybody to dig Charles's grave yet. Do you want to do it? I know you and Maddie-Jean can use the money."

"It doesn't matter to me," Kenny said sadly. "I've dug a lot of graves in my life. It isn't going to matter if I dig my own son's grave."

"It's all settled then," said Mr. Evans. "You can dig it Saturday or Sunday morning. If you dig it on Sunday morning, it's going to have to be early because my boys will be out there getting everything ready by nine o'clock."

"You ain't got nothing to worry about, Mr. Barry. I will make sure that the grave is dug. If it does not look like it is going to rain, I just might do it late Saturday evening. It'll give me something to do to keep my mind off everything for a while."

Barry looked over at Kenny and felt his sorrow. His own brother had been killed in an auto accident. Nobody could understand what he was going through at the time. The loss was devastating. Although everyone tried their best, they were unable to relieve the pain that he experienced. Today was the first time that he had thought of his brother in that way for many years. To think that one son could murder another…now that was truly beyond understanding. The pain was all over Kenny's face.

Barry kept his thoughts to himself, turned, and walked towards his car. It was all he could stand at that moment. He had to get out of that yard, back on the road, and out of Callawaytown. He had handled many funerals over the years, but this was certainly going to be a hard one. He negotiated his way around the kids that filled the front yard and drove slowly toward the main road. He noticed Kenny's face fading into the dirt as he glanced in the rearview mirror.

By the end of the week, all the kinfolk from up north had arrived. Everyone got there as fast as they could. They stayed with people in Callawaytown. It was common for doors to be opened to those who were in town for a funeral. Even Rachel and Rob made room for a few. The younger kids bunked on the floor in their parents' bedroom. Rachel and Rob wanted to do everything that they could to support Kenny and Maddie-Jean through these difficult times.

By midday on Saturday, everyone who was going to attend the funeral had arrived. No one talked about what had happened or why. No one wanted to bring up the subject of the trial. Everyone walked on eggshells.

Everyone should have been busy making plans for Thanksgiving and Christmas. Instead, they were all grieving Charles' death. The fact that he was gone was bad enough, but the way he had died was inconceivable. The fact that Lee Kenny had openly made those crazy statements about why he shot him and how he would do it again if he had the chance was unbearable.

There was talk around town that the judge should give Lee Kenny the death penalty. Poor white trash said it would be a lesson for the rest of the niggers. Most of the responsible whites in the community thought that it was very sad and unfortunate for Kenny and Maddie-Jean. They could hardly believe that such a terrible thing could happen in Callawaytown.

The feelings were mixed in Callawaytown. Everyone thought that it was sad for Kenny and Maddie-Jean. Since Lee Kenny did not show any remorse at all, most folks thought that the judge should severely punish him. But it would all have to wait; the important thing now was to get the funeral over and done with.

It was getting late in the afternoon, and a decision still hadn't been made about whether Charles's wake should be held at home or down at the funeral home. The problem was transportation. Many folks would not be able to come if it were held at the funeral home. But if she were held at the house, Maddie-Jean and Kenny would have to free up a room for the body. The discussion continued about what to do.

Rob and Rachel talked. "What do you think they're going to do about the wake?"

"I don't really know," Rob answered. Maddie-Jean and Kenny had to decide soon. "I think I will walk on over and see what's going on."

Rachel was relieved. She knew her husband would see that something got done.

Rob turned and walked out to the main road. He took short steps because he really was not feeling particularly good. The headaches were back and getting worse. He thought that maybe he should spend more time teaching Ernie and Lonnie the blacksmith trade. If something happened to him, someone would have to carry on the business he had worked so hard to build.

Ernie knew a lot about blacksmithing, but he did not know beans about business. He would have to know how to buy supplies and make deals. Rob suddenly realized he had better get on with it and get Ernie well trained. He shook off his mood. This was not the time to be thinking about such things. He had Maddie-Jean and Kenny to take care of.

Maddie-Jean had not had an easy life. Her mother died shortly after she was born. Her Aunt Linda had taken on the responsibility of raising the child. Linda was an interesting, but strange person. She always wore a pistol strapped around her waist. Some folks thought she was more of a man than a woman. She never had anything to do with men. Most of the time, she kept to herself. There was talk in the neighborhood that she had a few screws loose in her head. But one thing was certain, no one ever got in her way. Rob's father, Bent, and his uncles, Richard, and Eddie, were her brothers.

Eddie was married and had two young daughters. One day he came home, played with his two daughters, and told his wife that he was going down the road to buy some chewing tobacco from Linda. Eddie walked out of the house and did not return for twenty-five years. No one knew where he had gone.

There was talk in the neighborhood that he had gone to Georgia, met another woman, and started an entirely new family. They said he hadn't stopped at Linda's but had continued out of Callawaytown to the larger store, which was located at the intersection of Raft swamp Road and Highway 72. There he met up with some white trash gal who talked him into going south with her.

Although Eddie had straight hair and light red skin and could probably pass for white in some circles, he probably got caught once he crossed the North Carolina border. He was probably put in prison. That would explain where he had been all of these years. South Carolina had Jim Crow laws. The races were not allowed to mix, period.

His wife and daughters never gave up hope that he would return. Almost twenty-five years to the day, he returned home. He showed up in the afternoon when everyone was out working in the fields. No one was home. He returned with only the clothes on his back. He took off his shoes and sat down in his old rocking chair. His daughters were totally shocked when they returned home that evening.

Aunt Linda raised Maddie-Jean because her father never came forward. She was only twelve when Kenny showed up in the neighborhood. He was doing odd jobs for well-to-do white folks in the Lakeville area. Kenny rented a room from Linda and moved into the house. Everyone thought that Linda had finally found herself a man. But just under a year after Kenny moved in, he married Maddie-Jean. The entire neighborhood was surprised. Maddie-Jean was not yet a teenager, and Kenny was in his forties. The uproar was so loud that Linda was forced to ask Kenny to find someplace else to live. He purchased a little house from C.G. Baily on the small island next to Bent's lands.

Only a few months passed before Maddie-Jean gave birth to Lee Kenny. She was so young; she was always more like an older sister than a mother to him.

Rob approached the road leading up to where Kenny and Maddie-Jean lived. As he made the turn, he could see that lots of folks were at the house. He hoped that Kenny and Maddie-Jean had already made their decision about where to hold the wake. He called out, "Good evening!" Surveying all the people from Baltimore and Washington, D.C., he added, "How was the trip down?"

A tall man who had driven a lot of folks down with him answered, "Yes, it was incredibly good weather all the way down. I hope it continues to be good through Christmas and into January." Small talk was safe in this atmosphere.

Rob could see that Kenny was huddling with some folks at the other end of the porch. He talked for a while with the man from Baltimore. Finally, he made his way down to Kenny. "How're you doing?" he asked quietly.

"I am doin' okay, but Maddie-Jean isn't doing too good," Kenny said sadly. "We decided to have Mr. Barry bring Charles's body out here for the wake. We thought it would be better for everybody."

"Okay," Rob said gently. "If that is what you want to do, me and Rachel will help all we can. If you want us to do anything, just let us know."

"Well, I have to get down to the funeral home and let Mr. Barry know that he can bring the body out here sometime tomorrow evening."

Rob said kindly, "Don't you think if you have him bring the body out at around seven, maybe eight in the evening, that that will be early enough?"

Kenny looked over at him with blank eyes. "Yeah. I guess that will do. That'll give plenty of time for everybody to view the body. The ones who miss the viewing tomorrow will just have to go to the funeral on Sunday."

Ever practical, Rob asked, "Do you and Maddie-Jean have a room free for the body?"

Kenny shrugged. "No, we don't. Not right now, but we will by the time Mr. Barry brings the body out here."

Rob pursued. "Where will the folks sleep?"

Kenny was clearly overwhelmed. "Well, we ain't had no time to think about that. We been so busy with getting everything fixed with the church and all that, we just ain't had no time to think about where the folks are going to sleep."

"Don't worry about it Kenny," Rob said. "You can just send them over to us. We'll make room."

Kenny was relieved. "That sure is nice of you and Rachel to help us out like this. I really don't know what me and Maddie-Jean would do if we didn't have you here in the neighborhood. Y'all have really been nice to us." He added helplessly, "I just hope someday we'll be able to repay y'all for all you've done."

"Don't think about that now, Kenny," said Rob. "All we want to do is see that you and Maddie-Jean get through these times the best way you can. Terrible things happen to all of us. It's just your time now. Nobody knows when it'll be somebody else's time."

Rob moved on to make small talk with the folks that were sitting on the porch and standing in the yard. Most of the folks were caught up in grief and at a loss for words.

For so many years now, kinfolk had always made the trip down south for two weeks in August, four days during Thanksgiving, and maybe a week for Christmas or New Year's. This visit was totally unexpected. It shook the foundation of the family. No one would be able to return for the holidays. For the most part, they were all uneducated laborers or domestic workers. They had left the South for a better life up north. They were all victims of racial prejudice, Jim Crow, bigotry, and the backlash from poor white trash.

Rob was unique. Most Negroes had a very hard time, even in Callawaytown. They either had to do farm work, or they ventured out of the neighborhood to compete with the poor white trash for whatever work was available. Most white people did not treat them with kindness. Despite their rudeness and lack of education, the poor white trash was always considered to be one step above the Negroes.

The Callaway's carried the blood of Europeans, Cherokee and Lumbee Indians, and Negroes. However, their Zulu heritage was strong. It was clear that their lineage went back to the African continent. Many of the family members were as black as tar. At night, you could only see the white in their eyes. The whites did not regard those Callaway's as highly as those who were lighter.

That just made things that much worse for the other Negroes. When the poor white trash had a problem with a Callaway, they would, for the most part, take their frustration out on other Negroes. They knew that most of the Callaway's were closely knit with white people who were big shots in Lakeville. The Baily, Bitmaps, and Calwell families had a good relationship with the Callaway family. Bent had made sure of that during his lifetime, and Rob had followed in Bent's footsteps. Any problems with whites in Callawaytown that could not be resolved locally would be addressed directly to C.G. Baily or at least a member of his family. Most poor white trash knew that no matter who was really at fault, the Baily family would support most of the Callaway's.

The poor white trash was very jealous of Rob. They hated the fact that he controlled the blacksmith business in the area. They all thought that if a nigger could make it so good, then they should be able to make it with ease. In their minds, there was no way that a nigger could have the smarts to succeed at anything. But they never mentioned it to anyone in the neighborhood for fear that the word might get back to Rob.

After spending a few minutes with Kenny and the other folks, Rob thought that it was time to return and tell Rachel what he had learned. "Well, Kenny," he said. "I guess I better get back over to the house. Is there anything you and Maddie-Jean need for me and Rachel to do for you right now?"

Kenny looked over at Rob and said simply, "Nope." Then he thought. "But you know, Mr. Barry doesn't know that he gotta bring the body out here tomorrow. He still thinks we are going to have the wake at the funeral home. I really got to get down there and let him know to bring the body out here tomorrow."

Rob responded right away. "Well, I'll drive you down there. You can see if the body is the way that you and Maddie-Jean want it to be. I ain't doing nothin' now."

"That'd be good," Kenny said. "I'll go in the house and say something to Maddie-Jean, then I'll just walk back over with you."

"Okay, I'll wait." Then Rob had a thought. "Does Barry have all the clothes that he needs to dress the body?"

"I need to ask Maddie-Jean about that," Kenny mumbled.

Rob looked around and saw that the men from up north had either brought some whiskey down with them or they had run into the local bootleggers. A half-gallon jar was being passed around in the yard. No one passed the jar to Rob. It was clear that he was not in a drinking state of mind. Rob thought that it was a shame that these people could not even wait until after the funeral before they got into drinking. He worried that the police might come by. How would it look? All the police knew that whiskey was available for a price in the county. White lightning was brewed right here in Mills County. But Rob didn't want them to see the men drunk before the funeral.

Kenny came right back. He walked straight past the men who were passing the half-gallon jar of whiskey around. He did not want to see what was going on in his own front yard. "Okay, Rob," he said softly. "Let's go."

Rachel was standing in the front yard when the two men showed up. "What's going on?" she asked.

"Well, they're going to have the wake at home," Rob answered. "Kenny and Maddie-Jean decided to have the body brought out to the house for the wake. So, we've got to make some room for some more folks."

"That's not going to a problem," Rachel said quickly. "We'll just have to double up here and make room for them." She nodded toward Kenny. "How are you doing?"

Kenny was so tired. "I feel okay. I just want to get everything over with. I can't wait till all this is over."

"Yes, I know," said Rachel. "It's got to be hard on you and Maddie-Jean. But you do not have anything to worry about, the Lord will not put any more on us than he knows we can bear. He knows how heavy our load can be and he ain't going to give us no more than we can carry."

"I know," Kenny said wearily. "But sometimes you wonder why it all have to happen to you and all at one time."

"How is Maddie-Jean holding up to all this?" Rachel asked. "I hope she's putting her trust in Jesus. Lord knows he will see us all through this and more."

"She's not doing so good," answered Kenny. "She's laying down right now because she is mighty tired. But I know she's going to be okay. She just needs some rest."

Rob had walked past Rachel to the backyard where the car was parked. He went on the porch to where the pump was located, primed it, and started pumping water until the flow was ice cold. He took the gourd dipper from its hook, rinsed it, and had himself a couple of dippers full of water before going towards the car. "Okay Kenny," he called. "We can go now."

"Where y'all going?" asked Rachel.

"Rob is going to take me down to the funeral home so I can tell Mr. Barry that he's going to have to bring the body out to the house tomorrow," said Kenny. "He thought that we were going to have the wake down at the funeral home. After talking to Rob, me and Maddie-Jean thought that that would be the best thing to do. His eyes pleading, he asked, "Don't you think that's the best thing to do?"

"Yes," Rachel reassured him. "That makes a lot of sense. Everything is right here in the neighborhood. That's going to make everything much easier on everybody."

Rob got into his car and started the engine. He reached over and opened the driver's side door for Kenny. When he was seated and the door was secured, Rob turned towards Rachel. "We'll be back in a little while, honey."

"Okay, supper will be ready when you get back."

Rob backed the car out of the driveway and started the trip towards the funeral home. "Kenny, I know you'll be glad when all this is over and done with. These have been some terrible time for you and Maddie-Jean. And to think that you're going to have to go through that trial. But I know everything is going to be okay." Rob made the statement even though he knew that times would get even worse. Lee Kenny was still carrying on about having the right to shoot Charles. It did not look like he'd change his way of thinking. If he continued his attitude, the consequences were going to be terrible.

Although the crime was fit for capital punishment, no Negro had ever been given the death penalty for killing another Negro. They would always get the death penalty for killing a white person. It was an unwritten law that the loss of a Negro was nowhere near as important as the loss of a white person. However, there could always be a first time.

The Millsian newspaper had been writing articles about the shooting every day. All the articles were damaging to Lee Kenny. They had run a full-page editorial just two days before saying that the judge should give Lee Kenny the death penalty to set an example.

If there was ever a judge in North Carolina to listen to that advice and hand out the death penalty, it was certainly Judge Maddox. He was known by all to be tough on crime, especially crimes by Negroes. He had given Negro men the death penalty for lesser crimes. He had spoken openly about having little tolerance for "niggers and poor white trash."

"I don't really know what they are going to do at the trial," said Kenny softly. "I just hope they don't give Lee Kenny the death penalty or too much time. I know that he shot Charles 'because he was mad. Deep down in his heart, he didn't want to do him any harm." Desperately, he added, "Rob, you know how young the boys are, you've got Ernie, Lonnie, and Rob Junior. I know some time they must get mad with each other over one problem after another. Don't they?"

Rob had to be honest. "Yes, they do, but they don't get mad enough to kill each other." He made the left turn to cross the railroad tracks and enter the Negro township.

Kenny looked straight towards the jail. Rob asked, "Have you been to the jail to see Lee Kenny lately?"

The other man averted his eyes. "No, I have not been there for a few days. I was thinking about going in there and asking the jailer if he could come out to attend Charles's funeral. What do you think of that?"

Rob was shocked. He blurted, "What are you talking about? Have you completely lost your mind? Do you know what they will think if you go in there and asking such a foolish question? They'll think you've gone completely crazy. You know the jailer ain't going to let Lee Kenny out of that jail till he goes to the courthouse."

Kenny said nothing more. Rob made the turn into the funeral home and brought the car to a full stop. They both got out and walked towards the entrance. Barry was leaning against the doorway. He started to walk towards Kenny and Rob. "What can I do for you this evening?"

"I just wanted to come down here, Mr. Barry, and ask you if you could bring the body out to the house for the wake tomorrow. We decided, me and Maddie-Jean, that it would be better for everybody if the wake was held out at the house. That way all you must do on Sunday is come out and pick up the body and take it across the road to Middle view Church."

"Where do you plan to put the casket? With all those folks you got living there, I don't see where you're going to have any room."

Rob spoke up. "They are going to clear out one room. Some folks will come over to our house to spend that night."

Barry looked over at Kenny and then back at Rob. He wasn't sure who to address his next question. "What time did you say y'all wanted us to bring the body out to the house tomorrow?"

"I really don't know." Kenny looked over at Rob to get the answer. When it didn't come, he asked, "What do you think Rob?"

"Well, y'all got to get the room ready for the body. And nobody is going to be coming by to see the body before dark. I just bet you that it'll be after eight o'clock before anybody starts coming by. I'd say not before dark. Don't you think that's early enough?"

Kenny looked back at Barry before agreeing with Rob. "I reckon if you bring the body out there around dark, that'll be soon enough. By that time, I reckon everything will be the way it should be."

CHAPTER TWENTY-ONE

The next morning, Rob worked hard to get most of his small jobs done. But even before Rachel called him for breakfast, folks started coming around to see if their blacksmithing was finished. Then people showed up with horses or mules that had lost a shoe. Those jobs were considered emergencies and had to be done immediately. Finally, Kenny came down to the shop and asked, "You reckon everything's okay down there at the funeral home?"

Again, Rob assured him it was all going to be fine. Kenny rambled on. "We got everything we needed. We got him the shirt, tie, and suit that we wanted to put on him. As a matter of fact, Mr. Barry said the body will be ready for viewing sometime tomorrow morning. I don't know if you want to come down and see it before he brings it out. He said we could come down at any time. He's always open. Any time after nine o'clock tomorrow morning, you can come down." Kenny was sweating now. "He even said we could change anything we wanted to if we just let him know."

Rob knew it wasn't necessary to make several trips to the funeral home to check out what was going on. Pragmatically, he wondered, how badly could an experienced undertaker mess up a body? "I don't think there's going to be any need for you to go down there tomorrow morning, Kenny. Barry knows what he's doing. He's been doing bodies for a long time, and he knows how Charles is supposed to look. If I were you, I'd just let him bring the body out to the house after dark."

Barry did have years of experience. No one had ever accused him of screwing up a body or a funeral. But Rob had a different reason for repeating that to Kenny. He really did not have the time to drive him. He was willing to lend a helping hand, and he couldn't refuse to drive Kenny, but he had work to do.

Thankfully, Kenny looked over at Rob and stated, "That's going to be okay. I'll just let Mr. Barry bring the body out tomorrow after dark."

Rob was relieved. "Well, I think everything is set. Let me walk you on back to the house." As they got closer, he could see that the yard was packed with folks. Most of the men were drunk or well on their way. He thought again, that is plain shameful. But there is nothing I can do. I am going to stay away from Kenny and Maddie-Jean's house as much as I can.

When he arrived home, Rachel had the meal ready. He washed his hands and made his way into the kitchen. The children were already sitting at the table. Rachel brought the last few items to the table. Rob sat down, said the grace, and helped himself to the dish nearest to him.

"How's Kenny?" Rachel asked.

"He's okay. I think that Barry is a little bit off his old self. He went and asked Kenny if he wanted to come down and view the body tomorrow before they brought it out to the house. I don't see any need for that. So, I told Kenny to just wait until Barry brought the body out here after dark tomorrow. You know that Barry always does a good job. I couldn't see any need to go down there just to check on him."

"It was okay with Barry that they were going to have the wake out at the house?" asked Rachel.

"Yeah. Barry didn't seem to have any problem with that." Rob looked over at Ernie and Lonnie and said, "Did you boys feed and water all the animals?"

Ernie jumped on the question. "Yessir, we did everything. The horses, mules, cows, and hogs, all been fed, and we gave them plenty of water. We fed the chickens too and we gave them some water,"

"That's good," Rob said. He knew that he did not have to worry about his boys. For the most part, they did just as they were asked to do without any fanfare. He was proud of them. He had not had to deal with any of the problems that plagued even some of the most respected white families in the county. He was incredibly pleased with his family of nine sons and three daughters. And of course, he had a wonderful wife for whom he was grateful.

After the meal, there was not much talk in the household. Rob was tired and had a tremendous headache. At times, the pain in his head was almost unbearable. Still, he went straight back to the blacksmith shop. He had promised a lot of people that he would have their work done by the end of the week. Now it was Saturday, and there were certain to be folks coming over to check. He had let the boys help him. Ernie, Lonnie, and Rob Junior would help with the jobs that required at least two people to get done. George and Jacob would be there to turn the bellows.

As he walked over to the shop, the air was cool and crisp. It was only six in the morning. He would have at least an hour to work. Before he knew it, the children interrupted him and told him that breakfast was being served. He finished up what he was doing and told the men who had already come for their work that they'd have to wait a spell. He was going over to the house for breakfast. Rachel would come down and get him if he did not. Normally he would take a short break after breakfast, but not today. There was so much to do. He just could not afford the luxury of a break.

As he ate, he told the boys what he expected of them that day. After breakfast, he made his way back over to the blacksmith shop with them. Before dinner, he had completed every one of the jobs he had promised. He could close the shop and be free until Monday.

Rachel and the girls had prepared a three-course meal with all the trimmings. Rob ate to his heart's content. He really did not feel up to returning to the blacksmith shop. But he had one person who had not come before dinner come by and fetch the items that he had been badgering him about for several days.

After a catnap, he was up and out on the porch. He pumped cold water, caught it in his hands, and splashed it over his face. Fully awake now, he made his way down the steps and over to the blacksmith shop. He waited around for that one person who had been harassing him all week, but the man never showed up. Rob really wanted to get back over to the house, but he knew that as soon as he closed the shop, that bastard would come by.

Rob was irritated. When the customer comes by, he'd better have something to pay his bill with. Rob had problems with the man before. He was never satisfied. It seemed he always expected more than he originally asked for- and then he didn't pay his bill.

The man was an old white cracker. Everyone who knew him disliked him. Even the poor white trash did not have any use for him. All the Negroes referred to him as Mr. Lucky. The white folks called him Lucky. No one really knew the real reason for the name. The fact was that his luck was terrible. He had lived in the county for several years. Everything he touched Turned from sugar to shit. The poor man just could not succeed at anything.

Lucky was a sharecropper for one of the Raymond's. He planted it at the wrong time. He always waited until the last minute to gather the harvest, and then it would start raining before he was half done. Consequently, he'd always lose a good part of almost every crop. Furthermore, no one could tell the man how to do anything. He always knew what was best. He'd gone so far as to try to tell Rob how to shoe a mule. He'd stopped what he was doing and told him if he knew so much about shoeing mules, why didn't he do the damn chore himself?

Now, Rob had spent more than an hour in the blacksmith shop waiting for Lucky to show up. Sure enough, just as he was about to go back to the house, the man pulled into the driveway with his mule and wagon. Without a greeting, he called out, "Is my plow all ready?"

Rob kept his face calm. "Yeah, it's been ready for some time now, Mr. Lucky." He kicked his heel into the dust and added, "Thought you was coming by before now. I thought maybe you would have been by this morning. You know they got that wake tonight, and I did not want to be over here in this shop this afternoon. So, you can consider yourself lucky that you caught me open." He turned abruptly and went back into the shop to get Lucky's plow.

Lucky would never apologize to anyone for anything. Instead, he barked, "How much do I owe you for this?"

"It's going to be three dollars," said Rob patiently. "I had to do more than I thought."

For once, Lucky didn't make a fuss. He reached into his pocket and pulled out a roll of bills. He peeled off three and handed them to Rob. Without so much as a thank you, he picked up his plow, placed it in his wagon, and left.

At around six o'clock, Rachel was ready to serve supper. They would have two extra people at the table tonight. During the meal, everyone avoided talking about Lee Kenny. Finally, one of the guests looked over at Rob and asked, "What happened? What went wrong to cause a brother to shoot his own flesh and blood?"

Rob was caught off guard. Of course, everyone wanted to know why such a thing happened. But it was not a subject for the dinner table. He looked over at the man and said, "You know, it all boils down to one thing. The youngins of Maddie-Jean and Kenny never had any limits. They just do whatever they want to do."

The man nodded, grumbled, and continued to eat his food. Rob continued, "I can tell you that Kenny didn't even know that Lee Kenny had a shotgun. Now what kind of direction has a boy got when his own daddy doesn't even know that he's got a gun. I can tell you, you haven't seen the end of the problems yet. There's going to be a lot more things happening over there that nobody is going to believe, just mark my words."

By now, everyone had stopped eating. Rob went on, "I can tell y'all something right now, that Lee Kenny is an evil person. You know what he said when me and Kenny went down to the jail to visit him? He said he was glad that he had shot Charles and that if he had it to do over again, he would do the same thing. The only thing that he was sorry for was that 'the son-of-a-bitch is still alive.'" Now mind you that was before Charles died; he was still doing okay in the hospital. But can you imagine somebody shooting his brother and saying something like that? I could not believe my ears. And they tell me that he is still saying the same thing! And I can tell you something else. I know that Judge Maddox. He is about the meanest judge in Mills County. You will be coming down here for another funeral if Lee Kenny speaks like that in front of Judge Maddox. Cause he is going to give him the electric chair as sure as my name is Rob Callaway. Just you wait and see."

That was not what everyone sitting at the table wanted to hear. There was silence in the kitchen as Rob rambled on about what he thought of the situation. It was clear that although he had empathy for the Hooker family, he thought that this situation could have been prevented if Kenny and Maddie-Jean had raised their boy's right.

The couple spending the night both looked over at Rob rather judgmentally. After all, Rob was the leader at Callaway. If he knew that those youngins were so out of control, in their minds, he should have done something about it. He should have made Kenny and Maddie-Jean do something about the situation. Rob was closing the door after the horse was already out of the barn.

Silently, they blamed Rob. There was no reason for him to talk that way about the Hooker family. It was bad enough that one son had murdered another. Nobody really wanted to hear that this tragedy could have been prevented. Everyone sought an occasion to rejoice. Rob, though, continued and repeated his point multiple times.

After the meal and everyone was up and out of the kitchen, Rachel and the girls finished all their chores. The girls disappeared into another room. Rachel went outside to find Rob standing near the stable. Their guests had left for the wake. The boys were out in the back. Rachel saw a good opportunity to talk to Rob about what he had said. She had been embarrassed, even though she knew he was right. Some subjects were just for the family to hear.

Rob was a forthright man. When he had something to say, he always said it directly. That was one of his qualities that she really respected. But this evening she felt that he had talked behind Kenny and Maddie-Jean's back. She knew that what he said was going to get back to them.

As she walked over to where Rob was standing, he looked up at her. Before she could utter a word, he said, "You know, Rachel, I don't know how them folks who's spending the night with us took what I said at the supper table. But you know it's all true."

"Yes, Rob, I know it's all true." She patted his shoulder. "But, honey, you didn't have to say all that at the table. There was no reason to let them folks know how you feel about the situation. You know they're going to go right over there and tell Kenny and Maddie-Jean what you said."

"Well, I don't give a damn," Rob said angrily. "I didn't say nothin' that I didn't say to Kenny yesterday when I was driving him down to the funeral home. Kenny knows exactly how I feel about those youngins of his."

"You know what that asshole tried to do yesterday? He tried to compare our boys in his. I stopped him straight right away. Not only would I know if my boys had a gun, they damn sure would not have no gun. I am the only person in this house who's going to have a gun. I can tell you that if those folks go over there and talk about what I said, Kenny will have already heard it, and he will have heard it from my own mouth."

Rachel had a firm opinion on the matter. "Rob, there was no need to tell them folks about it. Everybody is trying to get ready for the wake tonight and the funeral tomorrow. That's the last thing they want to hear at this time of sorrow. I think we should go over for the wake as well tonight, don't you?"

Rob had his dander up. "Nope, I ain't going to go over there tonight." His chin was thrust out. "There's going to be enough drunks over there without me going over there." Then he mellowed a bit. "But you can go over with Shirley, Ernie, and Lonnie if you want to."

Rachel sighed. Her husband was a stubborn man. "I will go over it for a few minutes," she said firmly. "I need to go over and say a few words to Maddie-Jean and see how she's doing. I'll take all that leftover food with me. I know everybody is going to bring food, but I'll take that over there anyhow."

Rob agreed. "Don't stay too long."

Rachel leaned over and gave Rob a kiss on the cheek. "I won't be long. I'll go early. That way I can get out of there before the crowd starts coming." She turned and walked towards the house.

Rob walked around the barn and over to where the boys were playing. "Ernie, you, and Lonnie better go over to the house and talk to your mama. She's going over to Kenny and Maddie-Jean's for the wake. I told her that y'all could go with her and Shirley." The boys stopped what they were doing and ran over to the house. Rob walked around the edge of the fence, with Rob Junior, George, and Jacob following.

Rachel, Shirley, Ernie, and Lonnie went over to Kenny and Maddie-Jean's house. When they arrived, it was still quite early. As a matter of fact, Barry had just left the body for viewing. Maddie-Jean's eyes were red from crying, but she was glad to see them.

"Howdy, Rachel, girl, it's really good to see you. I am sho glad you have found the time to come. And girl, you didn't have to bring all that food. Folks have been bringing food all day. But Lord knows, the thought is good." She clung to Rachel's hand. "You don't know how much me, and Kenny appreciate all the good things you and Rob have done for us during this terrible time. Lord knows we really thank y'all for everything."

"That's what family and friends are all about. I know you and Kenny would do the same thing for Rob and me if we were in your shoes. How are you feeling? Kenny was telling me yesterday that you weren't feeling too good." Maddie-Jean teared up again, and Rachel put her arms around her. "I hope you're feeling better today. Just remember to put everything in God's hands, and Jesus will sho take care of it. You know God will never put more on you than he knows you can bear. Just trust in him, and everything is going to be okay."

Rachel and the children stayed for about an hour. They viewed the body, and Rachel commented on how Charles looked, like he was just sleeping. When they returned home, Rob asked about who was there, how the body looked, and so forth. They stayed up until their guests came back. When everyone went to bed, Rob and Rachel talked further about what had happened that day and how the funeral would go before they fell into a deep sleep.

It was a sad funeral and burial. No one knew quite what to say. Most folks still could not come to terms with the fact that Lee Kenny had killed his own brother. For the most part, the out of towners were leaving shortly after the funeral. The ones who came down by bus would leave soon. There was only one bus going north on Sunday. It left Lakeville at around 5:15 in the afternoon.

After the funeral, Rachel invited folks over to the house for a meal before they left for the bus station. At the dining table, no one mentioned the funeral or the Hooker family. They had small talk and commented on how good the food was. When they had finished eating, they said good-bye to Rachel. Rob drove them to the bus station.

"I'm glad this is over," Rob sighed upon his return.

"Yes, I am too. And we've got next week to deal with." Rachel looked over at Rob. "Now that the funeral is over, Lee Kenny will go up before that judge."

Rob shrugged. "I wouldn't be a bit surprised if Judge Maddox gave him the electric chair. They have been talking about that in the newspaper. A lotta folks want to see him get the chair."

"Kenny and Mary-Jean sure have never had any luck," Rachel replied.

"Well, there are many reasons why folks have bad luck," Rob pointed out. "You never know why things happen, but you just have to roll with the punches and don't let anything get you down."

CHAPTER TWENTY-TWO

Now that the funeral was over, Charles was buried, and the folks from up north had gone home, things were beginning to get back to normal. In just a few days, it will be Thanksgiving. The children would have a half week off, and everyone would enjoy a feast for that one day. For the first time in recent memory, no one would be coming down to visit from up north. They would not be able to come south until the following summer.

The following morning, Rob was up as usual, did his normal chores, went over to the blacksmith shop, and messed around for a few minutes before it was time for breakfast. Before he could get the bellows going, Rachel shouted from the kitchen window, "Rob, breakfast is ready!"

"Okay, I'll be there in just a few minutes," he called back. "I just want to get the bellows going now since I already started."

Rachel knew that it could take a few minutes or a half an hour for Rob to get the bellows going good enough. So, she called to the children, "Breakfast is ready! You all better get in here and eat. It's going to be time for school soon." Quickly, the kitchen was packed with all the school-age children. Rachel hurried around the kitchen. "You know, we don't eat till your daddy gets here, but if you got to get to school, you got to eat and get out of here."

By the time the children were half through the meal, Rob walked in from the porch. He looked surprised. "You all have already started eating. I did not think it would take as long as it did to get the bellows going today. For some reason, I just couldn't get the coal to burn."

Rachel brought him his food. "See, honey, I already fixed your plate. I wouldn't let them boys eat the best of everything while my man was out there working."

Rob smiled up at her. "Thanks baby. You don't ever have to worry about having enough to eat in this house. That's something' I can always say for sure. You always make enough to eat every time for a little army."

The children were soon on their way to school. Rob and Rachel were left alone with Mandy and Pope Junior. Rachel said quietly, "How have you been feeling, Rob? What with all the doings at Kenny and Maddie-Jean's, I haven't had time to ask."

Rob didn't want to worry her. "Don't worry about me, baby. I've been feeling good these days. I still have these headaches every once in a while, but it's nothing to worry about. If there was anything wrong with me, I know Dr. Bitman would have told me. So, I am not going to worry about it, and don't you worry as well."

He walked outside and back over to the blacksmith shop. As he worked on the jobs that were the most urgent, he noticed that there was a buggy wheel leaning against the side of the shop. Suddenly, he remembered that he had promised that wheel to Mr. Donaldson, who was a big shot in Flaterton.

Mr. Donaldson owned the country club and golf course. Of course, it was for whites only, and it just as well could have been for rich whites only. No poor white trash or crackers were allowed near the place. As a matter of fact, some of the local crackers' sons wanted to caddie out there but could not even get to do that. That was one job that was reserved for Negroes only. They would caddie eighteen holes for one dollar. Some would get even less. Still, it was a lot of money for the times.

Ernie, Lonnie, and Rob Junior were always out on the golf course to caddie on Saturdays and, from time to time, on Sundays. Rob knew every golf pro out there, so his sons always got the best jobs. The boys could keep half of whatever they earned. Rob always required them to set some aside for a rainy day. He put the money in envelopes with each boy's name on them. The envelope was kept in Rob's trunk, under his and Rachel's bed. The boys could use the money to purchase certain items of clothing or use it for the county fair. They could tap into it for birthday and Christmas gifts. They were incredibly pleased that they had one-half of the money to do with as they wished. That was more than fair in their opinion.

Rob put everything aside and walked back over to the house and shouted, "Rachel, you know what? I have got to go to Flaterton, to the hardware store. Just thought of something I need before I can finish Mr. Donaldson's wheel."

"I'm in here, and I can't hear what you're saying," Rachel yelled.

"Just wanted to let you know that I am going to go to Flaterton for just a minute. I need to pick up something before I can finish Mr. Donaldson's wheel! Got to pick it up now so I can get that wheel fixed before the end of the week."

Rachel came to the window. "Okay, honey, I'll be here, and if anybody comes by, I'll just tell them that you're going to be right back."

On that note, Rob got into his car and was on his way to Flaterton. He went straight to the hardware store to purchase the part needed for the wheel. He noticed Dr. Bitman walking out of the bank as he walked out of the hardware store around the corner and toward his car. He called out, "Howdy, Dr. Bitman!"

"Hi Rob," Dr. Bitman said as he approached. "I am glad I ran into you. I talked to Dr. Knox just before I came over here to the bank. He had time to look at the results of all your tests, and he talked to other specialists too."

Rob held his breath. "Interesting case you've got," the doctor said as he walked toward his car. "They want to see you again."

Rob's stomach dropped to the ground. What on earth was the doctor talking about?

Suddenly, Dr. Bitman stopped and looked over at him. "I'd like to go over the results with you in my office.

He hadn't been prepared to go to Dr. Bitman's office. He hadn't thought much about his experience at Duke. Right now, all he really wanted to do was get back to Callawaytown. But he was not a man to run. He'd go and see what the doctor had to say. If there was something to deal with, he'd best be doing it right away.

He nodded at Dr. Bitman to indicate that he would go with him. They walked toward their cars and talked about Rachel and the kids. They threw in everything else they could to avoid the subject of Rob's tests. They arrived at Dr. Bitman's office in less than five minutes.

By now, Rob had sunk into a state of dread. His dark eyes barely moved. It was as if someone had dropped a hammer on his head. But he summoned up his courage and asked, "What did Dr. Knox say about the headaches that I've been having?"

Dr. Bitman evaded the direct question. "Now let me tell you, you don't have anything to worry about. Everything is going to be okay. The specialist just wants to talk to you and me together. There just might be something we can do to correct those headaches."

Rob liked to deal with things straight on. "What are you trying to say? Is there something really wrong with my head that's causing these headaches?"

Dr. Bitman looked over at Rob and thought about all the times that he had treated him, his wife, children, mother, and father. He did not want to have to say what he was about to tell Rob. But he knew Rob was extraordinarily strong. Somehow, he would handle the news.

He lost the smile on his face, looked over at Rob, and said, "I talked to Dr. Knox this morning. He discussed all those tests you took at Duke with the other specialists there. There was something on the X ray. They are not sure what it is. They want to see you again and they want me to come as well. Dr. Bitman tried to lighten the situation. "They better want me to come. I don't want those fancy doctors up there making any decisions about you without me."

Somewhere along the way, Rob had started to shake just a little. Now he cried, "What do you think they saw on that x-ray?"

Once again, Dr. Bitman evaded the question. He said easily, "It could be several things. That is why I don't want you to worry about it right now. Whatever you do, don't tell Rachel, and get her all upset. It could just be a spot on the x-ray film. Let's just go up there together and see what they say."

Rob was not about to leave Dr. Bitman's office without having a better understanding of what was going on in his head. He wanted to know what the specialist had said. "Well, what do you think is wrong with my head? You know there's got to be something terrible wrong for these headaches to be coming back so often."

Dr. Bitman looked over at Rob and could not hold back the information he had received any longer. "To be honest with you, Dr. Knox thinks you might have a tumor on the brain that's causing those headaches." Not wanting to deal with Rob's understandable fear, the doctor rushed on, "But, like I told you, you have nothing to worry about, and I don't want you getting upset or going home and telling Rachel and getting her upset. We're going to just have to wait and see what happens when we go up to Duke together and meet with Dr. Knox and some of these other specialists."

Rob took a big breath and struggled to maintain his composure. "I am not going to go out and tell nobody about what you just told me. I just wanted to know for myself. You know a man is got a right to know if something's wrong in his head."

Dr. Bitman nodded soberly back at Rob. "When do you want to go up to Duke?"

"Well," Rob said. "I can just about get off any time I want to and go up there. How long do you think it is going to take anyway? As long as I know a day or two before, I am not going to have any problem getting away. Now that that funeral is over, you know that Charles Hooker's funeral, now that it's over, I am not going to be around so much."

Glad to have a different subject to talk about for a moment, Dr. Bitman rushed on, "Yes, that's right. They just had that funeral Sunday, didn't they? That was really a bad thing that that boy shot his own brother. Sometimes you just do not know what's going through young folks' heads these days. I'd never believe that a thing like that could happen out there in such a nice place as Callawaytown. Never heard of any trouble or problems over there. But look at what just happened. It's hard to say what's going to happen at the trial. That old man, Judge Maddox, is not going to take kindly to what that boy did. As for myself, I would be a little bit worried if I were in Lee Kenny's shoes. That Judge Maddox just might make an example out of him."

Finally, the doctor caught himself. "Well, you asked about when it would be a good time to go up to Duke. I am going to talk to Dr. Knox this afternoon. I will try to get everything set up for Friday morning. We will meet here at my office. We can go in my car. It is going to take about an hour for us to have that meeting. We should be back here way before dark. I know you can make up a story to get away from Callawaytown for a few hours."

Dr. Bitman was a special person. Although he was raised in the South, his family was originally from somewhere in Yankee country. For the most part, he treated all folks with dignity. If he knew someone had no money and nothing to barter, he would treat them free of charge. But the Callaway's were incredibly special to him. Privately, he believed the Callaway's would be leagues ahead of most whites if given the same opportunities. The Callaway's were not the type of folks to wait for handouts. They had built a school and a church in their own neighborhood and were as active in the county as the laws would allow. Even though all the ex-slaves in the area had been given equal amounts of land after the Civil War, somehow most of the land had ended up being owned by the Callaway's. That alone says a lot.

Dr. Bitman worked for changes in the laws and behavior between the races in the county and the state. He always used the Callaway's as an example to support his opinions. Negroes, Indians, and whites lived together and even had sex together. However, most whites wanted to keep the official policies of segregation. They did not want Negroes or Indians to have any real power. The poor white trash, crackers and rednecks knew that they would not have a chance if they had to compete on a level playing field with the likes of the Callaway's. Their only claim to superiority was their race. Without that as an excuse, they would have been left with no one to look down on.

Dr. Bitman was in an extremely dangerous position. If he openly supported Negroes and Indians, he would lose what little support he received from the whites in the county. But, in his heart, he knew what was happening was wrong and needed to be changed. So, whenever he could, he worked toward change. He talked to the golf pro about letting the Negro caddies use the golf course on Monday mornings. It took some time, but it finally happened–a great step forward in that part of the South.

Rob droves home after the meeting in Dr. Bitman's office and went straight to the blacksmith shop. He was not in the mood to talk to Rachel or anyone else, for that matter. He worked on a job and tried to think of a good excuse to be away from home for most of the day on Friday.

He was a man who was used to getting his own way. The thought that something could be seriously wrong with him was just not acceptable. He had a great life with a wonderful wife and children. His business was doing well, and even his siblings were no longer a problem. They never even asked about the farm, land, or proceeds from his father's rental properties anymore. Life could not be better.

He decided his brain would just have to be okay. Oh, he still had the headaches, but he rationalized they came from the extra pressure caused by the situation with Lee Kenny. There had been a lot of emotional upheaval and extra work. Now he was behind on his work schedule. Yep, he thought, that is why he had the headaches.

When Rob finished the day, he went over to the house and got ready for supper. As usual, the table fairly groaned with the bounty–three meats, veggies, potatoes, gravy, cornbread, biscuits, and plenty of lemonade. After eating to his heart's content, Rob went out on the porch to sit for a while. He stared out into space.

Rachel joined him on the porch. "What's wrong, Rob?" she asked gently. "Why are you sitting out here in the cold like this? Don't you know you're going to catch a cold sitting out here without a coat on?"

Rob just grumbled back. "I hadn't given it any thought. I am not cold. I feel just fine."

Rachel wasn't convinced. "I'll go inside and get you a sweater; you need something to keep you warm. I'll be right back." She returned shortly with a sweater, which Rob put on promptly. Rachel noted that he must have been cold after all. She sat down beside her husband and leaned her head on his lap. Looking straight up at his face, she asked. "What's wrong? Do you feel all right?"

Rob evaded her questions. "Yeah, I feel simply fine. Just got to go up to Durham again on Friday to pick up some more parts that I thought I had…some of those things that they don't have down in Flaterton. I asked today when I was downtown, but it's going to take them a few days to get them down here. So, I decided that I might as well go and pick them up for myself. I am not going to take a whole day. They already said, *'we have them.'*"

Rachel rubbed his chest. "You want me to ride with you up there? It'll give you some company."

Rob stood up at that point and said irritably, "You know somebody has to be here just in case a customer comes by. You can really help me in that way. Just tell them I had to go to Durham and that I'll be back for business tomorrow."

Deciding that her husband was in a rare bad mood, Rachel walked back inside the house. Relieved, Rob let himself relax for a few moments. Everything was set. He'd get up early on Friday to drive to Dr. Bitman's office and they'd leave for Durham.

Indeed, Rob was up bright and early. He took care of all the normal chores for the morning and had his usual hardy breakfast. It was still so early that the children weren't even up. Rob and Rachel were able to have breakfast together alone. They chatted about what had been going on over the past few weeks. Rachel brought up the fact that she had not had a chance to visit her family in Carriton for several weeks. Rob agreed to take her on Sunday. That decision had a side benefit–he would not have to see his sisters, who visited every Sunday around dinnertime. Furthermore, he had missed Rachel's father, Jason. He would shoot the shit with the old man and drink some of his homebrew.

Rachel was happy with his decision. "I can make some pies and cakes to take down with us."

Rob smiled, glad to see his wife so pleased. She was always in a great mood when she knew her family would all be together. "We'll leave here after breakfast," he said. "We'll have the whole day to spend with them."

"Well, you make sure you drive safely today," she said as she stood up and kissed the top of his head. "I'll have supper ready when you get back tonight."

"I am not going to be that long. You can bet that I'll be back here long before you even start cooking supper." He got up from the table, went outside on the porch, and washed his hands and face with the cold water. Now he was fresh again and ready for his trip to Durham. He said good-bye to Rachel and the children who had gotten out of bed.

As he drove, he let himself worry about the meeting he was going to have with Dr. Bitman and all those specialists at Duke. What would they all have to say? But Rob was always pragmatic. He knew that there was nothing that he could do to influence the outcome. Before he knew it, he pulled into Dr. Bitman's driveway. Even though it was still early morning, the light in the office was turned on. He knew the doctor was awake and ready to go.

Before he could get out of the car, Dr. Bitman stepped out of the office and locked the door behind him. "Good morning, Rob," he called. "Would you just move your car over to the side a few spaces? I wouldn't want anyone to think that I am renting parking spaces," he grinned.

"Yes, sir, I'll just move the car over. It doesn't matter a bit to me where I leave this car just as long as it's here when we get back."

After moving the car, Rob got out and walked over to Dr. Bitman's car. "Good morning, Dr. Bitman. I know it's not every day that you get up so early. I just want to say that I am very grateful that you're going with me to Durham. Must say that I am mighty happy that you are doing that for me."

Dr. Bitman shrugged. "Rob, don't worry about it. It is the least I can do for someone like you. I have known you Callaway's for God knows how long? My grandfather and great-grandfather all looked after the Callaway's, even when you were…"

At that point, Dr. Bitman collected himself and realized what he was about to say. But Rob just looked directly at him and said, "Dr. Bitman, you don't have to be careful about talking about slavery. My father and grandfather told me all kinds of stories about what went on. But you all have all been good to me and my family and that's what matters most."

The two men got inside Dr. Bitman's car and drove off. They were noticeably quiet all the way to Durham and Duke University Hospital.

Dr. Bitman parked in one of the spots reserved for doctors and special visitors when they arrived. The parking lot was located just outside the entrance to the clinic where Rob had visited before. It made Rob feel special–he was able to get out of the car and walk straight into the office.

Dr. Bitman and Rob left the car and stood at the receptionist's desk." Good morning. My name is Dr. Bitman, and this is Mr. Callaway. We've got a meeting this morning with Dr. Knox."

The woman behind the counter was the same person who had upset Rob the first time he made a visit to Duke University Medical Center. Today, her demeanor was completely different. She stood up hastily. "Yes,

Doctor. I'll go right back and see if Dr. Knox is available. I know he said something about having a meeting. I remember he didn't want to be disturbed while it was going on."

She gave all her attention to Dr. Bitman and acted as if Rob didn't exist. But that wasn't a surprise. When he'd been there before, she'd made it abundantly clear how she felt about black people.

Although people usually report to the receptionist and then take a seat in the waiting room, Dr. Bitman just stood there, so Rob did too. The woman looked over at him with irritation. But she said nothing and went to find Dr. Knox. Before long, he came out of an office and walked straight over to them.

"Good morning," he said. "Well, you can just follow me in here." He motioned to an open door. "I'll have some coffee brought in."

This really is a nice place, Rob mused as he viewed the paintings on the wall and the neat arrangement of everything in the room. Soon, the room overflowed with doctors. The coffee arrived. Everyone sat down at a round table. Dr. Knox introduced the doctors from Duke.

He took papers from his briefcase and passed them around to everyone in the room. At that point, Dr. Knox directed his attention to Rob. "As you can see, Mr. Callaway, we've been doing lots of investigation into what we feel is causing your headaches. We've come to some conclusions. It took the training and expertise of all these men in this room for us to figure out what is going on. But to be frank with you, I don't think there are better minds on this earth suited to make this type of judgment."

He paused for a moment and said, "We've concluded that you have a brain tumor."

Rob just stared over at the doctors. His mind could not absorb what the doctor had just said. No, he could not have said "brain tumor." No way. He could not have a brain tumor and that was that.

But Dr. Knox continued, "It is located in an area which is very difficult to reach."

Desperately, Rob looked over at Dr. Bitman, but he was busy listening to Dr. Knox.

"We only have two choices: We can do nothing and just wait and see what happens. We will give you something to ease the pain. Or we can operate."

Rob struggled to comprehend what the doctor was saying. Operate! On his head! Dr. Knox sounded far away. "The operation would be very risky. There would be less than ten percent of it being successful."

Mercifully, the doctor stopped for a moment. He seemed to be waiting for some reaction from Rob. When there was none, he went on. "Even if it was a successful operation, there is a very high possibility that you might not be able to use some parts of your body for the rest of your life."

Rob just sat in shock. In his wildest dreams, he had never considered the idea that his headaches could be so serious. He felt panicked. All he wanted to do was get out of that place and get home to Rachel and his children. If he just got out of here, everything would surely be all right. He began to get out of his chair. Dr. Bitman pressed his arm gently.

Dr. Knox seemed oblivious to Rob's distress. "We've discussed your condition repeatedly. We think the best approach would be for Dr. Bitman to monitor your condition. He can let us know what's going on and give you whatever medication you need to ease the pain." He added awkwardly, "However, the decision is certainly yours to make. We'll respect any decision you make." As though to ease his own discomfort with the situation, Dr. Knox said, "I must say that lots of folks live normal and productive lives just by taking it easy and having the medication available when it's needed. From what I have heard from Dr. Bitman, you are situated quite well in your life and can afford to kind of take it easy. With that in mind, I'd lean toward that."

Finally, Dr. Bitman said something. "Rob, I've known you and your family for many, many years. I think that you should just take things easy. I am going to be right downtown, and if you need anything, all you've got to do is just come on down to my office."

Take it easy! Rob had never taken it easy in all his life! What the hell were these men talking about? He could not believe they could all sit there so calmly and tell him that his life was basically over. What about his blacksmith business? He had worked hard all these years. What was he supposed to do, sit on a rocking chair like an old man?

Another doctor commented, "Now, on the other hand, I can tell you this is the type of case that makes history. Just let's say that you decided to have that operation, and it was a true success. You would certainly go down in history as making a major contribution to the betterment of mankind and medicine. But again, the decision is totally yours."

Rob had one objective, and that was to get the hell out of there and get back home. He did not give a rats' ass about the betterment of medicine and mankind. He had a wife and twelve youngins to take care of. He was not about to do anything that would put them in jeopardy. Yes, he had those terrible headaches, and sometimes he even had blackouts. Still, that was not enough reason for the doctors to get inside his head when even they were not sure about what the results would be.

No, hell no! No matter what happened or how bad the pain was, operating was out of the question. That was one option that he would never consider. "Well," he said a little loudly, "I can tell you now that I am not going to be letting anybody cut open my head."

Oh God! How would he explain all this to Rachel? How could she handle this kind of news? He looked around the room for reactions from the doctors, especially Dr. Bitman. When they said nothing, he rushed on, "That's nothing that I am going to even think about anymore. I'll just have to live with these headaches and see what happens."

"That's just what I think, Rob," said Dr. Bitman quickly. "When you have these headaches, I'll just give you something for the pain. That way, it won't disrupt your daily life too much."

The other doctors looked just a bit disappointed. They had lost their chance to make medical history. "Well, Dr. Bitman," said Dr. Knox,

"We'd like to see Mr. Callaway around once a quarter. It is a remarkably interesting case."

After some very awkward goodbyes Rob and Dr. Bitman left the building. They didn't exchange words as they walked toward the car. Rob got in, Dr. Bitman cranked the car, and they were on their way back to Flaterton.

There was a cool silence in the car for several miles before Rob broke in and said, "Well, I guess I'll have to go home and tell Rachel the story."

Dr. Bitman responded kindly, "I don't think that's a good idea, Rob."

It'll be much better if you just take it easy and do what we decided at Duke. Forget about telling anybody about what is happening. Why get them all riled up when there isn't anything they can do?"

Rob did not answer. A cold rage was beginning to take hold. He wasn't even fifty, and a goddamn specialist had told him that he had some kind of tumor in his head. He should have never gone to Duke in the first place. He would not have to deal with this shit. He should have kept his headaches to himself. Then he would never have gone to Dr. Bitman. He would not have known about this doctor's crap.

But Rob Callaway was a strong man. He decided to hold his head up high and accept whatever the good Lord had in store for him. He wasn't about to sit around feeling sorry for himself. Whatever was to be would be, and that was that.

Finally, Dr. Bitman looked over at Rob and asked, "What's on your mind? You look like you are miles away from everything." He drew his eyes back to the road just in time to avoid an old man with a mule and wagon. He twisted around to the left and missed the wagon by inches. Dr. Bitman swore under his breath. "Good Lord, what a day. Anyhow, what are you thinking?"

Rob realized that Dr. Bitman was all upset about this too. He answered, "I can't get over all these things that those specialists had to say. How would they know what's going on in my head when they haven't been in there with a knife? All that Dr. Knox did was ask me a lotta questions and took those pictures of my head. Just with that, he's able to say, *'What makes it hurt?'*"

Eternally kind, the doctor said, "Well, Rob, they are trained to understand the brain. That is all they do all day. I can tell you now that none of them could tell you how to put a shoe on a mule. They're good at what they do, nothing else."

Rob thought for a moment. "I've been thinking about what you said about not telling Rachel. I am going to take your advice. I am not going to tell nobody. I am going to just keep it between you and me."

Dr. Bitman nodded his agreement. "That's good," he sighed. "I was worried about how you were going to handle your condition and Rachel at the same time. She is a wonderful woman, but I really don't think she would be able to handle the news. And who knows? Lots of people live a normal life for many years with the same type of condition that you have. We just have to wait and see what happens."

Rob looked over at the doctor, glad to have some support for his decision. The two of them had been on the road for some time now. It was getting late, and they were ready to go home. Dr. Bitman made the turn onto the road where his office was located.

"It's sure been a busy day," Rob said. "I just want to get home and get something to eat. I haven't had anything to eat since I left home this morning. I am going to go straight to the kitchen and eat anything that's cooked."

Dr. Bitman negotiated his way from the main road and into his driveway. The driveway was empty. Evidently, his secretary and nurse had done a good job of keeping folks away from the office. This was just fine with him. Although he hoped Rob wouldn't notice, it had been a tiring day for him as well. All he wanted to do was check his messages and get over to his house. He was hungry too. Mostly, he just wanted to go to his study and rock himself to sleep in his old rocking chair.

As he brought the car to a halt, Rob opened the door on his side and got out. He looked like he had just lost the only friend he had on earth. "Well, Dr. Bitman," he began awkwardly. "I sure want to thank you for all that you've done for me. Most of all, I want to thank you for taking me up to Duke today. That was mighty nice of you. I know not being at your office and having all these sick folks come by and not get any treatment is not what you are all about. And to think that you took a whole day off just for me is mighty fine of you."

"Oh, you don't worry about that, Rob," Dr. Bitman replied. "Like I said to you before, you and your family have always been good folks and an example for all folks in this county, Negroes, whites, and Indians. It's just a pity what happened to that Hooker family, but that doesn't have anything to do with you Callaway's."

He gestured for Rob to come inside. "I just want to give you something for your headaches." He led the way up the steps and into his office. "But remember what Dr. Knox said. The best treatment is going to be for you to start taking it easy. I don't want to hear about you working all day, every day, in that blacksmith shop. That shop is too hot. I'd like to tell you to just stay away from it."

Only the nurse and the secretary were left in the office. Dr. Bitman was relieved to learn that not many people had come by. The nurse had been able to deal with everything. He and Rob walked through the waiting room and into his office. Dr. Bitman closed the door and asked Rob to sit down.

"Rob today was not a good day. You've got a lot of thinking to do. I want you to know that that's normal. It's okay for you to feel the way you do. Just remember that I am with you all the way. I want you to know that you can have my attention any time, day or night and don't you forget that."

Rob was moved by Dr. Bitman's sincerity. He wasn't seeking any special favors, but it was a good feeling to hear a white man say that he would go out of his way to help a Negro. He wanted to get home to

Callawaytown and his family. As long as he was near them, everything felt fine. His family and neighborhood gave him a special kind of energy. He could draw his strength from that. He needed the power in his own community now more than ever. Still, he was grateful to the doctor. "That's really nice of you to offer your support. But you got nothing to worry about. Everything's going to be all right, just wait and see."

Dr. Bitman reached into a cabinet over his head and fumbled for the pain medication. "I really think so," he said over his shoulder. "You've got the will and spirit that a person got to have to get through something like this." He stood on his toes and reached all the way to the back of the cabinet. "I know they're here. I put them here myself. They had to be here. Here they are. You should take one, maybe two if it's really bad, but don't take more than three at any one time. Try them two times a day for a few weeks. If it does not work out for you, try it three times a day. If need be, we can go up to four times a day, but I don't think you'll ever need to take that much." He handed the bottle over to Rob.

Rob placed it in his pocket. That is where he would have to keep them. If Rachel saw the bottle, she would certainly ask questions. When it was time to change pants, he would make sure that the bottle was placed under lock and key in his personal trunk under his bed. That way, Rachel would never find out about his condition. For now, he felt surprisingly good. It could be several days, weeks, or months before the terrible headaches returned.

"Yessir," he said to Dr. Bitman. "I'll take them just as you say, and I am going to make sure that I don't take any more than that what you said I had to take. I'm not going to tell anyone about what we did today, where we went today, what the specialist at Duke had to say, or anything else."

Dr. Bitman looked over at him, his face solemn. "I'll keep my end of the bargain. Just make sure that you keep yours. I don't want Rachel to get upset with me for not telling her everything."

"Yes, sir, I think you're right. There is nothing they can do. So, they are going to just worry about it, and that is not going to help." He shook Dr. Bitman's hand and left the office.

As Rob drove towards Callawaytown, he knew that things were not going to be easy for him. Those folks up at Duke had used some mighty big words. He had already known that there had to be something wrong with his head. There were times when he could hardly bear the pain. He did know for certain that he wasn't about to let those folks cut into his head. Every part of his body that he had when he came into this world, he was certainly going to take with him when he left this world, no matter how much it hurt.

He negotiated the right turn off the main highway and drove onto the road that led to Callawaytown. His story was all fixed in his mind. He knew his wife well. She would buy it. The groundwork was all laid. She knew that he was going to Durham that day to get some parts for a buggy. She knew that he was behind in his work because of all the upheaval over Lee Kenny. She would not ask any questions, and he'd have smooth sailing once he was back home.

It was midafternoon when Rob made the turn in his driveway. He brought the car to a full stop, got out, and walked over to the porch, up the steps, and into the kitchen. He shouted as he walked over to the stove in search of some sort of food. "Howdy honey, I am back!"

Rachel came around the doorway with a big smile on her face. "You're back early!" She gave him a hug. "I am so glad you're back early."

"Yeah," Rob said as he burrowed his face into her comforting neck. "Everything went well. I was able to get those parts that I needed and some other things that I know I'll need sometime soon."

Even after all the years they had been together, Rachel still admired her husband. "You always think of everything."

Rob lifted the covers off pots and pans in search of food. "You got anything to eat? I am starving. I didn't take any time to eat dinner because I wanted to get back on the road as soon as I could."

Rachel called out to her daughter, "Shirley! Go out to the icebox and get a mess of those leftover pig ears and feet for your dad. The oven is already hot. I am cooking corn bread and biscuits for supper. Put them in there so they can be warm in no time at all."

When Rob finished eating, he made his way over to the blacksmith shop to get things ready for work the next day. He checked the bellows and decided that it was not too late for him to start a fire. He went back over to the house to wait for the coals to heat up.

While he waited, he realized he had a perfect opportunity to put the bottle of tablets that Dr. Bitman had given him in his trunk. The bedroom was empty except for his youngest child who was sleeping. He eased the trunk out from under the bed, drew his keys from his pocket and opened the lock. He put the bottle under some old papers. After securing the medication, he locked the trunk and pushed it back under the bed.

He went into the kitchen and said casually to Rachel, "Well, it doesn't look like anybody is going to be coming by this late in the day."

When she looked up, she went over to him with her arms out. "Honey, you look like you're tired. Why don't you just forget about whatever you want to do over at the blacksmith shop and stay here, lay down, and get some rest?"

"Well, baby, you know I've got to do the work before the folks start showing up to get their stuff. I am going to take care of them. I started the bellowing before I came over here, so it's going to be really hot when I get back over there." Before Rachel could protest, he turned and walked out.

The sun was setting. When he arrived at the blacksmith shop, George and Jacob were there, turning the bellows. They were already tired, but they knew better than to question their daddy. He had let them go home only when he was ready. Rob was not accustomed to being questioned on his activities, especially by young folks. In due time, he would tell them to let the bellows go. That would be the signal that their work was finished, and they would be free to go. They knew their only hope was for their mother to call that supper was ready. Luckily, it wasn't very long before Louise came out of the house, running over to the blacksmith shop. She shouted, "Daddy! Daddy! Mama says supper is ready. She said everything was already on the table."

Rob didn't stop to look up. "Tell your Mama we'll be over there in a few minutes."

The boys looked over to their father and, at the same moment, cried, "Daddy, do you need the bellows anymore?"

He knew they were exhausted, so he gave them what they wanted. "You boys can go on over to the house and get ready for supper. Tell your Mama I'll be right there." He continued to tidy up the loose ends in the shop. When all was to his satisfaction, he left and latched the door behind him.

As he walked across the yard, it was plain to see that Rob had something on his mind. That meeting with the doctors had really upset him. He desperately wanted to talk to someone about it. Most of all, he wanted to share the information with Rachel. But that was out of the question. It would be too upsetting for her. At the moment, he felt just fine. So, he rationalized, chances were better than good that there was a mistake, and nothing was really wrong with his head or brain.

There was nothing to worry about. He was not that old. He would not even turn fifty until after Christmas. He did not have any bad habits. He would get through this, as he had gotten through tough times before. He'd just keep everything to himself. He would go to work just like always.

Rob went up on the porch and walked straight over to the pump. It was still primed, having just been used by most of the kids. There was a bar of lye soap nearby. He gave his face and hands a good soaping and then rinsed up. When he was finished, he took a rag that hung on a nail, dried himself off, and walked into the kitchen.

Rachel had his plate prepared. The children had already taken their food. That was not the norm. Rob was nearly always the first to be served. He had taken so long to get over to the house that Rachel had gone ahead and allowed the children to start.

She looked over at her husband with concern. "Rob, you don't look too well. Are you feeling, okay?" She saw that something was on his mind.

Rob flat out lied. He had to. "Yes, I am feeling okay." He pulled the chair from the table, sat down, said the grace and started to eat. There was not much conversation around the table. He finished his meal, got up from the table, and immediately walked outside. He walked around the barns and over to where the animals were housed. It was like he wanted to say something to the animals but was at a loss for words. He felt very strange. As he continued his walk around the old house, he thought about all the experiences in his life.

Although the Callaway's were well respected Negroes in the county, they were not above the racism that was rampant in the South during that period. One of his distant cousins was out and about one night. He was on his way home when a white woman stopped and offered him a ride. He made the worst decision of his life and accepted it. The woman had been in a fight with her father, who had raped and beaten her. When Rob's cousin saw that the woman had been beaten, he immediately asked her to get out of the car.

The woman stopped, but he had sat in the car and listened to her story. By the time he saw a car coming, it had blocked the front of the car. Two men jumped out and ran toward them. They pulled Rob's cousin out and beat him with the crank from their car. Not only did they break his nose, an arm, and several ribs, they left him to die by the road. Kenny Hooker was on his way back from fishing when he found him the following morning.

Kenny had set out fishing poles on the banks of the Lumbee River the evening before. This was routine for folks living in Callawaytown.

They'd get up very early the following morning and make their rounds, collecting whatever catch they might have. They would return home with the catch in time for the woman of the house to make stewed Catfish with green onions and gravy, which would be served with grits that morning for breakfast.

Kenny could not believe what he was seeing. The poor man was near death. He could only murmur a few words. Told Kenny that some white men had beaten him. Desperately, he tried to reassure the injured man. "Okay, you're going to be all right. I am going to get you up to Bent's house, and we are going to take care of you."

Kenny had put his poles and catches over one shoulder and pulled Rob's cousin up from the ground. When he found that the man couldn't walk, he threw his limp body over his other shoulder and walked the few hundred yards until he arrived at Bent's house.

Callawaytown was usually safe for the Negroes. Bent told everyone to just keep quiet about what had happened. They would wait and see what the white folks in and around Callawaytown and Flaterton said about it. They could not risk taking the injured man to a doctor. All the doctors in the area were white, and no one knew what the official story would be. They would take care of him as best they could and keep quiet about the whole situation.

When the Millsian newspaper arrived, the news was all over the front page. **"WHITE LADY BEATEN AND RAPED BY NIGGER NEAR CALLAWAYTOWN"**. It was just as Bent had feared–a Negro would be blamed for what a white person had done. After he read the article and the writer had identified the white lady and her family in further detail, he knew for sure that that was the case. Everyone in and around Callawaytown knew the family to be the lowest of the white trash. There were rumors of incest. Bent knew that they were in a no-win situation. If Rob's cousin went forward and identified himself, there would be no doubt that most of the whites would support the white trash. In the end, it would be awfully bad for Callawaytown. There was really only one choice- they had to keep quiet about everything and just let it work itself out. There was no doubt that the KKK would make some poor Negro pay the price.

Within hours, the local police arrested several Negro men. They had a line-up, and sure enough, the woman identified a Negro man who lived alone just outside of Callawaytown as the man who had raped and beaten her. Although the man proclaimed his innocence, no one would listen to what he had to say.

Bent knew that keeping his cousin safe while the other man was punished was not right. It was a terrible injustice. However, no matter what he said or did, the outcome would be the same. If Rob's cousin went forward, no one would believe him. The white crackers who had attacked him would never come forward with the truth. Therefore, Bent had to live with the knowledge that an innocent man would be punished for a crime that he did not commit.

The man was placed in the county jail in Flaterton. For several days, the newspaper inflamed the situation by demanding that action be taken immediately. It proclaimed that all white people were in danger. After three days, the man had escaped from jail. No one thought for a moment that the man had escaped from that county jail in Lumberton all by himself. Everyone knew that the KKK was involved. Several weeks had passed when the man's body was found hanging from an oak tree. He had been beaten to a pulp. His body was not even recognizable. His private parts had been torn from his body and placed in his mouth. The body was in decaying. The smell was so strong that it was almost impossible to get close to the body. However, someone who recognized a scar on the man's left leg positively identified the body. The man's body was laid to rest under the old oak tree.

Before he was buried, the county sheriff's office was notified, as was the newspaper. No one was interested in hearing the story. The Millsian printed one article, which stated that the nigger had escaped and other niggers and white nigger lovers had helped him get out of the state. This was just another example of how niggers get away with doing wrong toward white folks and then get away without being punished.

All the Negroes in and around the county were terrified about what had happened. However, they were well aware that there was nothing that could be done. It was just another example of how white folks, and especially the KKK, could harm Negroes in the South and get away with it.

There had been several lynching's in and around the county, but no action was ever taken. It was well known that the minister of the largest white Baptist church in the county was also a member of the KKK. He allowed the KKK to conduct meetings in the church. The death of the black soul had been planned in that Baptist church with the pastor's help.

The entire event was swept under the rug. Not one person came to the defense of the victim. Although most of the Callaway family knew what had happened, they were well aware that there was nothing they could do. If they defended the man who had been slaughtered, Rob's cousin would be placed in jeopardy. Even though the Callaway's were considered to be respectable niggers in the county, there were many members of the KKK who felt that they were no more than a bunch of niggers who had slipped through the KKK's net. They owned property that rightfully should be held by good, red-blooded white folks. In their minds, it was just not fair that those niggers in Callawaytown had so much land and even money stashed away. All they needed was an excuse to go into the neighborhood and lynch one of the Callaways.

Nobody had to talk about it. The Negroes knew that there was no way to win a physical or political battle. In the end, even the so-called white nigger lovers would side with the poor white trash. So, in the eyes of the Callaway family, it would be best to just keep what they knew to be the facts in this case to themselves. It would have to be a life-long secret, and that poor Negro had paid the price with his life.

Although many years had passed since that incident took place, it was still fresh in Rob's mind. He had always thought that the Callaway's should have moved forward with their side of the story. However, his father and uncles overruled him. They had always contended that the only way a Negro could survive was to out-think the white folks. In their minds, it was necessary to give the white folks the impression that all Negroes were dumb. In that case, white folks would let their guard down and leave themselves open for deception. This way of thinking was a matter of survival.

Rob considered all of these things as he walked around the barns, through the fields, and back to the house. He made a stop by the stables where his horses and mules were housed. The animals came out of the barn and walked over to the open area, where they were within arm's reach. Rob rubbed each of them over their face and nose as if to send them a mental message. Afterwards, he checked that they had been fed and had sufficient water. The older boys had accomplished their task for the day, all the animals were well fed and watered.

By this time, it was nearly dark. An early winter mist had set in, and it was turning cold. Rob walked up on the porch and into the house. He took his seat in his favorite old rocking chair. He twiddled his thumbs as he gazed at the fire in the open heater. There was not much conversation going on in the house. There was a sound from the outside that came from a special bird. The bird made a crying sound right before someone died. People believed the story so strongly that they considered the bird's sound to be a warning of death. Tonight, the bird sang very loud.

After Rachel had put the last young one to bed, she came in and sat down near Rob. "Sweetheart, how are you doing? Are you feeling okay?"

"Yes, I am feeling okay. I have never felt better," he answered quietly.

Rachel could see that he was only saying that to please her. She knew that something was troubling him…something that she could not put her finger on. Maybe he was just working too hard. She got up and walked out the door onto the porch, where Ernie, Lonnie, and Rob Junior were playing. "Ernie, you boys go out there and shoo that crazy singing bird away."

"No, no, don't shoo that bird away," Rob shouted. "That bird is bringing me a message. He's calling me home!"

It seemed like such a ridiculous notion that no one paid any attention to what he said. The boys continued to play. When they finished, the bird had already left.

Rob and Rachel made small talk until all the children were in bed. Finally, they went into their room and climbed into bed themselves. In the middle of the night, Rachel felt a strong shaking on Rob's side of the bed. She immediately lit the lamp so that she could see what was happening. To her amazement, Rob was quivering, and his body was stretched out as far as it could.

Rachel ran into the boys' room and called out for Ernie. "Ernie! Ernie! Your father is sick. Go down to your Uncle Henry and ask Johnnie to come and drive him to the hospital." Ernie was up and in his britches immediately. He returned with Johnnie. By this time, the house was in disarray. Little Jacob could see Johnnie, his older brothers and mother cover his father in a blanket and take him out the front door. Rob's body was still jerking and stretching as they put him in the car.

Panicked, Rachel told Shirley to take care of the other children. Then Johnnie roared out of the driveway. It was two o'clock in the morning. Johnnie drove as fast as he could.

Everyone in the car was in shock. They could not believe that Rob was so ill. His body was still shaking, and he had started to make noises from his mouth. His eyes were rolling from side to side, and foam was starting to drip from his mouth. The ride to the hospital seemed to take an eternity, but it was less than twenty minutes. Johnnie drove right up to the entrance of the emergency room. He stopped the car and ran inside, shouting, "We got a man out here who is really sick! We need to get him inside mighty quick!"

The woman at the front desk looked as if she had just met someone from another planet. "Is that a nigger you got out there?"

"It's my cousin Rob, and he's mighty sick. We got to get him in right now!" Johnnie cried.

By that time, the woman had walked from behind the desk and out to the entrance. She had a clear view of whether the sick person was black or white. Looking back over her shoulder at Johnnie, she stated. "I really don't know what we can do, because we do not have room for niggers tonight. All the beds for niggers are full. You know it's the weekend and a lot of niggers get shot and cut up when they have free time on their hands." The woman continued to ramble on without taking any action.

Rob received absolutely no attention for several hours. Finally, Rachel and Johnnie were able to beg the woman to make a call to Dr. Bitman. The doctor ordered her to admit Rob to the hospital, no matter what space they would have to use.

Very reluctantly, the woman called two orderlies to bring Rob into the emergency room and start giving him help. Dr. Bitman arrived almost immediately. He checked Rob's pulse and heartbeat. He looked back at Rachel, the two boys, and Johnnie. With total horror, Rachel could read his face. It was too late. Rob's body was very still.

Dr. Bitman quietly said the dreaded words. "Rob is dead. He could probably have been saved if I could have gotten to him right away. I am so sorry."

Ernie, Lonnie, and Johnnie became hysterical, weeping and crying out. Rachel dropped to the floor in a dead faint.

CHAPTER TWENTY-THREE

It was a perfect winter day in North Carolina, but Rachel was overwhelmed by sorrow. Why had God taken her beloved husband? She had been a good wife and mother. What was she being punished for? Why did God take Rob away?

She had always been a deeply religious person. Now that she was suffering, her beliefs were challenged, and her faith was put to the test. Nine boys and three girls would all look to her for support. She couldn't afford to be overcome by her grief for too long.

Rob had been the leader in their family. Now she would have to take over that role. She was a strong woman, but she had always relied on her husband. If Rob had been white, she thought bitterly, he would probably be alive today.

Dr. Bitman had told her that Rob would have had an excellent chance to survive if he had gotten immediate attention at the hospital. It was one thing to lose your husband, but it was quite another thing to know that he could have been helped. Why should the color of his skin have made any difference? This had been a matter of life and death! The irony was Rob's grandfather had been Irish and his grandmother was Cherokee Indian. When it came right down to it, Rob had not even been a full-blooded Negro. Of course, it should not have made a difference what color he'd been.

Rob was dead. Time could not go backwards. Rachel only had two choices. She could collapse and give up, or she could stand up straight and move on. The children needed her. Life would have to go on.

Tears ran down her face as she thought about the days ahead. It was going to be a tremendous challenge to keep everything in order and running smoothly. Rob had been a master at it. Now he was gone… forever. In one terrible night, the whole world crashed around her.

Dr. Bitman touched her arm softly. "There are a lot of things that need to be done," he said gently. "Right now, the body will be taken to the morgue. The Callaway's always use Evans' Funeral Home, right?" Glancing down at his watch, Dr. Bitman could see that it was almost eight in the morning. He continued, "You just as well go by Evans on your way home since you're down here. That will save you some time."

The world had just dropped out from under Rachel and her children and all the rest of the Callaway's. Johnnie thought about the fact that he had gone out night fishing with Rob and a couple of old boyhood friends just a while ago. Rob seemed to be in good health. He gave no indication that he was sick.

Now he lies dead on that stretcher.

Rob was the last person on earth that anyone thought would be dead this morning. And what about all those poor children that Rachel would now have to fend for? What would she do? Rachel was a good wife, mother, and housekeeper, but with the farm, the children, and the blacksmith shop, there was no way she could cope.

What that woman would need was a husband, Johnnie thought guiltily. He had always liked Rachel. Then he shook his head. This was not the time to be thinking about this stuff. His cousin wasn't even in his grave.

Rachel pulled herself up and thought about what she needed to do next. She would have Barry Evans come and fetch the body. They would have to go by Western Union and wire Rob's brother and sisters up north. Afterwards, they would go home, tell the other children, and decide on the funeral.

Once the word was out that Rob had passed away, folks from all over the county came to pay their respects all through the night. Rob had been so very well respected. His death would be a great loss to his family and his community.

Rachel had to rely on Johnnie to drive her from place to place. The chores that Rob had done were now hers. Although she was a strong woman and was smart in lots of ways, she knew nothing about managing money, paying bills, or bank accounts. Rob had taken great pride in taking care of the money in their family. He'd never talked to Rachel about property, money, or bills. Rachel had honored his pride and never asked any questions. Now, when she needed the information and training that would enable her to fend for herself and the twelve children, she didn't have it.

The local preacher was a regular visitor. He would pray with the family and give them assurance that Rob was in Heaven with Jesus and that the Lord would take care of them. Repeatedly, he said, "The Lord never put any more on somebody than he knows they can bear." But the minister wasn't as pious as he appeared to be. Rachel was a beautiful woman and looked much younger than her forty-three years. As he prayed, he kept one eye open; it wandered over Rachel's bare legs. He'd become so aroused at times that he'd lose his place in the prayer. He thought it was only a matter of time before she gave in to him.

It was not very long before the house was packed with Rob's family from up north. They had to be accommodated. The day before the funeral, Rob's body was brought to the house and placed in the living room.

Rob had been the head of the family; his sudden death came before he'd had time to train his sons to take over the blacksmith shop. Ernie and Lonnie would have to learn on their own. There were hard times ahead.

The funeral was held at a large church outside of Callaway town. It could not hold everyone who came to pay his or her respects. White folks and Indians stood outside. After the funeral, the casket was opened for a final viewing. When the hearse carried Rob's body to Callaway Cemetery, the line of cars behind it was more than two miles long.

Everyone felt that they should do something to help Rachel and all those children. The idea that Rob was gone forever was beyond the grasp of the Callaway and Pope families. Rob's friends were all in shock. His death seemed just plain wrong. It was so unexpected.

Rob had his faults. There were times that he was very difficult to get on with. Still, he was an excellent husband, father, and provider for his family. His absence was certain to affect the family, neighborhood, town, county, and state. He'd be missed professionally as well. No one could match his craft in his blacksmith shop. His work was better than anything that could be found in North Carolina, Virginia, South Carolina, or Tennessee. It would be years, if ever, that Ernie and Lonnie become as skilled at the craft as their father had been.

CHAPTER TWENTY-FOUR

When Rachel finally went through Rob's trunk, she found the pills that Dr. Bitman had given him. She also found ten thousand dollars in cash. All the money was in hundred-dollar bills. At the bottom of the trunk, she discovered Rob's bank savings book with a balance of $27,000! She found the deeds to their land and the house down on the riverbank. The titles for the car and the truck were there as well.

Rob had kept many secrets from Rachel, but now she was tremendously relieved. She and the children had plenty of money to live on. Not sure what to do with so much money, she thought she should get some advice. Surely her brother-in-law, Sonny Winsely, would be able to help her. She called out, "Rob Jr., you go over to Connie and Sonny and ask Sonny to come over here. I've got to talk to him." It was only a couple of hours before Rob returned with Sonny, Connie, and their children.

Sonny asked, "What can I do for you, Rachel?"

"Well, I've got something here I want to show you," she answered. "I just had time to look into Rob's trunk. I just want you to see what I found." She led him into the bedroom, opened the trunk, and showed him the contents.

"Boy, Rob really had some big secrets!" Sonny exclaimed. "Who would've thought he had all this money? He never told anybody." Sonny fingered through the hundred-dollar notes. "Rachel's, you've got to lotta money here. You can do just about anything you want with all this money. Just do not let them white folks in Lakeville get their hands on it. Cause you know all they're going to do is steal it from you." He continued to count the notes before Rachel interrupted him.

"Look here!" she said, and added, "Look at these bank papers. He had so much money in the bank."

Sonny was gleeful. "He's got a big account down there in the bank in Lakeville. Yes, girl," he laughed, "you've got enough money here to burn a water-soaked ox."

Rachel was determined. No white cracker or blackass nigger would get their hands on any of the money that Rob had left. She remembered what Rob had said about the stock market crash and failure of the banks in the twenties. Many good folks had lost everything. Folks had lined up at the banks only to be told that there were no funds left. She would never let that happen with Rob's money.

After having dinner with Rachel and the children, Sonny and his family returned home. They were not even out of Rachel's sight before Sonny broke the silence. "Did you hear us talking about all that money that Rob left Rachel?"

Connie answered, "Money? Rob had money. I was in the kitchen with Shirley and the children. I did not even pay any attention to what you were talking about in the bedroom. But when I heard that big laugh of yours, I knew that something was up. How much money are we talking' about?"

"A lot!" Sonny said it happily. "Rachel has got a lotta money now. I wonder if she would let me borrow some. This old car of mine is not running very well. I do not have money to get no mechanic to look at it, and if I did get it looked at, it would probably cost more to get it fixed than it's worth. It sure would be nice if I could borrow enough money from Rachel to buy me one of them new Chevrolets." Sonny's mind whirled with thoughts about the loan he would get from Rachel. He knew that he would get the money. It was a question of when, and not if.

For the next several days, Sonny went over to Rachel's to help with everything he possibly could. He ingratiated himself by taking Ernie and Lonnie out in Rob's car for driver's training. It was not many weeks before both boys were driving well enough to take their driving test.

He approached Rachel about the boys getting their driving licenses. "Rachel, you know Ernie and Lonnie have learned to drive Rob's car. You should consider letting them take the driver's test just to see how they do," he said carefully. "They just might pass the test. You know that would be good for you. Then you won't have to get Johnnie or anybody else to drive you around."

Rachel was hesitant. "I don't know if they could pass the test. The only time they've driven is when you've taken them out in Rob's car. Ernie is almost eighteen, but Lonnie is just sixteen. They won't be able to get any licenses until they get to be eighteen, and…"

"No, no, that's not the way it works," Sonny interrupted. "They can get their licenses at sixteen if you sign for them."

"Oh," Rachel said pensively. "I didn't know that. It would be nice if I didn't have to depend on anyone but my boys."

She would like to be free of Johnnie. Over the weeks since Rob's death, every time she needed to drive someplace, she had to call him. "Oh, Lord, how nice it would be to be free of that man."

Johnnie had been trying to get her to submit to him for many, many years. Rob once went to Washington, DC to do some work for a very wealthy man. During his absence, she had to fight Johnnie off. He would figure out when Rob's parents were away and show up with some excuse or another. The fact was, he wanted her. She had never submitted to him and had never mentioned anything to Rob. She knew that if Rob even suspected that Johnnie had made sexual advances towards her, there would have been a bloody scene.

After all these years, Johnnie finally had her in a situation where she was unable to fend for herself. Johnnie was more than willing to help her out with transportation–for a price.

Although the process was loathsome, she got out of bed in the early morning hours and quietly walked through the dining room, out the kitchen, and onto the porch. She stood there like a fool and waited for him to arrive. Most times, he was already standing there waiting for her. They'd leave the porch and go across the yard, around the barn, and to the trailer. There, Johnnie would demand his payment.

He was not as gentle as Rob. As a matter of fact, he was darn right rough. She never enjoyed having sex with Johnnie, but it secured her transportation. Now that the boys could possibly get their license, it was a blessing from God. Just the thought of not having to submit to that dirty bastard Johnnie was wonderful.

Several weeks went by before Sonny was able to make all the arrangements for the older boys to get their licenses. Finally, Sonny, Rachel, Ernie, and Lonnie went in Rob's car for the trip to Lakeville. Lonnie was not yet sixteen, so he was only going for the ride. Sonny encouraged them. "You boys don't have anything to worry about. You just go in that room where you are going to take the written test and remember everything, as I have been telling you all the time we have been out driving. I tell you everything is going to be okay."

Ernie was not so sure. "Sonny, I've been driving, and I understand all the signs, when I got to stop and when I got to go. But I have never taken a test like this before."

Sonny patted him on the shoulder. "Just answer the questions, do the best you can, and you are not going to have any problem."

When they arrived, Sonny was the first one into the office where driver's licenses were issued. "You all here to take the driver's written test?" asked the overweight, cross-eyed, white woman behind the counter.

"Yessome, I just came down here with my sister-in-law, Rachel Callaway, and her two sons," Sonny answered. "You remember Rob Callaway? Well, he died just the end of last year. This is his wife Rachel and her sons. She just wants to get them some licenses. It so hard for her to get around without anybody in the house with driver's licenses."

"Yes, I remember that nigger, Rob Callaway," she answered sharply. Then she thought for a moment. "Them there Callaway's are the best niggers in the county. We never have any trouble with them niggers. It was bad that he died so suddenly. That just goes to show you that we never know when the good Lord is going to take us away. It doesn't matter if you're white, Indian, or a Nigger. When the good Lord gets ready for you, he's going to take you."

Rachel didn't speak. She had heard it all before and was in no mood to listen. She just wanted her boys to get their driver's licenses. Nothing else mattered. The woman had to practically shout to get her attention. "Rachel, you know you'll have to sign for these boys, and you need their birth certificates. Do you have them?"

"Yes, I got both of them." She took the birth certificates from her bag and handed them to the woman.

The woman addressed Ernie belligerently, "Well, you know, you've got to take a written test before you take the road test. If you pass the written test, then we'll go out on the road and see if you can drive. "Mr. Wilkins over there," she pointed at a redneck down the hall, "will be giving the driving portion of the test. He will take you out and check your driving."

Rachel just looked down at the floor and waited. Finally, the woman got up and motioned for the boys to follow her. "Now that we've got all this paperwork completed, let's go and see if you boys know all the road signs, speed limits, and all."

The boys went into a small room and took a seat at a table. The woman opened a filing cabinet that contained large placards with various road signs and speed limits. She held up signs and asked the boys to identify them. The written test contained only twenty questions. The entire process took less than thirty minutes to complete.

The woman did not look happy, but she said, "Looks like you boys know everything you need to know in order to get your driver's licenses. We will just go back out here. Have a seat right there by your mama, and

I'll finish the paperwork and give it to Mr. Wilkins. He'll call you when he's ready to take you out for the road test."

"How was that test?" Sonny asked.

"It was very easy," the boys answered. Lonnie added, "I really didn't know the written test was going to be so easy. It only had thirty questions on it. Before that, all we had to do was identify the road signs."

"Well, I don't think the road test is going to be that easy," Sonny cautioned. "You're going to have to start, stop, and park. But you boys know how to do all that. We been over that so many times before. You'll be okay."

"You really think that they might get their driver's license today if they passed the road test?" Rachel said.

"Yes, they sure know how to drive. I really can't see them having any problems once they get on the road."

Rachel sighed. "That would really be great. Just the thought of not having to depend on anybody to drive me to Lakeville would be wonderful."

Mr. Wilkins came from behind the counter with several sheets of paper in his right hand. "Ernie Callaway and Lonnie Callaway?"

"Yes sir!" The boys came to their feet.

"Where are you boys parked?" asked Mr. Wilkins.

"Just outside in the front row of the parking lot," Sonny replied.

"I am going to take both boys at the same time. You can ride with us if you like," Mr. Wilkins said as he went out the door. Sonny followed behind.

Rachel relaxed in her chair. "I'll just be right here until you return."

"Which one of you boys wants to be first?" asked Mr. Wilkins.

Sonny pointed at Ernie. "You just as well give the test to him first. He's already near the driver's seat."

The test took no more than twenty minutes. Both boys passed with no difficulty. When they returned to the office, the woman who had given them the written test had already completed all the documents. She had not even noticed that Lonnie was not yet sixteen. She just assumed that he was old enough.

Lonnie immediately ran to the driver's seat for the trip home. "Mama," he cried. "I knew that I was going to pass that driver's test! There was nothing to it. You know, it was one of the easiest tests I ever had to take. No way like as hard as the ones we have to take in school." He cranked the car, backed out of the parking space, and began the drive home.

"You never had to take a driver's test before. How do you know if the test was easy or hard?" Ernie teased.

Rachel sat in the back seat of the car. "Well, it doesn't matter that much. The most important thing is that you boys have your driver's licenses now. That's the best thing that could happen in this family since your father died."

"You know that woman didn't even say anything about my age. When we get home, I've got to look at my license and see what she put in there for my age."

Ernie laughed. "That means, by right, you shouldn't even have a license, and here you are driving."

Sonny broke in. "You boys always find something to argue about. Just be happy that you can drive. From now on, your mama doesn't have to get that Johnnie to take her anywhere."

Rachel was incredibly surprised that Sonny was aware that she had been asking Johnnie to drive her on errands. How did he know? How much more did he know? No one seemed to notice her concern. She did the intelligent thing and didn't comment. Nobody acted any differently, so Rachel assumed they didn't know anything about it.

CHAPTER TWENTY-FIVE

Shirley, the oldest of the twelve children, was becoming more and more irritated. She had been placed in a secondary position. Once Ernie and Lonnie had their driver's licenses, they also had their mother's ear. Furthermore, they were able to use the car for whatever they wanted whenever they were not running errands for their mother.

The boys were always together. They used the car a lot, mostly at night. The only time Shirley was able to go any place was when she was out with her boyfriend, Buddy McMann. Buddy's father owned an old Model T. It was not enough for Shirley. She decided she was going to stop Ernie and Lonnie from using the car for pleasure. To accomplish this, she would have to convince her mother that it was in the best interest of the family if the boys only drove the car on business errands.

A few days after she had crafted her strategy, she put her plan in motion. On a Saturday morning, the boys were getting ready to drive their mother. Shirley piped up, "Mama, you know Ernie and Lonnie are not taking good care of the car. They're even driving the car without oil and gas. You know, if you continue letting them drive Daddy's car without oil and gas, it isn't going to be very long before it will break down, and then we won't have transportation."

Rachel and the boys looked over at her in astonishment. Shirley continued, "I think the car should only be used for them to take you where you want to go and take the family places. It is not a car to be used to go out riding in the neighborhood to pick up girls. That's just what I think."

Ernie defended himself with logic. "Shirley, you should know that you can't drive a car one inch without gas. If you can do that, we'll all be rich very soon."

Lonnie caught on and added, "That's right mama. You can't drive any car without gas, and we always check the oil."

Shirley retaliated. "Well, I just know that it's not good for Ernie and Lonnie to be using daddy's car when all they're going to do is have an accident or something with it. Daddy bought that car for the whole family, not just for them to be riding around and having fun. I just don't think it's right for them to be doing that."

Ernie and Lonnie were quiet now. They had noticed that their mother hadn't said anything. That indicated that she was not in agreement with Shirley. They couldn't know that she was thinking about how grateful she was to be free of Johnnie. Her past had been heinous. She was also constantly concerned that her children would find out. Once Johnnie was having sex with her out in the trailer. He had just finished and was in the process of buckling up his trousers. She heard someone approaching from the yard. "You've got to get out of here!" she had whispered urgently. "Somebody is coming! It's probably Ernie."

Johnnie had gotten himself together in a flash and was gone in an instant. Just as he disappeared in the dark in one direction, Ernie appeared from the opposite direction." Mama," he had asked, "what are you doing out here this early in the morning?

She lied to her own son. "I just couldn't sleep, so I decided to come out and walk around the barn. You know, like your father used to do. I really miss him a lot. Sometimes it is hard for me to sleep, so when that happens, I just have to get up."

She did not know if Ernie bought the story. He looked doubtful. But he didn't say a word. He walked over to his mother and embraced her. With tears in his eyes, he said, "Mama, I miss Daddy too. I just wished that I could just see and talk to him. It's not fair that he's not here with us."

Rachel had held him that morning. "It's okay. It's fine for you to cry. Just remember that the Lord never do anything that is not in his plan. He always knows what is best. We're going to be simply fine. The Lord is going to take care of us. Why are you up this early?"

"I couldn't sleep, and I heard something out in the yard, so I decided to get up and come out and see what was going on."

Rachel had investigated his strong, young face. "That's very responsible of you. You are the man of the house now, and your father would be immensely proud of you. You're such a big boy now." They both cried as they walked back towards the house. "Go back to bed and try to get some sleep before it's time to get up and get ready for school. I am going to cook ya'll a real good breakfast."

She had gone to the smoke house, which was stuffed with curing ham, bacon, sausage, liver pudding, and many other goodies that Rob had prepared the previous fall. She took what she needed and made her way into the kitchen. Alone, she reflected about how her life had been with Rob and how his death had affected her. If Rob was still alive, she would never let any man get anywhere near her. Now she had to contend with Johnnie, managing the rental properties, the farm, and the blacksmith shop. Only a few months ago, the responsibilities now on her shoulders would have been unthinkable. She had made a mistake by letting Johnnie into her bed, but she had justified it in her heart. It was a matter of necessity.

Rachel did not care about what Shirley said about the car. If it was ready and available when she needed to go somewhere, she was happy. All the complaints and accusations meant nothing to her. The boys could do no wrong if they stayed out of trouble and took no more than ten minutes to get home.

CHAPTER TWENTY-SIX

Rob had been dead and buried for less than three months, and Rachel was well on her way to being an independent woman. She had gone to the bank, confirmed the balance, and had her name placed on the account. Like so many others, the man at the bank seemed compelled to give his opinion about Rob. "You know he was a hardworking man. He was nothing like all those other black ass niggers we have here in Mills County. Sometimes I wonder, with that light skin and all, if maybe you Callaway's aren't really niggers."

Rachel did not respond. She was used to hearing ignorant people talk about her husband. She concentrated on all the forms in front of her. Rob's savings account did indeed have several thousand dollars in it. Still, then man went on, "I really don't understand how he was able to save so much money with a wife and twelve children. You know Rachel, I'd invest some of this money. You could put it in stocks, you know."

Rachel did not tell him that there were additional funds in the trunk at home. She was using that money to support her family. Many people were putting pressure on her to borrow money for a variety of risky investments and projects. She did not trust that they would repay the loans.

"Well, I don't really know anything about any stocks," Rachel said evasively. But she did know what Rob had told her about what had happened in October of 1929. She would never invest one dime of Rob's hard-earned cash in stocks, no matter who said it was a good investment.

The man persisted, "I do not know if you know it or not, but there's a company out there making adding machines and typewriters. It is called International Business Machines, or IBM for short. If I had this kind of money, I'd definitely invest some of it in that stock. If you need the money, you can always sell the stock and get your money out."

Rachel wasn't about to be moved, "I don't think I want to put any money in stocks. I will just leave it as Rob had it. I really think that is

the best thing to do for now. I don't want to do anything that I'll be sorry for later on."

"Okay, whatever you want," the man shrugged, "It's your money now."

Rachel was not used to having so much money. Eventually, her brothers in Carriton convinced her to buy some land. It was all woods and swamp. She paid much more money for it than it was worth.

That was just the beginning. Sonny convinced Rachel to give him the money to purchase the new car he coveted, a nice 1949 Chevrolet coupe. It was the best-looking car in the entire neighborhood, and that was the point of it for Sonny. Everyone knew where the money for the car came from. Many friends and family members worked hard to keep Rachel away from the money Rob had left for her and the children.

CHAPTER TWENTY-SEVEN

It had been a beautiful sunny day in late winter. Everyone had gone to church, returned home, eaten dinner, and was now relaxing in front of the fireplace. Ernie, Lonnie and Rob Junior had gone to the local private golf course to caddy. Rachel was not pleased with them for working on Sundays. However, she had agreed to it as long as they attended church first. After all, it was an excellent way for them to earn spending money.

Mr. Buddy, the professional at the golf course, knew the Callaway family very well. After their father died, he took a special interest in the boys. That was lucky because there were plenty of Negro boys who wanted the work. He always made certain that the Callaway boys caddied for big shots from Lakeville who gave good tips. The going rate for caddying eighteen holes was only fifty cents. But the men would buy their caddies a soda and snacks after nine holes and give them a dollar for their work. The boys would return home, give their mother half of their earnings, and keep the rest to spend during the week.

They would caddy every Saturday afternoon, most Sunday afternoons, and sometimes Wednesday afternoons. This Sunday, they just grabbed a bite to eat and made their way to the golf course. They were just in time to get to caddy for the Johnny Johnson foursome. These gentlemen were very good golfers and friends. They always played for high stakes, tipped well, and were a pleasure to caddy for. Johnny Johnson owned the golf course and all the surrounding land. As a matter-of-fact, Sonny and Connie lived on Mr. Johnson's land. The entire area had once been part of the vast Callawaytown Estate. However, Rob's father had sold a two-hundred-acre parcel, mostly woods and swamp, to Johnny Johnson. He had cleared enough for the golf course, clubhouse, a house for the club professional, and the greenskeeper. The professional's house was right near the pro shop.

Mr. Williams, the golf pro, was a cigar-smoking, temple-graying, short, fat man who appeared to be older than his 42 years. He could really hit a golf ball. He knew every trick in the book. Mr. Johnson had brought him into the area, and no one really knew where he had come from. His golf skills were so superior to everyone else's he became extremely popular with all the club members, workers and caddies. Before long, he allowed the Negro caddies to use the golf course on Monday mornings.

On this Sunday, the boys returned home for a wonderful meal that their mother had made. When they had finished their supper, the family gathered in the living room. They discussed the points raised by the preacher during his sermon. This kind of discussion would last anywhere from thirty minutes to one hour, depending on what time Shirley's boyfriend, Buddy McMann would arrive. His model T engine could be heard clearly once he made the turn at the Highway 72 and Callawaytown road intersection. He'd pull into the driveway in five minutes.

In those five minutes, the family would scatter and leave the living room for Shirley and Buddy. On this Sunday, Buddy arrived around six. It was a bit earlier than usual. Rachel and the children spoke to him and made their way to other parts of the house. But soon, Shirley's two cousins arrived. Their mother was Rob's sister, Susie. Art Lee was the older of the two. He drove his father's car. The boys got out of the car and went to the back porch.

"Howdy Aunt Rachel," they said simultaneously.

Rachel wondered what the boys were doing with their father's car. She thought it was a bit strange that Rick had let them use it. "How are you boys doing?" she called, "How are your mother and father doing? What brings you boys way over here?"

She wondered if the boys had gotten their driver's licenses. There really was not any reason for them to have a license. She had spoken to Susie just a few days ago, and Susie hadn't said a thing about the subject.

"We're all doing just fine," the boys answered. "We're just going to go for a ride over to the back swamp. We wanted to know if Ernie and Lonnie could ride with us. We aren't going to be gone very long."

Rachel's boys immediately began to plead. "Please, mama, please let us go. We just going over to back swamp and we going to be back very soon. Can we go mama?" Ernie and Lonnie were determined to get her to agree.

Rachel was not sure. "Well, I don't know if it's okay for you boys to be out tonight. You know you've got to go to school tomorrow, and you're going to have to get up exceedingly early."

The boys didn't give up. "You know, mama, we never get a chance to go anywhere with our cousins. We have never been out with Art Lee and Nathan. We went to church today and went to the golf course to work afterwards. Now we are home, and we can't even go out for a ride with our own cousins. And we even gave you half of what we made caddying today."

Rachel really did not have a sound reason to turn them down. "Well, it might be all right for you boys to go over to the back swamp, but nowhere else," she admonished, "And, be back in an hour."

Lonnie grinned with triumph. "Thanks, mama, we'll be back before you know it."

Art Lee quickly added, "That's right! We're going to be back even before you realize we're gone. I am going to drive really carefully. We just want to go over there where Buddy just came from." The four boys left, and within a few seconds they had gone around the curve and out of sight.

Rachel got the small children ready for bed. Within thirty minutes, she had read a chapter of the Bible to them, and they were down. Afterwards, she closed the house and went into the living room. She knew that Buddy and Shirley were in there hugging and kissing. Rachel moved chairs around in the dining room as she walked through to draw their attention. Her strategy worked. When she went into the room, Shirley and Buddy were only holding hands.

Rachel made small talk to smooth the situation over. "How are your mother and father doing?"

"They're doing simply fine, Miz Rachel. How've you been doing?" Buddy replied sheepishly.

"I am doing okay," Rachel said easily. "Been really busy the past week, but overall I am doing good." She made her way over to her favorite chair. "I am going to sit down here for a few minutes and relax before I go to bed, if you'll don't mind."

It was only a few minutes before there was a knock on the door. Rachel got up and made her way over to answer it. "I wonder who this is this time of night," she mused. "No one ever knocks on the front door." When she opened the door, Jake Summerfield stood there. The man lived down off Highway 72.

Jake's posture was rigid, and his voice boomed, "The Lord has spoken! He's come to take one of his children homes. Jesus has seen fit to find a better place for Lonnie." After that pronouncement he just stood there.

Rachel was totally confused. What on earth could Jake Summerfield be talking about? Lonnie and Ernie had just left to go for a ride with their cousins.

Jake spoke again, this time much more gently. "Rachel, it's Lonnie. There was nothing anybody could do. We just couldn't get to him. He's with the Lord now."

Rachel held on to the doorjamb as her legs threatened to go out beneath her. "What happened?" she whispered.

"Susie and Rick's oldest boy was just driving too fast. Right when he drove by our house, he lost control of the car, which ran into the ditch on my side of the road. Everyone got out except Lonnie." Jake paused for a moment and then added, "There was a fire, and Lonnie was still in the car." He stopped when Rachel's eyes began to roll back in her head. Then he added hastily, "But I tell you at this moment that boy is with his father in heaven, at the side of Jesus."

Rachel fainted. Buddy picked her up and laid her on the sofa. Shirley sank beside her mother, weeping and keening. Over the noise of grief, Jake preached about all the good things that could come from the accident. Still wildly sobbing, Shirley made every attempt to bring her mother around.

Feeling that there really was nothing he could do in the house, Buddy decided to go down to the site of the accident. When he arrived, the ambulance and police were there. The fire was out. The ambulance crew had removed Lonnie's body from the wreckage and placed it into the ambulance. The police would not let anyone near the body. Ernie and Nathan were both sobbing. Art Lee had been placed under arrest. He was in the back seat of the police car. The word had already gone out through the community. Sonny, Jeff, and Gary arrived and were speaking with Ernie and Nathan.

"I thought he was driving too fast when he went over that bump on Highway 72," Ernie cried, "but I didn't say anything. When he hit the bump, the car just kept going towards Mr. Jake's house."

Ernie struggled to speak, "When he tried to straighten it out, he almost hit the ditch on the other side. That's when he turned the steering wheel too much to the right and went straight into the ditch over there." He pointed to the burned car. "That's when we all got out. But Lonnie's coat was caught between the car door and the ditch bank." Ernie started to sink to the ground, but the men held him up. "We tried to lift the car over to the side, but we couldn't. The car was just too heavy, and we couldn't see very well. Art Lee lit a match." Ernie's face crumpled. "I could smell gas. When he scratched the match, everything just exploded. Fire was everywhere!"

"Oh Lord, we could hear Lonnie screaming, but there was nothing we could do. The fire was just too hot. Dear God, I don't know what I am going to tell Mama. She didn't even want us to go," Ernie wailed.

Sonny put his arm around Ernie's shoulder and tried to calm him down. "Rachel's going to understand everything," he said quietly. "She's going to know that it was not you boys' fault." Sonny handed the boys over to Jeff and walked over to the police officer standing near the burned car. "Sir, what happened?

The officer looked over at him and said solemnly, "Well, this boy was driving without a license. His brother told us that they stole the car from their father's yard while the rest of the family was inside eating dinner. I'm not sure what to believe until I speak with my father. Regardless of that, the boy's guilty of reckless driving and driving without a license. With Rob's boy being dead and all, there just might be a charge of manslaughter."

Sonny did not know what to say. He wondered how Rachel could possibly bear the loss of her son. The policeman added, "I really don't know what's going to happen. For now, we have got the boy that was driving the car under arrest. He is going to be kept in jail until we get some instructions from the judge. We do not want anybody messing with the body until the coroner has a chance to examine it. So, we going to have the body taken to the hospital."

By this time, the road was packed with spectators. A couple of policemen had already begun to rope off the scene of the accident, and the ambulance left for the hospital.

Lonnie was pronounced dead on arrival. After the medical examiner was finished, Barry Evans came over to receive the body. Before the body was released, it had to be positively identified. Sonny performed the gruesome task. The body was more than seventy percent destroyed by the fire.

Again, the Callaway family endured a tragic funeral. Art Lee was held in jail for only a few days before his father, Rick, was able to secure a bond. Rachel was furious with the judge's decision to release him on bail. She thought that the least the judge could do was hold him until the inquiry was held. She wanted to know for sure if there would be evidence to convict Art Lee of manslaughter. However, it was clear that the judge didn't see the picture the same way that Rachel saw it. The judge was a Free Mason, as was Rick. Although the Negroes and whites were segregated and attended separate lodges, the Negroes and white masons supported each other when the chips were down.

Rachel's family was also dismayed that the judge had let Art Lee out of jail. After all, he had stolen his father's car, driven without a driver's license, driven recklessly, and caused the death of one of Rob's sons. The way they saw it, Art Lee's release was just another indication of how little attention was put into a case when there were only Negroes involved. If a white boy had been killed in the accident, there was no doubt that any Negro responsible would be held in jail. There would not have been any way that a Negro's father could use his connections. It would have been impossible.

A few weeks later, the inquiry into the accident was held at the courthouse in Lakeville. It only lasted a few hours. Only people directly involved with the accident could testify. The judge listened as the county prosecutor questioned Ernie, Nathan, and Art Lee. The prosecutor never raised the issue of that Art Lee had stolen his father's car or whether he had a driver's license. The court ruled that he was guilty of reckless driving and gave him six months' probation.

Rachel and her family were beside themselves. She shouted, "I know the only way you got Art Lee out of this trouble was because of your connections with the Masons! You know he killed my boy, and now he's going to get away free. You know that's not right!" She continued to yell as she left the courtroom with her family. "The Lord will pay you for what you've done."

Rachel's brother added, "Lord knows that what they've done here tonight is a disgrace before God and man."

As they made their way down the steps of the courthouse, another man added, "There just isn't any justice in this county for any Negroes. It is bad when somebody can steal a car, drive without a driver's license, have an accident that kills someone, and get away with it. I just can't understand how that can happen."

Art Lee and his father walked out of the courtroom without saying anything to Rachel.

Jacob took Lonnie's death the hardest. They were so much alike that they could have passed for twins. To Jacob, it was as if he had lost a portion of his body. Lonnie always came to his defense after the death of his father. Now that Lonnie was gone, he stood totally alone. As big as Ernie was, Lonnie had been his protector. When Lonnie was not around, Ernie got physical with Jacob. He took all his frustrations out on little Jacob. When he saw it, Lonnie would always intervene. Now that Lonnie was gone, Jacob stood alone. He knew that Lonnie was dead and gone, but he was too young to really understand that he was never coming back.

One day Jacob went down to the river, where he had gone many times with his father. After Rob had died, he had gone to the same place as Lonnie. On this day, he noticed a small oak tree. It was only about six or seven inches high. With his bare hands, he pulled the tree out of the ground and carried it back to the house. He planted it just on the other side of the driveway. Afterwards, he placed a small rim from a wagon wheel around it for protection. He faithfully watered the tree and cared for it daily. The tree grew as he grew. If anyone went near it, Jacob told them that he planted the tree for Lonnie. He would never forget his brother if the tree were alive.

Jacob's spirit was broken. Just like his father would have done, he decided to take things one day at a time. Christmas had come and taken his father away. Now spring had snatched his favorite sibling. He wondered what the summer would do.

CHAPTER TWENTY-EIGHT

The summer was already hot. Rachel had managed the farm very well that first planting season. Now she could see the fruits of their labor. The tobacco was six feet tall, and the cotton, corn, and potatoes were plentiful. When Rob's sisters and their families visited on Sundays, they walked over what was once the land that belonged to their mother and father. They were not very pleased with the fact that Rachel now controlled it. Although they all had their own farms in Fair town, they believed that the land was really theirs. They could not live with the fact that now that their oldest brother was dead, Rachel and her children were using the property. They couldn't understand why Rachel didn't just pack up and go back to Bull County, where she'd come from. That's what their stepmother had done after the death of their father. Rob's sisters thought she should be forced to move.

Rachel received a visit from the sheriff's office not long after the harvest. She was informed that there had been a petition filed with the court. "I know you've been living here ever since I was a little boy," the sheriff said apologetically. "This property is certainly yours. However, I got to do what I got to do." He handed Rachel the court papers. "It's not up to me, Rachel. The judge will have to decide on who gets what." He stopped and kicked the dust when she did not respond. "I really don't think you've got anything to worry about. I can't see the judge giving anyone the house but you and your children."

Rachel was in shock. Rob's sisters had visited her several times after Rob and Lonnie died. They had never mentioned anything about wanting to take over the property. The least they could have done was to speak with her before getting the court involved! She hired the Brit Law Firm to represent her interests. She had the money and didn't hesitate to use what was necessary to insure a fair deal for her and her children.

It was a very dirty fight. In the end, the court had the property divided into equal shares. The house and the land that directly surrounded it were put together into one portion. Rob had purchased their stepmother's lifetime rights. That gave Rachel and her children the first choice of the house and the surrounding land. Rob's sisters were not pleased with the court's decision, and they were very vocal about it.

Rob's sister Mary shouted, "You know you should go back to Bull County, where you came from. You know this house and land do not belong to you. This is our father's house and land." The court had given her property just across the road from the family home.

Looking over at Mary, Rachel wondered what she had done to turn Rob's sisters against her and her children. She had always been nice and kind to her sisters-in-law and the rest of the family. She had acted as a buffer between Bent's children and their stepmother. Why were they acting like this? Why could they not be civil and work things out privately? Surely the whole world did not need to know that the family was in an uproar.

Rachel shouted right back. "I tell you now, if it were not for my children, I would give you everything and go back home! It is just not worth the trouble. I have got too many things on my mind to be worried about this house and land. But since the court has given us what is rightfully ours, we aren't going anyplace. If you want to act like fools, you can do it on your own land!"

The sisters did not speak to Rachel for many years. Two of them worked their land, while others rented it out to sharecroppers. Some of them just let the land go uncultivated. The encroaching forest soon consumed it.

The 1948/1949 school year was the last for Callaway Town Public School. It closed, and the elementary students went to Flathead, while the junior high and high school students went to Narrow Branch High School.

Ernie received his license to drive the school bus. Since Callawaytown was the last stop, Ernie lived in the perfect spot for the bus driver. He could pick up students all the way from Callawaytown to Flathead, drop off the grade school students, and continue onward to Narrow Branch to pick up students who lived en route. George and Jacob were just entering the fourth grade at Flathead. Louise, Rob Junior, and Shirley continued the bus with Ernie to Narrow Branch.

Because she had been able to live with her aunt and uncle, Shirley had only one year left before graduation. Ernie, Lonnie, and Rob Junior walked from Callawaytown out to the main highway, where they caught a bus to Narrow Branch. The Lakeville High School bus came by the house every day, but there was no way they could ride it. They were not allowed to go to Lakeville High School because it was for whites only. Lonnie had questioned the system from time to time. After his death, only Jacob ever asked any questions concerning the segregated school system.

Rachel never answered Jacob's questions. The boy couldn't understand why they had to ride so far to attend school when there was a school right near their home. The sad thing was that no one even tried to give the boy a straight answer. Jacob also noticed that the white children were never kept out of school. Negro and Indian children were kept home from school all year to work on the farms. This was very common during the planting and harvesting seasons. No matter how poor a white student's parents were, the student never worked on the farm during school hours.

Racism was very evident. Once a student completed high school, if he or she were unable to go off to an all Negro College, the only alternatives were to get married and continue living as usual or leave and go someplace up north. Detroit, Chicago, New York, Baltimore, and Washington, D.C., were common destinations. Some people went all the way out west to Los Angeles.

The only jobs available for Negroes were labor-intensive or domestic. There was no hope of ever getting out of poverty. One of Rachel's brothers had gone into the Army during World War II. He was stationed in California. Holmes came back home after the war but quickly returned to Los Angeles. He talked a lot about how the Negroes had a much better life out there. When Holmes visited Rachel and the children, they would all gather around him and listen to his stories about life out in California.

Jacob was especially excited about the possibilities of life out west. His imagination ran wild as he thought and dreamed about how it would be like to live in Los Angeles. Rachel listened and was happy for her brother. Still, she could not imagine living anywhere but right here in Callawaytown.

He had met his wife on a train while traveling from Jackson, Mississippi. They were in the same car, and he had helped her place her bags in the overhead bin. She mentioned that she was traveling to Los Angeles to marry her hometown sweetheart. During the two-day trip, they got to know each other very well. He was able to talk her into marrying him. When the train arrived at the station in Los Angeles. Rachel's brother and the girl saw the man looking for his wife-to-be. They ducked between passengers at the packed station and made their way out into a taxi without being seen. That was the first and last time Rachel's brother ever saw the man whom he had deprived of a wife. Now, he and his wife had been married for several years and had three small children.

He had returned to North Carolina to try to talk his youngest sister, Saral, into going back to Los Angeles with him. He hoped she would help his wife take care of their children. She had just finished high school and it would be an excellent opportunity for her to get out of North Carolina and make something of her life.

Saral had been dating Rob's cousin, Thomas. The relationship was not going too well. They had gone out on a date when Thomas stopped at a service station to get some cigarettes. When he went into the station, Saral opened the glove compartment and found a juicy letter from another girl. Saral could not handle it. Although they had been making plans for marriage, the letter killed everything. Her family thought that it was an excellent idea for her to travel to California with her brother. She soon married and had her own family.

After that school year, the work on the farm was very intense. A new tobacco barn had to be raised to cure the tobacco for the following year. Shirley would complete high school. Mr. Brooks, a Negro dentist in Lakeville, was very interested in her. She had developed into a beautiful young lady with long black hair. Mr. Brooks was of good stock. However, he had very dark skin, kinky hair, red eyes, and a short, stocky body. None of that went well with the Callaway or Pope families. But he was a very intelligent and kind man who had his sights set on Shirley. He was the only Negro dentist in the county, so every Negro who could afford it used his services. He met Shirley through contacts he had with teachers at Narrow Branch High School. He had been looking for an office worker that could also serve as a dental assistant. He went to Callawaytown and talked Rachel into letting Shirley work for him. Shirley benefited from the experience and extra cash.

During the summer, he asked Rachel if Shirley could accompany him to a convention in Washington, D. C. "Mrs. Callaway I would like it very much if you would allow Shirley to go with me. We will have separate rooms. It will be an excellent experience for Shirley. I normally take a different student with me on every trip. The student works as a secretary, gets lots of experience, and all expenses are paid. This time I've decided that I'd like to take Shirley. She is an excellent student, and she will learn a lot. She might even wish to be an executive secretary as a career after this trip."

But Rachel had not been too impressed. As she looked into the eyes of the dentist, she wondered what Rob would have done. Mr. Brooks had already spoken to Shirley, and she was very excited about the trip. She had never traveled out of the state, and the thought of going to Washington, D.C., was overly exciting. She had talked about maybe attending a private business school in Washington, D.C., after high school. Her mother had not given it much thought.

Rachel stalled for time. "Mr. Brooks, I really don't know what to say. I've never had to make a decision like this before. It sounds like it will be okay. But I am going to have to have some time to give it some thought."

"Well, there's not that much time left," Mr. Brooks said, "We'll have to be there by next Thursday. The convention begins on Friday. If Shirley is unable to go, I will have to find someone else. So, I really would appreciate it if you'd let me know as soon as possible."

At that point, Shirley came to the front porch where they were talking. "You know Mr. Brooks would like you to travel with him to a convention in Washington, D.C. What do you think about that?" Rachel asked.

"Oh mama! Please, can I go? I really want to go," Shirley cried. "Mr. Brooks has talked to me about the trip, and I know the student who went with him the last time. She said that it was a very nice trip. Please, can I go?"

Shirley had always been a good girl, and Mr. Brooks had an excellent reputation. "Well, Mr. Brooks, how many days is this convention?" Rachel asked cautiously.

"It's only three days. We leave on Thursday and return on Sunday evening."

Rachel had to do some fast thinking. She wondered what folks would think if she let her daughter travel to Washington, D.C., with a dentist who was a single man. But she had to think about Shirley first. The girl had mentioned that she was interested in attending that business school in Washington, D.C. Maybe this trip would give her a better understanding of how life would be away from home. Maybe it would not be all that bad. Rachel took a deep breath and gave her blessings. "Okay, Mr. Brooks. Shirley can go." She added sternly, "You take good care of my daughter."

"Don't you worry, Mrs. Callaway," Mr. Brooks smiled. "I'll pick her up on Thursday around noon, and I'll have her back here no later than nine, maybe ten, Sunday night. And as I said before, she'll have her own room. I am sure she'll enjoy the trip."

Shirley didn't tell her boyfriend, Buddy, that she was going to Washington. Her brothers and sisters didn't even know she was going with Mr. Brooks by herself. Rachel thought it would be better if only she and Shirley knew about it. If she told the other children, it would only create problems. Everyone would have an opinion, and no one would likely support her decision.

On Sunday afternoon, Buddy came over just like he always did. He and Shirley spent a few hours together alone in the living room before Rachel went in. After a few minutes of conversation, Buddy asked Rachel if he and Shirley could go to the store and over to see his parents. Rachel agreed.

They were barely out of sight before Buddy turned onto a back road between Callawaytown and the main highway. A lumber company used the road at night. Now, there was no one around. Buddy brought the car to a halt. Before Shirley could say anything, he kissed and fondled her. Before now, her mother had always supervised them. Shirley's first sexual encounter happened as a result of one thing leading to another. The entire process took less than five minutes. Although it was enjoyable, Shirley thought there should have been more to the process than that.

Afterwards, Buddy backed the car up and made his way back to the road. They did not talk about what had happened. Shirley sat quietly amazed, and then she started to get mad. Only an hour before, she'd been thinking about whether she should tell Buddy about her trip to Washington. After what had happened, she didn't feel she had any obligation to inform him of anything. He had lied to her mother and to her as well. He had planned to pull off the road and have sex with her, just like that! What kind of girl did he think she was in the first place?

As Buddy drove towards his father's and mother's house, there was silence in the car. Finally, Shirley said. "We won't be home next Sunday. We're going down to Carriton to visit my grandmother, aunts, uncles, and cousins."

"Well, I can come over to see you on Saturday," Buddy said confidently.

Shirley harrumphed. "You know that's not possible. I work for the dentist on Saturday. It will be late when I get home, and there will be lots of work for me to do. You know full well that Mama doesn't want us children to have any visitors on any day except Sunday. Maybe you can visit me the following Sunday."

"That's going to be a long time," Buddy complained. Then he said brightly, "At least we've got the rest of the evening together." They arrived at Buddy's home and spent a few minutes talking to his family before they were on their way back to Callawaytown. Buddy made a turn on the small road and drove to the spot where he had parked before. This time Shirley was more than reluctant. But he pleaded with her until she submitted. She had already gone further than she had dreamed she would. It was over within three minutes. Even so, she had to admit that she enjoyed it more the second time around. She thought about what her mother would think if she found out about what was happening. At least, Buddy had used protection. So, she would not have to worry about being pregnant.

Afterwards, they made their way back to Shirley's house. Rachel was still up, but the children were all in bed. Rachel went to the door when she heard the knock. Shirley came in and went straight to her and Louise's room. Louise was fast asleep. Shirley was undressed, in her nightgown, and in bed before Rachel came into the room to wish her a good night's sleep.

Shirley never told anyone what had happened that night. The week went by very fast. Her mother got her things ready for the trip. When Mr. Brooks arrived on Thursday, she was more than ready. He spoke with her mother for a few minutes before placing her suitcase in the trunk of his car.

They arrived in Washington, D.C., about six hours later. Mr. Brooks drove directly to the hotel, where he had made reservations for two rooms. Shirley was overly excited by everything she saw. It was the first time she'd ever been out of Callawaytown, Lakeville, Mills, and Bull Counties. She was now exposed to the big city. The buildings seemed huge. Mr. Brooks told her one of them was the Pentagon. It was built during World War II and was used to house the Department of Defense. She was very impressed.

Their hotel was in the Negro section of Washington. There were many people there who had arrived to attend the convention. Mr. Brooks had signed all the necessary documents, and the clerk gave him two keys. Their rooms were located on the first floor on opposite sides of the hall.

After Shirley unpacked her small suitcase and freshened up a bit, there was a tap on the door. She looked through the hole in the door and saw that it was Mr. Brooks. They would be going out to dinner, he had previously informed her. She opened the door after grabbing her sweater.

There was a nice little restaurant on the corner across from the hotel. They had a nice meal and made their way back. Mr. Brooks took her to her room and waited until she had opened her door. He wished her a good night's sleep before walking over to his room. That night, she could hardly sleep. Everything was so nice compared to Callawaytown. Everything was so much bigger! And there were so many more people. Not only that, but there were also people of all different colors, heights, sizes, and shapes. She had even heard some people speaking a language from a different country.

Mr. Brooks had treated her so well. Clearly, he considered her a lady. It was all like a dream. He was very knowledgeable. He always had the response to her questions on the tip of his tongue. When they were in the restaurant, he had taken the chair out from under the table for her. When they returned to the hotel, he accompanied her and waited until she was safely in her room. He was a gentleman.

The following day, she and Mr. Brooks went to the convention center. There were several hundred people attending. She did everything that Mr. Brooks requested. That was easy. For the most part, she was only required to keep track of the different papers he was given throughout the convention.

Shirley took a bus tour of the city while Mr. Brooks and other dentists were in meetings. He introduced her to someone who was working at the business school she was interested in. She was given informational pamphlets about the institution and informed she was welcome to enroll.

Shirley enjoyed herself to the fullest. After dinner on the last night, Mr. Brooks walked her back to her room and advised her to think about going to business school. He offered to talk to the school representative for her if she was interested. "She works in admissions," he said. "All I've got to do is give her a call, and she will make sure that there's a slot for you when you're ready."

Shirley thought for a moment, "Mr. Brooks, you know I'd like to go, but it's going to cost a lot of money, don't you think?"

"Well, I've already spoken to your mother," he replied, "And she said that she didn't think the cost would be a problem. If you really want to go, we should call Miss Johnson tonight."

Mr. Brooks continued to speak as he walked towards his room. Instead of going to Shirley's room, he went directly to his. He opened the door and walked in. "Come on in, and I'll make that call to Miss Johnson. She should be home by now. She said something about going to visit her father, but she's probably home now. Have a seat."

Shirley followed him into his room and now sat on the edge of his bed. Mr. Brooks picked up the phone and dialed Miss Johnson's number. "Hello, is this Miss Johnson? This is Mr. Brooks. You know that young lady that accompanied me here from North Carolina? Yes, the one I introduced you to yesterday. Well, I've had a long talk with her, and she is really excited about attending your business school. I wonder if you could reserve a seat for her." Mr. Brooks looked over at Shirley and gave her a thumbs up. "Yes, that's right, she wants to attend. Her name is Shirley Callaway. Thanks very much for everything, and give my best regards to your father. Bye now."

With that, Mr. Brooks placed the receiver on the hook and walked over to Shirley. He knelt on one knee, and she saw that his eyes were glowing with love. "You know you're an unbelievably beautiful young lady. I've never been married, and I'd really like to have children. I know that I am much older than you, but I think we could have a good life together."

Shirley was totally caught off guard. What on earth was he talking about? He knew that she had a serious boyfriend. She was just finishing high school, and Mr. Brooks seemed so old. Besides that, he was black as tar and had red eyes. Before she could gather her thoughts, Mr. Brooks put his hand into the opening in her blouse. He squeezed her breast while talking non-stop. She made a half-hearted attempt to push him away, but she really wanted him to continue. Then she was lying back on the bed, and he had his hands under her dress.

Before long, they were between his sheets. Mr. Brooks was a far cry from Buddy when it came to making love. He really knew how to make her feel good. He made love to her three times that night, and Shirley thoroughly enjoyed herself. After the third time, she got up, quietly dressed herself, and went to her room. Mr. Brooks was sound asleep.

Once she was alone, fear and regret set in. How could she have done such a thing? What would her mother think? What would Buddy do if he found out? She sat on her bed and cried. This was all a terrible mistake.

She would just have to put what had happened in the back of her mind. She would not mention this night to anyone… ever.

They returned to North Carolina on Sunday night. The return trip was noticeably quiet. Neither of them mentioned what had happened. Back at Shirley's home, Mr. Brooks arrived at the door carrying her suitcase. He thanked Rachel for allowing her daughter to accompany him on the trip. Rachel excitedly asked questions about what things were like up north. Shirley told her all about the tall buildings, the people, and the long bridge that they had crossed to enter the city.

Little Jacob sat on the floor with his legs crossed and his chin in his hands. He could not take his mind off the places that Shirley spoke about. In his heart, he knew that one day he would travel just like his older sister. However, it would not only be to Washington, DC. He would go to New York and maybe even further.

Eventually, the family went to bed for the night.

Shirley mentioned the business school to her mother. Rachel thought it was an excellent idea. No one in her family had ever gone on to higher education. If her daughter wanted to attend that business school and Mr. Brooks could get her in, Rachel would pay whatever it cost.

Shirley was indeed accepted into the school, and Rachel paid the entire tuition in advance. She went to live with her Aunt Lulu in Baltimore to attend. However, her attendance was short-lived. She had only been in school for a few months before she had to admit that she was expecting a baby.

"I don't know what I am going to do, mama," Shirley said. Her head was bowed, and her voice was quiet.

"Well," Rachel answered urgently. "You've got to keep it quiet. There is no need to let anyone know about it but Buddy. Then, you are going to have to set a wedding date. You're going to have to get married. No daughter of mine is going to have a baby without being married. So, you've got to tell him right away."

Shirley knew that she could not tell anyone what had happened to Mr. Brooks. She had practically convinced herself that nothing had happened. When she told Buddy, he was immensely proud of himself. He was ready for marriage and a family, and he had never cared business school.

Shirley and Buddy were married and moved to Winston-Salem, North Carolina, where Buddy worked as an insurance salesman.

CHAPTER TWENTY-NINE

The new school year approached. Ernie had graduated from high school the year before. The only person in Callawaytown with a driver's license was Rob Junior. Of course, he was anxious to drive the school bus. Once he finished school, the next person in line to drive the bus would be George. However, it would be several years before he would be old enough to apply for his driver's license. The children would have to walk out to the highway until George reached adulthood.

The Korean War was in full swing. Ernie was drafted into the army and was stationed at Camp Rucker, Alabama. He was very excited about being in the military. Rob's nephew, Adam, had also been drafted. Everyone was proud of him because he had gone to college and had become an officer. Every time anyone came near his mother's small shop, she told them about her son's accomplishments. She had pictures of him all over the store. Adam was a 2nd Lieutenant in the navy, and another son, Johnnie, had been an enlisted soldier in the army during World War II.

Since his father was dead, the military determined that Ernie was the family's provider. He could have been deferred from serving in the military, but he wanted to go. Since his mother was considered a dependent, he was required to give $40.00 each month from his monthly pay, and the military would give $51.00. Rachel would receive $91.00 each month.

After Ernie completed his basic training at Camp Rucker, everyone was afraid that he would be sent to Korea. That's where all the action was. Rachel and the rest of the children were very worried that he would go and never return. When he received his assignment, it was to serve in the Federal Republic of West Germany. There was a great sigh of relief.

Ernie came home for thirty days before he was to report to Camp Kilmer, New Jersey, before being shipped off to Germany. Rachel made sure that he received all the good home cooking she could provide. He visited everyone in the neighborhood and talked about the army.

He was actually sorry that he didn't get orders to go to Korea. "I really wish I could go someplace where I can use all the training that I've gotten over the past few months. It would've been great to be going to Korea instead of Germany," he said angrily. "I thought I was going into the army to fight for my country. There isn't any fighting going on in Germany." When he made the statements, it infuriated his mother. She had prayed that he would be spared. How on earth could he want to go over there when he knew that soldiers were being killed?

Ernie spent eighteen months in Germany. During the time he was overseas, he wrote home at least once a month. He never asked about the family or how things were going on the farm. Nor did he mention the blacksmith shop. He knew that he was the only family member that could do any work remotely close to what his father had been able to do. It was obvious that the blacksmith shop would be vacant till his return now that he was serving in the military.

What Ernie really wanted to know was how much of the $91.00 a month would be available for him when he returned. The first time he wrote about it, Rachel was shocked. She had thought that that money was sent to her for the benefit of the family. She'd had no idea that Ernie was thinking that she would save most of the money for him. She spoke with Sonny about the situation and made every attempt to save a portion each month, but to no avail. There was just not enough left after paying the bills, purchasing food, etc. It was far too late to make any recovery. By now, the funds that Rob had left were all gone. The money she had invested in the recommendations of family and close friends had all resulted in huge losses. The principle on the loans she had made to family members had never been returned. Everyone who had borrowed money had explanations about why they were not able to repay it.

"What on earth have you done with all that money?" asked Sonny when Rachel requested payment. He insulted her further by saying," You only let me have $7,550.00. I told you if you would give me $10,000.00, I could have purchased that land that's down there near my mother's land. Remember when I asked you about that? You said that you were not going to invest in any more land. If you had given me that $10,000.00, you would be all set by now." He did not mention the fact that he had never repaid what he had borrowed.

It had been less than five years since Rob's death. The money was gone, and the only thing she had to show for it was the dentures she had gotten for herself, a piece of land in Carriton, and a few dollars in the bank. She did have the house and a few acres of land that she farmed with the children, but other than that, everything was gone. Even her family came around only every once in a while. The family was filled with anger. Some of them thought that others had received more than they had. They figured that if Rachel didn't have any of the money left, she must have loaned or given it to some other member of the family. There was no compassion for Rachel and the children. The family acted like opportunistic parasites. George and Jacob were big enough to work on neighboring farms and as caddies on the golf course. They worked often and gave one half of their earnings to their mother. Times were hard.

Rob Junior was drafted into the army. After receiving basic training in Fort Jackson, South Carolina, he was sent away to train as a cook. He was unable to claim his mother and siblings as dependents. The army would only allow one son to claim the family. Rob sent his mother money every month. Never less than $40.00. She was really pleased to receive it. Still, she was unable to maintain the farm. She was forced to rent the land to a larger farmer, who in turn rented it to a sharecropper. Rachel received only one half of what the large farmer got. After covering the expenses for seedlings, fertilizer, etc., there was not much left. Sometimes, it cost her to lease out the land.

The fact was Rachel was cheated. The farmer added the costs associated with his personal farm and passed them on to Rachel. He assumed she would trust him and never question his figures. But she did figure it out. However, she always got the same response when she confronted the farmer. "You know, if you don't like the way I am running the farm for you, you can always get someone else to lease it to." He was aware that in Callawaytown, Rachel had no other options. Because of the war, there just weren't any other farmers around. Her only other choice was to place the land on the soil bank. This would allow her to receive a meager amount of cash each year. In return, the government would require that no cash crop be grown on the land. However, the land would have to be cultivated twice a year to prevent overgrowth.

Eventually, this was the option that Rachel selected.

When Ernie returned from the army, he was only interested in finding out how much of the $91.00 a month his mother had saved for him. "I just want to know how much money you got for me. I've been away in Germany for eighteen months, and all the time I was away, I sent you that money every month. If I were white," he said cruelly, "and sent that money to my mother, she would have saved every dime of it for me. I just cannot understand how you could spend all my money like that. Plus, all that money that daddy left. I'll tell you something. I want my money, and I want it quick."

Rachel barely recognized her son. How could he not understand that with Rob Junior gone and George and Jacob barely large enough to work on the farm, she needed every nickel of the money to survive? After she paid the bills every month, there was nothing left. How could he think that she should have money saved up for him when he returned? She could see that he was serious. Something must have happened to him in the army. He had never acted or spoken like that before, and she was scared.

"Jacob," she cried, "go over to Connie and Sonny and ask them to come over here. I need to talk to them."

Jacob was more than happy to obey his mother. "Okay, Mama, but can I ride my bicycle?"

Truly upset, she answered, "Yes, you can ride your bicycle, but you be sure and stop at the main highway, look both ways, and walk across the main road."

"Yes, mama, I'll be really careful and watch out for cars and trucks. I'll be back real soon." Jacob got on his bike and was on his way.

It was not awfully long before Sonny and Connie arrived. Sonny was a little out of breath. "What's going on, Rachel?"

"I don't know what's wrong with Ernie," she answered desperately, "Since he returned from Germany and the army, he has really changed."

"Yes, I know what you mean," Sonny answered, looking down at the floor. "He just doesn't act like the Ernie he was when he left. I just can't put my finger on what's going on in his head. He wasn't in Korea, so it can't be that he's shell-shocked. But like you say, there sure seems to be something wrong."

"You know what he said to me today?" Rachel sounded outraged. "You know how the army was giving me $91 a month while he was in the army? This morning, he said to me that he wanted that money. You know that I needed all the money that I got just to make ends meet. I was not able to farm. Sometimes I even had to work on the farm for folks to make ends meet." Rachel looked beseechingly over at Sonny. "I just don't understand how he thinks I could have saved that money for him." She paused and took a deep breath. "Sonny, I am scared for me and for the rest of the children. Simply put, I don't want to consider what he might do. I know that I can get some money from Mr. Bailey. But I'll need about a thousand dollars. With that, I think he'll be okay. I just got to make sure that I have at least that much when we talk again."

Sonny drove Rachel to Lakeville where she spoke with Mr. Bailey. He was very interested in why she needed so much money. He knew that

Rob had left her thousands of dollars. But Mr. Bailey had watched as the dollars had evaporated. But when it came right down to it, if there was one person in all Callawaytown that would be willing to help, it was certainly Rachel.

Still, he had to ask, "Rachel, you mean to tell me that you've gone through all that money that Rob worked so hard to save? That money he had in the bank, and whatever he had at home? You must have something to show for it." Instantly, he saw that he had gone too far. Rachel had suffered enough. Awkwardly, he added, "Well, I know how it is when you have children in school and small ones at home. Even though you have your own place, it costs money to live these days. I can very well understand that times can get hard in between. So, tell me how I can help you?"

Rachel was ashamed. "Well, Mr. Bailey, Ernie just came back from the army. He sent me some money every month while he was away. Now he wants that money back. Lord knows I would like to pay him back, but I don't have a dime to my name. Everything I've got is tied up in land. I just need to borrow about a thousand dollars so I can give it to him."

Mr. Bailey let loose a whoosh of air, "Rachel, that's a lotta of money! How do you plan to pay me back? You aren't working no place now and you're only tending that land you have just around the old house. I would sure like to help you, but I just cannot see where you are going to get the money to repay me. Ernie's home now. Does he intend to farm, or what is he going to do?

"Yes, he's staying at home," Rachel replied, and I think he is going to be there for some time. He never mentioned anything about moving. Sometimes I just wish he would go back into the army. Lord knows he sure wouldn't have to send me any more money, never again." She shook her head slowly and said, "Sometimes when I hear him speak, I can't believe he's my own flesh and blood."

"You know I've been listening to you, and I just came up with a good idea! You have a set of twin boys, don't you?" asked Mr. Bailey.

"No, they're not really twins, but they're the same size, look the same, and are in the same grade at school, and I dress them like twins, but really there are two years to the day between them."

Mr. Bailey continued, "Well, like I was saying, I thought of something to which you might want to give some thought. Let us say that Ernie will be willing to stay at the house with you and the rest of the children. I've got a lot of land out in Callawaytown that needs to be tended. You know, I even must put some of my best tobacco landthe soi in a soil bank. And hell, they don't pay me anything' for that. Not when you consider what I could make if I had a good farmer working on that land. You know a man can't even get a poor black-ass nigger to work the land any more. As soon as they get out of school, they're on their way up north somewhere. I just can't get 'm to work anymore. But why am I telling you about my problems? Let's get back to what I had in mind. Now take those ten acres of tobacco allotment I've got just near you, folks. I would be willing to let you farm it. You could let Ernie work it using two boys of yours. They could be a big help. I would give ya'll half of whatever is made. You could just give it to Ernie. After he paid the boys for their labor, he would still have far more than a thousand dollars. Then you wouldn't have to go into any debt. What do you think of that?"

Rachel actually smiled and said, "That's a really good idea, Mr. Bailey. I'll talk with Ernie about it today and see what he says. I really can't see him saying nothing' but okay. That's what I'll do. Thanks very much for your assistance, 'because I just didn't know what to do at this point. I can make money from working and farming them two pieces of land. But I would never make enough to pay Ernie a thousand dollars. So, this is going to work out just fine."

When she discussed the situation with Ernie, he was willing to take on the responsibility.

Everything went as well as it could for a few years. But the bad financial decisions and loans to family members eventually took their toll. The money went out much faster than it came in. Finally, the farm went into debt. Rachel had absolutely nothing to show for Rob's money other than the remodeling of the house, fifty acres of woodland in Bull County, and her dentures.

CHAPTER THIRTY

The seasons went by amazingly fast. The boys worked hard on the farm as well as on the golf course as caddies. Additionally, Ernie made some deals with the brother of one of his army buddies. His name was Roger Foster. A white sharecropper, he was about six feet five inches and around three hundred and fifty pounds. His wife was much younger and smaller than he was. They had six daughters and two sons. Two of the daughters were twins and about George's age. One daughter was Jacob's age. The oldest and the youngest were boys.

Ernie arranged with Roger to use George and Jacob for labor. He would pay their wages at the end of the tobacco harvest and sales. George worked with the men in the field, pulling the tobacco. Jacob was responsible for delivering the tobacco from the field to the barn. At the barn, the women would string the tobacco on sticks so it could be hung in the barn to be cured.

The harvesting took place once a week and required several steps. Once the tobacco was pulled, stringed, and hung in the barn, it was cured for five days. Then it stayed in the barn for the day and a night with the windows and doors open. This allowed the leaves to become soft. On the seventh day, the tobacco was removed from the curing barn and put into the storage barn to make room for the next week's harvest. During those five days of curing, the heat was kept at a certain temperature. That meant that the heat had to be checked several times during the day and night. Roger Foster's three oldest daughters took turns going to the barn during the night to check the temperature.

One day, Jacob was busy going back and forth from the field to the barn. He made a stop by the house to get cold water for the men who pulled tobacco from the fields. It was approaching eleven-thirty in the morning. Rogers' oldest daughter was returning home to prepare the dinner meal. Her mother had already cooked the food the day before. Her job was to set the tables, warm the food, and bake cornbread and biscuits. She also made cool-aid and lemonade. Jacob stopped the mule just beyond the kitchen porch, where the water pump was located. Rita came out of the kitchen door.

"Do you need a big gallon jar so that you don't have to take two?" she asked sweetly.

"Yes, that would be nice."

Rita was already on her way out with the gallon jar as Jacob was beginning to work the pump handle to clear the pipes of warm water. Rita walked over to him. Her blouse was open, and she was not wearing a bra. Jacob was an inch or two taller than her, so he was able to get a good look at her breasts. The nipples were pink and stood parallel to the ground. Her eyes were sky blue, and her hair was golden and curly and hung down to her mid-back. Before Jacob could say anything, Rita handed him the jar with one hand while she rested her other hand on his shoulder. Jacob looked down into her beautiful face, and his eyes met hers. He knew that he was not supposed to even be close to Rita. It was downright dangerous to be standing there with her hand on his shoulder. He had heard plenty of talk in the fields about why niggers and white folks should never mix. It was bad. According to God's law, the races just should not be together. Everybody knew that no decent white woman would ever get close to a nigger. Even if a white woman chose to have sex with a Negro, it would be regarded as rape. Scores of black men throughout the south had met their end by having sex with a white woman. Jacob was aware that it had actually occurred in Mills and Bull Counties.

Rita didn't say a word as she moved her right hand down Jacob's back. She touched his belt buckle with her other hand and worked her hand down to where his penis was already bulging. Jacob could not believe what was happening. Not only was she white, but Rita was also at least three years older than he.

He was unable to help himself. His hand began to shake as he placed the jar on the pump landing. They were totally alone. She was already unzipping his pants. He had his hand down her blouse and onto her bare breast. There was no going back.

Jacob had never had sex before. Rita's buttocks were even with the height of the landing. She pushed her tongue into his mouth and leaned over backwards with her legs spread apart. Jacob was on top of her, but he did not know quite what to do. Rita was not going to let this chance pass her by. She got up quickly and pulled Jacob's penis out of his pants and took him into her mouth. Jacob thought that was the most disgusting thing he had ever seen in all his short life. But Rita had moved from his penis to his mouth, where she pushed her tongue down his throat. At the same time, Rita had leaned over on the landing and had pushed herself onto his penis. After then, the action picked up speed and both of them had their climaxes.

Self-consciously, Jacob pulled himself together, emptied the half-filled jar and filled it with cold water. "You know," Rita said casually, "I am the one that goes down to the tobacco barn after twelve at night to check the temperature. Daddy gave me his alarm clock, so I can set it to go off every two hours. If everything is okay, I just come back home without waking anybody up. I have from twelve o'clock midnight until the morning to do whatever I want to do. You know we could really have a good time if you could come over to the tobacco barn. Nobody will ever find out. We could be together as much as we like."

Jacob did not respond. He was thoroughly shaken by what had happened. He wanted to get off that porch and back to the tobacco field with the cold water. He knew that he had been gone far too long, and it would not be exceptionally long before Roger sent someone to look for him. The men might stand around for about fifteen minutes, telling jokes, laughing, and having fun. Then, they would be mad when they didn't get their water.

But when he got back to the field, the men had not even noticed that he was late. He was tired and really wanted to lie down. He felt like he would fall asleep in seconds if he did. Sex had been a totally new experience for him. He did not know whether he should tell someone about it or just keep it to himself. Then his heart started to pound. It was impossible for him to ever talk about what had happened. He might be hanged like the other men who had sex with white women if news got out.

But after several days, Jacob really wanted to have sex with Rita again. She acted as if she had never spoken to him or knew him any better than she knew anyone else who worked at the farm. But he knew she was watching him. After midnight, the gathering at the tobacco barn might just be successful. He would have to figure out how he would leave the house without being noticed. He was still afraid of being out in the dark. He was only fifteen. He had never walked out of the neighborhood alone, especially late at night.

While he worked, he thought constantly about Rita. He really looked forward to just seeing her. He had a sneaking suspicion that she approved of him just as much as he did. He could see that she was genuinely happy to see him pull up to the edge of the porch and walk up the steps to the landing. Meanwhile, Roger would speak about blackass niggers and what he would do if any one of his children were ever involved with a blackass nigger.

"It's just not right! There's a place for blackass Niggers and there's a place for white folks. In no way should they be mixing."

Honestly, Jacob was not entirely clear into what category he and his family fit. Were they considered blackass niggers, or what? As he listened, he noticed that Roger used the term only in Callaway's presence. If any other Negroes were present, he would just stop and shake his head from side to side. Jacob was not sure what to make of that. Still, he knew that Roger would be extremely upset if he knew that anyone was involved with his daughter.

Jacob became all but obsessed with Rita. He forgot about his old sweetheart from school. Rita had taken center stage. He made a point to walk by the farmhouse where she lived whenever he returned from the golf course. He was dying to see her.

It was late one night, and Jacob had been working in the dry tobacco with his family. When they finished, everyone scattered for the night. Most of them were so tired that they were asleep within minutes. Still, it was so hot and humid that some of the boys took quilts and went off to find a cool spot outside. That is exactly what Jacob appeared to do.

He had other plans. It had been only days since he had been on the porch with Rita, but it seemed like years. He could not get her out of his mind. Tonight, he would walk over to the tobacco barn and see if she was there. He pretended to be asleep until he was sure that everyone else was out for the night. At that point, he got up and walked barefoot through the fields, across the main road, and over to the barn. He waited for what seemed like hours before he saw a light bobbing in the darkness. As he watched, it traveled from the house toward the barn. Even when he saw Rita, he didn't move. He had to make sure that she was alone. What if one of her sisters had decided to come along? He watched her check the temperature. When she closed the barn door, he whispered to her, "Rita, Rita."

She stopped in her tracks and did not make a sound for several seconds. Then, she said a little indignantly, "Jacob, I didn't think you were ever going to come here. You don't know how many times I've been down here, looking forward to you being here, and you never showed.

"Well, I didn't know if I should come or not. I just didn't know if it was the right thing to do."

By this time, they were in each other's arms. They stopped kissing long enough to get into one of the tobacco crates, and then they had sex. After they both climaxed, Jacob's penis rested inside her. It was a remarkably interesting feeling for him. Caught up in the sensation, he forgot all about what would happen to him if somebody discovered them. He knew that Rita would never say that he had raped her. Still, it wouldn't make any difference.

Right now, they were totally enraptured with one another. She felt as though he had become part of her. They talked about their feelings for each other and how crazy it was that they could not be openly affectionate. Before long, they had sex again. They talked again, until Jacob glanced at his Timex and realized that it was after 2 o'clock in the morning.

"I got to get out of here," he said urgently. "You've got to go back to the house, and I've got to get back to Callawaytown." They kissed, embraced, and whispered goodnight. Rita walked back to the house, and Jacob stood staring into her back until she faded into the night.

Jacob negotiated his way through the fields. He really was frightened of the dark. By the time he was almost home, he really got scared. The moon was full, and the shadow of swaying bushes and plants, especially corn, made him so afraid that it just about cancelled out his wonderful night with Rita. He finally got to Callawaytown. But he could see what looked like a shadow following him as he walked. He had never been so frightened in his entire life. All he wanted to do was get home in one piece. He had heard of ghosts, and now he was sure one was following him.

However, as he walked around the bend in the road, he could see that the trees, on the side of the road, at the bend, were preventing the shadow from following him. He then understood that the shadow he had been seeing was actually his own.

Jacob's relationship with Rita continued throughout the summer. It was a very closely kept secret. Jacob never told anyone about her. As far as he could tell, Rita never spoke with anyone about her involvement with him.

It was not long before Rita became pregnant. When she gave birth, no one talked about the fact that the baby was a bit darker than her mother and the rest of the family. The young girl was breathtakingly lovely. She was Rita's pride and joy. Jacob did not know how the pregnancy was handled within the family circle. The child had brown eyes and dark hair. This was simply fine since half of Rita's family had dark hair while the others were blond. Rita never talked to Jacob about the fact that the child was his and he never asked.

This was the way things happened in North Carolina. Everyone knew that Negroes, whites, and Indians mixed regularly. However, it was never discussed. If a white woman's child was born with darker skin, or curly hair, the whites would say that she'd been frightened by a mule during her pregnancy. That would be the end of the discussion. When no white people were present, the black people would be aware of what had occurred and would make fun of it.

Once, a white woman with seven children became pregnant and gave birth to a very dark baby with curly hair. The local white minister gave a sermon about how God works in mysterious ways. During her pregnancy, the woman had gone to the farm to bring her husband some water. Apparently, a mule had frightened her. Even though a Negro man lived right next to the family, this ridiculous explanation was enough to stop the gossip. The Negroes made fun and laughed about the situation. They confirmed that she had been scared numerous times by the same mule.

CHAPTER THIRTY-ONE

Summer came to an end, and all the tobacco was harvested. The time came for Ernie to pay George and Jacob for their work. Ernie came home one day and called George and Jacob. He walked them outside and told them that times had been hard. He bemoaned how challenging it was to manage the farm and work for the county at the same time. He told them he had lost a lot of money on the farm. "I really shouldn't have messed with no farming this past year. I really lost a lotta money messing with all that tobacco, and the price of tobacco was nothing' like I thought it would be when I first started last spring. I don't know what I am going to do, but you boys don't have anything to worry about. I said I was going to pay you for working on the farm and I am going to do that."

George looked as if he believed what Ernie was saying, but Jacob was not impressed. Ernie pulled out a roll of bills from his pocket. He peeled off a twenty and a five-dollar bill and handed them to each of them. George acted as if he was pleased. But Jacob looked at the twenty-five dollars and then back at Ernie.

"You mean you worked us this whole year for just twenty-five dollars?" Jacob said incredulously.

Ernie went ballistic, "I don't know what's wrong with you. You are just a little stupid son-of a-bitch. You are crazy. That's what's wrong with you. Why can't you be like George? You see, George took his twenty-five dollars and was satisfied. You've got to act like a fool. Boy I tell you, you going to be in prison or dead before you get to be thirty, just you wait and see."

Jacob shot right back, "We should have more money than twenty-five dollars! We cannot even buy any clothes for school this year with this little money. And now, we aren't to have time to work somewhere to make money for school clothes."

Ernie took a step toward Jacob, saying, "You can just give that back if you don't want it. Mama said that you boys were going to work for me to pay back that money that I sent to her when I was in the army. So, I really didn't have to give you anything'. It was out of the goodness of my heart that I even gave you the twenty-five dollars. You don't want it just to give it back."

When Jacob just stared at him, Ernie continued, "You know, Mr. Walker asked me if you boys could go up to High Point and drive new school buses back before school starts. I told him that George could go and drive a bus back, but I wouldn't let that crazy Jacob drive nothing.' I told him that you were crazy. Now I am glad I told him that, cause today you proved to me that you are crazy. There isn't any doubt about it boy. You just aren't the same as George."

George brightened up and asked, "Is it true, Ernie? Did Mr. Walker ask if I could go up to High Point and drive a new school bus back down here?"

Ernie nodded, glad to have suckered George. "Yes, he just asked me that yesterday. He did not tell me what day yet because he wants to make sure he's got enough drivers before he sets a date to go. He also asked me if you wanted to drive the school bus this year. I told him that that would be great. Now I can say to him that you can do all these things, but I'd never, in my wildest dreams, tell him that Jacob could ever drive a school bus. I really don't understand how he ever got his driver's license."

As they walked back to the house, Jacob was really hurt by what Ernie had said. What had he done to his brother for him to speak so negatively about him? Well, there was nothing' he could do. He was forced to spend one more year at the house and in Callawaytown. This was his last year in high school. He decided right there that he would never be around for another harvesting season. Not even to be with Rita.

Ernie had a job with the Mills County Department of Education. He worked at the bus depot. His job was to go around the schools each day and make certain that all the buses in the county had gas and were well greased. The white men who worked at the bus depot were mechanics. They never performed any of the dirty work. Even when there was a tire that needed to be changed and a white mechanic was there, he would call for Ernie to come and change the tire. Afterwards, the white man would sign the documents, indicating that he had done the work. However, it was common knowledge that only the Negroes had to do that type of work.

Still, Ernie was pleased to have the job. The only other work available in the South for Negroes was domestic, farm, or other types of hard labor. This job gave Ernie an opportunity to add to what came from the farm and his late father's blacksmith shop.

He would visit every school in the county at least once, maybe twice a week. It was the first year since Rob Junior had left that anyone in Callawaytown was available to drive a school bus. Three of the four bus drivers had graduated from high school the previous spring. Therefore, three new drivers had to be identified before the start of the new school year. Mr. Walker, the white manager responsible for the transportation of all the students in the county, was interested in getting at least one bus driver from Callawaytown, since that was the end of the bus line. It would be ideal to have two drivers from that area. One bus could take the children from that area and proceed straight once it arrived at Highway 72. The other could take a right at Highway 72. Both buses would meet again at Flathead Elementary School. Once they dropped the children in grades 1st through 6th, they would go in different directions, picking up Negro children throughout the countryside until they arrived at Narrow Branch High School. The entire route would take an hour and a half to two hours. The drivers would have to leave home sometime between six and six-thirty each morning.

When Ernie arrived at the bus depot the following day, Mr. Walker held a meeting. "We got several buses to be driven from High Point to here," Mr. Walker said. "Right now, I've the buses covered with drivers except two. I think I've got one more covered, but I don't know for sure yet." He paused and then looked over at Ernie. "You mentioned that your brother George could probably drive one for us, right?"

"Yessir, that's right," Ernie replied. "My brother George can drive a bus. I know for sho that he won't have any problem driving one of them new busses."

Mr. Walker nodded his agreement, "So that leaves us with only one driver short. We've got to find one more driver and then we'll be all set."

At that point the bookkeeper, an old and longtime friend of the Callaway family, piped up. "Ernie, what about Jacob? I know he's got a driver's license because he drove my boy to the pool one day when my wife was busy. She said he drove very well and came back just as he was supposed to. He even told her that he would come back if she needed him. I do not know, but he seemed to be a very fine boy. Mr. Walker, what do you think of him driving that last bus?"

Before Mr. Walker could respond, Ernie said angrily, "I tell you now, that Jacob is crazy. George is okay and can drive a bus, but that Jacob, no, never. All he is going to do is have a wreck. I sure would not trust him to drive no bus. I really do not know how he ever got a driver's license in the first place, but he did, so somebody messed up, somehow. That is not important. The important thing is that he can't drive no bus and that's that."

Mr. Walker didn't agree, "Well I don't know about that. The boy might not be too bad of a choice to fill my empty slot. If he can sit behind the wheel and his feet can reach the foot paddles, he just might fit the bill."

Ernie wouldn't give up, "I can tell you right now Mr. Walker, that Jacob can't drive no school bus. If you want to have a wreck on your hand just let him drive a bus and you'll surely be sorry."

Mr. Walker could not believe his ears. If Jacob was that much of a problem, why hadn't he heard anything about it before? Hell, his office was not that far from Callawaytown. A neighbor had just spoken up on his behalf. So why was Ernie so hard on his brother Jacob? He would have to investigate on his own. The only way to do that was to go out to Callawaytown and speak to the boy and come to his own conclusions.

Everyone on Mr. Walker's staff except Ernie was white. They looked over at Ernie after his harsh comments about his brother. "We still have that one bus which we've got to find a driver for. But I will work on that and see what I can do. As it looks like now we'll probably be going up to High Point some time before week's end. I'll let you'll know when I make my decision." Mr. Walker closed the meeting, and everyone went to their daily activities.

Mr. Walker went directly to his pickup truck and drove to Callawaytown. When he arrived at Rachel's house, drove to the back of the house. As always, all the children gathered around the truck soon after Mr. Walker brought it to a complete stop.

Mr. Walker looked over at George and asked, "Are your mother and Jacob around?"

"Yes, mama is in the kitchen and Jacob is around here somewhere. I'll tell mama that you're here Mr. Walker."

But before George could make his way into the house Rachel stepped out from the porch, "Howdy Mr. Walker, what can I do for you?"

"Well, I heard that you have two schoolboys that have driver's licenses. Is that so?"

Rachel nodded. "Yes, I got George and Jacob. George drives just about anything, but Jacob, I do not know how much he can drive. I do know he can drive the tractor. He drives it just about all the time around here on the farm."

Jacob overheard the conversation as he entered the yard from the field. He said excitedly, "I can drive Mr. Walker! I can drive a car good! I got my driver's license the same day George got his and he's two years older than me. I can drive really good."

Mr. Walker looked over at the young boy and gave him a look of approval, "Miss. Rachel I'll tell you why I am here. We have got to go up to High Point to get some new school buses for next year. The way it stands now, we have got a driver for every bus but one. As a matter of fact, we are going to have your son George drive one. I was talking with my staff today and it was mentioned that Jacob has his driver's license, and somebody said that they had seen him driving. I just want to know if it would be okay if he drove that one bus from High Point down here. That would really help me out a lot. What do you think about that?"

Rachel answered honestly, "Well, Mr. Walker I really don't even know if Jacob can even drive a bus. I know he can drive a car, because I see he's driving around here from time to time. But a bus, that, I just cannot say he can do. He drives the tractor too, but a bus, that just might be too much."

Mr. Walker thought for a moment, "I'll see that he is able to drive the bus before we go up to High Point. All I need is for you to give me permission to use him. I'll make sure the rest is taken care of."

Rachel still wasn't quite convinced, "I am not got no problem with him going with you up to High Point and driving a bus back. I just don't want to be getting into no trouble if he happens to get into an accident."

The boys were extremely interested in what Mr. Walker was saying to their mother. George wanted to do whatever he could to prevent Jacob from participating in the project. Jacob, meantime, was exerting every effort to support his mother's choice.

"Mama, you don't have to worry about me getting in no accident. I'll tell you. I can drive just as good or better than George. Just because he is two years older than me, doesn't mean that he can drive any better.

Remember, we got our driver's licenses the same day. So, I'll just bet you that he'll probably have a accident before me."

Mr. Walker was overly impressed with Jacob's confidence. Now he wanted to take the boy for a drive just to the nearest crossroad to convince himself that the boy was trainable, "Miss Rachel do you mind if I take Jacob for a ride just over the third bridge to the crossroad. I just want to see for myself how good he drives. What do you say?"

"Jacob, you go inside and get your shoes," Rachel ordered to Jacob's delight, "And you do everything that Mr. Walker tells you. You understand?"

Jacob ran into the house to the bedroom he shared with his brother, reached under the bed, and retrieved his only pair of shoes. In his haste, he put them on without socks and returned to the yard.

"Jacob, you think you can drive this truck?" asked Mr. Walker.

"Yessir, I tell you, I am not going to have any problem driving this truck." Jacob replied as he approached the driver's side.

"Just a minute!" Mr. Walker laughed, "Let me just go back out of this driveway, get on the road, and I'll tell you when I want you to drive. Just get in on the other side."

Mr. Walker backed out of the driveway and made his way down the road. He said, "You know you've got to be careful when you're driving. It's one thing to drive a car, but it's altogether different when you're driving a truck or bus. Not only do you have to drive for yourself, but also, you have got to drive for all of them fools out there. It is not easy, but if you take your time and use your head you aren't going to have any problem. Now I am going to drive to the crossroads and then I will let you drive back. Let's see how you do." He brought the truck to a full stop on the side of the road.

They exchanged places. Mr. Walker taught him about the gears and other features of the truck, and then Jacob took off as though he'd been driving for years. Mr. Walker was impressed. As they approached the driveway, Mr. Walker asked him to make the turn into the driveway and negotiate his way to the area where he had parked when he arrived. Jacob came to a full stop just as Mr. Walker had asked.

Jacob got out of the truck even before Mr. Walker could exit from the passenger side, saying, "Mama, Mama, you know I can drive this truck. I can drive it just as good as I can drive a car. It was fun! I really like to drive a truck!"

Mr. Walker wore a wide smile, "Yes Miss Rachel, this boy can drive quite well. I don't see that he's going to have any problem driving a school bus. I tell you, I'd sho like to use him for sure. In my opinion he can drive just as good as any of the other boys I am going to have driving. To tell you the truth, he can probably drive better than most of them."

"Well, like I said, it's all up to you. If you think that it's going to be okay, then I don't have no problem with him driving a school bus for you."

Except for his experiences with Rita, this was the happiest moment of Jacob's life. Now he would be on equal footing with his brother George.

"Okay, what I'll do is inform Ernie of what I've decided, and we'll take it from there. Thanks for your time. We'll be getting in contact with you very soon."

"It's okay, Mr. Walker. I am glad that I could help. It's always nice if you can help the county, especially the school department," answered Rachel.

When Ernie returned from work that evening, he was very upset. He turned his car into the driveway like a mad man. The instant the car stopped, he jumped out and ran over to when his mother was standing on the porch.

"What in the hell is going on around here?" He shouted. "I thought I told everybody that that crazy Jacob couldn't drive no school bus! What happened? Did Mr. Walker come out here? Who told him that Jacob could drive a school bus? You'll know damn well that that fool can't drive no school bus. All he is going to do is have a wreck and get this family in a world of trouble. Just wait and see. You can just forget about me having anything to do with him. If Mr. Walker want to use him to go up to High Point that's up to him, but I am not having no part of it."

George saw his opportunity to get ahead of Jacob, "I told mama that Jacob couldn't drive no school bus, but she just wouldn't listen to what I was saying when Mr. Walker was here."

Rachel held out her hands to ask for peace, "Well Mr. Walker took him for a ride in his pickup and when they came back Jacob was driving. Mr. Walker said that he did not have any problem with his driving and that he would be responsible if anything should happen. He has been driving around here on the farm for I don't know how long. He has not had any accident. I do not see nothing' wrong with him helping with them driving that one school bus that one time just from up there in High Point."

Ernie growled at his mother, "I know it's your son and I know you just can't get it into your head that you had one child that is crazy, but I don't want him making me look bad before all of them white folks down there at the county. It's one thing when he's acting crazy here at home but when comes to being out in public, I just don't want him around me. I tell you now! Tomorrow when I go to work, I am going to tell Mr. Walker that Jacob can't be driving no school bus from all the way up there in High Point. I am going to stop it. He isn't going to be making me look like no fool out there before everybody."

Jacob was sitting in the yard on the root of a tree. It was clear that he was very sad about the cruel things Ernie had said. He wondered what he had done to make his brother feel that way about him. He felt worthless at that moment. His shoulder was wrapped by Rachel as she approached him, who also ran her fingers through his long, curly hair.

"Mama, Mama, why do Ernie feel that way about me?" Jacob said brokenly. "I never did anything to him. When I was driving with Mr. Walker, he said that I was driving exceptionally good. He said that I could drive a school bus for him. I just don't know why Ernie don't want me to drive."

"Don't worry, Mr. Walker said you can help. He is the boss. So, it isn't going to matter what nobody else has to say," Rachel soothed.

When the time came for the delivery of the buses, Ernie took George and Jacob with him to the county office. Ernie did not repeat any of the things he said days earlier at home. Mr. Walker thanked all the boys who had participated and gave them each twenty-five dollars. Ernie finished what he was doing late in the afternoon, gathered his belongings, and yelled for George and Jacob.

As they drove towards Callaway town, Ernie finally broke the silence. "You'll know that you never would've got to drive a school bus back from High Point if it hadn't been for me. I'll tell you right now Jacob. For sure, if I hadn't gone to Mr. Walker and told him that I knew for sure that you could drive a school bus, he would have never in a million years let you drive. You boys should give me at least twenty of them dollars each. There was all kind of white boys that Mr. Walker could have got to drive. I think twenty dollars would be good. You haven't got nothing to do with all that money. You just going to throw it away."

The boys looked over at each other but did not respond. Ernie waited until he could not stand it anymore. "Well, I can understand that you want to keep most of it, but you got to give me something. There isn't no way you are going to tell me that I had to drive you'll +down to the county this morning and to High Point and now back home and not get nothing'. That is +just not fair. You got to +give me at least a five spot each."

The boys did not dare open their mouths. They knew that if it came down to a debate with their oldest brother they would lose. The only way to win was to not say a word. They had made the turn onto the road leading to Callawaytown. Mercifully, it would be a very short period before they would arrive home.

Once they were home the boys jumped out of the car and went to their mother. "How did it go?" she asked. "I can see that you didn't have no accident."

"No, mama, it was fun!" Jacob answered. "We drive a school bus all the way from High Point back to the county. We did not have any problems at all. And you know what? Mr. Walker gave us twenty-five dollars each. He gave us a five-dollar bill and a twenty-dollar bill."

They pulled the money from their pockets and handed their mother twenty dollars each. She smiled over at them. "Why thank you, but don't you boys need this money for school? Maybe to buy some school clothes or something?"

The boys answered simultaneously, "No, we don't need anything but the five-dollar bill. When we needed to buy school things, we'll be caddying at the golf course on the weekends."

Ernie was angry that he had been unable to get any of the money from the boys. Hell, he had put everything in place for them to make that money. This was the thanks he got for everything he had done. He would fix them. He had told Mr. Walker that George could drive the school bus and had recommended him and now even that little bastard was turning his back on him. He had given most of his money to his mother. Yes, he would fix George. He would make certain that someone else would get that job.

It was not exceedingly long before Mr. Walker had his school bus driver's + assignment meeting. First discussed the white schools and the Indians. Lastly, he came to the Negro schools. He walked over the black board, "We got to a big problem with those Flathead and Narrow Branch schools. We need two more drivers. The way the district is set up we ++ a big problem over in your area Ernie. Callawaytown is the end of the line. Any driver we get is going to have to drive into Callawaytown and make a U-turn at the church and old schoolhouse. Now on the other hand we have got a golden opportunity. Ernie, we have your two brothers, George, and Jacob. Both of them boys can drive, and I know that Jacob can drive really well. When I went out there to talk with your mother, I took him for a ride in my pick-up and let him drive back. He really did a good job." Looking over to the lead mechanic, he asked, "We didn't have any problem with them boys when we went up to High Point to pick up them buses, did we?"

The mechanic shook his head, "No, not at all."

Ernie broke in, "I'll tell you now Mr. Walker, I don't think either one of them boys is able to drive no school bus. I sure would not trust them with no bus. You are just going to be asking for trouble if you go and let George or Jacob, but especially Jacob drives a school bus. The boys just aren't got what it takes to drive no school bus."

Mr. Walker ignored what Ernie had said, "I think it would be perfect if we let both boys drive a school bus. I have never heard of no Callaway having no trouble driving no school bus. Ernie, when you were in school, you and your other brother, what is his name, cannot remember, but I know he drove until he finished school as you did. You boys never had any problems. That would satisfy all our needs. We are going to add one new bus to that area. One bus would turn left at Highway 72 and the other would continue straight. That's all we'd need. What you boys thank?"

No one was about to disagree with whatever idea Mr. Walker had. It would be career suicide. Nobody said anything.

"Well, I guess it's final. Since George is the older of the two and he was in line to drive the bus in any case, we will give the old bus to him and the new one to Jacob. He can have the new route. I think that will be the best thing to do. Anybody have any problem with that?" Mr. Walker knew that once he had made his views known, he would not receive any opposition. As far as he was concerned it was all settled.

Ernie was amazed, he could not believe his ears. Not only would George and Jacob be driving this year, but also Jacob would have the new bus. That bus should certainly go to George. All Jacob was going to do was a wreck. That was going to make things bad for everyone in Callawaytown. It was just not right for Mr. Walker to be deciding like that! However, since he was unable to affect a change, he would make use of a difficult situation and still make it work out to his benefit. Indeed, he would find a way to improve a hopeless circumstance.

When he returned home, he told the boys that he had talked with Mr. Walker, "You know he's got a new route for our school this year. He is going to probably want to have another driver. Right now, he isn't got no body in mind to drive that bus." He looked right at Jacob as he lied.

"I can probably talk with him and see if maybe I can get him to let you drive that other bus. It is going to be one of the new buses that we picked up in High Point. I will tell you what I will do. I will talk with him and see if he will let you drive it Jacob, but I tell you now that it's going to be a long shot. You know you get twenty-five dollars a month for driving the bus if he allows you to drive. So, if I can get him to let you drive, how much will you give me a month out of that twenty-five?"

Jacob thought for a moment, "I don't even want to think about driving the school bus now. Now I know Mr. Walker is not going to let me drive the school bus for the whole school year. So, there's no use thinking about what I'll give you."

Ernie knew at that point that Jacob had outwitted him and would not be giving him any money.

The day came for the new school year to begin. George and Jacob rode down to the county office with Ernie. Neither of them knew what bus they would be driving. They only knew that Mr. Walker had spoken to their mother, and she had agreed. When they arrived at the county Mr. Walker gave them an overview of the routes and schedule for each stop. They reviewed the documents and familiarized themselves with the various stops, times, and schedules. Both routes were amazingly simple. George was very sure that he would be given the new bus to drive. He knew that he had his older brother Ernie's support. Furthermore, why would Mr. Walker trust that crazy Jacob with a brand-new bus? All he was going to do was eventually have an accident, so why not let him have it on an old bus?

Mr. Walker gave them a ten-minute break and five cents for a soda. Afterwards, he told the lead mechanic to gather the boys in the same conference room where they had spent the better part of the morning.

Mr. Walker entered the room and walked straight to the front. "Well, I think we've got one of the best crops of young bus drivers we've had in this county for some time. This is surely going to make things much easier for my staff. We've added another route to Narrow Branch High School. It will start at Callawaytown, go to Flathead, and drop off the elementary school children at that point. Then it will pick up any Junior High and High School students and continue to Narrow Branch."

George knew that he was already scheduled to drive the original bus route. Because of this, the only option was to give him the new bus route and the new bus, while giving his younger brother Jacob the old route.

Mr. Walker gave all the assignments except the two for Callawaytown. Then he walked over to the board and wrote #'s 301 and 311 on the black board. He turned around and faced the boys. "These are the two routes that will originate in Callawaytown. There will be no change in the current route and proposed driver. A new bus will support the new route. For the first time, we have two brothers driving school buses during the same year. The Callaway boys will be driving for us this season. George, of course, was already scheduled to drive the old route. Jacob will be the new driver for the new route and new bus. As you'll know, the old bus is the number 301. The new one is 311. That's the bus that Jacob will drive."

George could not believe what Mr. Walker had just said. How could he allow Jacob to drive the new bus and have the new route when he was two years younger than him? Even Ernie knew that wasn't right. There was no way that Mr. Walker should do a thing like that when he knew that Jacob was crazy and would only wreck the bus. Why was he taking such a chance like that with Jacob? Now everyone in school would be laughing at him for driving an old bus when his younger brother was driving a new one.

But Jacob was incredibly pleased. He had never imagined that Mr. Walker would select him to drive a school bus in the first place. That alone was amazing. Now he would be driving that brand-new bus. I just can't wait to get home and tell mama, he thought joyfully. Mr. Walker closed the meeting after giving the boys the keys to the buses. George and Jacob drove them home and parked them in the front yard near the road.

It was an interesting year. Both boys drove without incident during the entire school year. They received twenty-five dollars each month and gave twenty dollars to their mother.

When the year was over, on the last day of school, Mr. Walker came to Narrow Branch High School and presented Jacob with a certificate for the safest and youngest school bus driver in the state. This was of course only for the Negro schools. George received a safe driver's certificate. However, all drivers in the state received that certificate if they were not involved with an incident or accident during the year.

But that last day was very rainy. The paved roads were wet and slick. The dirt roads were very muddy. Jacob was driving on one of those dirt roads. One of his school buddies was sitting behind him in the front seat. Most of the students had already been dropped off. There was a very sharp curve just a few miles down the road. Jacob's buddy goaded him, "I bet you can't go around that curve without putting your brakes on."

"How much do you bet?" snorted Jacob.

"I tell you what. If you go around that curve without putting your foot on the brake I'll give you five dollars."

Jacob looked over at the certificate that he had just received less than five hours before. He looked at the five-dollar bill, which his buddy had already taken from his pocket. He knew that the road was very slick and that it would be difficult for him to negotiate that curve on a rainy day without the use of his brakes. However, it was his last day in school. He would not be driving the bus next year and for all it was worth, he would be finished with the school bus and Narrow Branch Hill School for good. So why not take the chance?

"Give me that five-dollar bill," Jacob said grimly. His friend handed him the money. He pushed it into his pants pocket and braced the steering wheel with both hands. He took his foot off the gas pedal and let the bus continue its speed as it entered the sharp curve. The bus began to skid from one side of the road to the other. The students began to yell and scream. Jacob was fighting the wheel to prevent the bus from slipping into a ditch on one side or the other. But there was just too much speed, and it was impossible to negotiate that sharp curve. The bus swerved twice before coming to rest in a ditch on the right side of the road.

Jacob panicked. He made several attempts to back the bus out of the ditch. However, the rear wheels on the left side were not even touching the ground. A man drove by in a car, saw what had happened and yelled, "What's going on here? What happened? Is anybody hurt?"

"No, sir, isn't nobody hurt," Jacob answered ruefully. "We're all okay. I was just going around this curve and as you can see it's very slippery. I just lost control and I slid in this ditch."

"Well, I'll stop by the county and tell them that they have a bus in the ditch over here. They should be here in a few minutes to pull you out." The man returned to his car and drove off.

One could clearly see by the skid marks left on the road that the driver had been going too fast for the road conditions. Jacob knew that what he had done was wrong. He knew that within the space of five minutes, he had destroyed all the faith that Mr. Walker had placed in him. Now, everything that George and Ernie had said had come to rest on his shoulders. What could he do? There was nothing that he could do that would change the situation. Not only had he let Mr. Walker down, but he had also let down all those who had voted to give him that reward. He had really brought shame on himself and all those who had supported him. Now he would have to face up to the result of his actions. For a meager five dollars, he had taken that stupid risk. What a dumb thing to do!

It was not long before the lead mechanic arrived with the wrecker. He did not have to ask what happened, for he could see the skid marks. He backed the wrecker up behind the bus and connected it. He pulled the bus from the ditch. He checked it for damage, but there was none. He informed Jacob that he should drive carefully in this bad, rainy weather and sent him on his way.

Jacob was scared about what Mr. Walker would do. He berated himself. Why hadn't he just ignored his friend? He knew better! It was a foolish thing to do. Oh, God, how he wished he could reverse his actions. Well, now it was over and out of his hands. He had screwed up, and whatever the price for his actions, he would have to pay. Mr. Walker would surely take some sort of punitive action. Everything would depend on what the lead mechanic put in his accident report. If he indicated the skids on the road, Mr. Walker would know that Jacob had been driving too fast for the weather and road conditions and was at fault. On the other hand, if the lead mechanic's report made no mention of the skid marks, Mr. Walker would no doubt conclude that it was probably an unpreventable accident, and therefore there would not be a tarnish on Jacob's driving record.

Jacob was terrified. After he had delivered the last students to their stop, he made his way to the county where he was to deliver the bus. He was the last driver to arrive at the county school bus depot. He parked and went towards the building where the other drivers were. He moved slowly and with a lowered head, walking like a scared animal. He could feel the eyes of all those in the room piercing his body like pinpricks. However, he continued his journey down the sidewalk, into the building, and down the hallway. Once he was inside, he felt relaxed. It was clear that the drivers were not aware of the details of what had happened. Although they were made aware of the incident, the lead mechanic failed to inform them of the skid marks.

Furthermore, he had not informed Mr. Walker of the details. The man gave a short speech about the school year and thanked the boys for their good driving and for taking good care of the buses. Afterwards, Mr. Walker came and spoke to the boys. He gave an overview of the year and the county driving record. In closing, he thanked the boys for good driving. He made no mention of the accident. Jacob was extremely relieved. He had been praying to God and Jesus ever since the accident.

"Oh, Jesus please have mercy on me. I did not mean to get into no accident. Please make it so that Mr. Walker wants to take my certificate away from me. If you'll just do that for me, I'll go to church every Sunday. I'll pay attention to the preacher, and I won't ask any more questions about things that I know the preacher can't answer. As the preacher always say to me when I ask, I will rely on faith and faith alone. Please Jesus, just help me this time and I'll do anything you ask."

A spontaneous prayer was granted. Ernie was completely unaware of the incident. The lead mechanic had kept the event between him and Mr. Walker. They had gotten Jacob into the school bus driver's program and supported the award he'd received. They knew that if the word got out that Jacob was involved in an accident it would be an unfavorable reflection on their judgment. They were determined to prevent it from happening. When Mr. Walker heard of the accident, he immediately made an excuse. "I know it's bad out there on them dirt roads. It's always bad for even driving a car and when it's raining and them boys are driving a bus it's not easy to negotiate that one real sharp curve."

The mechanic caught on quickly and supported Mr. Walker's story. "Yeah, I tell you, that Jacob was doing everything he could do to prevent an awfully bad accident. You should have seen how he maneuvered that bus to keep it from running into a truck that was approaching him. He did an excellent job. I tell you, a lesser boy would have been afraid of hitting a ditch and would have run straight head-on into that truck."

Mr. Walker knew full well that Jacob had been acting like any other teenager. He was fooling around on that road and showing off just because it was the last day of school. He had driven that route on numerous occasions in the rain, mud, and sometimes sleet. But revealing what Jacob had done would be of no advantage to him. Therefore, the story reported by the lead mechanic became official.

Jacob was very afraid that someone would find out the truth of what had happened on that dirt road that afternoon. However, he was not about to say anything about it. He knew that his friend had already left to visit his grandparents. They would not be interested in what he had to say about the accident, even if he brought it to their attention. They were all involved and too busy working. The chances of the truth getting out through him were little or none. Now that he was home and everything was quiet, he could breathe with relief.

May went by. Summer had robbed spring of its last month. The sun was very hot, and the corn, tobacco, cotton, and other crops were being plowed for the last time. If there had been lots of rain during late spring, it would have required that the crops be plowed once. If the crops looked as if they could use some assistance, fertilizer would be distributed down each row. A single wing plow would be used to turn the soil from the center of the row towards the crop. The process would require three steps: spreading the fertilizer, turning the soil towards the crop with a single wing plow and opening the center with the double wing plow.

Ernie did not allow George and Jacob to use the tractor. He was convinced that they would destroy the crop as they negotiated the turns. They had to use the mule or horse, which seemed to take forever. The boys worked every day from sunup to sundown to complete the task before the very hot summer days arrived. Jacob told himself that he would not spend the entire summer on the farm. He had worked the year before for a meager twenty-five dollars.

He had been writing to his brother Rob, who lived with his wife in New York City. Rob told him that he could come to New York and live with him after he finished high school. However, Rachel had promised Ernie that George and Jacob would both be available to work on the farm during that entire year. This was in an attempt to satisfy his request for the money the army had sent her during the time that he was in service. However, what she didn't realize was that that Ernie would never be satisfied. Even if the boys worked for the remainder of their lives, he would forever consider her in his debt. What Ernie was really after was the rights to his mother's property. As the eldest son, he thought that he should have it. The fact that the army had designated him as head of the household only gave credence to his position. He had no desire to look after his mother and siblings. All he wanted was the house.

Ernie had been dating several nice, educated girls around the county. Any one of them would have made him a nice wife. But he'd just date a woman for a few months at the most and then lose interest. Then a black family from the state's northern region relocated to the county. The father had been married before. He had two boys and two girls by his first wife. When she died, he married a friend of his eldest daughter. She was at least twenty-five years younger than he. They had two boys and two girls.

David Raymond owned the farm they lived on. He was well known in the county, even before he was involved in a plot to murder someone.

Kenny Hooker brought the news. He opened the screen door and walked onto the porch and into Callaway's kitchen. "You know somebody killed old man Wilson last night. He was down at the barn getting ready to feed his mule when somebody hit him on the head with a two by four. They found him in the barn near the stable yesterday morning. One of his daughters went down to look for him when he did not return for breakfast. She found him lying near the stable, at the stairs leading to the hayloft."

Rachel, please think of any reason why anyone would want to murder Mr. Wilson. He, his wife, and their two daughters were one of the nicest families in the county. They were very nice to the Negroes. Never gave anyone any trouble and was always able and willing to help everyone in any way they could.

"Why would anybody want to kill Mr. Wilson?" she asked.

Kenny just shook his head and said, "I really don't know. I just don't have any notion of why anybody would want to kill that old man."

Tom Lee Hooker worked on David Raymond's farm, doing odd jobs. From time to time, he also worked for Mr. Wilson. The Wilsons were one of the white families that treated black people with dignity. Mr. Wilson was married and had two grown daughters. They had respectable jobs in Lakeville. His wife was always out visiting poor Negroes in the county and especially in Callawaytown. She collected clothing from well to do white folks in the county and gave them to disadvantaged people, mostly Negroes. She had visited Kenny and Mary Lee just a few days before to drop off a box of clothing.

Kenny said, "You know they came over to the house this morning and picked up Tom Lee. I don't know why they came out here to get him, but I guess we'll find out soon enough."

"Who came over to pick up Tom Lee this morning?" asked Rachel.

Kenny scratched his head, and said "The police from Lakeville, they just came right out here and picked him up."

"But why would the police want to pick him up? What do they think he did?" replied Rachel worriedly.

Kenny responded, "I really don't know. They said something' about wanting to talk to him about where he was last night. I don't know why they couldn't just ask him while they were out here. You never know what's going to happen once they get him down there in that jail."

"Well, I am sure Tom Lee didn't have anything to do with the murder of Mr. Wilson," Rachel said firmly.

Kenny nodded, "Yes, he's been working for that old man a lot over the past few months. As a matter of fact, I think he worked for him just a few days ago. He's always over there giving him a hand with one thing or another."

The news about the murder was all over the county by mid-morning. However, only the people in Callawaytown knew that Tom Lee had been arrested.

Kenny went to the jail to attempt to speak to Tom Lee but was told that he did not want to meet or speak with anyone. Kenny was alarmed. He knew that Tom Lee would never tell anybody that he did not want to see his father. But there was nothing he could do. Helpless, he had to wait until he could see his son. There were no Negro attorneys in the county and no white attorney would take the time to investigate why the young man was being held in jail. In general, they believed that all black males should be imprisoned in case they ever commit a crime.

Several days went by. Then, one day the headlines in the newspaper screamed: "NIGGER FROM CALLAWAYTOWN ADMITS TO THE MURDER OF A WHITE MAN." The article said that Tom Lee had confessed to the crime after several hours of questioning. However, it was more like several days of torture. When Kenny was finally given permission to see his son, there was no doubt that Tom Lee had been beaten. Kenny could see the fright in his son's eyes. They were bloodshot and he looked as if he hadn't slept for several days.

Tom Lee stated that he had murdered Mr. Wilson because he'd caught him attempting to have sex with his mule. No Negroes believed that story. However, true to form, some of the ignorant whites thought it was a reasonable explanation. Respectable white folks, including Mrs. Wilson and her two daughters, thought otherwise. They went from house to house and to every church in the county to speak in Tom Lee's defense.

They knew that there were white folks who were not happy with their stance about Negroes. The poor whites saw the Wilson's as being instrumental in assisting Negroes, liberal whites, and northerners in destroying their way of life. They desperately wanted to keep the status quo.

The Supreme Court had made their historical decision concerning Brown vs. The Topeka, Kansas Board of Education. That decision struck down the old Jim Crow law concerning separate education. Segregation in the nation's public schools would soon be a thing of the past. The majority of southern whites found it extremely challenging to accept the concept. The well-to-do whites could always send their children to private schools. But the poor whites had no option except to disobey the law and that's just what they did. Several years would come and go before the school systems in North Carolina were integrated.

Even so, many educated and well-to-do white folks in and around the county knew that what was reported by the newspaper about Tom Lee was too outrageous to be true. Mrs. Wilson and her daughters were convinced that there was more to the story. She went down to the jailor and demanded to speak with Tom Lee. However, her request was denied. So, she met with Mary Lee and Kenny Hooker.

Mrs. Wilson arrived at their home in the late morning. Mary Lee was busy preparing the dinner meal while Kenny worked in the fields, just as he always did from sunup to sundown. Mrs. Wilson negotiated her way through the maze of children that were running around and playing in the yard. Once she brought the car to a full stop, she exited and walked towards the front porch. Mary Lee was walking in her direction with her hands up and palms out.

"Oh Mrs. Wilson, I am so sorry for what happened to Mr. Wilson. It's very sad. But I tell you, I can't believe for one minute that my boy did that terrible thing to Mr. Wilson. You know he worked a lot for your husband, and he never had one bad thing to say about him. I just do not see how he could do a thing like that. It just doesn't make any sense to me."

Mrs. Wilson was painfully gracious. "I know that Tom Lee is a good boy. He has been working for—I do not know how long. There has got to be something behind what has happened. I came out here today to let you know that me and my daughters have no ill feeling towards you folks. You've always been nice to us, and we know for sure that when the truth comes out, there will be somebody else behind the murder of my husband."

She paused to catch her breath. "I just came from the jailhouse. I wanted to talk with Tom Lee. But the jailor said that he did not want to speak with me. I cannot believe that he just killed my husband for the reason given by the newspaper. There has got to be more to the story. I was thinking that maybe you or Kenny would go with me to the jailhouse. Can we do that?"

Mary Lee thought for a moment, "Everybody is working out in the fields right now. It's getting to be dinnertime, and they are going to be coming here looking for some food mighty soon. I got a lotta cooking to do yet before they break for lunch. Can you come back after dinner? I will go with you."

Meanwhile, Kenny could see Mrs. Wilson from the field. But he didn't come in. What could he say to her? His son was accused of murdering her husband. He decided to wait until she left.

Mrs. Wilson returned, picked up Mary Lee, and drove down to the jail. The jailor was very suspicious. He knew that the false confession had been beaten and tortured out of Tom Lee. He was part of the conspiracy. But Mary Lee wouldn't be turned away this time, "I want to see my son, I know you'll got him locked up and don't want anybody seeing him, but I am his mama! There isn't no reason why I can't see him."

The jailer glared at her, shuffled his feet, and then deferred, "You can see Tom Lee," he snarled, "You just remember that he's charged with first-degree murder. He already signed a confession. So don't be talking to him about the case." He pushed the sign-in pad over to Mary Lee.

She signed in and handed the pencil over to Mrs. Wilson. The jailor looked over at the white woman as if he wanted to say something. He could not believe the old white bitch wanted to speak with the nigger, who had already admitted to the murder of her husband. Sometimes he just could not understand his own people. Why wouldn't she just accept things the way they were? After all, a nigger could commit the most terrible crime at any time. Everyone in any sense knew that. They just happened to be able to beat out a confession from this nigger. He decided to let it go and remained silent. Everything was all said and done anyway. There was nothing she could do now to change it.

It wasn't long before Tom Lee was brought out to the meeting room, "Mama, mama, I don't know what happened," he cried, "I feel so confused. They made me sign the papers. I really don't know what's going on, mama." Desperately, he reached for her hand. Mary Lee and Mrs. Wilson were shocked at what they saw. Tom Lee looked as if he had not had any sleep in several days. It was clear that he had been beaten.

The jailor could see that Mary Lee and Mrs. Wilson were well beyond being upset. He scrambled to make excuses, "Tom Lee had some misunderstandings with the other inmates over the last few days. That is why we decided that it would be best if we put him in a cell alone. Things are working out okay with him since we did that." Mary Lee and Mrs. Wilson did not respond. They knew what had happened, but there was no way to prove it.

Tom Lee said plaintively, "Mrs. Wilson, I want you to know that I didn't kill Mr. Wilson. You know I would never do any harm to Mr. Wilson. He has been so nice to me and has given me work to do. There is not no way I could harm Mr. Wilson."

Mrs. Wilson looked him straight in the face and said, "I know you didn't do it. I can see in your eyes that you are telling the truth. Tell me what you know."

Tom released a big breath, and said, "Well, I was fishing back in the swamp behind your barn. When I finished setting them, I decided to go up the hill to the barn and get some water. Just as I was getting close, I could hear Mr. Wilson talking very loudly to somebody. I heard Mr. David Raymond say, 'I am going to kill you, your old son-of-a-bitch. I knew it was Mr. David Raymond, 'cause after he said that Mr. Wilson told him to get off his land and get back out to the highway. You're just as crazy as your brother Billy, and Billy aren't got but one brother and that's Mr. David. Plus, I know Mr. David's voice. I was so scared that all I wanted to do was go back to my fishing poles. So, that is what I did. After I fished for some time more, I decided to go out to that little shop of Mr. David's and get me a soda. When I got out of there Mr. David gave me the soda and a pack of cookies free. He asked me what I was doing and where I was going. I told him that I was fishing in the river back there behind Mr. Wilson's barn and that I had my poles in the bank and had just come out there to buy a soda. He asked me if I would do him a favor. I asked what he wanted me to do. He said, 'I owe old man Wilson fifteen dollars. He handed me a five and a ten-dollar bill and asked if I would go by and give it to Mr. Wilson for him. He also said that I did not have to go to the house because Mr. Wilson was working down at the barn. He had already given me that soda and the cookies free, so I did not see any harm in doing him that favor. I took the fifteen dollars with me and walked by Mr. Wilson's barn on my way back to the swamp. When I got to the barn, I hollered for Mr. Wilson but got no answer. I walked closer to the barn where the ladder was leading to the hayloft. When I got near the ladder, I could see that somebody was lying down under the hay, with only their feet showing. I thought that maybe Mr. Wilson had fallen from the loft, but when I got to him and turned him over, I could see that he was dead. I could see that somebody had murdered him! I realized that Walker knew he was already dead when he sent me down there. I did not know what to do. So, I ran as fast as I could back to the swamp where my fishing poles were."

The jailor said hurriedly, "This is the first time that nigger has ever said anything like that before. That's the first time I've heard that story, and I've been here every day." Then he snarled and added, "I don't know where niggers get all these crazy stories from. They lie with a straight face. Ain't nothin' that nigger said is true. The only thing that I have heard a nigger say that is true was what the newspaper printed. Everything else he's just making up in his head."

When Mrs. Wilson started to say something, the jailor went on, "Now we know that the fifteen dollars he had in his pocket when we arrested him came from your husband's pocket.

There's no telling what a nigger won't do for fifteen dollars."

But Mrs. Wilson just looked over at Mary Lee and said, "This is really something that must be investigated. We got to go over to the judge and speak with someone about this situation."

The jailor just sneered, "Well, I'll tell you this for sure, isn't anybody here in this county going to believe anything this nigger got to say. He made that confession yesterday, and we have no reason to believe that he's doing anything but lying now. There's no need to get out of this jailhouse and talk to anybody about what you just heard. All it's going to do is stir up a lotta confusion among the folks in this county." He led Tom Lee back to his cell.

When he came back to the front office, he rushed behind the counter, opened a drawer, and grabbed some papers. Pushing them into Mrs. Wilson's hands, he snapped, "You can see for yourself! This is the confession he signed yesterday. We got everything we needed for a conviction. There's no need for you to start any trouble. Now you just take Mary Lee back out to Callaway town and watch over your daughters. All you've got to do now is let the court take care of everything."

Mary Lee was speechless. She knew that this kind of injustice had happened in the county before. But now it was happening to her own flesh and blood. She believed her son, and she knew that he had been beaten and tortured. However, she was powerless. At least Mrs. Wilson had heard what Tom Lee had said with her own ears. It was just a matter of what she would do.

Mrs. Wilson had great dignity. She said, "I read what was in the newspaper, and I see what you've got here, but I don't believe Tom Lee murdered my husband. He's just not that type of person. I want to know the truth about all this."

The jailor screamed back at her, "I don't know what you don't understand! Here, your husband has been murdered, and we caught the nigger who did it. He made a confession, and now you want to muddy the water by getting other people all riled up! All you got was some lies that the nigger told you just to save his ass. He knows he's going to the electric chair for killing Mr. Wilson. So, you know he's going to say anything he can to save his black ass. You just got to forget about what you've heard and get on with your life and let us handle everything down here."

Mrs. Wilson just looked at him. Her gaze made it clear that she was going to take her concerns further. She and Mary Lee signed out of the jail and walked out on the street. She looked over at the black woman and said, "I think most of what Tom Lee said is true. I don't know how we are going to prove it, but I am sure there's more to the story. I tell you, I am going home to discuss everything with my daughters and see what they have to say. Let me drive you home, and you'll hear from us soon."

Mrs. Wilson discussed the situation with her daughters and found that they were convinced that David Raymond was involved in the murder of her husband. He had had several run-ins with her husband. She had been afraid that they would do bodily harm to each other. After listening to Tom Lee's story, she knew that David Raymond was guilty. Now she had to convince the authorities that the case warranted further investigation. That would not be easy. David Raymond was white, and most white folks in his neighborhood were like him, *plain white trash.*

To be white and side with a Negro in a situation like this was going against the grain. No white person in their right mind would take such a risk. Mrs. Wilson would have a very difficult time if she made an attempt to set the record straight. Nevertheless, she was determined to do something. She was not a person who could sit and let injustice prevail. So, she contacted a lawyer in Lakeville. Next, she and her daughters made a trip to the town hall to speak to anyone who would listen. Their words fell on deaf ears. Everyone thought that they were out of their minds.

The chief of police was outraged, "That nigger's going to the electric chair for what he did to your husband!"

But Mrs. Wilson was not daunted. "I want the truth," she said quietly. "I want to get to the bottom of whatever happened. We just cannot believe thestory in the newspaper. I tell you, I talked to that boy today, and I don't for one moment think he killed or was even involved with the murder of my husband," Mrs. Wilson said vehemently.

"What makes you think like that, Mrs. Wilson? I can tell you that I was there when that nigger made that confession. We had been talking to him for some time when, finally, he said that he wanted to make a statement. And God knows the statement he made is exactly as the newspaper reported it."

"Was that before or after he got into a confrontation with other inmates?" asked Mrs. Wilson.

"I have not heard nothing about no mixing it up between the inmates," the police chief grumbled.

At that point, Mrs. Wilson and her daughters knew without a doubt that Tom Lee was not guilty. They walked over to the courthouse and up to the judge's chambers. However, they were not able to speak with the judge. So, they went down the street to the newspaper office and went past the reception desk. The editor, a big, tall, burley, and overweight fellow, was a typical southern redneck. "Howdy, Mrs. Wilson, what can we do for you today?"

Mrs. Wilson looked him straight in the eye and said, "We're wondering where you got the information about the confession of that Hooker boy. Frankly, I don't believe what you reported in your newspaper."

The man pulled on his suspenders and ignored what she had said, "I can surely understand your feelings about that nigger boy killing Mr. Wilson. That was bad. I just don't know what we good white folks are going to do to protect ourselves. Seems like every time you look around some nigger is committing a crime. Do not worry. Just wait and let the court take care of everything. With that signed confession, he's as good as dead."

Mrs. Wilson had none of it. She said firmly, "I was down there to the jail yesterday with Mary Lee Hooker, the boy's mother. I can tell you now that I do not believe a word that you printed in your paper the other day. As far as I am concerned it was all one big lie. I do not believe for one moment that that boy killed my husband. I'll go even further to say that I don't even believe that he was involved with the murder. It all sounds like a frame-up. I want the truth." She looked at the editor skeptically, "Did you even talk to that boy?"

"No," he replied, looking a little sheepish, "I must say that I've not seen him." Then he gathered his courage, "You know all our news sources are confidential. We can't speak about where and how we acquired our information."

"Well, I can tell you it would be a good idea to talk to him. I think you would see he's telling the truth."

At that point, the editor became visibly angry. His face turned bright red, and he broke out in a sweat. His hands trembled as though he wanted to hit something. "I can't understand why you want to get involved with the law. Why don't you just let the court work things out? The police have done an exceptionally good job of getting that confession out of that nigger. He is going to pay for committing that crime against your husband. So, there is no need for you to get all upset about nothing. Because it is just a matter of time before they have the trial, and that nigger will be on death row. Now you just go on home!"

Mrs. Wilson was not going anywhere until she had her way. "Then write an article about the conversation me and Mary Lee had with Tom Lee yesterday. That is all, just write what he said to us and let the readers decide what they want to believe."

The editor all but exploded, "We're a respectable newspaper! We can't be writing junk like what you've been saying. I tell you now, at this point, you and your daughters have got total support throughout the county. But if you start causing problems for the police, and getting other folks involved, you are going to start losing it. Good folks in this county thought that maybe Mr. Wilson brought everything by himself. He has always had them niggers around him. Some folks go so far as to say that you are nothing but nigger lovers. Now you know me, and my paper never thought anything like that. But when you come in here and want me to print some shit like you have said to support a nigger who has already confessed to the crime, I wonder if I should rethink my position. How can you possibly believe a nigger over your own people? It's beyond me to understand how you can do it."

Mrs. Wilson shouted right back, "Well, if you won't write it, I will pay to have it published in your paper!"

The editor had taken as much as he could handle at that point. He just wanted to get Mrs. Wilson out of his office. He knew that Tom Lee was innocent. But the editor was part of the original conspiracy. There was no way he could accommodate her. The time for being polite is over. "Mrs. Wilson, you are going to be able to print any article in this paper, and all you going to do is stir up a lotta problems. No good Christian white person is going to support you. Just about everybody I've spoken believe the police. They aren't going to change their mind over what that nigger said to save his ass. Now, if you want to go on and make a fool of yourself, that is your decision. But do not think you'll get any support from this newspaper. I am not going to lift one finger to help that nigger."

Mrs. Wilson and her daughters left the editor's office and the newspaper. As they walked down the streets, they talked to anyone who would listen. They repeated what Tom Lee had said about David Raymond. When the news got to C.G. Bailey's ears, he was overly concerned. He had had a run-in with David before. He knew the son-of-a-bitch could do anything. He was aware that Mr. Wilson was having problems with David. Only a few days before, Mr. Wilson had been in his office and mentioned that he might have to take him to court to settle some sort of claim. Why had Tom Lee confessed to the murder and signed the confession one day and then changed his story? Why did he have all those bruises on his body?

Out on the streets, Mrs. Wilson was making no progress. Most of the well to do white folks were aware that the confession signed by Tom Lee was beaten out of him. However, the thought that David

Raymond was somehow involved with the murder was just too much to acknowledge. That would mean the police department had engaged in a cover-up.

The fact that an innocent black man was going to be punished for a crime he did not commit was a normal occurrence in most of the South. However, Mills County believed they were above that kind of blatant injustice. Most well to do white folks in the county got along with the Negroes and Indians with few problems. The Indians kept to themselves for the most part. They lived in and around Flathead and controlled the town. They had their own college and owned some land. The Negroes performed all the farm labor and domestic work. If everyone stayed in their place, and it was to the advantage of the well to do white people to get along with them.

A railroad track and the Lumbee River split Lakeville. No Negroes lived east of the Lumbee River or north of the railroad tracks within the city limits. As a matter of fact, no Negroes were allowed in the area after dark or before sunrise, unless of course, they were live-in help. In that case, they were not allowed to leave their place of employment during that timeframe. It was an unwritten law that everyone accepted. The last thing that the country club folks needed was to have racist practices unveiled for all to see. They didn't want anyone to know that a white man had killed another white man and framed a Negro for it. That would certainly shatter the myth that all was going well in Mills County. Folks might say it was time to change things.

Mrs. Wilson was one of a kind. She marched down Fourth Street and throughout the town. Everywhere she went, she shouted, "I know that that David Raymond was involved with the murder of my husband! We've just got to do something about Tom Lee."

Everyone ignored her. The well-to-do white community did not want to hear it, nor did the poor white trash community. They were ready to put the blame on any Negro they could. That was one way they could fool themselves into believing that they were always better than the best of the Negroes. That was an idea they had hung onto since the Civil War.

If David Raymond stated that he was not involved with the crime, then the Nigger had to be lying. There was just no other way to see the situation. Under no circumstances could a Nigger be equal to a white man.

Meanwhile, most well-to-do whites in the area thought that the in-bred poor white trash was a disgrace. They were stuck in the middle of a situation, but they refused to take control over it. They decided to let the court deal with it. Everyone already knew that the judge would let the confession stand. The nigger would be convicted and sentenced to death. In a few months, everything would be back to normal.

Despite Mrs. Wilson's efforts, that is exactly what happened. Tom Lee's appointed attorney told him to plead guilty to try to escape the death penalty.

A man from across the railroad tracks and across the Lumbee River got in contact with Kenny, "I know what you're going through. Something' like that happened to my cousins a few years ago in Polk County. You got to do something' before it's too late."

Kenny had already begun to weep. "Isn't there nothing I can do now?" he wondered. He has already signed the confession. The judge already said they could use that confession."

"Well, I tell you, I've seen you bring wood down here to make these no-good white crackers ever since I've been in this town. I bet they do not give you more than five dollars a load, and it takes you two days to cut that wood. Now you need help, and none of them bastards are going to come forward and speak up for you and your son. From now on, you should forget about them crackers and live for yourself and your family. Let me tell you something'. They got some folks in New Orleans. They called the seven sisters. They have the power. I tell you, for one hundred dollars, they're going to do a lot for you and your boy that the judge would never do." The man pulled a pad and pencil from his pocket.

"Somehow you've got to get one hundred dollars and get your ass down to New Orleans, see them sisters, and let them give you some help. Cause you aren't going to get anything from these crackers here but a death sentence for your son. And they know he's not guilty. It's really a damn shame that a man must go to such lengths to get even partial justice." He tore the strip of paper from his pad and handed it to Kenny.

Kenny was confused. "I don't know what those folks can do to help me. And why would they want to help me anyhow?"

"Man, just do as I say. You don't have to be concerned about why or how they will assist you. They are black folks like us. They have got the power, and they will help you if you give them the money. You go there, tell them your problem, and they are going to take care of everything. You just get your hands on one hundred dollars and a bus ticket and get down there. You have got to do what you can while you still have some time. There isn't any need in going after the trial. You are going to be surprised at what you get for your money. Just you wait and see."

Kenny did not waste any time. There was nothing else he could do for his son. He went home and gave the piece of paper to his wife. "I got this in Lakeville today. I understand that these folks can do something' to help Tom Lee. I heard they would help for one hundred dollars. I don't know, but I think we have got to do it. If we do not, Judge Maddox is going to give our boy the electric chair. Tom Lee done said he killed old man Wilson. You know and I know that our boy did not do it, but it isn't going to make any difference to the judge. You know what all the folks around here are saying. They say that the only way to stop niggers is to send a few to the electric chair. We can't just sit around here and let it happen when we got to way to do something."

Mary Lee was horrified, "What's this you got here? You know we can't get involved with Voodoo or anything like that! And where are we going to get that kind of money from? Even if we had the one hundred dollars, we don't want to get involved with no voodoo."

Kenny was insistent, "We got to try anything that we can. Just as sure as my name is Kenny Hooker, that judge Maddox is going to kill our boy if we don't do something."

"You mean that you'd go down to New Orleans and see these people just because of something you were told by some man in Lakeville? I tell you, I think that's just plain crazy."

Kenny was beside himself. He practically shouted, "Well, he's not just another man in Lakeville! He's been down there to see these folks, and he said that they're well known and very good at what they do. I really do not care if it's voodoo or not. The most important thing now is to keep Tom Lee out of the electric chair. If this is the one chance I've got, that's what I am going to do. I will just have to borrow the money for the trip and pay the folks once I get down there. But I tell you now, nothing' going to keep me from trying anything I can to keep Tom Lee alive."

"But you can't even read. How you going to be able to find a place like this when you can't read?"

"I'll figure out something. I tell you now, I am going to figure it out soon."

Mary Lee just looked at him and handed back the piece of paper he had given her. Kenny folded it and placed it in his shirt pocket. He left to find the man who had given him the information about the women in New Orleans. Then he went downtown to several of the places where he had delivered firewood over the years. Somehow, he got the money he needed. When he returned home, Mary Lee was waiting for him in the kitchen.

"What happened to you? Where did you go? I was just getting ready to talk to you about something when I knew what had happened and you were gone. Where on earth did you go?"

"Well, after you reminded me that I can't read, I knew that I couldn't go down there to New Orleans to find that place by myself. So, I went back to Lakeville to find that guy who gave me the address. He was there. I told him I would pay for his bus ticket if he'd go with me. I went across the river and talked to some of the white folks that I cut firewood and deliver to ever year. I was able to get money for my deliveries in advance. Plus, I borrowed a little here and there. So now I have just what I need for two bus tickets and a little bit left over. We going to be leaving tomorrow morning for New Orleans."

Mary Lee shook her head in astonishment. "All I got to say about that is that you surely move fast. I sure didn't think you'd be making any move this quick."

Kenny was irritated with her. "Woman, you just don't seem to get in your head that the white crackers down there in Lakeville is getting ready to kill our boy. It would be something' if he was guilty. But knowing what we know, how can we stand idle by and let them kill our boy when we just might be able to save him? I got to move fast before it was too late. That judge Maddox already made up his mind. I am leaving here tomorrow morning. I'll be back when I get back."

Mary Lee knew by the tone of Kenny's voice that he had made up his mind and that there was nothing she could do to stop him.

The next morning Kenny was up early, and he was down to the bus station before it opened. The bus driver wondered if he was running away from Mary Lee and that house full of children. After she saw him buy two tickets, she waited patiently to see who was going with him. The colored area of the station was near the rear of the building. The bus stopped right by the white section. The Negroes would have to walk around the side of the building in the weather in order to board the bus. The man showed up just as Kenny had started to give up on him.

The trip took the better part of two days. It was late in the afternoon when they arrived in New Orleans. Luckily, the man knew the city well. He and Kenny made their way through the side streets toward Bourbon Street. Kenny had never seen anything like it. There was so much to see. The city was filled to the brim with odd people.

They walked down Bourbon Street, and Kenny purchased a drink and some gumbo. He leaned over to the street vendor's ear and whispered something to him. The other man looked up and pointed down the street toward a door with black curtains.

Kenny saw many strange objects hanging in the windows and on the walls. The man led the way through the curtains. The room had no windows, and black curtains covered the walls from floor to ceiling. There was a small desk and three chairs. A heavyset black woman with long black hair, long fingernails, and very long eyelashes occupied one. She really was a sight to see. Kenny was thrilled and scared at the same time.

Kenny's companion said, "This is the friend that I wrote to you about. His name's Kenny Hooker. I didn't have nothing' going on so I decided to come for the ride."

The woman smiled, showing broken teeth. "Come on in, Mr. Hooker. I know exactly why you're coming down here. It's bad when we can't get justice in this world. The white folks just won't give us a chance. But we've got the power that everybody on this good earth has. We got to use it to make sure that we could balance the scale a bit. Just sit down there in that chair on the left. We're going to see what we can do to keep that boy of yours out of the electric chair." She directed Kenny to a chair on her left. Looking over at the other man, she said. "You can stay in here if you want to, or you can go and wait out in front until we get our work done."

"I just as well stay here. There isn't nothing for me to do out there. Just as well be here and see what's going to happen."

The woman cackled. "Well, I tell you, it's going to get very busy and hot in here, but it's okay with me."

There were Tarot cards, a crystal ball, and some other strange items on her desk. The woman began to chant words that Kenny could not understand. Suddenly, a strong breeze came out of nowhere and the candle went out. The atmosphere in the room became very strange. She placed her hands on Kenny's hands and then on the crystal ball. A chill went through his body and goose bumps appeared.

"I know your boys are going to be okay," she said in a faraway voice. "I can see that things are going to work out just fine for him." Then she pronounced firmly, "We're going to give you something to take back with you." She reached over and picked up a large jar, screwed off the lid, and poured a little of the contents into a smaller container. "When you get back, you take this, and you just sprinkle a little bit around the judge's doorstep. You've got to do it at least four times a week, every week, until the end of your son's trial. Never sprinkle twice on the same day. Your son is going to plead guilty. Everybody is going to think he is going to get the death penalty. But do not worry! On the day that the judge gives him his sentence, he's going to give your boy life."

Kenny's eyes opened wide, and his heart raced. There was hope! The woman continued, "That's not the end of it. Your boy is going to be out of that prison in less than five years. One day he is going to just walk away from a work detail and never return. Your son is not guilty of that crime. He was framed by one of those white cracker rednecks who never had a use for the fellow he murdered. That man's never going to get caught and punished for what he has done. But, not to worry, his payment is coming. Before your son's trial is over, his family–I can't see who, but somebody from his family, like a sister, brother, wife, or one of his children, is going to go over to your house and bring some food for your family. Take the food, but do not eat it. Cause I can see what is in that food. You just take the entire contents, including whatever it is packaged in, and bury it at least one hundred yards from your house. Never mention anything about any of this to anybody." She returned the large jar to its place, screwed a lid on the small jar and handed it to Kenny.

Gratefully, he put the jar in his pocket with one hand and took a roll of bills from his other pocket and attempted to hand them to the woman, but she waved him off. "I do not help my people with money. I do it because as a people we must do something' to balance the scale. On the other hand, if you have something' that you brought here for my service you can just drop it in that bucket by the door on your way out."

Kenny could feel the power of unseen forces coming from the powder in his pocket. The entire process took less than an hour. The two men left the building, and Kenny dropped the roll of bills in the bucket. As they walked down the narrow street towards the bus station, the man said, "Man, I do not know why I didn't think to tell you that the women don't take any cash. Everyone knows what they charge. But they just do not take any money straight out. You've got to give them something', but it's not like they're charging you for the service. Everybody knows what to drop in the bucket. If they don't have that much, it's good if they just leave what they have or can afford. But if they try to cheat, it's going to be bad for them, 'because not only will that shit they have not work to help them, but it will work against them. I sure hope you put all that we talked about into that bucket."

Kenny shook his head and said, "You do not have to worry about that. I put just what you told me it cost. No more and no less. Do you really think any of that shit she had in that room is going to keep my son from the electric chair?"

"Yes, if you do everything, she told you to do, I'll bet my life that it's going to work. This is the first time I have seen this woman. As I said, there are seven of them. That is why they are calling them the seven sisters of New Orleans. I heard that sometimes they work together. They have three or four little shops around here in the city. But this is the only one that I know about."

"I've got to admit that I feel better about my son," Kenny said quietly. It was strange in there. I could not wait to leave. But if it is going to help Tom Lee, that is the only thing that matters."

The trip back to North Carolina seemed to take longer than the trip down. When they arrived in Lakeville, Kenny thanked the man and walked home. He hid the small jar in the smoke house behind some hams. The next day, he went to town and onto the street where the judge lived. He did as the woman told him to do. He did not draw any attention. Everyone in town knew that Kenny sometimes came by the well to do folks houses and looked through the garbage for anything of value. From time to time many of the folks would give him two or three-days' worth of leftovers. Kenny would gladly take them and offer his assistance around the house in exchange.

Just as the woman had told him, a Raymond family member came over and brought some food one day. Kenny had just returned from the field to the house to get some cold water. Kenny met Raymond's daughter as she came in the yard and made a U-turn so that she was pointed towards the main highway.

"Good morning, Uncle Kenny," she said brightly. "I just want you to know that there are not any hard feelings between us and you and your family. It is just so sad that Tom Lee is so confused. That poor boy is just saying anything to keep out of the electric chair. I know, you know, and everybody knows that my father had nothing to do with the murder of Mr. Wilson. I really do not know why niggers try to get nice and decent white folks into trouble just to save themselves. It is sad that some folks think my father was involved. Just because we do not have a takin' to niggers and nigger lovers does not mean that we want to harm them in any way. Me and my mamma made some fried chicken for you. We just want you to have it to show that we hope the best will work out for Tom Lee."

Kenny hides his feelings well: "Thanks, Miss Raymond. That is nice of you. Lord knows we can use it with all these mouths to feed. I do not know what else to say, but we really appreciate you bringing it over to us." He took the bag carefully.

David's daughter left immediately, and Kenny stood staring after the car until it turned onto the main road. He opened the bag and took a good sniff. It was very good chicken, well-seasoned and cooked. The woman in New Orleans had just passed the first test. He could hardly believe that anyone from the Raymond family would even speak to anyone in his family. But things were happening just as she had said they would. How could she see all this in the future?

One thing was certain. He was not going to deviate from her instructions. He would go straight out back and bury this bag. No one in the family would ever know that he had received the food. If Mary Lee or any of the children saw it, they would surely not understand why they were not allowed to eat it. Often, they ate spoiled food that Kenny had retrieved from the garbage of the well to do whites in downtown Lakeville. He was just going to do as he was instructed and hope for the best. He walked in the back, taking the shovel with him, and buried the food and the bag.

The days went by, and Kenny continued to do what the strange woman in New Orleans had told him to do. When it was time for the trial, everyone in the entire county thought that it would be a closed case. Although no one in their right mind believed that Tom Lee had confessed willingly, the fact was that he had signed the confession. Only the Negroes in the county thought about the case. But they had no power and would have no input concerning the matter.

North Carolina regularly executed Negroes for crimes that involved white people. In most cases, a Black man never made it to trial. The Klu Klux Klan made certain of that. Lynching was a normal way to deal with Negroes who were considered out of line. The KKK did not forgive crimes against white people. Just being involved with a white female was enough for them to justify killing a Negro. Furthermore, Negroes were expected to "keep their place." That meant that a Negro had always to show full respect to a white person, no matter what. The trashiest white folk knew that even they were above the noblest Negro.

The day of the trial, Kenny and Mary Lee were the first in the courtroom. Then, Mrs. Wilson and her daughters arrived. Tom Lee pleaded guilty before the judge, and the judge accepted it. Then he asked if anyone had anything to say on behalf of the convicted murderer. Mary Lee got up and pleaded for her son's life.

Ms. Wilson made a statement that left the whites in the courtroom baffled. Most whites could not understand how one of their own could get up before the judge and plead for the life of the person who murdered her husband. No white person thought that the judge would give Tom Lee anything less than the death penalty.

Although Tom Lee was connected to the Callaway's by blood, the KKK was certain that justice would be applied just as it always was. If they had had any idea that the judge would spare his life, they would have administered justice in their usual way. Tom Lee would somehow "escape" from jail during the night and later be found lynched in the woods. That would be the end of it. There had never been a murder said to be committed by a Negro against a white person where the Negro didn't receive a death sentence.

During the sentencing phase of the trial, even Kenny lost hope. He was already trying to accept the fact that Tom Lee would be sent to Raleigh, where he would be executed. He had all but forgotten about his trip to New Orleans.

Several folks got up in court to speak on behalf of Tom Lee, and many others spoke on behalf of Mr. Wilson. They remembered what a nice person he was and, most of all, how much he had helped Negroes in the county. Then the judge recessed the court for lunch.

Judge Maddox walked the few short blocks from the courthouse to his home. Kenny had already been by his house that morning and sprinkled a heavy dose of the powder that the woman in New Orleans had given him. The judge smelled a peculiar aroma when he walked up the steps to the porch. However, he gave no thought about what caused it. As usual, he placed his briefcase in the doorway and continued through the kitchen and into the dining room, where his wife sat.

"You know that case I got now with that Hooker nigger from Callaway Town is something. David Raymond was involved with that crime. I think he may have murdered Wilson himself. It just does not make sense to me that Tom Lee would kill that old man. He just had no reason to do it. David had all the reasons in the world."

Mrs. Maddox could hardly believe her ears. She was a nice lady but had little use for Negroes. Her grandfather had fought in the Civil

War and fallen to General Sherman's army. As far as she was concerned, niggers should all be either in prison, working on the farm, or dead. "You mean to tell me that you are going to believe a nigger over a white man? David Raymond said that he had nothing to do with the murder. That nigger killed that poor old man. There is no doubt in my mind that he did it. Just think for a moment, the nigger was over there messing with that mule when old man Wilson caught him. He had to kill him to try to save his skin. Sounds just like something' a nigger would do. When are you going to send that nigger to the electric chair? He is going to burn in hell, and that's going to be just what he deserves. He is the brother of that nigger who shot and killed his brother a while back, just for stealing his boat, isn't he?"

Judge Maddox considered what she had said for a moment before saying, "Yes, he's Lee Kenny's brother. Now I do not feel any regret for sending that boy to prison for 25 years. He had no remorse at all. That was a very easy case to deal with. But there's something' that is not right about this case. The pieces just don't fit to the puzzle."

"Well, everyone knows you are going to do the right thing. I have heard from some of the girls in the country club that poor old man Wilson's widow and his two daughters were all saying wonderful things about that nigger. I cannot understand how they can say anything good about anyone who admitted to murder, especially a nigger. Even if they feel that way about him, they should keep their mouths shut until after you have a chance to do your job."

"Yes, they were in court this morning. They spoke very strongly in favor of that nigger. I just do not know what to think. It sure makes my job harder."

Mrs. Maddox put her hand on her husband's arm reassuringly. "Now, you do not have to worry. You know that the nigger is guilty. They always try to do anything they can to save themselves once they get into trouble. And I do not know what's going on with our own people these days. You would think that some of them even go as far as to think that niggers are equal to white folks. Everybody on earth knows that a nigger was created to serve the needs of white folks. You can just look at them and see that they are nowhere close to being equal to any white person. Just take a moment and look around you some time, and you will see that you will notice the difference right away. It just does not make sense to me that any white person can even think any other way."

Meanwhile, the house cleaner was listening. She continued her normal routine. She just wanted to get out of that house and back across the river to the Negro side of town. Judge Maddox and his wife were nice to her, paid well, and gave her lots of food and clothing. The last thing she wanted to do was lose her job. She tried to let what they were saying go into one ear and out the other.

When Judge Maddox finished his dinner, he relaxed for a few minutes before walking back to the courthouse. He arrived just a few minutes after one o'clock. The courthouse was packed. Not that anyone thought there would be any surprises. They just wanted to watch Tom Lee get sentenced to the electric chair.

To everyone's amazement, Judge Maddox sentenced Tom Lee to life in prison. The courtroom went silent when the verdict was released. Mary Lee cried tears of joy. Mr. Wilson's widow and daughters were also incredibly pleased with the sentence.

Kenny thought that the woman in New Orleans was incredible! Now his son would be alive. He might even be out of prison within the next five years. Kenny was not going to hang his hat on that, but at least his son was not going to death row. That was a miracle.

The entire community was outraged by the sentence. It was a given that no nigger would get out of Judge Maddox's court without a one-way ticket to the death house in Raleigh. At the next meeting of the KKK, the white men were outraged that the clan had not just taken things into their own hands from the beginning. One clansman went as far as to suggest that they should still see to it that justice was meted out to the nigger. As far as they were concerned, the nigger was guilty of murdering a white man, and that was enough to justify their action. Hell, if they let this nigger get away with murder, who knows what doors would open. This nigger had killed a white man and was going to live to talk about it. Niggers had to be kept in their place, and it was up to the clan to live up to their responsibility.

But in the end, they decided that they should leave the case alone. Tom Lee was from Callawaytown. The clan might do more damage than good if they stirred the shit and did not get the support they required from the white community. The Callaway's were just too popular and respectable. As much as the clan did not want to admit it, Callaway blood ran in many of the white families in the county. Then there was the issue of Rachel's grandfather in Bull County.

The clan left things as they were. Tom Lee spent just under five years doing hard labor on a North Carolina chain gang. One day he walked off, just as the woman in New Orleans said he would. The news was all over the papers. When he came back home to visit his family, nobody ever asked about how he got out of prison. It was as though a magical spell had been cast over everyone's mind.

Tom Lee could have stayed in Callawaytown without any flak from anyone. However, he chose to head east to a small town near Newburn, North Carolina. No one in the neighborhood took any special notice when he appeared in the neighborhood. Tom Lee was a free man. Ms. Wilson and her daughters had campaigned to connect David Raymond to Mr. Wilson's death. After a time, most folks thought that David had participated in some way. When the word got out that Tom Lee had been spotted in the area, most folks thought that he had been released on a technicality or that the governor had seen the wisdom in giving him a pardon.

CHAPTER THIRTY-TWO

Now sixteen, Jacob had some difficult decisions to make. He was in his final year of high school. His grades were excellent. He hoped that he would get into the army via West Point Military Academy. He had spoken of the possibility with his teachers, classmates, and, of course, his mother. However, no U.S. President, Senator, or Representative had ever appointed a Negro from North Carolina to a military academy. His chances of breaking through were slim to none.

But nobody had the heart to tell Jacob that his dream was impossible. Instead, everyone brushed the subject aside when he tried to bring it up. Finally, his Principal, Mr. Richardson, asked, "What do you want to be when you get out of school, Jacob?"

Jacob looked straight at the older man and said, "I want to go to West Point and be an officer. What do you think? Do you think my grades are good enough?"

"Yes, I think your grades are much better than many of the boys that will get appointed to attend West Point this year." Jacob had not realized that someone was going to need to appoint him to get into West Point.

Mr. Richardson went on, "There isn't any way you are going to get into any academy. I haven't seen any colored or Indian person being appointed from this county. The senators and congressmen from this state do not seem to have any room for colored or Indian boys. Your best bet is to try to go to college and get into the Reserved Officers

Training Corps (ROTC). That is where you would have your best chance of becoming an officer in the army."

Jacob knew that he had almost no chance of going to college. The money that his father had left had long disappeared. The farm and most of the property generated only enough revenue to support the family. Any profits went straight to Ernie. He did not really need the money since he had a job, but he used it to live the good life.

Jacob graduated near the top of his class. He immediately went to meet with the Air Force recruiting officer, but he was turned away because he would not be seventeen before July 16th. Although that was only about two months, it seemed like a lifetime to Jacob.

He had already let his family know that he would be leaving as soon as he turned seventeen. He did not care what branch of the military he ended up joining–all he wanted to do was get away from Ernie. Ernie pressured his mother to not sign the permission papers. Indeed, she had assumed that both George and Jacob would work on the farm during the planting and harvest seasons. Once it was clear that Jacob was leaving, he was determined to get every ounce of energy out of the boy while he had control.

He worked the boys from sunup to sundown six days a week. To ensure maximum results from Jacob, he put George in charge. That meant that Jacob worked harder than ever.

Times were hard for Jacob. At one point, he went as far as to change the date on his birth certificate to try to get into the service early. But it was noticeably clear to the recruiter that the document had been tampered with. Rather than discuss it with Jacob, he suggested that he take it to another recruiter in another county. But Jacob had second thoughts and destroyed the document. He purchased an official replacement for fifty cents.

He wrote a letter to his brother. Rob Junior was out of the army and living in Harlem in New York City. He explained what was happening at home. Rob immediately sent a one-way bus ticket to Jacob, letting him come to New York.

No one had ever thought that Jacob would get away from Ernie. If anyone left, it would be George. Despite all the evidence to the contrary, people still believed that Jacob was crazy and would always live near home. They thought that he would have to be protected and cared for by others for the rest of his life. People laughed at him when he announced that he was moving to New York to live with his brother.

Jacob checked the mail every day. He met the mailman when he drove into the yard and ran up to him with his hand out. Several days went by before a letter arrived from Rob Junior. When Jacob saw that it had finally come, he could hardly contain his joy. He immediately separated the letter from the rest of the mail, folded it, and pushed it into his back pocket. He walked back to the house and placed the mail on the kitchen table. He then went to the outhouse, where he was sure that he would be alone.

He opened the envelope and saw that Rob Junior had sent the ticket to New York along with twenty-five dollars and a note. "My dear brother Jacob, here is the ticket I promised to send you and a little pocket money. I will be waiting for you when you arrive. Just get off the bus, walk straight to the first bench you see, and sit down. I will see you Sunday morning!"

Jacob had three more days to deal with the physical and mental abuse Ernie threw at him. Later that day, he blurted, "I am going to leave this place! I am going to live with Rob Junior and Mary in New York City, just you wait and see."

Ernie just sneered at him, "You aren't going to no New York City, how you going to get there? You don't have any money and it cost money to buy a bus ticket to New York City and if you did have the money for a bus ticket, Rob Junior won't have you living up there with your crazy self. You just get back out there in the field and get the plowing finished before the rain come!"

Jacob did not bother to respond. He already had the key to a new life in his back pocket. Nothing was going to prevent him from leaving that Saturday. He would work as hard as he could for the rest of the week. But come Saturday, he would be gone.

He planned to tell everyone that he was going to the movies in Lakeville.

If he worked hard and did everything that Ernie and his mother asked of him, there would be no reason for them to question what he did with his free time. Jacob knew that George had been invited to go along with Ernie to one of the local Saturday night joints where most Negroes would get to talk, listen to music from the jukebox, eat chicken and fried fish, and dance. Ernie always invited George, but never Jacob. On this coming Saturday night, that would be a blessing.

The days went by very slowly; it felt like Saturday would never come. When it did, Jacob's plans were in place. He had gathered his clothing and placed it in a brown paper bag. He had almost nothing. After he finished working on Saturday, he went down to the swimming hole in the Lumbee River and took what he considered to be his last dive from his favorite oak tree. The water was fresh, clean, and cool. He played with some of the boys in the river for a few minutes before he returned to the house. He took a nap under the old chimney berry tree. Afterwards, he got dressed and told his mother that he was going to Lakeville.

In the end, he had looked over at her and told her the truth, "Today is my last day in this house. I am going to New York City to live with Rob Junior and his wife."

"Why are you talking about going to New York?" his mother cried. "You know Rob Junior and Mary don't want to be bothered with you. They have their own lives to live. You just forget about going anywhere and stay here. We got the tobacco ready to harvest in a few weeks. After that, we have all the rest of the crops to harvest. There's no way we can do it without you and George."

When Jacob just looked back at her, Rachel went on in a rush, "I already promised Ernie that you boys would be here to work for him on the farm for the rest of this year and next year. I do not want to hear anything else about you leaving and going anywhere, do you understand?"

Jacob listened to his mother, but he was leaving. He knew he could not say anything more to her. As it was, she had not really believed him.

He waited until his mother walked down toward the vegetable garden, then came out with his brown paper bag. Unexpectedly, tears came to his eyes, "I'll see you later, mama!" he shouted. "I am leaving now, and I love you."

"Okay, son, you be careful and don't get into any trouble," Rachel replied without turning her head.

Jacob made his way down to Lakeville, where he went to a small hot dog stand where people of all races would gather, order food, and stand to eat. Jacob made small talk with his old classmates, who were in town for the afternoon. He had hours to kill until the bus would TOOK him to New York City. It was all he could do to keep the secret from his friends.

When it was finally time, he presented his ticket to the driver and took a window seat in the back of the bus. The bus driver closed the door and drove off.

As the driver negotiated his way to the main highway, he watched the streets go by. Once the bus picked up speed, Jacob laid his head in his hands and thought about what it would be like once he arrived in New York City. What he was doing finally sunk in.

Jacob was finally free. He closed his eyes and went to sleep.

www.ingramcontent.com/pod-product-compliance
Lightning Source LLC
LaVergne TN
LVHW061540070526
838199LV00077B/6854